Praise for Dylan Newton

ALL FIRED UP

An "utterly delightful romance."

—*Booklist*

"A unique, romantic, and engaging read."

—The Nerd Daily

HOW SWEET IT IS

"Newton's debut romance is laugh-out-loud funny, with enough antics, fast pacing, and chemistry to keep readers as engrossed as any of her hero's bestselling horror novels would. A hilarious rom-com romp that delivers on both sweet and heat."   —*Kirkus*, starred review

"Brimming with witty banter, sweet characters and sizzling charm."   —*Woman's World*

"The funny moments that had me laughing out loud. The end of this book was super romantic and very fitting! *How Sweet It Is* exceeded my expectations."   —The Nerd Daily

CHANGE
OF PLANS

ALSO BY DYLAN NEWTON

How Sweet It Is
All Fired Up

CHANGE
OF PLANS

Dylan Newton

FOREVER

New York Boston

Forever
Hachette Book Group
1290 Avenue of the Americas, New York, NY 10104
read-forever.com
twitter.com/readforeverpub

First Edition: August 2023

Forever is an imprint of Grand Central Publishing. The Forever name and logo are trademarks of Hachette Book Group, Inc.

The publisher is not responsible for websites (or their content) that are not owned by the publisher.

The Hachette Speakers Bureau provides a wide range of authors for speaking events. To find out more, go to hachettespeakersbureau.com or email HachetteSpeakers@hbgusa.com.

Forever books may be purchased in bulk for business, educational, or promotional use. For information, please contact your local bookseller or the Hachette Book Group Special Markets Department at special.markets@hbgusa.com.

Library of Congress Cataloging-in-Publication Data:

Names: Newton, Dylan, author.
Title: Change of plans / Dylan Newton.
Description: First edition. | New York : Forever, 2023.
Identifiers: LCCN 2023003974 | ISBN 9781538703724 (trade paperback)
   | ISBN 9781538703700 (ebook)
Subjects: LCGFT: Romance fiction. | Novels.
Classification: LCC PS3614.E74 C53 2023 | DDC 813/.6--dc23/eng/
   20230202
LC record available at https://lccn.loc.gov/2023003974

ISBNs: 978-1-5387-0372-4 (trade paperback), 978-1-5387-0370-0 (ebook)

Printed in the United States of America

LSC-C

Printing 1, 2023

To those currently serving in the military
and to our veterans:
thank you for your sacrifice and service.

And to the hardworking moms and
mom-like creatures everywhere:
give yourself grace.
You are doing great things!

CHAPTER 1

Bryce Weatherford examined the pull-ups section of the grocery aisle, baffled by how much information you needed to buy a kid diapers.

She glanced over at her twelve-year-old niece. "June, how much does Addie weigh? She's not fifty pounds yet, is she?"

June snorted, her face buried in her phone. "How would I know? That's a question for a responsible *parent*. Why don't you go find one?"

Bryce gritted her teeth and beckoned Addison closer. Her five-year-old niece was flitting from black square to beige square on the grocery store floor, the yellow, glittery wings vibrating on the harness around her back as she jumped, singing something under her breath.

"C'mere, Addie-bell. Let me pick you up."

Trying to remember what it felt like to haul in those fifty-pound bags of rice at Chez Pierre—a lifetime ago when she'd been their sauté chef and completely in control of her kitchen and her life—Bryce hefted her youngest niece, who shrieked and giggled.

"I'm flyin', Aunt Beamer! See me?"

Bryce grunted, holding the little girl up by the arm-pits. Her gold-glitter-glued sneakers dangled a foot from the floor.

"Oof. You're flying, all right. All thirty-five pounds of you. Maybe forty, but you get medium-sized pull-ups." Bryce set her down. "Don't run, Addie-bell, and stay in this aisle where I can see you."

Addison grinned at her, her blond hair and pixie-like face all sweet innocence. "Only, fairies like to run, an' I'm the fastest fairy runner in all the worlllllldddd!"

And like a hummingbird, she was off, dashing from one side of the aisle to the other, snatching at low-hanging packages of baby toys, squeezing three of them to see if they squeaked, then trying and failing to re-hook them onto the strip where they'd dangled, tantalizingly, just for grabby hands like hers. With a backward grin at her aunt, she tossed the baby toys atop a shelf of formula and twirled away before Bryce could decide whether this was what the counselor would label "a scolding event." Probably not.

Nothing was broken. Addie got so much joy from playing fairy, and Lord knew these girls had experienced little of that lately. Bryce figured any responsible mother figure wouldn't get uptight about Addison ruining a baby toy display.

Right?

Selecting the proper pull-ups, Bryce winced at the price. Addison had been wetting the bed at night for the past six months. Initially it had worried Bryce, yet the court-required therapist assured her that regression was common in grieving children. While she'd rather be spending this same amount on a really good Roquefort, the pull-ups—

and not being woken at 2 a.m. to change the sheets—beat the cheese.

Yet she weighed the package in her hand, debating. Dry sheets? Or an aged blue cheese to go with her last bottle of sauternes wine? The debate she'd never anticipated having seesawed in her sleep-deprived brain as she pushed the grocery cart down to the end of the aisle.

"Aunt Beamer, you're missing a kid," June said, interrupting the mental conundrum. Her tween niece wore a pair of black jeans, zombie-killer boots, and a black long-sleeved tee that said *It's a beautiful day to leave me alone.* Her long brown hair was tied in a low ponytail. She rolled her eyes, lowering her phone just enough to gesture with her chin behind them.

Following the chin-point, Bryce groaned, tossing the toddler pull-ups into the cart as she spotted her third niece sprawled on the floor trying to reach something under the bottom shelf of the baby food aisle.

"Cecily! Stop messing around and get out from there," she hissed, bending to tug on the dirty ankles of her eight-year-old niece. Cecily had refused to wear weather-appropriate clothes for the cold, drizzly day that passed for spring in Western New York, insisting that her long basketball shorts were as warm as jeans. "What's wrong with you?"

"I dropped my lucky rock, and it rolled under," came Cecily's muffled voice from beneath the shelving unit. "I had to reach really far to get it, and now I'm stuck. But you wouldn't believe how much change is under here. How much is two dimes and a quarter?"

"Forty-five cents," Bryce answered, belatedly realizing

she should've let the girl figure out the math on her own. Another caregiver fail, and she was about to commit one more parenting sin: bribery. "Let go of the change and the rock so I can pull you out, and I'll give you a dollar."

"Two dollars," bargained her niece, "and I get to pick out the cookies this week."

"Done," she muttered, flipping her braid over the other shoulder as she knelt down to peer under the lowest metal shelf, her palms on the store's dirty floor and her cheek perilously close to the same. "Now let go so I can unstick you."

Out of the corner of her eye, she spotted a tall man with a baby in his cart pull into the aisle. She levered herself onto one hand, snapping her finger at Addison, who was currently twirling in circles close to the approaching stranger, oblivious to everything as she sang and stared at the lights overhead.

"Addison, stop twirling and come here! You're going to knock something over." Then she turned to Cecily, tugging on her shoulder, but the girl was either resisting or was really stuck. Bryce figured it for the former and sighed in exasperation. "C'mon, Cici! The manager is going to kick us out if you guys can't behave."

"You know, we all identify as female in this family, and calling us 'guys' is sexist and promotes the toxic belief in male superiority." June speared her with a green-eyed glare. "And before you resort to 'girls,' keep in mind society uses that term for groups of females as a pre—a per...prerogative."

"Pejorative," Bryce corrected, clenching her jaw against the urge to swear. "And it's not an insult when the group of girls you're addressing aren't yet old enough to vote. As for calling you 'guys,' that's my bad. But you can't work for eight years in an all-male kitchen and not have sustained testosterone poisoning from it all. Now, can you put your phone down and help me here?"

With the amount of all-suffering, put-upon-ness matched only by biblical martyrs and hormonal teens everywhere, June stuffed her phone into her pocket and shuffled in her black chunky boots to half-heartedly tug on Cecily's leg.

"Owwww!" Cecily howled.

Bryce closed her eyes, wishing for the millionth time that her brother was here. Bentley would have his daughters sweetly compliant in a heartbeat, his wife and his sister laughing over it later, everyone succumbing to his easygoing charm and ability to put things in perspective. If Bentley were here...Bryce wouldn't be wrangling her nieces. She'd be over a thousand miles away, standing at her ten-burner Vulcan range as she crafted another soup to complement Pierre's menu, dreaming of the next starred review for the Tampa restaurant.

But Bentley was dead, and his wife with him.

All she had left of her brother were his children and his wish that she be their sole guardian.

Bryce shoved thoughts of Bentley to the background where they'd been on constant simmer and focused on the dumpster fire that was today.

"Cecily, stop yelling!" Bryce hollered over her. She gave up on avoiding the gross factor and lay down on the grimy floor in her white chef's coat, pressing her cheek against the tiles, using her cell phone's light to peer into the darkness at her niece. It appeared she'd wedged herself between two support legs of the store shelves. She'd somehow have to twist the girl to the left and pull at the same time to get her out. "Cici, turn your head until your cheek is lying on the floor, like mine."

Bryce shoved her own arm in up to the shoulder, attempting to put her palm between Cecily's face and the sharp edges of the metal shelf above her, but it was too close. Her niece was truly stuck. Panicked thoughts of having to call the police or worse—the girls' maternal grandparents—and explain what had happened made sweat prickle at her scalp.

No. She was going to figure this out.

And she'd do it without any injury to Cecily that would require paperwork to be completed and add to the mountain of reasons Adele and Harvey Payne already had for why Bryce wasn't capable to act as their granddaughters' guardian.

"Are you a pirate?" Bryce heard Addison ask someone as she pressed down and pulled on Cecily's shoulder. "'Cause I'm looking for Captain Hook, who stole Peter Pan's ship."

Bryce glanced up from the floor and noticed two things at once: the man Addison had called a pirate was standing a few feet away.

And he was hot as hell. He had close-cut dirty-blond hair, and a hard-edged face with thick eyebrows that bunched over a pair of deep-set blue eyes that gave him a sexy brooding vibe, like a grumpy Viking. From her position on the floor, the guy appeared tall and muscular, and he looked vaguely familiar. Bryce figured maybe she'd seen him come into PattyCakes—her tiny workstation at the bakery's kitchen stove gave her a partial view of the dining area and she'd gotten to recognize most of the regulars in town—but she couldn't place him. He was dressed like he'd come from the gym in a Buffalo Bills cap and black long-sleeved shirt with a matching pair of long mesh shorts. Her niece was currently clutching the man's left leg...which ended in a metallic spring-like prosthesis below the knee.

The pirate comment suddenly made the worst kind of sense.

The man glanced down at Addison and gave a half smile. The expression transformed his face, like the sun emerging from behind a storm cloud, and that momentary softening of his fierce expression was as surprising as it was mesmerizing.

"Aye, lassie." The man's faux brogue made her simultaneously think of the *Outlander* series and every sexy, pirate-themed movie she'd ever watched. Like a gas burner twisted to medium-high, Bryce felt her dormant libido tick to life. As his voice continued in that sexy rumble, flames, hot and eager, raced through her body. "But I'm retired from the high seas, and not even Davy Jones himself can make me return! 'Tis not me yer lookin' for, little Tinker Bell."

"I'm not Tinker Bell. I'm Addie-bell, and I think you're lyin' to me, pirate." Addison yanked a plastic cutlass from her pants, and Bryce wondered how that child always managed to stuff toys in the most unlikely places. "Now, fight me, Hook!"

Then she gave the hot guy—who happened to be pushing a cart with a baby inside—a mighty jab with her sword.

Right in his junk.

With a surprised *Oof*, the guy doubled over, hands on both of his knees.

"Addie, no!" Bryce yelped.

Addison brandished her sword in triumph, a manic grin on her elfin face. "Ha! Got you, pirate! Hand over my friend's boat, or I'll make you walk the flank!"

With that odd threat, her niece jabbed again.

Bryce had lunged to her feet, hoping to stop the fake sword from bashing the guy in the head but knowing she'd never get there in time, when the man's hand shot out, fast as a snake.

"Nay, lassie. I am not your enemy." The man held the pointed end of the cutlass, his grip unwavering, even as Addison tugged on the weapon with all her fairy-sized might. He straightened slowly, but his free hand stayed down by his balls in a defensive cup Bryce recognized from playing football with her brothers and his friends.

The guy must be cramping so bad.

Unbidden, a giggle bubbled out of Bryce, attracting the man's gaze. When the laser-like blue stare hit her, she clapped a hand over her mouth, willing away the laughter she'd always had for pratfalls and slapstick situations. This was serious. Her niece had nailed a guy in the prunes. He might really be hurt.

Recalling when these mishaps had happened to Bentley when they were growing up, she sprang into action, snatching a bag of frozen vegetables out of her grocery cart.

"I—I'm sorry," she stumbled over the words, willing herself not to laugh again. It wasn't funny. The man was obviously suffering. She saw the pained lines of his mouth as he held his ground with the furiously fighting fairy at his feet. The guy was intimidatingly handsome, so Bryce moved only close enough to snatch Addison by the upper arm, reeling her and her plastic sword out of fighting range.

Bryce held up the vegetables, like a peace offering.

"Here. Hold this on there. It'll help with the cramps."

She tossed the bag of frozen corn at him. But she'd been so distracted by those sensuous lips and perfectly stubbled jaw that her aim was off. She'd misjudged the distance and force of her underhand throw, and the bagged corn swooped up and between his legs.

Scoring him in the jewels once again.

"Mmph!" The frozen package smacked the floor next to his sneaker, and the cute baby buckled into his cart's front seat burbled a laugh, pointing with one chubby finger at the unintended crotch missile.

"I—I didn't...I'm sorry." Bryce choked back a giggle, biting the inside of her lip. It was totally uncool to laugh while the guy was doubled over after a plastic cutlass and a bag of corn to the nuts. But damn, was it funny! A few snorting giggles came out before she was able to rein herself in enough to ask, "A-are you okay?"

"Depends. If I say yes, are you going to sic the rest of your pack on me?" the guy asked, without a Scottish accent, his forehead even with his baby's in the cart. Delighted, the little one gave up her stuffed book to grab her father's ears, twisting them and shrieking in glee. Bryce noticed that the man's left ear had a notch taken out of it, high up on the stiff ridge of the cartilage. He continued speaking, his head bowed under his baseball cap.

"Because if that's the case, I'll surrender my pirate vessel and my grocery cart, both. Just no more shots to the groin. Please."

Bryce bit both cheeks, feeling her abs contract with the laughter she held inside as she managed to squeak out, "I'm sorry. I was trying to help."

He lifted his head enough to look the chortling baby directly in the eyes, and the hard lines of his face softened. He touched his nose to the girl's teeny button nose, rubbing to the left and right in what Bryce's dad used to call "polar bear kisses."

"You think that's funny? I can't believe you're ganging up on me, too, little Lisi."

Bryce's urge to laugh evaporated as the sweet sight left her heart melting like butter, oozing into a puddle at the bottom of her chest. If she captioned this picture in her mind it would read: *Find a man who gazes at you with the adoration this father has for his baby.*

"In-garden!" Addison, sensing weakness, tugged away from Bryce to brandish her plastic cutlass again.

This time, Bryce snatched the weapon away and swooped to grab the frozen vegetables from the floor, putting both in her grocery cart. She set the gallon of milk on top of the toy sword as insurance against her niece using it once more for evil.

"It's *en garde*, and you're done fencing. You hurt this man, and you need to tell him you're sorry," Bryce said.

Addison mumbled an apology, then twirled away. She dashed to the cart, where she swung herself up to stand innocently grinning, while her blue eyes darted to gauge the difficulty in reclaiming her cutlass.

Bryce gave her own apologetic smile as the man straightened. "Sorry. She likes to play fairy. All the time. She won't take off her wings, even for school—since her parents passed, she's confused fairies with angels and—"

Suddenly, Cecily shrieked from under the shelving unit. The high-pitched sound was like an ear-busting fire alarm, both in its inability to be ignored as well as decibel-topping tone.

Bryce jumped and spun in one movement, rushing toward the sound before making a conscious decision, and Cecily stopped squealing enough to shout.

"Quit pulling! You're ripping off my arm!"

"What?" June asked, in faux confusion, holding her hands up in an "it wasn't me" gesture as she sat back on her heels. "You told me to pull and get her out, didn't you?"

Bryce made herself take a calming breath. It didn't help.

June must've sensed she'd pushed a little too far because she let go of her sister and joined Addison next to the cart, pulling out her phone once more. Bryce knelt on the floor next to Cecily, heaving a frustrated sigh. "Cici, you've got to scoot yourself backward and to the left. Or you're going to spend the night sleeping under the baby food."

To her surprise, the man with the bruised balls wheeled his cart over. "Can I help?"

Bryce looked up, noticing with appreciation his muscled arms. His shirt was one of those Dri-FIT jobs and she could see his well-defined biceps. She felt herself staring a beat too long, but before she could refocus, her gaze caught sight of the guy's forearms. Suddenly, it was as if Bryce's brain stuttered to a stop. Some girls were chest and ab girls, some dug a guy with a nice ass—and that was great, but Bryce herself was an arm girl. Give her bulging biceps and strong, corded forearms, lightly dusted with hair, and she was off. And this guy's sleeves were shoved up, showing every glorious inch up to the elbow...

She dragged her gaze away from his arms—although she did note he wasn't wearing a wedding ring—and she nodded.

"I'd appreciate it. I don't want to call the manager. If they have to bring in the Jaws of Life to get her out, I'm screwed from ever getting guardianship of my nieces." Bryce knew she was babbling, but the man had bent down to peek under the shelf at the situation, sending a whiff of his warm, woodsy cologne or body spray or whatever her way, and she sensed her libido moving from simmer to a rolling boil. "June and Addie—can you please watch Mr....uh, what is your name?"

"Ryker," he replied, straightening. He released his hold on the cart when Addie came bouncing over with June at her heels.

The unusual last name pinged in her head, but Bryce was certain she hadn't met him before. Surely, she'd have remembered those forearms? But then again, these past months in Wellsville had felt similar to stepping on dry land after a day spent Jet-Skiing in the choppy waters of the Tampa Bay—she was in a constant state of dizzying vertigo as she struggled to keep her feet pointed in the right direction. So it was possible she'd met this guy, and in her exhaustion-fogged brain she'd forgotten.

"Watch Mr. Ryker's baby while he looks to see if we can get Cecily out from under here?"

June huffed but obeyed, stashing her phone and pulling

his cart out of the middle of the aisle as the man looked on, trepidation in his face. But when June and Addison began a game of peekaboo, making the baby erupt in deep belly laughs, his expression relaxed, and he crouched down, peering under the shelf. Seconds later, the laser-blue eyes were on Bryce once more.

"My arms are longer, so I'll take that side. Her shoulders are stuck, and she'll have to wiggle in deeper, get her arm down by her side, and then dip her shoulders around the shelf's floor brace. Then we can tug her out. Ready?" At Bryce's nod, the guy stepped over Cecily's prone body, switching sides with Bryce. Without hesitation, he lay flat on the grocery store floor, adjusting his baseball cap to put his face right up to the edge of the bottom shelf that held the larger jars of baby food as well as some disgusting concoction of pasta and vegetables so overcooked and oversalted she wondered how anyone would feed the crap to a defenseless baby.

Bryce flopped down on the other side, her hand patting Cecily's calf in reassurance.

"Hey, Cecily, Mr. Ryker has an idea of how to get you out. Listen to him, okay?"

"'Kay," she said. "Before I get out, can I roll my rock to you, Aunt Beamer?"

It was useless to argue, so she agreed, and a flat, gray rock came shooting out. Bryce caught it, lifting up on her hip long enough to get it into her pocket, then activated her cell phone's flashlight, shining it under the shelves.

"Hi, Cecily." Mr. Ryker's voice came from the other side of her niece. "Looks like you got wedged in there. Once when I was a kid, my dad had to cut the back off our kitchen chair because I got my legs stuck sitting in it backward. But this'll be way easier. Scoot your head up to where you dropped that dime, and don't stop until your nose is even with the coin."

Cecily's little body wriggled in farther, and Bryce swallowed her objections as most of the shelving unit devoured her niece's legs, leaving only her untied sneakers visible.

"Good." The man's voice was calm and cheerful as he coached her through putting her arm down to her side, and then wriggling backward first in one direction, then another, as if this were a standard, grocery store catastrophe he'd seen a million times. "Now, use your left arm to push yourself to us and keep your right one by your side, and your aunt is going to pull. If anything hurts, tell us and we'll stop."

Slowly, Bryce dragged Cecily's body out by the ankle, then by her knee, then holding her narrow hips. The girl's black athletic shorts were covered in massive dust bunnies comprised of dirt, wadded hair, and God only knew what else.

Cecily tried to get up on her knees and pull herself the rest of the way out, and then she yelped.

"Ow! Something's poking me!"

Bryce shoved her hand up, feeling immediately what it was—the bottom of the shelving unit had a plastic pricing tag holder that dipped slightly lower than the shelf, and it was scratching down the middle of Cecily's back.

"It's this." Bryce turned off her cell light and pocketed her phone. She wrestled with the plastic holder, but it was bolted to the shelf.

The guy sat up and watched Bryce struggle with the bolted holder.

"Here. That plastic is going to cut you if you're not careful. I've got it."

His large hand replaced hers, callus-roughened palm brushing against the outside of her hand. A prickle of awareness went through Bryce at the warmth of that brief touch, and she caught the flash of his glance. Had he felt it, too? Remnants of the old, easygoing Bryce loomed up inside her, and she had a sudden desire to flirt. Smile, maybe crack some joke and—

There was a metallic pop, and her gaze returned to Cecily. With one quick jerk, the man yanked the entire contraption out of the shelving unit, bolt and all. Although his muscles bulged, Bryce averted her gaze, focusing on her niece. She wasn't the old Bryce. Not anymore.

Addison oohed in appreciation behind them. "You're the strongest pirate I've ever seen!"

Bryce shook her head. "Addie," she said, warningly, but then Cecily was wriggling out and Bryce was helping her niece to her feet, scanning her from dirty head to grubby toe. No blood. No limbs broken or hanging at odd angles. Cici was okay. Bryce gave her a quick hug.

"Thank you," Bryce said as the man pushed off the floor to stand easily, dusting off his workout attire. "I don't know how much of a scene we'd have made if it weren't for you saving the day. We owe you, don't we, Cici?"

Before she'd prompted her to thank him, Cecily crossed over, going in for a hug. She wrapped her scrawny arms around the guy's waist. The man's whole body stilled as she embraced him, and his face took on a funny, almost wistful expression.

"Hey." He patted Cecily's back awkwardly. "Glad I could help."

"Thanks, Mr. Ryker." Cecily released him. Then, turning to grin at Bryce, she opened her fist to reveal a handful of coins she'd hauled out with her. "Plus, now I'm rich. Can I get gum when we leave, Aunt Beamer?"

Without waiting for an answer, she headed for the grocery cart with the man's daughter, cooing along with her sisters at the beautiful, wispy-red-haired baby inside and showing her sisters the booty she'd discovered.

Bryce wiped herself off, noting with a grimace that her chef's coat was now smudged with grime all down the front, and walked with Mr. Ryker to their respective carts. The girls, seeing him approach, did one more peekaboo game with the baby—he'd said her name was Lisi—and then scattered to their own cart, June hauling out her phone and Cecily counting her change as Addison twirled in circles just out of reach and always in the way.

"Well, thanks again for the help," Bryce said. "You were the hero we didn't deserve."

"Your little fairy had it right—I'm more pirate than hero." He tossed the ruined price-tag holder into his cart next to a bottle of baby shampoo and two sad cans of pour-and-heat soup. Then he hesitated, his expression guarded as he adjusted his baseball cap. "Hey, uh, I didn't get your name—"

Suddenly, it was as if a bomb went off behind them.

Bang! Bang-BANG!

Before Bryce registered the sound, she, her nieces, and the cart with little Lisi were corralled to the aisle's endcap. In two heartbeats, the guy had placed himself between them and the noise, like a human shield.

"Get down!" he yelled, smooshing them toward the floor

while huddling over the baby in the cart. They all ducked at his command.

Her heart hammered in her throat as she clutched her nieces to her, even June scuttled to crouch under Bryce's arms. But after a few seconds, as The Weeknd's "Save Your Tears" continued to play and there was no emergency announcement, Bryce peeked around the man's leg.

There was no crazed, gun-toting shopper.

But there was a mess.

Three jars of baby food lay smashed on the floor. Bryce put the clues together and realized she and her nieces had likely caused this upset.

"Um, I think we're good now," she said to the Viking-strong man crouching over them. "It was just baby food. We must've thrown those jars off-balance while we were rescuing Cecily."

Mr. Ryker looked over his shoulder, confirming her words. Then he stood. His ears flushed bright red, and before she could say anything, he'd unlatched his baby and scooped her out of the cart. Cradling her head with his free palm, he rounded the endcap, his long legs eating up massive chunks of aisle as he fast-walked through an empty checkout lane and through the exit as if escaping a flaming building.

"Wow. He was like a superhero," Cecily said after he'd disappeared through the swooshing automatic doors, her eyes as big as pearl onions. "A genuine supermarket superhero."

"No. He's a pirate, and he's tired. He tol' me so." Addison fixed her bent fairy wings. Then her eyes alighted on the mess in the middle of the aisle. "Are we gonna get yelled at, Aunt Beamer?"

Suddenly, a public announcement came over the grocery store's speakers.

"Cleanup on aisle five, please. Cleanup on aisle five."

"Nope. But we're going to check out." Bryce snatched the baby shampoo and canned soup from the man's cart, then rushed the girls out of the aisle and toward the cashiers. "I think we've worn out our welcome here."

CHAPTER 2

Ryker bolted from the store, leaving everything but Elise behind in his rush to outrace his humiliation. But as good as his prosthetic was, he couldn't outrun his PTSD or his embarrassment. Every day since returning from deployment to Afghanistan seven years ago, he'd fought the feeling that he didn't fit in the real world. Some days, months even, it would lessen. He'd hang out with guys from his old high school football team or his Marine brothers, and things would run smoother, like his life had gotten a much-needed oil change. But then, inevitably, the gears would gum up. Life would feel... heavier. Some days when he appeared in public, that sense of not belonging—of being out of sync with the rest of the civilians—became so painfully intense it was all he could do to clench his jaw and gut through the sensation.

On those days, it was just easier to skip the VA therapy appointments, rationalizing that it wasn't worth time away from the shop. It was easier not to leave the garage at all; the grocery delivery app was the best thing created, in his opinion. He'd planned to just stay home with the baby…until she'd shit herself all the way up to her hair. Twice.

Ryker wondered if somehow Dr. Kirkland had arranged the entire fiasco, just to prove his point. Ryker could hear the doc's calm, unruffled voice in his head.

"You know PTSD comes in waves, and avoidance is not a therapy. PE and CPT are," the calm, patient tones of Dr. Kirkland explained for the thousandth time the benefits of prolonged exposure and cognitive processing therapy for both veterans and anyone who'd experienced trauma. "Just like Notre Dame had a binder full of plays to get into the end zone, I've got a binder full of ways we can tackle PTSD. All you need to do is participate with me. Suit up. Be in the game."

In every telehealth session, Dr. Kirkland always managed to slide in a reference to his four glorious years of collegiate football. At first Ryker had been suitably impressed—even sharing with doc his days as the Wellsville Lions Varsity quarterback—up until Doc admitted he was the team's kicker. And the backup kicker, at that.

"I just want to be on the sidelines. Or the bench. The bench would be good," Ryker muttered to himself, then, as his niece grabbed onto his left ear, he forcibly pushed those thoughts from his head. He unhooked her chubby hand and lifted her in the air to blow a raspberry on her little belly until she drew her legs up, screeching in her throaty baby voice. "First things first: get you back to the garage, little Lisi."

He unlocked the door to his truck and carefully slid baby Elise inside her car seat.

"Frigging thing," he said under his breath, wishing the makers of this moronic ninety-point baby harness were here so he could strangle them. He'd finally clicked it all together when someone tapped him on the shoulder.

"Excuse me, Mr. Ryker?"

Whipping around, he let his muscles relax. It was the friendly woman from the grocery store with the loosely braided hair and white chef's coat. The one the kids had called Aunt Beamer. The one he'd "saved" from jars of baby food. His muscles tensed again as his neck burned with embarrassment.

He stood at stiff attention, throat working to find something to say, until he finally blurted out the first words that popped into his head.

"Just Ryker. No mister. I mean, I *am* a mister, but..." He stopped his babbling with effort. What in the hell was wrong with him anymore that he couldn't even handle an introduction? He took in a lungful of air, finishing the dangling sentence. "Ryker's my first name."

"Oh." She smiled and nodded, seemingly unbothered by his verbal foaming at the mouth. "Well, Ryker, I just wanted to say thanks again for getting Cecily unstuck and all. I'm Bryce, by the way. Bryce Weatherford." She stuck out her hand and he shook it, appreciating how strong her grip was at the same time he muscled past his embarrassment to meet her eyes. Momentarily, he was distracted by her frank, blue-gray gaze, looking away only when she dangled a plastic bag from her other hand. "Thought you might need these."

Elise yammered "dadadada" in her seat as he took the bag. Inside was the baby shampoo and the two cans of soup he'd left behind in his cart.

Glancing back up, he could tell from Bryce's expression that his face was set in its usual rigid lines—the look his younger brother, Zander, had coined his RBF, or resting bastard face—and he fumbled to pin on a suitable expression.

"Uh, thanks." He paused, recalling the moment in the store when he'd been about to ask her name and then maybe ask her out. Maybe it wasn't too late? His mind desperately tried to come up with a segue, and he spotted the cans of soup. "I'm the stereotypical bachelor—I don't have the time or skills to cook, so canned stuff is my go-to."

"Growing up with a short-order cook for a mom taught me how to whip up a good meal in under ten minutes." Bryce shrugged, her hand coming up to brush an escaped strand of her brown hair from her eyes as the wind whipped around them in the parking lot. "It's all in the prep."

He was hoping she'd zero in on the "bachelor" part versus the cooking part of his statement, and was puzzling out another conversational transition to get her number when she gazed over his shoulder, her lips pursing. She pointed with two fingers to her eyes, then to something outside of his gaze, then back to her eyes in a classic "I'm watching you" gesture.

He swiveled his head to see a canary-yellow BMW the next lane over, with two girls' heads—the one with the fairy wings and the one who'd been stuck under the shelf—pressed up against the glass of the car's rear window. They were both taking turns smashing their lips into the window and puffing out their cheeks until they looked like blowfish under the glass, then pointing and appearing to giggle at each other.

"Your nieces are cute," he said. Then snapped his fingers, finally figuring it out. "Oh, I get it. Aunt Beamer because you drive a BMW."

The woman took her gaze off her car with a laugh. "Other way around. My initials are BMW, so I've been nicknamed 'Beamer' my whole life. I thought it was only fitting I owned one, and this was my first, non-parent-funded car purchase. It's not very conducive to hauling three girls around, but it does the job until I can afford something bigger. Something road-trip friendly."

Ryker found himself repeating the nickname in his head. Beamer. How appropriate for this woman who seemed to be a grinning ball of sunshine and light. Belatedly, he noticed it was his turn to do the reply thing. Clearing his throat, he looked at the plastic bag.

"Thanks for tossing my stuff in your cart. What do I owe you?"

"Zilch. It was the least I could do when your quick thinking saved my niece. And if it had been an active shooter in there, we'd have been in good hands. Are you in the military?"

He nodded, shifting uncomfortably. "I was."

"Let me guess—Marines?" she asked, and when he nodded again, her face brightened as if she'd won a prize. "I knew it—you were fast on your feet and fearless. Well, thank you for your service. Is that how you lost part of your leg?"

Wow. She went there.

Her bright smile hadn't lost any wattage as she awaited his response. Typically, people would studiously avoid looking at his leg, or else they'd stare at it. They rarely asked any questions.

He blinked and moved his head up and down. Damn it—what was wrong with him? He felt as tongue-tied and reclusive as his horror-writing older brother, Drake, had been before he'd met Kate and she'd dragged him into society. Clearly, Ryker needed to get out more.

Yet the woman appeared undaunted by his conversational ineptitude. Her easy expression never shifted as she slid her hand into her jeans pocket underneath the white chef's coat like she had all day to wait for more than a nod to her question.

"Yeah. In Afghanistan." The sting of the word was still there, but as promised, seven years of PE therapy had dulled the barb to a scratch versus a stab. Yet something must've shown on his face, as she was quick to reply.

"I wasn't trying to pry. My dad was born with a leg-length discrepancy and a big port-wine stain on his face, and the thing he hates most are people staring and pussy-footing around it. Nobody likes to be pussyfooted around, right?"

The p-word, twice, falling from the lips of this gorgeous woman made the edges of his mouth quirk up. "True," he said. "Pussyfooters are the worst."

She nodded once, as if he'd passed a test. "Well, I appreciated what you did in there and wanted to pay it forward somehow. I've been really blessed to have met some kind people in town who've helped me adjust to being a single...whatever I am. Mom-like creature, I suppose. But I use the term loosely." Her eyes darted to the yellow BMW, and her expression lost some of its luster. "Truth is, I feel like a failure. Every day is a crisis—the disharmony is exhausting, my self-care is nonexistent, and I've given up finding a work-life balance. Who knew caring for small humans was so hard?".

He knew from the gutted tone of her voice that she needed something. Empathy, or, more likely, she just wanted to be heard. Seen. Validated. Ryker knew the feeling. But coming up with a response was like turning the key in the ignition of a car left sitting in a dusty garage too long. His vocal cords were seized up with disuse, and he wondered if they might squeal from rust as he cobbled together a few sentences.

"Yeah. This is my first whole weekend with little Lisi, and I've been on high alert the entire time. Hard to believe a kid this tiny could fill a diaper so full that it ran up her back and into her hair." He shook his head with the memory of getting crap out of baby Elise's fine, red-brown curls. When he stopped speaking, the woman's bright, inquisitive eyes and expectant expression wrung more words from him. "It took a half bottle of baby shampoo to get the mess out—it was like washing a greased seal. I thought it was tough playing football in the rain, but bathing a wet baby is next-level difficult. Just as I had her clean and wrapped in a towel...she pooped again, and now the whole bottle's empty and I'm sure when I hand her back to her mother on Sunday, there's going to be some rapid-fire questions."

"Oh, I can top that." The woman's lips curved in a wry smile, her eyes glinting with something like competitive mischief. "Last week, Cecily set off the emergency flare she'd dug out of the roadside kit I kept under the seat and nearly blew us all up. We piled out right in the middle of Main Street. The inside of my car looking like the Fourth of July and everyone around us just started taking pictures and making judgments. I had no idea parenting was so hard—did you? I mean, someone should write a damn manual."

Ryker had been marveling at how he and his brothers had never managed to set off a flare inside the car—they'd likely done everything else to drive Mom crazy after Dad died—when the rest of her words made it through his rarely used conversational filters.

She thought he was Elise's dad. He rushed to explain.

"I'm not—"

Suddenly, the horn sounded from the nearby BMW. Both girls were still messing around in the rear window, so it must be the oldest girl beeping for her aunt.

"I've got to run, or they'll find a way to destroy my car." The woman grinned. The smile brightened her whole face, crinkling the skin next to her eyes.

In his head, Ryker tried to classify her eye color as blue or gray, while at the same time, he berated himself. Why hadn't he asked her out when he had the chance, before he'd acted like a kook?

Suddenly, he realized she was still talking. He struggled to catch up with her words.

"...the baby shampoo, but honestly, as far as the canned soup goes, take my advice and save that crap for a blizzard. Next time, soup's on me. We caregivers have to stick together to survive these tiny humans. Agreed?"

Dumbly, he nodded. Then he noticed he was standing at loose attention, his posture rigid and his hands at his thighs, thumbs pointing straight down where the seam of his trousers would be, if he were in his dress blues. Her voice had a crisp, no-nonsense, "this woman is in charge and means business" cadence that his Marine-trained brain reacted to by standing at the ready to receive orders. He made a concerted effort to relax his shoulders and take the business card she'd thrust at his chest.

Bryce Weatherford, Sous Chef
PattyCakes and Coffee Café
Wellsville, NY

He blinked, details of past conversations with his family sifted through the teeth-like gears of his mind. This was the woman his mom had hired a few months ago to take over the kitchen and expand the menu. The same new employee she'd been trying to not-so-subtly suggest would be a nice person for Ryker to "get to know" if he would only stop by the bakery—one more woman in the seemingly never-ending stream of them his family was always thrusting in his path, as if he were incapable of finding his own dates.

"Don't let the title fool you," Bryce said, misinterpreting his pause. "Patty gives all her employees business cards with fancy titles, because she says words matter. Although I've told her whipping up sandwiches and soups hardly qualifies as a sous chef, Patty insists. Since she had these cards printed, I didn't want to seem ungrateful—she's been good to me and the girls—so I occasionally give them out as a promo-type thing."

He squinted at her, wondering if she truly didn't know who he was, wondering if somehow his mom had orchestrated this whole meetup. Then he noticed writing

bleeding through from the back of the card. He flipped it
over to read a quickly scrawled note:

Redeem for a free bowl of soup—Bryce.

"You're giving me a coupon? To PattyCakes?" The
words were his way of digging into her motive, yet his
tone must've been wrapped in barbed wire from the way
she winced.

"Um, yeah. It's a really good café." Her smile fled as she
shrugged. "Feel free to swing in sometime."

Then she was gone, jogging over to her car, where she
put both hands on the trunk, pushing up and down to
make the car jump like an amusement park ride. The two
girls in the back giggled and shrieked, the sound muted
but still carried by the spring breeze.

He watched her get in the car, still trying to figure out
if this had all been some strange, elaborate setup by Mom,
or Drake, or even his younger brother, Zander. But then he
recalled Cecily, and the way she was stuck under the shelf.
That couldn't have been premeditated. He might've spent
more time figuring it out, except just then the unmistakable stench of baby poop hit him like a cloud of tear gas.

Cupping his hand over his nose, he turned to Elise, who
grinned, flashing those eight tiny teeth, and the swollen
gums of teeth to come—which, according to his brother,
were the reason for the diarrhea. Erupting teeth apparently
came with erupting diapers.

He glanced at his watch, then at the baby.

"If we hurry, we have enough time to get you hosed
down before Staff Sergeant Mahoney arrives."

* * *

As it happened, he was right. At exactly 11:30 a.m., after he'd cleaned up Elise and dressed her in the last clean outfit in the diaper bag—a black long-sleeved onesie with the words *My Little Black Dress* spelled out in glittery gems above a scratchy tutu-like frill—the door to his garage banged open.

"Staff Sergeant Matthews!" came Tarun Mahoney's crisp bark from behind the '69 Cougar Eliminator Ryker had suspended on the lift. "Front and center."

"Here." Ryker held Elise with one hand on the makeshift changing table he'd rigged atop a rolling metal toolbox as he battled with the diaper. "Give me a sec, Mahoney."

"I'm not asking for a blow job. But a salute would be nice." Tarun appeared carrying a pink pastry box, his face expressionless under his close-cropped hair. Yet his eyes glinted with pride as he pivoted in his woodland cammies to show off his insignia: three chevrons above two rockers, a set of crossed rifles in between. "Especially when I stopped at your mom's place for celebratory cupcakes."

His best friend, his brother-in-arms, his fellow staff sergeant, had finally been promoted.

Ryker's stomach plummeted to his knees. "You made Gunnie. Congrats, man. I'd salute," Ryker said, wiping his hands on the fiftieth wet wipe, buying time as he fixed his face. "But I'm digging baby crap out from between my fingers."

Gunnery sergeant was the next rank Ryker would have achieved, had he not been injured. It was the last rank before master sergeant—the same level as his late father.

It was all he'd ever wanted, to achieve master sergeant. And it was forever out of reach.

"Did someone finally make you a father?" Tarun squinted at Elise as he set down the pastry box. "Funny, your mom never mentioned it when I chatted her up a few minutes ago. All she said was to drag your ass out of this place. Not in those words, of course, but Patty always gets her point across. It's one of the things I love about her—that, and her cooking. Those new soups and sandwiches are incredible. She gave me a sample as I was waiting for the cupcakes. Why didn't you tell me your mom had hired a new chef and expanded the menu?"

Because I didn't know. Because I avoid the café, my family, and all civilians as much as possible. That may make me a rotten son, but my presence lately is far worse.

Ryker kept those words to himself, his gaze on Elise. He lifted the baby to his shoulder, thankful for her warm, baby-powder-scented body between him and his friend.

"This is my niece, Lisi. Well, her parents call her Elise, but I think the name is far too serious for such a little one. Officially, I'm watching her for the weekend so Drake and his wife can focus on the upcoming book launch they're having at an abandoned sanitarium up in Rochester." Ryker allowed Elise to lean forward and grab at Tarun's lid.

Tarun ducked his head, obliging the baby's tiny hands, and allowing her to take off his camo cap. He smiled as she screamed in delight, then focused his perceptive brown eyes on Ryker.

"And unofficially?"

"Unofficially, it's another ploy by my family in their never-ending quest to fix me. Make sure I'm not...at risk."

Tarun was quiet for a beat, his gaze penetrating. "Should they be worried?"

Ryker grabbed a premade bottle of formula from Kate's diaper bag and headed toward the makeshift coffee bar. It was situated next to the dilapidated front end of a vintage yellow-and-white Volkswagen bus he'd bolted to the garage's wall. Jabbing the hot-water button on the Keurig, he handed Elise to Tarun.

"Hold her while I warm up a bottle," he said. Tarun obeyed, holding Elise under her arms a good distance from his chest, as if she were a delicate bag of something toxic. Which, with her latest diaper explosions, wasn't far from the truth.

Elise's chubby little legs kicked delightedly and she belly laughed as Tarun made faces at her until Ryker at last had the bottle sitting in a bath of steaming water inside an old coffee can. Yet Ryker knew his buddy wasn't going to let him off without a direct answer. He waited until he'd retrieved a rolling stool for them both and took Elise.

Ryker snagged the baby blanket from atop the VW bus's front end and draped it on Elise, settling her in the crook of his left arm. "I'm not suicidal. I want to be left alone. That's all."

"Is it?"

Ryker bit back the immediate *Yes,* searching for his truth—an excavation that was always excruciating when he was with Tarun. Something about their shared past— the fact that they were both middle siblings, Tarun from a Vietnamese family where he was the first ever to enlist, and Ryker from a family whose men had been Marines practically since the battle against Montezuma—

had brought them together in basic training. Then, after they'd both been deployed to Afghanistan, fought side by side there...well, it made sense Ryker was unable to lie or hide the truth from Tarun as he did with civilians and even his family. Ryker finally spoke.

"I'm sick of watching my brothers live out their happily ever afters."

Tarun's eyebrows rose.

"Brothers? I mean, Drake's been married to that event planner who got him to write romance in addition to horror—what's her name?"

"Kate."

At the name, Tarun snapped his fingers on both hands in a three-snap, staccato gesture, an old habit he'd had ever since Ryker had met him in boot camp years ago.

"Yes, her. So if it's not Drake, I assume something's new with your baby brother, then?"

Ryker shook his head, snagging the bottle from the coffee can and testing the temperature by dribbling a bit of it on his left wrist, jostling Elise's head into a weird angle to do so. Luckily, the kid was so good-natured she just gave a gummy smile at the awkward manhandling, grabbing at his hands as he guided the bottle to her mouth.

"Nothing new, exactly. Zander and Imani are still engaged. No date for the wedding, but they're madly in love." Ryker watched Elise sucking contentedly on her bottle, her eyes slipping closed. He envied her security and innocence. "I'm happy for them. But it feels like the universe is giving me the middle finger."

"And?" Tarun prompted, doing a rolling, "give me more" motion with his hand. "What's really got your RBF in turbo-mode? I noticed you favoring your left leg. Are you okay?"

"I'm fine—"

"Don't lie. Not to me." Tarun traced the chrome VW emblem, lingering on the ragged hole in the outer edge of the "V," the other piece of evidence in this room of the damage done by the IED's detonation. "When you save a guy's life, it's a rule—"

"That you get to be up in his business for eternity?"

"It's your HO rearing its ugly head again, isn't it?" Tarun asked, undeterred by Ryker's words. "Have you gotten any bloodwork?"

Ryker supposed it was the bond forged from their shared wartime experience, as Tarun was practically psychic when it came to the bizarre twists and turns of Ryker's mind and mood. While his family knew of his battle with trauma-induced bone heterotopic ossification, only Tarun knew the extent of the mental and physical pain the rebellion of his own cells caused Ryker, growing in soft tissue and muscle, with no way to halt the sneaky enemy other than radiation . . . or more surgery. The latter was what kept him up at night.

"It might be HO." It was all Ryker could make himself admit, even to Tarun. "I'm due for bloodwork in another month."

"Maybe you should get a bone scan—see if there's any shit forming in there," Tarun said, and when Ryker didn't answer, he shook his head. "John Wayne used to say, 'Life is hard. It's harder if you're stupid.' Don't be stupid. I'll drive you to Walter Reed, or maybe your brother can hook us up with the fancy copter he rents to take you in an hour—"

Ryker cut him off. "You know what'll happen if I say anything. Drake will drop the rest of his book tour, Zander will postpone his classes, my mom will freak out and close down the bakery to hover. All because I've got some renegade cells acting up. It's not serious enough yet to be an attention whore. I'll double down on my ibuprofen."

"Allowing your family in your life isn't being an attention whore. It's being a real boy."

Ryker smirked at the familiar accusation. "Who wants to be a real boy when you can be a cool-ass cyborg?"

"You got any swelling?" Tarun asked.

Ryker knew his best friend wouldn't drop it until he had visual proof, so he shifted Elise and hefted the edge of his gym shorts. With one hand, he rolled down the sleeve above the cuff of his prosthetic, revealing that the scarred pink-and-white tissue of his residual limb was only mildly puffy and irritated.

"See? It's fine."

"If it's not your HO, what's going on?"

Ryker gazed at Elise. She was such an angel. Such a blessing...then his mind strayed to the beautiful woman from the grocery store. Bryce. The one he'd almost asked out on a date—a first for him in more months than he cared to admit. Then she'd said that comment about parenting, assuming he was Elise's father, and the comment had ignited in his belly and bottomed out his chest at the same time.

"These never-ending trips for radiation on my hip and knee to keep the HO at bay. Although they're careful, the docs told me it's pretty unlikely I'm ever going to...have kids."

"And?" Tarun asked, as if that weren't enough of a buzzkill.

"And that makes me not an attractive target. For women."

"Oh, but your winning personality and ready smile is winning hearts the world over? You think the possibility of your sterility is the only reason you're not lighting it up on Tinder?"

Ryker scowled. "I deactivated that account ages ago. I've had so many radiation treatments I practically glow in the dark. My sterility is more than a possibility. It's a promise."

"Not all women are sniffing out sperm donors. Bunches of them are looking for love, I hear." Tarun's mouth curved in a smile. "Quit being so doom-and-gloom and get yourself out there. Date someone. If you find the right person, you can always adopt, like my parents did."

Ryker gave a soft snort, careful not to wake Elise, who'd fallen into a milk-drunk sleep, formula oozing from the corners of her mouth. He eased the bottle from her lips and used the blanket to sop up the mess.

"If dating and falling in love is simple, why haven't you done it?"

Tarun's gaze was steady. "Because of the dreams. Same as you. Or are you going to tell me the blanket and pillow I spy behind this '72 VW front end is folded up there because you lack storage?"

Ryker flinched, regretting that he'd told Tarun about his night terrors; how he sometimes relived the IED explosion and the memory of the Marine brother he couldn't save, and how the sight of the vehicle's yellow front end bolted to the wall of his garage calmed him. It was ridiculous—the part-metal man crouching behind his metal safety blanket wishing for the nightmare to release its claws from his heart, wishing for the morning, wishing...

But of all the people in this world, Tarun understood. Too well.

"I know I'm lucky to be here. We're both lucky to be here." Ryker examined Elise's face, slack with the kind of innocent sleep he hadn't had in years. "But when my mind rebels with PTSD moments, and this bone shit acts up, 'lucky' feels more like..."

"Cursed," Tarun finished, his gaze glancing off the metal surfaces of the garage like a ricocheting bullet. "While I was training the next batch of recruits, I met a girl at Camp Lejeune. She worked on base at the day care. We dated a few times, then she slept over. I thought it was all cool, except the next morning I found her locked in my bathroom. She'd slept in my tub. Apparently, in the middle of the night, I'd given a solo performance of the 'Best of Afghanistan,' a one-man soliloquy. Super stirring. But she didn't stick around for a curtain call."

Ryker knew better than to offer a hug or dole out some form of pity. All his friend wanted was to be heard without judgment. Understood. And nothing said you cared like a little game of PTSD one-upmanship.

"That's nothing. I protected five innocent civilians from baby food jars today." Ryker gave his friend a rundown of this morning's adventure at the grocery store. He played up the ridiculousness, channeling his younger brother's humor and ability to lighten the mood until, finally, they were both hooting with laughter.

Elise's eyes opened and she gave a perfect imitation of his

sister-in-law's green-eyed glare until they swallowed down the rest of their hilarity.

"Wait." Tarun wiped the leaking tears from his eyes, still chuckling. "She gave you her number *after* you herded them like goats? Sounds like a keeper. Or at least a good segue into the dating market."

"It wasn't her number. It was a coupon to my mother's place." He didn't tell his best friend that when he met Bryce their connection was like a spark plug to his chest. For the first time since leaving the Marines, his heart had chugged to life. But like becoming a gunnery sergeant, having a happily ever after was no longer in his future.

Ryker forced thoughts of the woman out of his head. Best he be like the metal in his leg: sturdy, reliable, without emotional rust. Like a robot.

Tarun leaned against the VW front end. "You need a service dog, my friend. I'd have one, but you can't still be serving and qualify. Vazquez got one—a German shepherd named Valor—and he says it's a game changer. I can't force you to date, but I can hound you about getting your application in to Paws of War."

"Done," Ryker said. "Submitted it right after you lectured me at Thanksgiving. Got my paperwork in from Dr. Kirkland to show I was in therapy and everything. The wait list is almost two years, so don't go tattling to everyone about this. My family will get their hopes up, Drake will call his publishing contacts to pull strings, someone will write a freaking article about it, trying to get me moved up the list, and it'll be smeared all over hell. This is my journey. My load to carry."

"No tattling. Roger that." Tarun gave a salute with only

his middle finger. "But for the record, it's not only your load. You are surrounded by people who love you, and—"

"Where are they sending you next?" he asked Tarun, his voice clipped.

Tarun took the hint and changed the subject. As his best friend launched into a story about his promotion, Ryker held a baby who wasn't his and listened to a career path forever gone from his reach. He nodded along, smiling and saying all the right words.

Just as if he were a real boy.

CHAPTER 3

"But what if he really was Superman?" Cecily asked as Bryce drove them to dance class. Her eight-year-old niece had to yell the question to be heard over Addison's full-throated singing of "You Can Fly" from *Peter Pan*.

"He's not." June scowled at her younger sisters from her spot in the shotgun position. "Quit kicking my seat, Stinky."

"Don't call names." Bryce shot June a death glare, which her oldest niece matched with the same competitive intensity that Bentley had, and the jab of pain at the memory of her brother made Bryce blink rapidly, gripping the wheel hard.

"What? She smells like feet. And spoiled milk." June sulked, staring out the passenger window. "Maybe if you made her take a bath like a *real* parent—"

"He's not Superman," Addison piped up, halting her song mid-chorus. "Mr. Ryker's a pirate, but now he's tired again. He tol' me so."

"Tired?" Bryce asked, frowning as she turned in to the dance studio's parking lot. The man had seemed anything but tired—the only thing exhausting about him was his continual reappearance in her dreams since their encounter earlier in the week. "He said he was tired?"

"No, he said he was *re*tired." June huffed out an annoyed breath. "A retired pirate."

"That's a pirate who is tired all over again," Addison explained in her "that's what I said" tone of voice. "He's got a baby and they make you re-tired every day. Right, Aunt Beamer?"

"Mmm," Bryce hummed. She'd learned this was the best way to handle her nieces' unanswerable questions. "Get your shoes on, Cecily. We don't need another pair of ripped tights."

Cecily grumbled about the fact she liked ripped tights better, but Bryce ignored the argument bait. Last time she'd forgotten tights, Cecily had a meltdown when Bryce offered to go back and get them. The middle Weatherford girl was the easiest by far, so she tried to be patient with her quirks.

"Shoes on, Cici."

Pouting, Cecily slid on her dingy, untied sneakers over her pink tights. When Bryce opened the door, it was like releasing a greyhound. Her niece blew past the other parents and kids, blasting toward the dome-shaped building of Dancing Through Life.

"See you after class." She waved to her nieces, blowing Addison the required number of air-kisses—three—and trying not to growl at June as the tween rolled her eyes and sauntered away without a goodbye or a backward glance.

"If she rolls her eyes at me one more time, I swear..." Bryce muttered under her breath and was startled when a singsong voice behind her answered.

"Swearing won't help," said Imani Lewis, the girls' dance teacher and the studio's owner. The woman's chestnut hair was pulled into a ponytail, and her eyes glittered with mischief as she hugged Bryce in greeting. "I teach enough teens to know, and who can blame them for the attitude? Middle school is terrible. But I think your nieces—and you—are doing fine, all things considered. It just takes time."

Bryce felt sudden moisture in her eyes and blinked furiously, caught off guard by Imani's heartfelt comment. The dance teacher had extended a hand in friendship when they'd met, telling Bryce how she'd lost her own mother in high school and offering to help with the girls anytime.

Bryce smiled. "Thanks, Imani. Do you need me to stay, or—"

"We'll call if we need you." Imani made a "shoo" gesture. "You go enjoy some 'me' time. Maybe grab a milkshake at the Texas Hot? That always makes me feel better. I've got Lactaid if you need it."

"I think I'm going to go for a run. Clear my head."

Imani nodded enthusiastically. "Great idea. See you in an hour."

From her pocket, Bryce pulled a ring of keys as full as if she were a medieval jailer. She flipped through the ones for PattyCakes and the upstairs apartment she and the girls rented from Patty, the one to her post office box, and finally past the one for her Jet Ski, which she'd left, along with her single life, floating forlornly in the Tampa Bay region. Plucking off her car's key fob, she stripped down to the sports tank and leggings she'd worn under her clothes. She'd been hoping to grab time for a run. Spring days in Western New York were unpredictable, with snow one week followed by balmy and warm days, like today. It would have been a shame to miss out on some fresh air and exercise. Stuffing her car's key fob into her leggings, she set off.

Ten minutes later, Bryce felt the tension of the day, the week, the past half year, lessening. It was temporary; as soon as she stopped running, she'd become Aunt Beamer, with the hectic-craziness that title now entailed.

She jogged over the curved bridge above the dance studio, turning toward Maple Avenue. Her lungs burned, and thoughts of running with her brother—he'd always help her train for soccer season—flooded her mind, making her smile.

"C'mon, baby sis—you're tougher than that. Show me who runs this field," Bentley would say as she'd race against him in suicide sprints, using his words and his presence to encourage her. He was always there for her, but especially in sports, making it to every soccer game, even after he'd graduated high school. Bentley was her support, her person to make her challenge herself. Dig deeper. Be better.

But now he was gone.

Unbidden, thoughts of that night came to her. She'd been at work, prepping for dinner, when her cell phone rang. On her stove simmered her latest creation, toasted orzo chicken soup, named for the way she roasted the orzo in butter before cooking it, lending a nutty, caramelized flavor to the soup. When she'd seen it was Bentley calling, she'd immediately answered, grinning.

"Hey, Bentley. Wish you were here to taste tonight's soup. You're missing out—"

Another man's voice interrupted, his tone solemn.

"This is Sheriff O'Grady from the Wellsville Police Department, and there's been an accident. You were listed in Bentley Weatherford's cell phone under emergency contact?"

All the kitchen sounds receded.

"Yes. I'm his sister. What happened? Is he okay?"

Then, before Bryce was ready for his next phrase, it was on her, strangling the breath from her lungs. "I'm sorry to inform you Bentley Weatherford and his wife, Heather, were in a head-on collision with a driver who ran a stop sign. His wife is in critical condition, but Bentley...he died on impact."

The sheriff's voice continued, telling her facts she heard but didn't absorb until later: Heather was on life support in the hospital, the children were not in the vehicle during the accident, and the at-fault, uninsured driver of the other vehicle had also perished. Bryce had stood there, ladle dripping toasted orzo chicken soup in scalding-hot splats down her arm, leaving raindrop-shaped welts she didn't feel and wouldn't notice until the next day as she boarded the plane for New York, where the process of burying Bentley and understanding the ramification of his death began...

Bryce stumbled, remembering that horrific weekend and the surreal funerals that followed, first Bentley and then, a few days later, his wife, Heather, who had finally succumbed to her injuries. After the funerals, their will was read and Bryce discovered she'd been named as her nieces' guardian. Her shock was probably as profound as Harvey and Adele Payne's—the girls' maternal grandparents—as they discovered they were the executor to the meager estate but had no guardianship role.

That's when the lawyering up began.

Her mouth twisted, recalling how her formerly plump nest egg from working as a sauté chef in Tampa had shriveled to the size of a jelly bean. Despite her job at PattyCakes and the occasional catering clients she booked, Bryce knew that when the judge viewed her budget in the custody trial next month it would be glaringly obvious that the funds going out were greater than the funds coming in.

"The court will look at three prongs in this guardianship challenge," Lillian Goodwin, her attorney, had said. "Who has been in the children's lives? Where do the kids want to go? And who can support them best, both financially and otherwise?"

Bryce had lived in Tampa until recently, so the only times she had been in the girls' lives was on her vacations to New York, or when the family came down to Disney World. Being local, the Paynes had a larger claim on the girls' past. As for the second prong, she knew her nieces had initially been enthusiastic about living with their aunt. However, that feeling cooled considerably when Bryce began enforcing rules, like chores and homework done before using electronics. Now the maternal grandparents were the "fun" ones.

Lately, Bryce had been hyper-focused on ensuring that the third prong of the guardianship trial—the finances and the "otherwise" piece of the decision—might be in her favor. So far, it wasn't looking amazing. While she adored her nieces, their life together was a mad scramble from the moment Addie startled her awake until well past the time June reluctantly switched off her bedroom lamp.

Bryce's life was like a bunch of kitchen buzzers going off

at once, all the time. How did she figure out what problem took priority?

Like June's hostility. She'd passed it off as typical teen angst, but what if it was more? Addison's bed-wetting was almost as disturbing as her refusal to take off her yellow, glittery fairy wings. Bryce had been forced to argue with the teacher and then escalate to the principal, who'd finally agreed to let Addison wear them only because Heather had been such a big part of the school's PTA before she'd passed. Then there was Cecily. She fought against Bryce washing her clothes, and she stank like a goat. Getting her to shower was a weekly battle.

If only Bentley were here.

Then she'd still be fun Aunt Beamer, and her brother and Heather would be dealing with tween-aged sarcasm grenades, middle-of-the-night sheet changes, and the WWE-style moves required to decontaminate grubby kids.

Shoving useless if-onlys from her mind, Bryce pushed her body faster, as if to outrun it all. She sprinted up the hill toward the brick-red Victorian mansion owned by horror writer Drake Matthews—Patty's infamous oldest son. A crowd of people mingled outside, posing for pictures next to the gates designed to look like bat wings that surrounded the old house. As Bryce slowed to a walk, she caught snippets of their conversations.

"Can you believe they have a *baby* living in there? I mean, it's sweet he wrote a romance, but it's not like one book with a 'happily-ever-after' ending offsets his reputation as the Knight of Nightmares," one woman commented.

A guy in a Buffalo Bills sweatshirt nodded, stuffing his hands into his pockets as he peered at the mansion. "Yeah.

Did you know Drake Matthews eats his meat raw? Who does that?"

Bryce rolled her eyes, coming to a stop. She hated it when people made snap judgments. She'd seen enough of that while traveling with her dad to last a lifetime.

"I can tell you who." Bryce used the no-nonsense voice she'd developed to carry over the din of a busy, all-male, five-star kitchen. "Anyone who enjoys the fine delicacy of steak tartare." She didn't care if sweat was running down the sides of her face, or that her hair was probably sticking out of her braid like it always did when she ran. She wasn't about to let a bunch of looky-loos shit all over Patty's son. "It's sinfully good. At the restaurant I worked for in Tampa, I'd make a sauce relevée for it that's so delicious it'd make you forget your momma's name."

"Hear! Hear!" came a male voice, along with a slow clap. Bryce couldn't tell whether it was sarcastic or sincere until the speaker worked his way through the parting crowd, revealing a tall guy wearing a black Under Amour baseball cap with a figure that should be chiseled in granite.

It was her supermarket superhero. Ryker.

His expression was almost a smile, with his lips canted up on one side. Many gawked at his prosthetic leg, clearly revealed under his long athletic shorts as he made his way through the throng to stand in front of the gates.

He stopped clapping, then looked toward the Victorian, squinting an eye.

"You know, if you go around to the back, you'll see the attic. Some say a little girl haunts the place. But I think it's a woman—you can sometimes see her shadow in the turret window."

Ryker hadn't finished the sentence before the flock of onlookers fled down the sidewalk and around the corner, cell phone cameras pointed at the house as they jostled for position. Soon the area in front of the bat-winged gates was empty except for Ryker and Bryce.

"You really believe those ghost stories?" Bryce asked, opting to forgo the niceties. The guy hadn't bothered to stop by PattyCakes all week long. Clearly, he wasn't interested in either her or her soup, and she wasn't about to make a fool of herself by giving him an opening like she'd done before.

He shook his head.

"I practically grew up there, and the scariest thing I ever saw was a dead mouse in the basement. I wanted to intervene before my brother's fans decided you were a colossal buzzkill and revolted."

Bryce blinked, processing this. "Your brother is Drake Matthews?"

"One of them. I can, um, get you an autograph, if you want?"

Bryce snorted. "I have zero interest. No offense. I'm sure Drake's talented, but I only read cookbooks." Then her stress-addled brain finally made the last connection and she gasped. "Wait. If Drake's your brother, then your other brother is Zander, and your mom is my boss, Patty Matthews."

Ryker shrugged, his hand coming up to rub the back of his neck. "Guilty."

The ping of his name from the grocery store finally made sense. Patty had mentioned her son Ry a few times, and she'd assumed Ry was short for Ryan. Since there weren't any recent pictures on the wall of Patty's café and he never came in—at least not during the forty hours a week she was there—Bryce hadn't recognized him at the grocery store. "Why aren't you ever in PattyCakes?"

Ryker's already stony expression got downright granite-esque. "I don't get out much."

Bryce got the feeling there was a lot to unpack in that sentence, but a glance at her watch told her she didn't have the time to try, even if he'd been in a talking mood. Which, gauging by his monosyllabic answers, he wasn't. She flashed a polite smile. "I've got to run. I need to pick up the girls from dance, but it was nice to officially—"

"Can I join you for a run? Got my fast leg on and everything." He gestured to his black, spring-like prosthetic. When she hesitated, he lifted his left eyebrow, his tone sardonic. "Don't worry. I'll slow my pace so you can keep up."

Bryce felt her polite smile widen at the challenge, then she shrugged. "Suit yourself."

She pivoted from the house and began to jog, figuring he might need time to warm up, and she'd already logged at least a mile. But he kept up with her, stride for stride, his breathing unlabored. Silence pressed in on her, threatening to drag her own thoughts back to the forefront of her mind. She grabbed for the easiest conversational filler.

"Is it hard to have your brother be so famous that his readers mob the town?"

"Sometimes." He was quiet then, and Bryce glanced sideways at him.

"Care to elaborate?" she asked. "Or are one-word responses a specialty of yours?"

The corner of his mouth twitched. "Drake's writing really started to catch fire when I was on my first deployment, so I missed the gradual, organic rise I'm told happened. By the time I'd returned Stateside, he was like a rock star, jetting around the country for signing events. But since we grew up in Wellsville, everyone here takes his fame in stride. It's usually newcomers or tourists we have to watch out for."

"Well, you don't have to watch out for me. I've been here for..." She did the quick math in her head. "...almost seven months. Your mom can vouch I've never once asked about Drake."

"It's hard not to ignore my oldest brother's presence in there—the pictures are everywhere. Her café is like a Drake shrine."

"Damn firstborns. Always stealing the spotlight." She remembered her parents' pride at Bentley's football games and with each A he effortlessly earned in high school, while she struggled to make C's. Then, like someone took a meat cleaver to her gut, she gasped, stumbling. Bentley was gone. He'd been the apple of her parents' eyes and her hero. And now he was buried in a double plot with his wife, never to be a spotlight-stealer again.

"You okay?" Ryker asked.

She wasn't okay. But she wasn't about to dump her sorrow on this guy. Instead, she went for her favorite position. Offense.

"Yep. I'm fine. In fairness, your mom has pictures of Zander in there, and I recall seeing a few photos that must be you. There's one behind the counter of a guy in dress blues. Patty said the picture had been taken when you got your Silver Star and Purple Heart. Pretty impressive stuff."

He ignored the compliment. "How long have you been working for my mom?"

"Patty's been my mentor since I arrived from Florida. I stopped into the bakery to buy cupcakes for the girls before the...funeral." She tripped over the ugly word and the memories it conjured. "I asked if she needed any help at the café and told her about my time at Chez Pierre. She hired me on the spot. Said she'd been trying to figure out a way to do some menu expansion, and that I was a godsend. Your mom even convinced me to move into the empty apartment above the café when my brother's landlord wouldn't let me take over their rental."

Ryker gave one nod. "Makes sense. Mom just used it for storage. I'm sure she's happy the place can be useful."

"Your mother is amazing. Actually, your whole family is Hallmark-movie perfect. Imani is my nieces' dance teacher, and Zander helped me move into my apartment. He said he was born to haul things, and I've never seen furniture move upstairs so fast in my life."

"Yeah. My brothers are superstars, and Mom is next in line for sainthood." His tone was neutral, but Bryce sensed something behind his words.

"And you're the middle brother. Don't tell me the stereo-types about middle siblings are true? That you're all..." She paused, searching for a word.

"Undervalued and unheard?"

"I was going to say 'complicated,' but your description sounds way more angsty. I'd love any tips to surviving my nieces' angst, so please. Say more."

He gave a low chuckle, like an engine rumbling in the distance. "Not angst. More like..." He paused. "...never being all that important. Even when you're the first to achieve something—like football quarterback or a military rank—it's slotted between what the angel oldest is doing and the needs of the baby of the family."

"That explains so much of Cecily's behavior," Bryce said. "She's the middle, too, and with her older sister's anger at the world and the constant, make-sure-she-doesn't-die work involved in caring for her younger sister, I bet poor Cici doesn't know where she fits in. Except for bath times, she's quiet and just goes with the flow. It's easy to accidentally overlook her."

They were quiet, their feet hitting the sidewalk at the same cadence until Bryce couldn't stand the silence. She blurted the question bubbling up in her mind since she'd seen him in the grocery store with his child. "So, you're not married?"

As soon as she spoke, she regretted it. She'd been wondering about the baby-daddy situation he had going on with baby Lisi's mother, but realized belatedly that this topic was too personal, too soon. She opened her mouth to apologize when he replied.

"No. You?"

"Nope. My job ate up all my free time in Tampa, and now that I'm here...well, I don't exactly have game anymore."

He flashed her a look, the very edges of his mouth quirked up in a way that might be his version of amused. "Not true."

"But you didn't stop by PattyCakes," she said. When he shot her a puzzled glance, she clarified. "I gave you that coupon, but you didn't come in to redeem it. My game clearly is off."

She'd expected him to be taken aback by her bluntness. People—especially men—usually were.

But he replied with equal candor. "I figured it was either an elaborate setup from my meddling mother or maybe a pity move. After my grocery store...incident, I thought you were just being nice."

"It wasn't a setup, and for the record, I don't have much use for that flavor of 'nice' in my life." She gave him a sidelong look as she picked up her pace. Yet he kept up without a hitch in his stride, so she continued, enjoying the wind against her skin. Evening had begun to fall, and they jogged from streetlight circle to streetlight circle, glorying in the cool night air. "I find being honest is much more effective. Cuts the bullshit and saves time. Besides, I saw enough of those kinds of looks at my dad growing up, and pity is debilitating and demoralizing. It's about as useful as 'thoughts and prayers' if you're really in a bind. I say friendship, a smile, or even a good bowl of soup is worth more than a bucketload of pity, thoughts, or prayers."

For the first time, the storm clouds on Ryker's face cleared. Then the most miraculous thing happened. He smiled.

The expression transformed his face, making him look years younger than the permi-scowl he'd worn all evening. The shadow of whiskers darkening his cheeks and chin were contrasted by the gleaming of his teeth as he grinned.

His smile was like looking at the sun—all sparkle and blinding brilliance.

Bryce was mesmerized. Until her toe caught the crack of the sidewalk.

A yelp of surprise burst from her lips, and her feet *smack-smack-smack*ed against the pavement, trying to recover from her trip-up. Her belly lurched as she realized she was going down.

She scrunched her eyes closed, yanking her hands into fists in front of her face a millisecond before impact...

But she never hit anything.

Instead of face-planting, she was snatched up by the back of her tank top and bra like a plush toy in a kids' claw machine. Her lids flew open to see the dark sidewalk receding as she was yanked back, giving her a close-up view of the metallic aspect of Ryker's prosthesis. The curved, spring-like metal crunched on the sidewalk once before his right sneaker came down to bring them to an abrupt, skidding stop.

He helped her stand, and she grabbed his shoulders to steady herself. Her face was inches from his as she gasped, breathless with adrenaline.

"You okay?" he asked.

She heard the genuine concern in his voice. His eyebrows were drawn together and he squeezed her forearms gently, as if probing for injury. Suddenly, something inside her shifted. She became hyper-aware of the corded muscles under her palms, the heat of his hands on her arms, the minty smell of his breath. His hand came up to brush away hair that had fallen into her face. She stared, mesmerized, at his full lips. They pursed slightly as he gazed at her. Giddily, she wondered if he was going to kiss her...

"Bryce, are you hurt?" he asked, instead. "Talk to me."

It was like shaking herself out of a really hot fantasy, and she shivered, finally mustering the strength to take a step back.

"Holy shit. You have super-fast reflexes," she said with a

shaky laugh. She dropped her arms from his shoulders, her heart at last settling into a more normal pattern. "The girls call you the supermarket superhero, and I think they're right. Seriously, you need a cape."

His lips quirked up at the edges. "Supermarket superhero? Those are big shoes to fill. Plus, I don't like wearing costumes." Ryker's eyes flicked down her body, then to her face, and his almost-smile grew tight. "Speaking of costumes, I think you might be having...an equipment failure?"

Bryce looked down.

Her mouth dropped open as she realized she looked like a bad actress in a porn movie. Her boobs had spilled over the top of the DD jog bra she'd worn under her tank. The top, thankfully, hadn't ripped, but her nipples jutted out against the thin fabric, as if celebrating release from their former jail.

"Whoops. Can you, uh, turn around while I harness these puppies?"

He pivoted, his expression still intense, except the corners of his mouth had lifted to what might be called a restrained grin. He faced the empty street, blocking her from view of any potential traffic. Amusement flavored his voice when he spoke.

"I'm sorry. Did I rip your shirt?"

"Nope." She hefted each breast and stuffed it back into her bra, which was considerably looser now since he'd grabbed it to save her from falling. "Okay, you can turn around. Turns out you may be a pirate, but you are officially *not* a bodice ripper. But unfortunately, this 'jog' bra has been downgraded to a 'peacefully strolling' bra."

A low chuckle rippled the air between them as they walked. Ryker's full-wattage smile had been replaced by a subdued grin. Bryce was surprised by the desire to do or say something funny to provoke that full-on joyous expression once more.

As if sensing the direction of her thoughts, he spoke as they entered the dance studio's parking lot. "What's the soup tomorrow? Maybe I'll swing by PattyCakes. I mean, since you're sure it beats my canned stuff."

"Creamy potato and Italian wedding soup are tomorrow's specials, but I always have homemade chicken noodle and tomato. And every soup I make *owns* your canned crap— like 'slaps it on the ass and pulls its hair' owns it." The words had barely left her mouth when she realized she'd released her inner trucker, the dirty-mouthed vocabulary that she got away with in the all-male kitchen but wasn't appropriate in regular society. She cleared her throat, wishing she could suck the words back into her lungs. "I mean, yes. My soups are good."

"You had me at 'slaps it on the ass' good. I'll be there." He stopped short of the dance studio's front doors, and for the second time that night she found herself bathed in the full power of his smile. It lifted his cheeks and, like rolling back the sands of time, made him look boyish and playful. And wickedly hot.

"Ohkmph," she garbled out some sort of word, her brain still in smile-shock. When had making a man smile ever been this...erotic?

He held the studio door open, and she ducked under his arm to enter, noting that the guy smelled amazing, even though he had a light sheen of sweat on his skin from their run. How was that possible? She was pretty sure that in addition to her boobs looking odd in the newly deformed workout tank and bra, she smelled like garlic and onions from today's fantastic, if aromatic, French onion soup. Yet when she glanced up at him, his gaze tracked her with the same blue-eyed intensity he'd had last week in the grocery store—as if each time she'd been dressed to the nines, freshly showered, and in full Instagram-worthy hair and dress.

It was weird.

But hot damn, it was so freaking nice she wanted to put her hands once more on those bulging biceps of his and give him a kiss. On the cheek. She didn't know him well enough for a full lip-lock, after all, and besides—

"Where in the blue blazes have you been?"

Hearing the unmistakable nasal tone of Adele Payne was like being dunked in an ice bath. Bryce's brain spun off the quasi-naughty thoughts of Ryker to face her nieces' grandparents. The ones contesting her guardianship of the girls, despite what Bentley and Heather's will had stipulated. The duo blocked the dance studio's entryway, hands on their hips. Behind them stood Imani, looking worried.

"I tried to call you," Imani began, gliding forward on silent ballet slippers to usher Bryce inside, away from Adele and Harvey and into the relative seclusion of the shoe and coat cubby. "June's in the bathroom. Crying. I think she got her period and she won't come out. Then Cecily and Addison started crying, blocking anyone from coming near the bathroom door, and I had to stop class to call you. After you didn't pick up the third time I tried your cell, I got worried. So I called the emergency contact on the girls' registration forms..."

Bryce fumbled for her phone. The tiny front inside pocket of her leggings had her car's key fob, so she patted at her back pockets... and realized that when she'd taken off her workpants to run, she'd forgotten to grab her phone.

"Damn. I left my cell in my car. I'm sorry I put you in an awkward position, Imani. I totally get why you called them." Bryce shot a glance at the Paynes, dressed in matching frowns and navy-blue outfits. Adele was in a dress, and Harvey wore a shirt in the exact hue of his wife's outfit.

They sidled over, not exactly inserting themselves into the conversation but not keeping far enough back for it to be private.

Imani winced. "I really am sorry."

"Don't be." Bryce squeezed her friend's hand and gave her a reassuring smile as she moved out from behind the cubbies, spotting Cecily and Addison standing next to the studio's bathroom door. Addison's yellow wings sagged off her shoulders, and she had a finger in her mouth, crying in a horrible, hitching-guttural way that made Bryce's insides twist in sympathy. Cecily had one of her ballet shoes in her hand, holding it over her head. As Bryce watched, one of the dancers got a little close to the bathroom and, fast as a snake, Cecily leaped out, bopping the child over the head with her pink shoe, sending the tiny dancer into face-crumpling hysterics. Undeterred, Cecily moved back into position, shoe over her head, ready to bop the next gawking kid who dared get too close.

Her nieces were the stars of a shit-show spectacle, and it was her fault.

Again.

CHAPTER 4

You did the right thing, Imani." Bryce tucked her sweat-plastered hair back into her braid, giving Imani a weak smile as her friend retreated to gather up the other dancers and continue class.

"Which is more than we can say for you." Harvey practically vibrated with indignation. "Some guardian you are, if you're not there when the girls need you. You're lucky we were eating at the Beef Haus around the corner. We left our dinner and got here five minutes ago. We'd have been here sooner if we were the first ones listed on the emergency contact form instead of you."

Bryce restrained her urge to say something snarky about how they always seemed to be hovering, waiting for her next mistake, tallying them all for the trial next month. But that was her inner bitch rising up. She owned this. Not the Paynes.

"I'm here now. Why didn't you grab Addie and Cici?"

"We tried," Adele said. "They refused to leave until June comes out."

Luckily, her nieces' dance class was over, and Imani's assistants were attempting to corral the last class as the new ones—much older girls—began to arrive to warm up. Bryce slipped off her sneakers before she stepped on the shiny, wooden studio floor.

She wended through the clump of ballerinas, girls in buns and various-colored leotards, and saw in the studio's massive, full-wall mirrors that the Paynes had stopped before the wooden floor as if it were uncrossable lava. Before they found a free chair, sat to pull off their shoes, and made their way over here, Bryce had planned to get June and the girls out of the studio.

"Addie-bell, I'm here. Don't cry." She rubbed the little blond head as Addison rushed her, tackling her with a hug. She chucked Cecily under the chin, and the girl reluctantly lowered the ballet shoe. "Thanks for holding down the fort, kiddo, but you can re-holster your shoe. Can you take your sister over by Nana and Pop-Pop and help her get her shoes on? The next dance class is starting, so as soon as I get June, we're gonna leave, okay?"

Cecily straightened, a good soldier, nodding and grabbing Addison's hand to lead her tear-streaked sibling to the shoe cubbies.

Thankfully, Imani clapped her hands, calling the new ballet class to attention and starting the classical music—all a great cover for Bryce as she set down her sneakers to rattle the locked doorknob, calling softly through the studio's bathroom door.

"June? It's Aunt Beamer. Let me in." Bryce pressed her ear to the door, hearing the sniffing and low sobs of her almost thirteen-year-old niece but no telltale movement toward the door to unlock it. "Open the door, honey."

"Go away! I'm not coming out! They're all going to

laugh at me." A loud wail rose from the bathroom, competing with and briefly overwhelming the tinkling strains of piano music. Heads swiveled in Bryce's direction, despite Imani's best efforts to gain the attention and warm up the next class of dancers.

Bryce thunked her forehead against the white wooden door, stymied.

"What do you need?" came a low voice from behind her, and Bryce jumped. It was Ryker. Somehow he'd gone behind the building to the back door, let himself in, and was standing next to the dance studio's small office.

Bryce lifted her head, speaking in a low voice. "A blanket, or something to cover her, would be great. She...I think she got her period for the first time. I know you're a guy with two brothers, but take it from me, this is DEFCON 3 level in the teen-girl freak-out meter."

He pulled his baseball cap lower, nodded, and disappeared into Imani's office. Moments later, he reemerged holding a purple towel.

"There's a back entrance behind the office. I'll have the door open for you when you're ready."

Bryce gave him a look of wordless thanks, and knocked on the door with purpose.

"June, I've got a towel and nobody is looking," Bryce said in the most reassuring stage whisper she could manage. "Let me in and we'll put this around you and scoot you out the back door."

As soon as the lock clicked, Bryce was in, nearly barreling over June, who was holding a wad of folded brown paper towels between her legs that did nothing to hide the splotch of red on the fabric of her leotard and tights, confirming

Imani's suspicions. The poor kid had gotten her first period at dance class. In a pink leotard. That sucked.

June's eyes were swollen, and the skin on her face was blotchy. Her normally defiant expression was absent, and her tears rolled down cheeks still rounded with youth. She looked so young, so bereft, that Bryce's breath caught in her throat. With the calls in to the principal's office and complaints of belligerence and sarcasm from her teachers, it had been easy to overlook the fact that June was only twelve. A kid. One whose mom and dad had died without warning, leaving her to muddle through puberty and the hell of middle school all alone.

Except for a screw-up aunt.

"June, honey, it's okay." Bryce reached for June, but her niece pulled away.

"Don't touch me. Ms. Lewis tried to call, but you didn't answer. You always say we're a priority, but when we need you, you're not there." June glanced down at the mess of paper towels between her legs, her chin quivering. She snatched the towel away from Bryce's hands, winding the fabric around her waist. Then she shook her head, glaring up at her aunt. "Why couldn't you be dead, and not my mom? I—I hate you."

Bryce swallowed a hot lump of shame, anger, and hurt big enough to choke her into momentary silence. She gathered the soiled paper towels and shoved them deep into the bathroom's garbage, burying the mess. By the time she'd washed her hands and turned back to June, Bryce had composed herself enough to speak.

"I know you hate me. I hate me right now, too, because I forgot my phone and I let you down. I'm sorry, June.

And you're right. There's no good reason why your mom and dad are dead and I'm...what's left." Bryce stumbled over the last of it, hating how those words hit like a gut punch but knowing that however much she hurt, her nieces hurt more. Their whole world was gone, leaving Bryce as a weak substitution. "But that's life. Sometimes it's sweet and sugary, like cotton candy, and living is so wonderful it melts in your mouth. But being alive can also have those bitter times—times when you think you'll never enjoy anything again. You've got to get through the bitter bites in order to appreciate the sweet."

"Whatever. Just take me to the apartment." June was always careful not to use the word "home" and chastised her sisters if they ever slipped, reminding them their home was gone along with the rest of their parents' things to settle the estate. "You do have...things there I can use? Or are you not even prepared for this?" June swept her hand in a circling arc around her midsection, her bloodshot green eyes an accusatory laser.

"Of course I'm prepared." Bryce prayed she had pads in the house. She couldn't give her niece a tampon, after all—it was her first period and that was curveball enough. No need to instruct her on how to shove a wad of cotton up there to add insult to injury. Thinking back to her own first period and her mom's advice, she added, "We'll get you some Tylenol and a heating pad, too. It'll be fine. My friend opened the rear door, so you don't have to walk in front of the class on the way out to the car, okay?"

June nodded, crossing her arms in front of herself, holding her towel close and hunkering behind Bryce when she opened the door to the studio.

Ryker was standing by the back exit like a Marine sentry, his athletic form all muscles and tense readiness. Bryce vowed to make him a soup so good he'd understand the level of her gratitude as she shoved her feet into her sneakers and ushered June outside, sensing Ryker behind them as they left the studio.

Cold wind gusted as she dug the key fob from her leggings pocket. Bryce unlocked the passenger door and whisked away her purse and clothes so June could sit, then quickly shut the door, promising to return in a minute with her sisters. Ryker had kept a ten-foot distance, allowing them privacy, but approached as Bryce jogged to the front of the dance studio.

"She okay? Can I run to the store and get anything for you?" he asked, keeping pace as they ran to the studio's entrance.

She snorted a laugh that felt closer to a sob.

"Please. We barely know each other." She shook her head as he stood there in military mode, his blue eyes a shadowed gray in the early evening light. "I'm not going to ask you to get sanitary napkins for my niece. I'm pretty sure I have stuff at home. Maybe. But thank you for running interference in there for us. Swing by PattyCakes for lunch and I'll make sure you go home so full you'll burst. My treat—"

"I hate to break up your...whatever this is." Adele Payne stalked out of the studio with Harvey and their two grandchildren in tow. Addison and Cecily appeared content—like the drama from ten minutes ago was ten years ago—and their mouths wore dark remnants of something that looked suspiciously like chocolate. "But these girls are exhausted, and I'm sure June needs some care right now, not to mention it's a school night. I wonder how you think dating is a priority with everything going on—"

"It wasn't a date." Bryce stepped away from Ryker.

He took the hint, his eyebrows drawing together before giving a quick nod and disappearing around the building. Bryce stifled the urge to jog after him, anticipating the lecture Harvey was about to deliver.

"It's ten past seven," he scolded. "Luckily, Adele always carries those miniature candy bars. We gave the girls some because the poor things were starving."

Bryce felt her blood pressure rise five hundred notches above normal.

"They weren't starving. These girls had French toast, scrambled eggs, and fruit for breakfast, soup and sandwiches for lunch, and I fed them apples and peanut butter before dance." Feeding people was the one thing she did well—even if she felt like she failed at everything else. But the word "starving" brought back the times of volunteering with her mom in soup kitchens growing up. She knew what starving looked like. "They were hungry for dinner. A dinner I have waiting for them at home. And you just filled them up with chocolate."

Adele's genial face—all pink cheeks and gray-blond, helmet-shaped hair—fell in a shocked expression. "We were just trying to help. Ms. Lewis called, and we came right away. You know these girls mean everything to us." The older woman misted up, making Bryce feel simultaneously like hugging her and like running away to avoid the sight of her sorrow. "They're all we have left of Heather..."

Then it was as if a really shitty fairy had come and sprinkled sob-dust on them all.

Adele began to cry; first one tear, then twenty rushed down her face. The girls gawked up at their grandmother, and then Addison started, mustering more tears from what had to be a well practically dry of them. Finally, Cecily started to sob, a face-contorting, howl-at-the-moon type of all-body crying that made her boneless, causing her to sag against her grandfather's leg. Harvey staggered at the onslaught, looking on helplessly.

Bryce closed her eyes, wishing she was somewhere—anywhere—but here. She'd give anything to be standing at her ten-burner Vulcan stove in Tampa, master of her domain and third in rank in the most prestigious restaurant in the area. Or going on a solo road trip in her BMW, the windows down, pop tunes playing without a single thought to bleeping out the curse words on the Cardi B songs. Hell, even a trip to the dentist would beat this scene.

But she was stuck in the present.

Mustering kind words, like squeezing a lemon for juice after it had already been in the press, she made herself say the right thing.

"Thank you for coming when Imani called. Although it wasn't an emergency on my end—I forgot my phone in the car—I'm glad you came so quickly for the girls."

Bryce gathered her sobbing nieces to her, one on each side, shuffle-walking them to the BMW, where she made sure they were buckled, then got in herself. June's face was covered in new tear tracks, and as Bryce started the car and put it in drive, her headlights picked out the figure of Ryker standing by the side exit of the dance studio. He looked on, the parking lot light above cutting him right down the middle, casting half of his body in shadow.

He waved once.

Bryce stared straight ahead, refusing to blink, refusing to wave back.

As she pulled out and turned toward Main Street, her car full of crying girls, she reminded herself that this, *this* was why she couldn't date right now. She didn't have time for the load she was already carrying, let alone the energy it would take for a relationship.

For once, the Paynes were right. Dating was not a priority.

Bryce clenched her steering wheel, refusing to join her nieces and cry. Tears solved nothing. Action did, and so did good resolutions. She adjusted the rearview mirror until it captured the half-light and half-dark figure of the man with the leg of metal and the heart of gold.

She may not be a genius, but Bryce knew ingredients. In this case, the elusive recipe for an easy life was proving hard enough to master as it was. Adding a man to the mix was insane.

She turned onto Main Street, her gaze flicking to the mirror as the man grew smaller and smaller. Until he was gone. And she resolved to keep him there. That was the smart decision—and the safe one.

Bryce clenched her jaw until her chin stopped wobbling.

Once she pulled into her tiny, off-street parking spot, she ushered the girls up the side stairs in the doorway to the right of PattyCakes with promises of a fondue dinner. It was their favorite meal, and an easy one to get them to eat, considering the candy bar "snack" their grandparents had given them earlier.

Thirty minutes later, she'd popped the last of the apple wedges, dredged in melted Kerry Irish cheese, into her mouth when her phone dinged a text notification. Pulling it from the waistband of her pajamas, she saw it was from Imani and wanted to forehead-slap herself for not texting her friend once she got home, reassuring her that all was well and thanking her again.

But it wasn't the "I hope everything is okay" text she expected. It was bizarre.

> Imani: I hope June and the girls are okay, but I've been asked to give you a message. From Ryker Matthews, my soon-to-be BIL whom I haven't seen out in public since my Christmas dance recital.

Imani's incredulity came through even without a bugged-out-eyes emoji, as she double-texted without waiting for a response.

> Imani: He said you have a delivery sitting outside your apartment, and since he didn't have your cell number, he made me text you. He wants to know if you picked it up?? What the hell is this all about?

Bryce swallowed her apple wedge and scraped her chair against the wood floor as she rushed out of the tiny kitchen, fingers flying as she replied.

> Bryce: June is ok. In bed with a Tylenol, heating pad and a horror novel. I'm heading downstairs.

"What's wrong?" Cecily dropped her fondue fork to stand, her little legs spread as if readying herself for battle in her dark-blue Moana pajamas.

"Nothing. Someone made a delivery out front. I'll be right back. No choking, you two—small bites, you hear me?" Bryce grabbed her keys and called out to June's closed door that she'd return in two seconds. Then she jogged down the stairs in her bare feet, one hand holding her boobs against her chest, cursing the fact she had on only her skimpy sleep bra, having ditched the stretched-out jog bra. "Who the hell is delivering something now?"

Outside, the night was cool and clear, and Main Street's pretty lampposts lit up the nearly empty sidewalk on both sides like a vintage black-and-white print. Thinking there had been some weird delivery for PattyCakes, she'd brought her massive keychain so she could heft the boxes straight into the café's kitchen. But the bags stacked neatly by the restaurant's entrance were flimsy white plastic ones with the bright red CVS logo emblazoned on the front.

"What the hell?" she mumbled, stepping onto the cold sidewalk, the pavement rough beneath her bare feet as she crossed to the bags. She stooped to look inside, and then barked a laugh so close to a sob she clapped her hand over her mouth.

The bags were overflowing with period products. She spotted packages of pads in every size from normal flow, to overnight, to maximum "better take some iron pills when you're done with this cycle" variety. There were a couple boxes of tampons and five tiny pink packages of panty liners thrown in for good measure. It was as if someone without a clue about monthly flow went to the store and, when confronted with the dozens of options in the feminine product aisle, swept the whole mass of it in the cart.

There were enough blood-absorbency products here to handle the aftermath of a Quentin Tarantino film.

She dashed the sudden moisture from her eyes, scanning the sidewalks and parked cars more closely. Halfway down Main Street, she spotted a red truck idling at the curb, its lights off. The figure inside was indistinguishable except for a baseball-capped head and broad shoulders.

Ryker.

As soon as she spotted him, he put his truck in gear, did a U-turn, and left in the opposite direction. It was as if he were worried she'd be mad about the gesture. Or maybe he didn't want to be hovering as she processed these feelings— being so absurdly thankful her chest hurt with it.

The gesture was next-level kind.

Right now, that sort of gesture might break her.

Her phone rang, the tones muted against her hip, and she took out her cell. Imani.

"So? Spill it!" Imani said in a singsong, her voice breathless. "What was the delivery, and don't tell me it was for PattyCakes. If Ryker is involved, there's no way it's about anything culinary. I've seen the crap he eats, and I'm convinced he has no taste buds."

Bryce cradled her cell with her shoulder as she gathered the bags—five of them—dividing them up and threading them on her wrists. Then she wrestled all that absorbency into the stairway of the upstairs apartment, having to nudge them out of the way with her hips as she threw the lock and bolt on the door.

"He, um, bought practically every kind of menstrual product at CVS. As in, I think the shelves are bare. He must've been worried when I said I wasn't sure if I had supplies at home for June." Bryce stuck the ring of keys in her pajama pocket and hoofed it up the stairs, feeling like Santa—if Santa was stocking up for a vee-jay apocalypse.

The silence on the phone was so long Bryce thought she might've accidentally hung up the phone with her cheek, but then Imani's high-pitched incredulity shattered her eardrum.

"Ryker bought you PADS? And TAMPONS? You're sure it was him? He raided the feminine product section just for you?"

"No, for June." Bryce finally reached the apartment landing. She hesitated outside the inner door, not wanting to finish this conversation in front of the girls. "It was a nice gesture. Truly. Can you let him know I—"

"No way. I'm texting you his number. You two don't need me as a mediator, or matchmaker, or chaperone. Seems to me you've got this handled."

"There's nothing to handle. I'm not in the market for a relationship. I've got enough trouble as guardian—the last thing I need is the role of girlfriend on top of that. Can you text him for me, please?"

"Nope. That's on you. And for what it's worth, the Matthews brothers are the ones to hang on to. Just sayin'."

Imani hung up, and two seconds later, Bryce's phone dinged with a text notification from her.

It was ten numbers, followed by an eggplant emoji next to a peach, with a string of fireworks at the end.

Bryce shook her head, snorting. No way was his eggplant worth the trouble to introduce to her peach.

Although she agreed the fireworks would be amazing.

CHAPTER 5

Ryker kept his word, watching the garage's clock, counting down until he could break for lunch. Yet when he arrived at PattyCakes at noon, he was surprised—and bummed out—to see a line snaking out the door and halfway down the block. By the time he'd reached the café's inner sanctum, every tiny table in his mom's place was taken.

He looked around furtively. No Mom—she was likely either in her back office or out making a delivery. No Drake, Zander, or either of his sisters-in-law. Ryker stood in line, marveling at the café's business. Typically, Mom's place was hopping in the morning, or late afternoon—times when the sweet tooth hit. However, come to think of it, he hadn't been physically in the store in ... how long? Since before Elise was born?

Instead of thinking about that, he spent his time in line staring at the menu board options. His mouth watered. Did he want chicken noodle soup, or was he in the mood for that special Bryce mentioned—the Italian wedding soup?

Finally, he reached the front. A young woman whose right arm was sleeved in a gorgeous garden of black-and-gray flowers stood at the cash register. He realized with a jolt that he didn't recognize her—his mom had hired at least two new employees and he'd never even known.

"Can I say hi to the chef?" Ryker asked the woman, whose name tag read *Willow*, after finally ordering the Italian wedding soup. When Willow put it on the counter and proceeded to look to the next customer in line, he stopped her, adjusting his ball cap and attempting to peer through the swinging door's window into the kitchen beyond. "I haven't paid yet."

Willow refused his money, one pierced eyebrow raised in surprise.

"I know. It's on the house. Bryce told me you might stop by, and said to tell you she had to step out."

His eyebrows drew together. He hoped everything was all right. "Okay, I'm Ry—"

Willow held up her hand, pointing to the picture on the wall behind the register of him in his Marine dress blues, his face impossibly young, his goals impossibly high. Then her impassive expression broke into a sly grin. "Oh, don't worry. I know who you are, Ryker Matthews. You're Patty's reclusive son who does hero work on the side. Ten out of ten agree that was very rad of you, Mr. Super Absorbency. Here's a free tip, though. Next time when she texts to thank you, hit Reply. We women like it when you reply, and if you can manage punctuation or an emoji, even better."

Her advice was the final bullet to his mood, which deflated as he left, his mission of the day a complete bust. But when he got into his truck, the savory smell of the soup made his stomach growl in anticipation. He'd just dug in, his mouth full of soup and a massive hunk of the baguette chaser, so when someone knocked on his truck passenger window, he choked.

Coughing and thumping his chest, he turned to see Bryce. Her white chef's coat was buttoned to the neck, hiding the goodness he knew existed underneath. Her dark hair was done again in a braid that lay against her shoulder, and her expression was a strange mix of annoyance and ... worry?

Leaning over, he rolled down the window with the vintage crank until she popped her head in, elbows resting on the window frame.

"You need the Heimlich?" she asked, brows drawn together as he continued to sputter, a fist over his mouth to avoid splattering soup everywhere. When he shook his head no, blinking choke-tears from his eyes, she nodded once. "Well, I have a mind to give you a good thump anyway for how much money you spent on period products last night."

He continued to cough, looking at her narrowed eyes and shaking his head in some kind of apology.

"Oh, for Pete's sake." She tossed her water bottle at him. He managed a one-handed almost-catch, trapping it between his fist and the steering wheel, causing the old Ford's horn to give a wheezy beep, making them both jump. Dropping the baguette on his seat, he unscrewed the cap and guzzled water until the lump of bread slid down his throat.

"Sorry," he wheezed, rapping a fist against his chest one last time. "And thank you for the comp'd lunch. Your soup really is 'slap your ass and pull your hair' good."

Bryce raised an eyebrow. Then she shook her head, giving a small laugh.

"You're welcome. And thank you again for the menstrual supplies last night. I didn't find a receipt in the bag, but you must've spent a fortune. One free bowl of soup doesn't cover what I owe you." Then Bryce leaned away from his window, her gaze on the storefronts down the block. "Look, I've got to roll. I got a call from Mrs. Simon at the elementary school. Apparently, Cecily is getting teased and I need to do something about it..."

She trailed off, her face flushing and her eyebrows coming together in a fierce scowl. Ryker was immediately on guard.

"What's she getting picked on about?" He felt defensive for her, although he barely knew the kid except to pull her out from underneath the grocery shelves.

Bryce scanned the sidewalk, then she met his eyes. She blew an escaped wisp of hair off her forehead in a breath of defeat. "They call her Garbage Girl because she's always grabbing things out of the classroom trash can. I swear, she thinks everything is a treasure. Rocks. Scraps of paper. A broken pencil. It all ends up in her lunchbox, her backpack, her pockets, and even stuffed into the side of her sock. Plus, she's got B.O. But I can't get her into the shower unless I wrestle her into the tub, and forget about me washing her clothes. I have to wait until she's asleep, or she screams bloody murder. The last time I did, a neighbor called the cops, thinking a child was being tortured." After the rush of words, she barked out a hollow laugh. "Yet one more example of how I'm failing as a caregiver. Then, this morning, my BMW started to rattle, like I have the time to figure out what's wrong there. I barely squeezed in an oil change and tire rotation last week, and now I have to get it into the shop to search out a mysterious rattling noise? Honestly, it's like the world is conspiring against me. Do you ever feel like that?"

He'd been listening. Of course he had. But the passion and emotions flickering on her face were so mesmerizing, he'd lost track of the conversation. Scrambling, he clung to the piece firing an alert in his mechanic's brain.

"You've got an intermittent rattle? Swing by my garage on State Street. I can put your BMW on the lift and take a look for you."

She blinked, then flushed. "That's a nice offer, but my bank account won't support a mechanic's bill, and I'm already in your debt for the mountain of menstrual products you left on my doorstep. I was taught to live within my means, you know?"

Ryker nodded. He remembered all too well the feeling of having no funds.

Bryce lifted her forearms off the car's passenger window, making as if to say goodbye. In desperation, Ryker searched for a way to prolong their discussion.

"Mom taught us the same. 'Neither a borrower, nor a lender be' is one of her favorite sayings," Ryker blurted, and although it went against every fiber of his Marine training, he cracked open a little of his personal diary. "But if it weren't for Drake lending me money to start up my garage, I don't know where I'd be right now. See, I accidentally screwed up my credit when I was nineteen."

Bryce leaned in, those piercing blue-gray eyes interested. "Really? How?"

"I'd gotten a credit card to help cover expenses to outfit my first apartment, but when I got deployed to Afghanistan,

I never thought about setting up a system for automatic payments. After I returned, I found out I was in collections. While I paid off that debt, it left a mark on my credit. Banks refused to underwrite a small-business loan, let alone a mortgage." Ryker couldn't believe he was spilling his guts like this. But her open, rapt expression acted like lubrication to his seldom-used conversational skills, and he was unable to stem the flow of words. "Drake took out a mortgage in his name for me and lent me the start-up funds for State Street Garage. I've been rebuilding my credit these past years, and soon I'll be able strike out on my own, without my brother's backing. Maybe do something different."

She nodded. "There's nothing like the feeling of charting your own life's road trip." She barked a humorous laugh. "I miss feeling like I was winning in this world."

When Bryce's expression went all lost and vulnerable, Ryker couldn't help himself. He jumped in.

"Winning is a matter of perspective. Sure, you've had a change of plans. But when you change lanes in a race, you appear to lose ground, when all it takes is being on the low side of the curve to be back on top. Battling grief is tough—I should know. It takes time, and requires you to occasionally accept a boost from others." Ryker saw her face close off. Figuring she wasn't likely to accept his charity with her car—she barely knew him—he decided to go for another tactic. "I have a proposal. Bring your car over tonight after five, and I'll take a look. See if I can fix it. In exchange, you bring me a quart of soup. Deal?"

"But I'll have the girls with me, and they're...a lot."

Ryker squinted an eye. "So? Bring them. I'll make sure the road flares are all safely tucked away."

She snorted but didn't smile. Her gaze flicked over everything in his truck—the soup container, crumbs on his shirt from the baguette, his hands attempting not to throttle the steering wheel in nervous anticipation.

Her lips pinched, then she pushed out a gust of breath.

"My bank account can't argue with that math." Her agreement was reluctant. "Deal. As long as I can bring you over a homemade dinner in addition to the soup."

She stuck out her hand, and he shook it, surprised by the steely strength of her grip.

"I can't wait to see what tops a sexy 'smack in the ass' soup." He raised his eyebrow, the playful comment falling from his lips surprising even himself.

At last her expression brightened, and her lips twitched up in a smile.

"I'll do my best to make it a 'shout out my name when you finish' sort of experience."

* * *

Five hours later, a knock came on the garage's main door. When Ryker opened it to the blustery March evening, it was like inviting in a giggling, chatting whirlwind as Bryce and her nieces blew inside.

"Aunt Beamer made me leave my sword behind." The littlest one, Addison, shoved her sisters out of the way to present him with a mighty scowl. She wore a purple, glittery tutu over a pair of neon pink leggings and a white shirt with a rainbow-sequined heart on it. Her wispy blond hair was barely held in a ponytail, and while her yellow wings were still attached to her back, one of them was bent and held together with a large safety pin. "I tol' her pirates like you expect us to come with our own swords. Only, she said it wasn't 'propriate."

Before he replied, the girl he'd help pull out from under the grocery store shelves—Cecily—brushed by him, then stopped dead in her tracks. Dressed in dark jeans and a camouflage shirt, she stood in the center of his garage, next to the empty lift. Then she threw her arms out and spun in a circle, trampling on and stumbling over the untied laces of her Chuck Taylors as she cried out.

Ryker jumped, startled by the high-pitched scream. Was she hurt?

"What—"

"Don't worry." The oldest girl spoke over the screams. Her green eyes flicked a dismissive gaze at the garage, then at him, before turning her attention once more to her phone. "She's taking in the dirt and grease, and feeling like she finally found the place where she belongs."

Ryker blinked at this information relayed in a flat tone from the oldest girl—he recalled her name was June—who wore a black shirt with the sentence *What Would Wednesday Addams Do?* written in gothic lettering on the front.

Bryce followed June inside, plucking the cell phone from her hands as they entered and giving her a look. June flushed an angry red. She slunk to the small café table and chairs next to the front end of the VW and plopped down, her expression an exaggerated sulk.

Bryce pocketed June's cell phone, then boomed out, "Cici, volume off!"

The spinning girl's screech stopped as if her aunt had found a real-life mute button. Wobbling a little after the spin, she raced over, standing next to Addison, who had claimed Ryker's right hand and was tugging him toward the pile of boxes in the corner.

"What are those?" Addison asked.

"Can we help you work on Aunt Beamer's car?" Cecily shouted over her sister. "I've always wanted to touch stuff underneath the car!"

"Did you want me to open the garage door and drive in the BMW?" Bryce asked over her nieces, hooking a thumb toward where her vehicle likely waited outside. Then she caught sight of the VW front end, and whistled. "Holy cow. Are you restoring a vintage VW bus? My dad had one of these when I was a kid and we used to take the most epic road trips in that."

Ryker's head was on a swivel. State Street Garage officially had the most females in it since he'd first hung his shingle outside the door. For a moment, he was overwhelmed by the din of their chatter. Then he felt little Addison's hand so trusting in his. His anxiety melted away.

"Those boxes are for you to play with." He directed his words to the little blond fairy at his knees. Then he caught Cecily's gaze. "You can help with the car if your aunt says it's okay. The button for the garage door is there," he said finally to Bryce, pointing to the side of the door. Then, forcing his face to remain neutral, he answered her last question about the VW. "And the bus restoration is . . . stalled. I only have a front end, nothing else for her."

Seconds later, he'd corralled the two younger girls into the corner of his garage where he'd stashed a load of boxes given to him by a buddy down the street who owned an appliance store. Ryker held out a roll of silver duct tape and a box of crayons.

"My favorite thing to do as a kid was build forts. I thought you might want to—"

"We'll build a pirate ship!" Addison shrieked at a decibel he was certain cracked a glass somewhere. She snatched the crayons as Cecily snagged the duct tape. They each moved so fast it was like being besieged by cute piranhas. "Can we build a pirate ship?"

"You can build whatever you want." Ryker felt his lips lifting into a grin. Then he spotted June, arms crossed over her chest next to the VW's yellow front end. The misery on her face reminded Ryker that these girls—Bryce included—had recently buried loved ones. Although he'd been inclined to leave the older girl to her own devices, something in her belligerent expression called to mind another grieving teen who'd buried a parent. He'd been about June's age when his dad died. After the garage car door trundled open and Bryce drove her car inside the bay, he waved June over. The girl sidled up, curious as he handed her the box cutter, then spoke to her sisters.

"Here's the deal—while I look at your aunt's car, only June is old enough to use the box cutter. You two decide which boxes you want cut, and draw it out. Then June can do the cutting." He waited for the little girls to nod before he turned to June. "I never lend my tools to someone who's not trained to use them. Does your aunt let you use blades yet?"

Bryce had exited the car in time to hear the question.

"Hmm, it hasn't come up. But she's watched me unbox supplies at PattyCakes. I suppose she's old enough. Hell, I was using a jackknife at her age. Why not? Cut away from your body because if you slice yourself open Nana and Pop-Pop's lawyer will torture me in court for it."

June gave her aunt a dark glance, her eyes narrowed. She mumbled in a tone too quiet for Bryce to hear, "Might be worth the stitches."

Ryker kept his expression blank. He recognized her anger—similar to his dark passenger, transforming him into a person he didn't recognize for months after his dad had died.

"You good?" he asked, his voice low. "No shame in asking for a tutorial."

June stared at her combat boots. "Can...can you give me a refresher?"

Ryker's opinion of the tween rose ten notches. He took one of the medium boxes, flipping it over. June handed back the box cutter, and Ryker made a show of telling the little girls to stand clear, then thumbed open the blade. He sliced the box, angling the sharp edge away from his body.

"Sheath it when you're done." He showed her how to slide the button until the blade sank into the holder. "If it gets dull, tell me. I'll show you how to nip off the old blade to reveal the new one underneath. Dull tools are dangerous, and in my garage it's safety first."

She took the box cutter.

"Junie, cut this out first!" Cecily called.

The little girls had poured the new box of crayons out onto the concrete floor and had already sketched out what could either be a large porthole or a small doorway on one of the long appliance boxes. He watched as June knelt, shooed her sisters away, then carefully unsheathed the blade and cut the circular hole perfectly before sliding the sharp edge back down. She glanced up, giving him a questioning look.

He nodded. "Well done. Call if you need help."

June drew up tall, not hunched as if heading into a stiff wind. While she didn't smile, her mouth softened, losing some of its sourness.

Tools and gears—he knew how their power to fix broken things extended to broken people. The girl had just learned the same.

Bryce's voice came at his shoulder. "Well, look who is the tween-whisperer."

He pivoted. Bryce thrust a paper bag at his chest, and he reached for it reflexively.

"Your dinner. Go ahead and eat. My car can wait, but this hot dinner won't." Her left eyebrow cocked up as he hesitated, and she leaned in to speak in a voice her nieces couldn't overhear. "It's okay if you call out my name as you mouth-gasm."

He barked a surprised laugh. His brain tried to come up with a funny response, but just then, the paper bag gaped open, and the scent of dill, mustard, and something buttery and delicious wafted to his nose. Ryker's stomach growled, switching his brain to "off" mode.

Peeking inside, he counted only one soup-sized container and one plate covered in aluminum foil. "Aren't you eating? Or the girls?"

"Are you crazy? I'd never willingly travel with my nieces on an empty stomach, and I certainly wouldn't subject you to their hangry tantrums. Or mine, for that matter." She snorted, then snaked an arm through his elbow, guiding him toward the tiny table by the VW. "C'mon and eat while the girls play. I need to make sure I haven't lost my touch."

He sat. He watched her pull out soup and then whip the foil off the plate with a flourish.

"We have cream of mushroom soup, followed by mustard dill chicken, with a side of chive mashed potatoes alongside tender asparagus with lemon and pecorino." She beamed, tucking a napkin into the neck of his garage coveralls. Her fingers grazed his skin, but it felt like a trail of tiny shocks where she touched him, and he wondered if she felt the same as she hastily pulled away, shoving a set of silverware across the table. Her cheeks were slightly flushed as she gestured to the cutlery. "Go on. Dig in!"

He gazed down at a dish that looked like something from one of those foodie magazines in the grocery checkout. The soup steamed, the scent of something creamy and decadent tickling his nose. On the plate, her mashed potatoes were whipped in a swirl, like the frosting on his mom's cupcakes, with the green chives scattered on top like sprinkles. He didn't know what pecorino was, but he figured it was the little white flakes draped over the asparagus sprigs, and the chicken was seasoned, seared, and covered in some mustard concoction that must've come straight from the angels, it smelled so divine.

Holy shit. This was fancy.

And he...he was the opposite of fancy.

He gazed down at his mechanic's coverall. It'd started out clean, and now it pretty much told the story of his day. There were dirt smudges along the arms from changing the flat tire this morning for Mrs. Foltz, Imani Lewis's grandmother, and a ketchup stain from his lunchtime hot dog. Plus, he wore a big streak of grease across his front from helping Drake's neighbor Mr. Penny get ready for a hot date by giving the old man's vintage Chevy Bel Air a much needed tune-up.

Striving to look more presentable, Ryker unzipped and slipped his arms out until the work covering lay like the peel of a banana in his lap, revealing his black short-sleeved undershirt. He removed his baseball cap, running a hand through his hair to eliminate as much of the hat-head look as possible. Then, as he re-tucked the paper napkin into his collar, he caught her staring at him.

"What?" he asked.

"Nothing. I wondered how much you were going to take off there, for a second." Her lips were curved in a smile, and her chin rested in her hands on the opposite side of the tall bistro table next to the VW. "You done?"

He gaped at her. If he didn't know any better, he'd think she was flirting with him.

But it couldn't be. She was just . . . friendly.

To save himself from speaking, he speared four of the asparagus and was about to shove them into his mouth when he recalled she was a fancy chef. And she was used to men with table manners—not some dude who ate like a Neanderthal. He picked up the knife, carving the asparagus into bite-sized pieces then piling on some potatoes and finally a chunk of the tender chicken into the perfect bite.

As soon as the fork left his mouth, all thoughts of her flirting and all thoughts in general flew from his mind. It was as if all his senses but taste had taken a knee.

The food was outstanding.

Flavors of dill and chicken and velvety potatoes along with the caramelized goodness of asparagus exploded in his mouth, rich and complex, yet comforting all at the same time. His jaws chewed automatically, and just as soon as he'd swallowed it down, his fork and knife had magically carved another slice of heaven. He shoveled it into his mouth, forcing himself to chew slower and savor it.

He groaned, closing his eyes. God, it was incredible!

Bryce chuckled, the throaty sound making his mind detour from flavor to the woman across from him. When he opened his eyes, he found her gazing at his mouth.

"Best. Compliment. Ever," she breathed. "I've missed watching people lose themselves in my cooking. It's like food porn. I'm going to watch you eat every single bite."

Wait. Had she said . . . food porn?

He swallowed before he choked. Her dilated pupils, lips open in breathless expectation—almost like she was into him. The expression reminded him of the other night when he'd hauled her up after she'd tripped, and she'd gazed at him with what had looked like wonder and something that felt like . . . desire? No. He didn't trust his instinct—rusty as it was—that he'd done something to turn her on. She just missed cooking for someone who appreciated her skills. He needed to get his mind out of the gutter and enjoy the fact that she was here. In his garage. And not staring at the grease lodged in the creases of his knuckles. Or the side of the prosthetic peeking out from the gap between his coverall and work boot.

"It's a blue-ribbon winner." He took a mouthful of soup, then wiped his lips with the paper napkin. "Outstanding."

Bryce looked pleased.

"It was one of my most requested dishes at Chez Pierre."

"You miss it? Your old job?" he asked, carving off another

hunk of the chicken and popping it into his mouth. He could eat this every day for a year and not be tired of it.

She shrugged. "Being a saucier, or sauté chef, I didn't always get to make the dishes I wanted, but what Pierre's patrons wanted. That's one of the biggest perks about working at PattyCakes. Patty lets me create my own menus, which has been liberating. Plus, she's teaching me the business side of the restaurant, and while I'm not a massive fan of baking, your mom's showing me all her pastry chef tricks."

"You hate baking?" he managed, between bites. God, this food was good. He couldn't recall the last time he'd shoveled every morsel into his mouth because it tasted amazing, and not due to the urge to satisfy his body's hunger with the least amount of time and effort.

"Baking is a science. Cooking is an art." Bryce's words sounded like something repeated often. "Having to learn the baking side of PattyCakes is like...having to take science class before I can go back to my stove for recess. I'm super grateful for Patty and this experience, but working at Chez Pierre felt like finally achieving all that I wanted...and now I'm sort of flailing. You know what I mean?"

He nodded, scooping up another spoonful of soup. "Absolutely."

She waited for an expectant beat, then rolled her eyes. "Carrying on a conversation requires you to string together more than a couple words. C'mon. Make me feel better. Tell me when you felt like you were flailing once, so I can envision my life looking normal someday."

Her tone was lightly mocking, and he winced. He'd thought he was holding his conversational own with her.

Clearly, he needed more social interaction. Maybe his brothers and his mom had a point: never leaving the garage for weeks on end did have its drawbacks. Steeling himself, he wiped his mouth and rummaged in his brain for his truth.

"When my dad died, I was twelve, and it screwed with my head. I found some peace playing football, but I spent my angsty middle school years in trouble, usually skipping classes to hang out with a bunch of former military guys my dad knew, who owned a garage."

"Aah, that's how you became a gearhead. Why the military after you graduated, and not trade school, then?"

"If you're a lost kid like I was, the military provides order and purpose. Dad was a Marine, and Grandpa Matthews and his father before him, too, so I'd be lying if I said I wasn't influenced by family legacy. After boot camp, I discovered I loved being a Marine. When I was in Afghanistan, it was everything I'd ever wanted. I had respect. I had discipline. I knew my place in the world, and my future was mapped out with logical precision." He paused, taking another bite as his mind recalled the years before the IED explosion. The times in the field with his unit—the feeling of watching a bunch of strangers coalesce into a single fighting force. "You live in the moment. Fighting for the Marine to the left and the Marine to the right. It's all that I was. It's all I ever wanted to be."

Bryce nodded. "There were days I covered for another chef, in at six in the morning to prep, then working both the lunch and dinner crowd. Twelve or fourteen hours on my feet, stopping only long enough to pee and shovel food into my mouth before returning to the stove. It didn't feel like work, though. It felt as easy as breathing. But now...my whole world has shifted. The universe dealt me a change of plans, and I'm..."

"Off-balance. Like you've slipped a gear," he finished, recalling that hazy time after the IED detonated—those blank places in his mind that were like a camera being switched on, taking a picture, then turning off, the photos a mismatched jumble. "Losing what defined you...I get it. I mourn my Marine career more than my left foot. These past years taught me my limits. Both good and bad."

He hadn't meant to get personal. Yet she didn't look discomfited by his honesty.

"Fixing cars for you is like cooking for me, then—therapeutic?"

He nodded. "I'd always liked cars, and when Dad passed, tinkering with engines was the way I dealt with the grief. After my honorable discharge, I threw myself into starting this vintage vehicle resto/reno business. I figured while God saw fit to take my left foot in Afghanistan, He didn't take the right one for a reason." He gave a wry grin. "So I could push the gas pedal."

"And you found a new purpose. Maybe it's not as comfortable of a fit as the Marines, but you adapted. Then thrived." Her serious expression slowly morphed into a smile, like the sun coming out behind a bank of storm-gray clouds. She slapped the table and stood abruptly. "You give me hope, Ryker. I'm going to let you finish your dinner in peace while I go check out this beauty on the lift over here. It's a Cougar Eliminator, right? Is it 1970? Or is it a '69?"

Ryker gaped. "She's a '69. How'd you know?"

"My dad loves all things car-related. In fact, he says he originally dated Mom because her name was Shelby, like the Mustang, and his name was Hudson, like the defunct car manufacturer. He drove car transporters and collected posters of his favorites." Bryce peered through the driver's-side window. "He had one poster of the Mercury Cougars through the ages, and I always thought the snub-nosed 1950s-era models were my favorite. Then he let me drive a 1970 Eliminator off a transporter once, and the whole car literally rocked when you goosed the gas. It was pretty sweet."

"You . . . drove cars off the transporter?" he asked, trying to picture a tiny version of Bryce clambering up into a big muscle car. "I mean, your dad trusted you to do that?"

"My brother and I spent summers traveling with him in the big rig. There are few hands and much to be done, so we'd both drive the cars off the transporter. Dad taught me to drive stick by the time I was ten, although he'd had to rig up a wooden block for me to reach the clutch. One summer, I worked a construction gig alongside my brother. I thought about getting a crane operator's license my senior year, but decided to apply to culinary school, instead." She gave him that hot-as-hell assessing look, lifting one eyebrow. "I can drive anything with wheels. Probably have driven everything with wheels. Except those behemoth crawler-transporters NASA uses to haul the rockets to the launchpad—although I doubt it's any harder than operating a Trojan loader. The NASA crawler is a hell of a lot slower, anyway."

For a second, he thought she was purposely punking him, like he was being set up for some type of hidden-camera joke. How many people knew muscle cars, let alone drove everything from Cougars to construction vehicles? How was she this perfect? Then she squatted down to snag a stray crayon, and he caught sight of a double-wing tattoo on her lower back. It looked like a pair of squared-off angel wings, but a little different, like the logo of a . . .

"Bentley," he said out loud as soon as the car's name came to him.

Everyone in the garage froze.

Too late, he realized the car emblem was symbolic. Bentley, as in Bentley Weatherford. The man who had been the girls' father. Bryce's late brother.

The box cutter June was holding clattered to the cement floor. Bryce gasped as if she'd been stabbed, while one of the little girls gave a piteous whimper.

And Ryker wished he'd kept his big mouth closed.

CHAPTER 6

U h." Ryker's brain scrambled to come up with something to defuse the situation after accidentally pulling the pin on the dead-dad grenade.

"That's my daddy's name," Addison said in the softest voice he'd ever heard her use. "Did you know him?"

His face felt singed, as if he'd jacked up a welding torch too high. "I...I met him once. He brought his plumbing truck in for a part. He was a good man."

Addison nodded. "I've been waiting to see him in his fairy wings. Only Aunt Beamer says the fairies don't leave heaven 'cause the gates are locked. Have you ever seen a fairy, Mr. Ryker?"

"N-no. Never have. I was—I was talking about your aunt's tattoo. It's the logo for a car called a Bentley."

Bryce stood, pulling her shirt down to cover the ink on the base of her spine. She looked embarrassed, and Ryker immediately kicked himself. That's what happened when he loosened the hinge on his jaw. Unplanned shit spewed out.

"I got it after my brother...passed." She said the last word as if she had to handle it carefully in her mouth to avoid being jabbed. "He always lifted me up in life, so I got it on my lower back, as if he were giving me a boost."

"Yeah, Aunt Beamer's first tattoo is a tramp stamp." June leaned against the garage door, her shoulders hunched. "Imagine that."

Bryce's body deflated like a tire with a nail in its rim. Her eyes lost their sparkle, and she put a hand out on the Cougar's metal frame as if to steady herself after a punch to the gut.

His mouth was moving before he realized what he would say. All he wanted was to deflect the girls' attention and reverse the heavy fog of sadness descending in his garage.

"It's a beautiful tattoo, but my ink story beats your aunt's." He shoved his sleeve up to his shoulder, motioning for the girls to look at the black-and-gray rendition of the eagle, globe, and anchor tattoo. "You know what this is? It's the insignia of the Marine Corps."

"What's 'signia' mean?" Cecily asked, approaching him first to peer at the ink on his arm.

"Insignia means our emblem. It's what represents us as Marines. I'm proud of this tattoo." He caught Bryce's gaze before speaking to the girls again. "But I'm not proud of what's underneath. I bet on a football game with some Marine buddies of mine. None of us had any money to bet, so the loser had to get a tattoo of the winner's choice. I lost. And got stuck with a tattoo of a...unicorn. Jumping over a rainbow."

Addison immediately jetted to his side, her bent yellow wings flapping. She squinted at the black-and-gray outline, her little hands grabbing his biceps. "Where? I don't see it."

"It's under the feathers of the eagle. See? The unicorn's horn is here." He pointed to the beak of the eagle where the artist had blended it into the existing tattoo. Then he traced the curve of the globe. "Here's where the rainbow was, and the clouds on either side of the rainbow are hidden under the dark parts of the anchor."

Addison shrieked as she spotted it.

"There it is! I love unicorns!"

"I still can't see it," Cecily grumbled.

Out of the corner of his eye, Ryker saw June and Bryce approaching from different directions. Encouraged that he'd done a Zander-like maneuver to deflect tension by using himself as some sort of human stress ball, he pulled a black Sharpie from his coverall's pocket and handed it to Addison.

"Trace it out for them." He waved off Bryce's small noise of protest, winking at Addison but directing his words to Cecily. "I get as grubby as I want during the day because I've got a special soap. This'll wash right off with my dirt-magnet."

Addison did a pretty accurate tracing of his first tat, only adding a few embellishments to the original—like a pair of oddly shaped stars above the unicorn's head. Then she drew a big, sloppy smile on the unicorn's face.

"There. Now Lady-Glitter-Sparkle the unicorn is perfect!" She capped the Sharpie and handed it to him with a twirl of her purple tutu. Then she gazed at the VW, her bright blue eyes lighting up. "Hey, is that a fort? I see pillows back there."

Before he could do anything, the little girl had flitted behind the yellow front end, her wings getting caught up as she wedged herself into the small space behind where it was bolted to the wall. Soon her little moon face appeared behind the curved windshield, her tiny hands reaching for the rearview mirror his Marine brothers had brought from Sangin, Afghanistan.

Panic welled up and he jolted up from the bistro chair. His hand went to the notch in his left ear.

"It's not safe." He'd meant for the words to come out easily, but they had the hard-edged, clipped bark that reminded him of the loudest Marine he knew. His father. Clearing his throat, he fought down the rising anxiety, forcing a more kid-friendly tone. "It's only loosely bolted to the wall. I don't want you to get hurt."

Bryce sprang into action, fast-clapping her hands as if trying to startle a flock of birds instead of a five-year-old girl.

"C'mon out of there, Addie, and go play with the boxes. June, go pick up Mr. Matthews's box cutter before someone gets hurt."

June's eyes widened. "Wait. Did you say Matthews? Is... is this guy related to Drake Matthews?" At Ryker's nod, the girl's angry annoyance melted into an expression of wonder. "Are you freaking kidding me? The Knight of Nightmares is your brother?"

Ryker gave a nod. "One and the same."

"Wow," June breathed. "I loved *Dark Dolls* and just finished *Halloween Hacker* and can't wait for the movie— although books are always better. Did you know he was going to be a famous writer when you were growing up?"

"I don't think any of us expected that. When we lost our dad, Drake stepped up for me and my brother. That's when his writing played a big role in his life—he used his pen and paper to escape reality when things got...hard." Then, although he never offered up his brother to anyone, he figured after reminding the girls of their dead father he could toss out this bone. "If you ever want to meet him, I'm sure we can make that happen."

June's face flushed. "Th-that would be great." Grabbing Cecily's hand, she called to Addison, who was still flitting around the VW hood. "Let's finish the pirate ship and save Peter Pan. That dumb boy can't seem to stay out of trouble."

The little girls flew to the cardboard boxes, and June went back to playing sentry by the garage door, where she alternated between reluctantly helping her sisters and gazing off into the distance with a look that reminded Ryker of his oldest brother.

"Thank you. That was kind," Bryce said.

Ryker shoved down his shirtsleeve. Covering his leftover chicken meal with the foil, he shot Bryce a glance. Her face was thoughtful. And sad.

Damn.

He cleared his throat. "Sorry. I didn't mean to...dredge it up for all of you. For the record, I like your ink. It's a hell of a tribute to your brother."

She blinked the moisture from her stormy-blue eyes. "Thanks. At the time, I thought the placement was perfect, but June has a point. Low back stamps have a bad rep. I should've—"

Ryker stood, shaking his head. "Nope. Don't do that. Thoughts starting with 'should have' are a waste of time. Or so says my PTSD therapist."

Double damn. He hadn't meant to tell her he was in counseling. She barely knew him, and now that info was splattered like a fast-flying bug on a windshield.

To his surprise, she lit up. "Your therapist and mine should get together. Except I'll warn you—mine is a stickler for writing in special notebooks. Ordinary paper won't do. We have to have individual journals for both the girls' court-mandated counseling sessions and our group ones. That's eight notebooks to keep track of, and she gets pissy if you accidentally bring the wrong one. It's a little ridiculous. Does yours make you keep a journal, too?"

Bryce followed him to the BMW, stepping into his field of vision, one hand on her hip. She wore jeans and a brown sweater that clung to her curves, and instead of her usual black sneakers, she had on a pair of brown boots that hugged her calves and were hot as hell. She was so distracting, he'd missed a good portion of what she'd said—something about therapy and notebooks?

Disguising the fact that he hadn't heard all of what she'd said, he pivoted to his toolbox, opening the top. "Okay, let's talk about this rattle. What is it and when do you hear it?"

She snort-laughed in derision, and he quit rummaging through his tools to look at her. She was smiling the way women sometimes did when they were anything but happy.

"Man, you rock at dodging conversational chitchat. Me? I see lags in speech and am compelled to fill them, usually by oversharing. Sorry." She glanced toward her nieces playing with the boxes. "Apologizing. It's what my entire existence has become, a big-ass apology to everyone for everything.

Okay, moving on. This rattling noise: it's mostly when I accelerate, but sometimes when I turn, so I don't think it's a belt problem. It sounds like a pebble tumbling in the dryer. Like when I don't empty Cecily's pant pockets before washing them."

Ryker felt frozen, like a computer given two combatting commands. He knew he should address the first part of what she'd said—comfort her or empathize in some way. But damn, he wasn't like Zander, all comfortable with talking about feelings. Instead, he focused on the second part— the actionable part. He could do actionable all day long.

Snagging his black-and-green padded creeper, he lay on it and scooted himself under her BMW. His mechanical side took over, hands testing bolts and fittings, then, to probe further, he reached into his chest pocket for a tool...and found nothing.

Swallowing a curse, he rolled half out. "Forgot my wrench." Before he'd positioned his prosthetic leg under him to stand, Bryce was poking through his toolbox.

"You want a three-eighths?"

He nodded and wiped the surprise off his face as she handed it to him.

Right. Her dad was a trucker. She drove everything, *and* she knew all about tools.

He kicked the creeper under the car, then allowed himself to smile as his hands went to work on the underside of her yellow BMW.

She was so freaking hot.

After checking that everything looked normal and finding no obvious reason for the rattle, he rolled out and had her pop the hood. She gazed under there with him, and he tried not to notice that she smelled delicious, like lemons and rosemary. He forced his brain and mouth to work together.

"Answering your earlier question, I don't use notebooks in therapy. Dr. Kirkland at the VA was a kicker for Notre Dame. He knows better than to assign a jock turned gearhead a writing assignment. I'd never come back." He barreled on, feeling her gaze on him like a spotlight. "Working on civilian encounters—that's my therapy homework. Being in the real world. That's my struggle."

She was quiet for a beat, and he looked studiously at the work his hands were doing as he checked the caps for the oil filter housing and the power steering, as well as the clamps for the air filter cover. They were tight and weren't the source of the rattle.

"For what it's worth, I'd give you an A-plus. Thanks for what you said to June. I forget she has all these grown-up thoughts and feelings. It was easier when the girls were tiny." Bryce nudged him with her elbow, her expression playful. "Fair warning: your little Lisi is going to be a handful soon, so enjoy these days while you can!"

He'd opened his mouth to tell her Elise wasn't really his handful when Cecily came running over.

"Hey." She tugged on his coverall's belt loop. "Can I see under the car, too? Please? I'll be super careful, and I promise not to touch anything."

Ryker gave Bryce a questioning look, and when she shrugged, he led the girl around to the side where he'd left the crawler. After giving instructions on what she'd see under there, he guided the crawler under with her on it. When she wheeled out, her hands were covered in the salty grime kicked up from driving on the here-now-gone-again snow on the March roads.

Bryce clucked her tongue. "So much for her not touching anything."

"Daddy said that dirty hands were a sign you worked hard," Cecily said, looking defiantly at her aunt. "And I'm not washing it off."

"Dirt and grease are my best friends at work, but I do my best to get some of it off when I'm done." He tossed her a shop towel, demonstrated how he wiped his hands, and she grudgingly copied his movements. He'd put a hand out to lift her from the creeper when his gaze caught on the front wheel of the BMW. The beginnings of a smile crept over his mouth, and he grabbed another tool from his box. Snagging his rolling stool, he wheeled himself closer to the car. "Cecily, take a look at this front wheel. Tell me what you see."

Cecily obeyed, her thin brown hair a riot of static electricity from lying on the creeper.

"Hey, it's missing a thingy here." Her dirty finger pointed to the lower point of the star-shaped pattern of lug nuts surrounding the blue-and-white BMW logo.

"Fu—dddge," Bryce breathed, revising the curse word in mid-utterance. "They didn't tighten the lug nuts when they did the tire rotation. That's what I've been hearing— I can't believe I didn't think to check. I don't suppose you have an extra lying around?"

The next half hour, Ryker was in mechanic's heaven. He got to jack up the car, get out his lug wrench, and do what he did best: fix shit. He checked the owner's manual stuffed in Bryce's glove box, and he happened to have an extra twelve-millimeter lug nut to replace the lost one. He put on the lug nut and allowed first Cecily, then Addison, to get the feel of tightening it, and, finally, June, who came over to shyly try her hand at securing the nuts on all the wheels using his lug wrench. A couple more were loose, and Ryker felt the back of his neck getting that prickly hot feeling that meant he was steaming mad.

"I'm not going to ask which mechanic you went to," he prefaced his words to Bryce as he replaced his wrench in his toolbox, "because I'd be tempted to go over there and rattle their cage. Someone didn't do their job right. You don't let someone drive away with loose nuts."

Bryce winked. "Ha, you know it." She lowered her voice, checking that her nieces weren't within listening range. "I've got a better one. What does a mechanic do after a one-night stand?"

Ryker shook his head.

"He nuts...and bolts."

Ryker burst out laughing. "That's so wrong."

"Instead of dad jokes, my father was full of these rude, car-related one-liners." Bryce rolled her eyes. "He wouldn't let up until he made everyone laugh. I wish Mom was in better health, because they'd be here in a heartbeat. They came up for the funeral...but I don't think they'll make the trip again. Mom has early-onset dementia and Dad is managing her medical issues. Losing Bentley hit them hard..."

Bryce trailed off, and Ryker felt the unmistakable tug of another who was desperately trying to overcome loss—a feeling he knew well. He sifted through replies in his head, like rummaging through a junk drawer, coming up with only a few, oddly fitted sentences.

"Although my ears aren't pretty, they work. I'm here if you need to talk." He winced inwardly at how awkward he sounded. He really needed to get out more. Suddenly, a phrase his therapist used popped into his head, and he lobbed it out there. "It's a judgment-free zone."

Bryce's easy grin slipped a little, showing the vulnerability under her armor. "I—I could use a little of that zone in my life."

Then, to his surprise, she lifted herself up on tiptoe and placed a kiss on his cheek.

Her lips were warm and impossibly soft, and he was self-conscious of how bristly his own unshaven face must be against her mouth. Unsure what to do, he stood stock-still. The lemony herbal scent of her rose to his nose and as he breathed her in, something inside him loosened, as though her gesture had unclenched a muscle he hadn't realized was tense. And while he wasn't a cheek-kiss expert, he thought hers lasted maybe two beats longer than a "you're a great new pal" gesture.

Had it even ventured into "hmmm, could we be a thing" territory? He was so out of practice he didn't know.

She was the first to pull away, and he noted her face was flushed. Was that a good thing? Or a bad thing? Damn, he had no idea.

Her voice was low and almost timid when she spoke next. "Thank you, Ryker. For everything, but especially taking your evening to help me with the car while also entertaining my nieces. We should—we should get out of your hair. Come on, girls!" Bryce pivoted away, and in no time had rounded up the stray crayons, stacked the unused cardboard boxes into the corner of the garage, and had the girls corralled by the BMW ready to go. "Girls, say thank you for—"

Ryker snapped his fingers. He'd almost forgotten.

"No thanks needed. Hold on, I've got something for Cecily." He rushed into the garage's apartment, coming back with an extra bar of Lava soap.

"What is it?" Cecily's face was a mixture of excitement and confusion as he handed the red package over to her.

"Soap. Specially designed for people like mechanics and plumbers. People who aren't afraid of dirt or of getting dirty." He nodded to her as she looked at him, wary. "But I'll warn you—the soap is made from pumice. That's rocks that were thrown up by volcanoes, so you have to use it with caution or it'll rub the skin right off you."

Cecily gasped. "This is . . . volcano vomit soap?"

"Let me see!" Addison jumped, wings flapping, as her sister held the Lava soap box above her head, retreating to their aunt's car.

"Cici, what do you say?" Bryce called, hands on her hips.

"I'm going to use it tonight!" Cecily called, before squabbling with Addison and piling into the back of the BMW.

"What she meant to say was thank you." Bryce squeezed his arm, smiling as she picked up one last crayon from the floor, stuffing it haphazardly into the pack. Then, as an angry shriek came from the BMW, she thrust the rest of the crayons at him, wincing. "I've got to go before they kill each other. Thanks for helping with my car—I can't believe it was something so stupid as loose lug nuts. You saved me a bunch of money, and I'd like to return the favor. Maybe another dinner? Just us adults this time?"

He blinked. This sounded suspiciously like a date. Was it? He cleared his throat, forcing his lips into an expression he hoped didn't look as gobsmacked as he felt. The engine responsible for the conversational centers of his brain ran hot as he pushed it to the limit to find something funny to say. "Name the day, and we're there. Me and Lady-Glitter-Sparkle, that is."

She looked over her shoulder at her nieces, safely enclosed in the car before whispering, "I don't do threesomes, but for this I'll make an exception."

He barked a laugh and shook his head. She was always going to win in the dirty joke competition. Damn if that wasn't his kind of sexy.

Giving him a final wink, as if she'd read his thoughts, she got into her car and reversed out of his garage. Addison and Cecily popped their heads up to peer out the rear window, waving manically until their aunt pulled away.

He chuckled, waving until they'd disappeared down the block.

He touched his face after the garage door clanged shut. His cheeks were sore—from smiling. A first. And he'd laughed tonight. Truly laughed. And flirted—something he hadn't done in . . . he didn't know how long.

Smiles, laughter, flirting, cheek kisses . . .

What the hell was happening?

He looked at the cardboard stacked in the corner. The girls had managed to tape together four or five boxes in what might be construed as a ship. If you were drunk and you squinted at it.

Snorting, he stowed the crayons in the corner of his toolbox and closed the lid. He crossed to the bank of light switches, intending to flip everything off and go inside the teeny garage apartment to take off his prosthetic, shower, then lie in bed and watch ESPN until the sports banter put him to sleep.

But the would-be pirate ship caught his gaze. The portholes weren't aligned. And the bow of the ship was the flat side of a box—if they'd angled that box, the corner could've been the wave-slicing part of the bow, then all they'd have to do to fix the portholes was make the center one a cannon gunnery opening . . .

The vision of the girls scrambling around a cardboard ship, little Addison brandishing her plastic cutlass, flared inside his mind. He looked down at his modified tattoo.

Lady-Glitter-Sparkle peeped out from the edge of his short sleeve, distinct from the eagle, globe, and anchor tattoo, with her drawn-on lopsided grin.

His heart lurched with something like excitement. Before he knew it, he was striding over to the pile of cardboard, retrieving the box cutter as he went.

Maybe he'd tinker for a while.

The pesky smile returned to his face, but this time he barely noticed.

CHAPTER 7

"Frickin', frackin' fudge," Bryce ground out through gritted teeth as she read the text from Shama Patel—a labor and delivery nurse who'd since retired and now juggled three side hustles—teaching Lamaze classes, working as a doula for laboring women, and helping when needed as a babysitter for the Weatherford girls.

> Shama: Sorry for the late notice but have to cancel.
> One of my moms is in labor, three weeks earlier
> than expected.

Once upon a time, Bryce had hated to ask favors. That notion seemed quaint now as she stared down at her phone with the text notification from her babysitter canceling an hour before a meeting with a potential weekend catering gig. She'd already rescheduled with the future Mrs. Strickland once before, when Cecily woke up with her hair tangled in a wad of gum she'd clandestinely gone to bed chewing. It had taken three screeching hours and a jar of peanut butter to get her strands untangled from the gooey mass. Bryce couldn't afford to cancel again.

Literally. Every cent she earned from PattyCakes drained out of her checking account like water through a colander, covering extra expenses for the girls she didn't feel like fighting about with the executors of her nieces' estate— Harvey and Adele Payne. Plus, she had to earn enough for the attorney fees to fight the contested guardianship. The catering side hustle she'd been cobbling together after hours—with Patty's full approval—was the financial edge she hoped would prove to the judge that she, Bryce, was just as financially viable a guardian for the girls as the retired Paynes.

Bryce's thumbs flew as she texted a desperate reply.

Bryce: Do you know anyone who could babysit the girls instead? Any names would be appreciated!

Sharma: Maybe the girls' grandparents can stand in?

Bryce: Can't. They're playing in a golf tournament.

Sharma: Sorry. ☹

Bryce felt sweat prickle at her scalp as she checked on the nibbles she'd prepared for today's taste meeting, warm in the oven, the sauces in their dishes all ready to go. She couldn't cancel on the Stricklands-to-be. The wedding was in two months, and they needed menu options or they were going to walk, and she needed this gig. What was she going to do? Having the girls upstairs alone was a broken limb waiting to happen, and having them downstairs in the closed café with her while she met with clients was asking for professional embarrassment when the girls inevitably fought.

"How do you spell 'column'?" June asked, frowning down at the notebook paper only a quarter filled for the eight-hundred-word book report due on Greek architecture for her social studies class. Technically, it had been due a week ago, and Bryce had received an email from June's teacher announcing that she'd already lost twenty points on the essay, but if she turned it in Monday, she may still get a passing grade. Bryce was making June work on it in the kitchen, where she could ensure that her horror-infatuated niece's nose didn't end up in another Drake Matthews book instead.

"C-o-l-u-m-n," Bryce answered, scrolling through her limited Wellsville contacts for another sitter option and coming up empty.

"It's got an 'n' in it? Damn. Who knew?"

"Damn has an 'n' at the end, too, and you owe me ten push-ups for the swear." Bryce rubbed her eyes, trying to find the motivation to start a load of laundry as she puzzled out a solution to the sitter quandary. Starting the laundry wasn't the problem—it was remembering to flip it to the dryer, followed by the Herculean task of sorting the billions of socks, that made it daunting.

"Spelling is whack." June speared her with a crafty look in her green eyes. "And it's not a swear if the little girls aren't here to rat you out. That's what you said last week when you broke the yolk on Addie's fried egg and said 'shit-balls.'"

Bryce glanced out into the middle of PattyCakes, where

Cecily and Addison were splayed out on a blanket and pillows they'd dragged down, excited to have the closed café dining area all to themselves as Bryce cooked. They were watching the millionth playing of *Tinker Bell and the Pirate Fairy* on an old portable DVD player with such intense interest the whole building could've collapsed and it was unlikely they'd notice.

"Fair. Okay, who do we know that can babysit?"

"We don't need a babysitter." All the savagery was back in June's voice. "I'm twelve and can watch them for an hour."

Bryce snorted. "Without fighting? Or completely tuning them out to text your friends? Please. You can't get your own homework done without a babysitter. Case in point." She swept her hand over the café table strewn with her niece's school iPad and notebooks. "You gotta prove you can handle your own self before you can be responsible for your sisters."

"Oh, and I have such a good role model. You're the one who can't handle her own crap." June gestured at the disarray of the desk in the tiny café's office, blanketed by a flurry of invoices and sticky notes. "Case in point."

Bryce felt her eyes narrow. "Why don't you show me you're responsible enough, then, and take your sisters upstairs. Finish your paper. Then we'll talk about future paid babysitting opportunities."

June slammed her book closed with enough ferocity that most of the girl's notes flew in the mini-tornado. Gathering them up and giving a terse bark to her sisters to follow, the tween headed out the front door to the apartment without a backward glare in her aunt's direction.

Bryce let out her breath.

June was right. Bryce's to-do list, both in the daily tasks of caregiving and fighting for guardianship of her nieces, was massive. Add to that working forty hours at PattyCakes along with her fledgling catering business, and life had become so unwieldy it was easier to put out fires versus be proactive. Whenever she had a spare moment—not cooking, or caring for her nieces, which amounted to maybe a half hour every day—she attempted to tackle the chaos. But it was a Sisyphean task. Inexplicably, the harder she worked at reducing the boulder of her responsibilities, the heavier it became.

It was only a matter of time before the thing rolled down, crushing her.

Bryce scrolled through her contacts. Imani was out of town with Zander. Patty was on a clandestine date—one she was keeping from her sons—and Bryce didn't have Kate Sweet-Matthews's number. Willow, Patty's amazing front end manager, was in Buffalo for a rock concert. There was nobody left to ask, except...

Her gaze landed on Ryker's name and their multiple texts with terrible mechanic jokes—a daily thing they'd been doing since that night at his garage. Her stomach fluttered at the thought of seeing him—the good anticipatory feeling she hadn't had in forever. When she'd kissed his cheek, his expression had hinted that he'd felt the same sparks. But asking him to babysit? The bubbly feeling soured at asking a favor from a guy she was crushing on.

Then her eyes spotted her checkbook. Although it was closed, she knew the figures inside, and it wasn't good.

Shame was a more expensive emotion than she could afford at the moment.

She hit the icon for Ryker, and when he picked up, she asked her favor in a rush of words.

"I already owe you for buying out the downtown pharmacy of period products and for fixing my rattling car, but I need help. Can you watch my nieces for about an hour in my upstairs apartment while I meet with my clients at PattyCakes?"

He didn't hesitate. "Yes. When do you need me?"

Bryce winced, her voice strangled as she admitted, "My clients are due in a little over twenty minutes."

"I'll be there in five."

* * *

A half hour later, Bryce was seated with the future Mr. and Mrs. Strickland with taster plates and linen napkins in front of them, explaining each nibble, writing down their preferences and reassuring them it would really be this good when there were two hundred, versus two, of them.

But in her head she wished she was upstairs.

Ryker had shown up, as promised, in five minutes. He was in a pair of garage coveralls so clean they looked like they were for show versus work. He wore black Chuck Taylors, and smelled a little of cars and the spicy scent of whatever cologne or body spray he bought—the one Bryce was convinced must be manufactured in some illegal pheromone laboratory whose goal was to cause clitoral explosions everywhere.

The smell of him made her want to cancel her catering clients to breathe him in. All. Night. Long.

Instead, she smiled politely at the young couple sitting at the fifties-style red-and-chrome table. The two were tall, blond, and had teeth so blindingly white they might've been models for wedding cake toppers. The guy was a tanned Ken doll who might easily double as a Hollister mannequin, and Bryce found herself mesmerized by the future Mrs. Strickland's symmetrical perfection. You could draw a line down the woman, fold her in half, and she'd match right down to the same cup size. Bryce guessed the bride-to-be was a card-carrying member of the Itty-Bitty-Titty-Committee but was wearing a cheater water bra that gave her a generous B cup. She fantasized how awesome it must be to wear a lacy bra with wispy-thin straps, never worrying if you had on the right bra for your DDs to handle any high-impact activity. Like jogging to catch the UPS guy to mail a package.

Bryce shook herself out of the IBTC fantasy, recovering her sales groove.

"This is the latest trend in wedding dining—the mini-bites. Everyone will have a salad to start, then hit the buffet, which will be filled with these choices. Stuffed portabella mushrooms for your vegetarian guests, teriyaki chicken drumettes, mini stuffed shells, shrimp, and of course they'll have me—a chef to sauce it all up for them." Bryce smiled, indicating the variety of homemade sauces she'd prepared for each of the menu options.

The groom-to-be began stuffing everything into his mouth at once, sans sauce. But the bride had a chef's palate. She carved a perfect triangle out of the portabella, dipped it into Bryce's fresh green goddess sauce, then bit into it.

She closed her eyes, then moaned. "This is incredible."

Bryce suppressed a smile. The IBTC bride-to-be was hers.

The rest of the appointment flew by as the picture-perfect couple tried various bites: yes to the mushrooms and mini-quiches; no to the shrimp-deviled eggs. Yes to the field green salad drizzled with a lemon-poppyseed dressing; no to the mini Caesar salads with the homemade croutons. Although, Bryce noticed, they both ate every bite of the "no" items, clearly impressed.

Almost two hours later, she had the deposit check in her hand and the Strickland wedding date inked in her calendar. Bryce was elated, but as she took the stairs two at a time—holding her hands over her boobs because she'd worn the T-shirt bra for its nipple-hiding and smoothing effect, which had absolutely no support for the girls at all—she worried. She'd thought she'd heard someone on the stairs earlier and was stressed that something had happened, but nobody came into PattyCakes. While she hadn't heard any shouting or overly loud wrestling-match-type shenanigans in the time she'd been serving the future Mr. and Mrs. Strickland, she had spent the whole meeting anxious.

Had the girls survived Ryker as a babysitter? Had Ryker survived them?

Throwing open the door, she moved to go into the living room but heard the girls' voices in one of the bedrooms.

"Hello?" she called, and suddenly they all came tumbling out of Addison and Cecily's shared room. First June, with a bemused grin replacing the sarcasm typically etched on her face, then Cecily, who was so excited she almost fell as she skittered out in her dirty sock feet. Trailing them was Addison, who exited the room fairy wings first as she tugged a reluctant Ryker into the hallway.

As soon as they came into the light of the kitchen, Bryce figured out why.

Ryker looked like he'd been given a makeover by a drunken, blindfolded Kardashian.

The guy, still dressed in his mechanic's overalls, was completely transformed from the neck up. He was all glittery blue eyeshadow and glopped-on mascara. He held his baseball cap in his hand, because twenty different-colored barrettes were clipped to his short dirty-blond hair. His perpetual five-o'clock shadow was gummed up with peach blush, which clashed with his punk-rock-purple-painted lips.

"Hey." That was all he said. And really, what else was there to say?

Apparently, the girls got bored with the princess movie and strong-armed the Marine into a Barbie makeover. They'd pulled out all the stops and raided June's stash, as well as Bryce's limited supply of cosmetics, to give the Marine a whole new look.

It was terrifying.

And funny.

"Look what we did, Aunt Beamer!" Addison shouted, her high-pitched voice shrill with excitement. "Doesn't he look bee-autiful?"

To her surprise, June chimed in, grinning wickedly. "Do the duck-lip face, like I showed you."

Ryker pursed his lips in the way thirsty women did on their 'gram, cocking his head to the side and raising an eyebrow in a parody of a come-hither look.

Bryce giggled, then laughed, then bent at the waist as the humor took over, racing through her body like water over dry, parched earth. She felt as if she were suddenly lighter, the laughter lifting some unseen weight inside.

"What? You think the purple lipstick is too much?" Ryker deadpanned.

"I think you pull it off nicely."

His mouth widened in a smile. Even with the blue eyeshadow, insanely long, mascara'd lashes, and the purple lips, the expression melted Bryce's heart.

She'd opened her mouth to make some joke...and noticed the girls were no longer hovering behind Ryker but were babbling to someone in the living room.

"...Grandma Payne, you've got to come see Mr. Ryker's face!" Cecily's little gravelly voice insisted.

And suddenly her nieces' grandparents appeared in the apartment's narrow hallway. Adele and Harvey's expressions radiated disapproval.

"You let them in?" Bryce asked Ryker, feeling like someone had kicked the chair legs out from under her when she'd been leaning back, relaxing.

"He didn't have to. We have a key you gave us months ago in case of emergency, and besides," Adele said, her face the same pinky-red color as her shirt, "we got a text from June. She wanted us to come get her."

Bryce's head swiveled to her oldest niece. "What?"

June stared down at her chipped, black pedicure as she spoke. "I told you. I'm too old for a babysitter."

Hurt, anger, and annoyance swept Bryce's buoyant jubilation away like a fast-moving hurricane.

"Even when I win, I lose," she muttered, then faced the Paynes. "I was downstairs meeting with clients so I can make enough money to cover my attorney fees. My sitter

canceled at the last minute, and I had nobody else to call—
you were at a golf tournament, weren't you?"

"Harvey's gout was acting up, so we didn't go." Adele
held up a hand to forestall Bryce's response, adding, "Besides which, we are always available for our grandchildren.
They are our priorities. As they should be for you."

Bryce felt as if her face were blasted with the heat of a
450-degree oven.

"I'm trying to make a living here. I was only downstairs, and besides, Ryker is more than a capable sitter,"
she argued, gesturing toward the man in full face makeup
beside her, who appeared to be attempting to blend into
the faded wallpaper. "He told me he cares for his daughter
on weekends, for God's sake."

Adele gasped. Then she rounded on Ryker, eyes narrowed
and her finger wagging in his face as her voice rose.

"Your mother will be appalled to hear the lies you're spilling, Ryker Matthews. Don't think that I won't tell her how you
tried to take advantage of Bentley's grieving sister. You should
be ashamed of yourself, pretending to be a father. What were
you doing? Using Drake's baby as some kind of . . . lust lure?"

Lust lure? Drake's baby? Adele's words hung in the air
around Bryce like an exploded bag of flour until they finally
settled into her brain.

"You . . . you're not Lisi's father?" she finally managed.

Ryker's face got that closed, Marine-tight expression
and he shook his head once. "No. I'm Elise's *god*father.
I was . . . babysitting for Drake and Kate while they were
away." He paused, a muscle ticking in his jaw, then the
next sentence plopped from his mouth. "I'm sorry. I forgot
you didn't know—"

"Spare me the apology and leave. Actually..." Bryce pivoted to face the Paynes, the flames of her anger boiling off her former tears. "You can all leave. Feel free to tattle about this to your attorney, Adele. I'll email mine and tell her I was doing the best I could in a hard situation, and I'll be sure to include the fact that you barged in to handle the texting tantrum of a twelve-year-old instead of simply calling my cell phone first."

"We aren't the enemy," Harvey began. "We're all on the same side—the girls' side."

"Right. Well, it'll be in the judge's hands soon enough. I think you should leave." Bryce's gaze swept the Paynes to include Ryker. "All of you."

Ryker, in full-face makeup and plastic barrettes, executed a military-looking pivot and was out the door as fast as if his ass were on fire, with Adele and Harvey lumbering down the stairs after him. When she turned, Bryce saw her nieces standing there, mouths agape.

"And for you, I expect your rooms to be spotless and the makeup put away. No dinner until it's done, and no dessert unless it's done well."

Cecily's eyes narrowed, and Addison's lower lip began to quiver.

"B-but, Mr. Ryker said we could." Fat tears rolled down Addie's face. "An' he looked bee-autiful! Why are you making us clean like Cinderella?"

"Because she's the evil step-monster," Cecily growled. Then she took her sister's hand, leading her into their shared bedroom. "C'mon, before she makes us sweep the fireplace, too."

"I'm not a step-anything. I'm your aunt. And we don't

have a fireplace," Bryce called as they ran to their room. "But there's bathroom floors to clean if you're going to get sassy!"

The sound of June snorting made Bryce spin to glare at the tween.

"That went well." June's green gaze, so like Bentley's, hit her guilt like a searchlight. "Making friends and stealing hearts, Aunt Beamer."

Bryce snatched the iPhone from her. "I'll add this to my steal, then. Cell phones are a privilege, not a right, and you just lost this privilege for the rest of the week, Smarty-McFarty."

"It's not fair!" June shrieked, then raced to her room, slamming the door with enough violence that the picture of Bentley and Heather fell off the wall, landing with a crash of glass.

Bryce stomped over, snatched the frame off the floor, and took it to the kitchen, scraping the broken bits of glass into the garbage.

Suddenly, hot fire laced her index finger.

"Shitwaffle!" She set the broken frame on the kitchen table, racing to the sink to wash her finger. Blood welled up along with her tears as she washed out the cut, the pain in her hand less than the hurt in her heart. Ripping off a mass of paper towels, she wadded them around her finger.

Then she slid down the counter to sit on the floor.

Shame, embarrassment, and the sickening feeling of failure congealed into a lump at the pit of her stomach. Bentley and Heather grinned down at her from the table, a large, triangular shard of glass pointing at their happy expressions as if to highlight the differences between capable people and her.

"Now what am I supposed to do?" she whispered, glaring at her brother's smiling face. "I'm ruining everything. And it's all your fault. I hate you for leaving me in charge."

Then she put her head in her hands, and cried.

CHAPTER 8

Sometimes Ryker hated living in a town where everyone knew everyone else's business. Like now. Only two hours after being kicked out of Bryce's apartment, his brothers were banging open the door to his garage gym and interrupting his chest and biceps workout for what had to be some sort of intervention.

"Ah, we're back in town just in time to catch you doing the glory muscles. Again." Zander ran a hand through his shaggy locks as he crowded over the weight bench, examining how many plates were on the bar. "And you're lifting like a bull, man. You need a spot?"

"Your leg looks swollen." Drake's keen eyes never missed a thing. "Is that why you're not wearing your prosthetic? I thought you went to your prosthetist guy, Jeff, last month. Didn't he adjust it for you?"

Ryker shifted his position, eyeballing his socket, which he'd left leaning against the bistro table by the Volkswagen front end. After getting home from Bryce's, he'd swept the barrettes out of his hair, carefully dumping them into a compartment in his toolbox. Then he'd changed into shorts and a T-shirt and taken off his prosthesis, eager to have his leg free. He'd used his crutches instead, hoping to ease the blistering pain at the front of his shin about three inches below his knee, almost at the end of his residual limb. The hot spot screamed for attention, despite his prosthetist's best efforts to carve out a bubble in the prosthetic to protect him from the outcropping of HO bone growth there.

"I don't need a spot, Zan. And Jeff did adjust my leg." Ryker answered his brother's questions truthfully. Drake was an expert at sniffing out lies, and it was best to give a lie of omission versus an untruth unless he wanted his brother poking his nose in his business more often. Which he did not. "I had a couple hours free to work out, and I didn't want to sweat inside my liner, so I took it off. What's up?"

Although he didn't come right out and ask "Why are you freaking here?" his tone implied it, and his brothers both picked up on it.

"We just got in from checking out an abandoned sanitarium for a potential reader event Kate and Imani are planning, and figured we'd swing by." Drake peered at Ryker's residual limb. Ryker knew he was seeing the red, irritated skin on the front of his shin where the bone had decided to grow, the cells there basically on overdrive, growing a useless, cauliflower-like offshoot on what remained of his amputated tibia. "You sure you're okay, Ry? Your leg is really red. Mom called and said she'd heard there was some sort of dustup."

"I'm fine." Ryker bent his left knee back and forth to show his brothers his leg still worked. "There wasn't a dustup. I was helping . . . a friend, and things got—"

Zander put out a hand. "By the blue eyeliner smeared all

over your eye, and the...interesting shade of blush stuck to your sideburns, we get you, bro. No need to explain, and we are here for you in this transformational journey. What pronouns should we use, going forward?"

"Dick," Ryker cursed at him. He swiped at his eyes, then his sideburns, growling at the evidence still there—evidence of another moment where he'd tried to do the right thing and it blew up in his face.

"Roger that. Dick/Dickish. Unusual choice for pronouns but fitting." Zander sidestepped Ryker's fist, and Ryker glowered at him.

"I'm not changing genders. Bryce's nieces got bored, and I let them...You know what? It's not any of your business."

Ryker grabbed his crutches from where they leaned against the Smith machine and made his way over to the garage workbench for his protein shake, eager to put some distance between himself and his brothers. He knew they only wanted to help. But their help wouldn't resolve the chaos he'd inadvertently caused for Bryce—a woman he was attracted to, but more than that, a woman he respected and admired. How many times had he relived the moment when he'd held her after she'd stumbled? How many times had he caught himself chuckling, recalling her funny mechanic jokes? Something about being with Bryce and her nieces was transformative. He'd felt like a different man this past week—one who smiled, was lighthearted. Almost as if the PTSD-addled Ryker were gone.

And look what letting down his guard had done.

He glared at the rearview mirror and emblem, recalling what happened when he let himself get distracted. You'd think he'd have learned.

Zander snapped his fingers, bringing Ryker's attention back to the present. "Wait. You're secretly practicing a drag routine so you can be the newcomer act at Hamburger Mary's, aren't you? For what it's worth, I think you'd rock a Britney Spears look." Zander tilted his head in consideration. "Although your voice is more Miley Cyrus. With a little manscaping you might be able to pull it off, but you'll have to get some fresh razors, dude, because you're as hairy as a Yeti in winter."

Ryker narrowed his eyes at his younger brother, mentally counting how many strides it would take to tackle him to the ground when Drake, interpreting his bro-lephathy, intervened.

"Zan, quit it. He obviously likes Bryce. His epic run to CVS was pretty much an all-caps billboard announcing the fact." Drake's dark eyebrows rose, a pensive look on his face. "Which, by the way, I have to know: did the cashier say anything to you? The scene keeps replaying in my mind, and I need some resolution. Or at least some dialogue."

Ryker felt his neck and ears burn. He chugged the rest of his protein shake and slammed the metal Tervis to the table, making a terrific clang.

"Can't a guy buy a box of tampons without the whole town losing their damn minds?"

"Yeah." Zander scoffed as Ryker crutched over to take his place on the overhead press. "But you practically bought the whole *aisle*, dude. Everyone's curious who this woman is that has a tough Marine panic-buying period products. She must be something special."

"Mom says Bryce is incredible," Drake intervened, his voice neutral. "But Mom wasn't super thrilled to hear through the rumor mill—and by rumor mill, I mean Adele Payne—who told Mom that you, uh, pretended to be—"

"Elise's baby daddy," Zander finished, shaking his head. "Dude. What were you thinking? No good relationship starts with a lie. You should be up front about who you are: scars, PTSD, and all. That's what I did with Imani, and she still fell in love with me."

"Proof there's a sucker born every day." Ryker ground his teeth, racking the bar and sitting up on the bench, feeling like he'd get more satisfaction from jabbing a fist at his brother versus this workout. But inside he was debating about coming clean to everyone, not just Bryce. What would it be like to tell his family that despite the fact it had been years since his last deployment and injury, his PTSD seemed to be worsening? How would it feel to admit that his HO was getting to the point where he was going to have to take action—drastic, under-the-scalpel action— to get it resolved? Could he ask them to help shoulder the weight he'd been carrying?

His eyes flitted to the yellow VW front end bolted to the opposite garage wall.

No. While he might not be actively serving, once a Marine, always a Marine, and Marines endured. Pain was just weakness leaving the body.

"Zander's right. You need to fix this," Drake said.

Frustration boiled in Ryker like an overheated radiator. "Fine! You two are so brilliant with women, what do you want me to do?" He'd meant to sound sarcastic but was embarrassed when it came out as a desperate plea. He cleared his throat, choosing a firm, military-approved, tone. "I should've corrected Bryce a long time ago when she'd assumed I was Elise's dad, but I didn't. I screwed up and it's over!"

"You're being a tad dramatic, bro." Zander shoved him off the weight bench. Ryker stood, watching as his younger brother inserted himself under the bar, pressing it up easily a few times before re-racking the weights, gesturing for Drake to take his place.

Drake shook his head, taking the standing leg press machine instead as he spoke. "Fixing this is as easy as pie."

Zander cried out. "Yassss, that's it! Bake for her. She's a chef, right? She'll dig that."

Drake shook his head. "No offense, Ry, but I'm not confident anything you'd bake would be...edible. I was thinking more along the lines of an act of service. Something *helpful* to her."

Ryker shrugged. "My only skills revolve around cars and engines, and guess what? She can drive anything—literally anything—with wheels, plus she's got her own tool set. She doesn't need a grease monkey."

In frustration, he used his right leg for the short, six-inch jump to catch the chin-up bar with both hands. Although he'd already done a set there, he did a few more to beat away the feeling of ineptitude that rose up to swallow him whole.

"But she does need help with the kids, right? I mean, we only have one child, and it's all Kate and I can do to manage Elise and work full time. I can't imagine how much harder it is as a single caregiver." Drake lifted his chin to forestall Ryker's argument. "You've got a truck with plenty of room to haul little girls. Start there. Go to the school and complete whatever paperwork you need to help with the back-and-forth to school, then offer up your services."

"That's not going to..." Ryker stopped speaking, his brain finally catching up to his brother's words. He hopped down onto his right leg, his body alert. "Wait. Could I do that? You're not fictionalizing solutions, Drake?"

Drake scowled. "I never fictionalize solutions—"

Both Ryker and Zander burst out laughing.

"Duuude," Zander snorted.

"Bro." Ryker lifted an eyebrow. "You write novels for a living."

Drake rolled his eyes, but he was laughing.

"I'm not making this up. You'll probably need Bryce's signature for permission, but at least you'll have the first step done."

"Imani had to get background checked when she taught a dance for the elementary school's PE class," Zander said. "You could do that, then if she needed someone to stand in as a tutor, you'll be ready. Nobody can object to helping kids with homework, right? You'll be a hero. After you sincerely apologize for being an ass-hat, of course."

Ryker gave in. "If it'll shut you two up, I'll check into the school's paperwork. But I doubt it's that easy."

* * *

Turned out, he was wrong. It was that easy.

He'd gone to the Wellsville School District and filled out the papers to be a volunteer and got background checked for all grade levels. If Zander was right and Bryce needed help for pickup or drop-off, he could fill in. All he needed to finish both forms was her signature...and the opportunity to apologize.

That part wasn't as easy.

Between garage clients, he started out by texting an apology, being as forthright as possible. He even used Zander's words.

> Ryker: I was an ass-hat and I'm sorry I didn't tell you straight up that I was Elise's godfather. I'd like to apologize in person for causing you unnecessary conflict.

> Bryce: Apology accepted. No in person necessary. Life is complicated enough over here. It's best to leave well enough alone.

He winced at the short, choppy sentences, so different from their previous text exchanges. What had his brothers said? Give her what she needed.

Even if what she needed wasn't what he wanted.

He waited a couple hours, mulling over his answer as he changed a customer's oil, and then, as he closed up his shop, he texted back.

> Ryker: Copy that. I have a delivery to drop off to you. Is it okay to leave it behind PattyCakes in the loading area?

> Bryce: ??What is it??

> Ryker: It's for the girls.

> Bryce: Check to see if Patty's cool with it, but it's okay as far as I'm concerned.

Before overthinking it, he loaded everything into the bed of his truck. He called his mom as he drove, surprised that she answered on the first ring. Ryker knew from texting with his brothers that Mom had been taking off every Wednesday for a pickleball league she'd joined, so he'd figured she'd be busy with her gal pals.

"Hi, sweetheart. Everything okay?" Her voice was a little breathless, like she'd just gotten done laughing.

"Fine. Mom, do you mind if I commandeer the loading dock in the back of PattyCakes for the rest of the week? It's—it's important."

Fully expecting the third degree—at the very least, a lecture about how he hadn't even bothered to stop by the café to apologize for her having to hear about all this drama from Adele Payne—Ryker was surprised to hear his mother hum in assent.

"Sure, whatever you need." His mom giggled, then Ryker heard the unmistakable sound of a man's low voice. There was a smooshing noise on the other end of the phone, followed by his mom continuing in a breathless voice. "Is that all, honey?"

Ryker's eyes widened in surprise as he pulled up behind the closed café. This didn't sound like a pickleball game. Was his mom on...a date?

"That's it. Thanks, Mom. Have a...have a good night."

His mom chuckled. "I intend to."

Ryker hung up, shaking his head, refusing to think about his mom on a potential date. He had to focus. It was an apology mission comprised of three parts: deliver the goods, say his piece, then leave. He'd picked Wednesday night because he knew Bryce and the girls would be home, but now he was nervous. He wasn't sure how this gesture would be perceived, and like dropping off the feminine hygiene supplies, he'd rather not be present when they saw it. Just in case it was a bad idea.

He backed his truck into the narrow alley behind Patty-Cakes. He flipped down the tailgate and hauled everything out. There was some last-minute construction that needed to be done, and he was using his teeth to rip off another piece of duct tape when there was an eardrum-piercing scream above him.

"Holy shit." He jumped, ramming his elbow into the side of his truck, making the nerve endings in his funny bone tingle and ache. He gazed up and saw two little girls peering at him through screened windows in the upstairs apartment.

"Is that what I think it is?" Addison shouted, her yellow wings flapping as they caught the cool spring breeze through the window. "Did you build us a pirate ship?"

He shrugged. "I didn't build it, you girls did. When I woke up, it looked like this. I'm just bringing it over. Is... is your aunt home?"

In answer, both girls left the window, and he heard screaming and loud thumping and slamming of doors. He continued taping the rest of the boxes together, willing his jangling nerves away, and a few minutes later, the alley door opened and a gaggle of chattering females exited. Addison gave another trademark shriek, followed by a hoarser, lower-octave version from Cecily, and even June gave a laughing gasp of surprise.

Bryce remained silent, staring alternately at him and the cardboard pirate ship gleaming red in his taillights and the exhaust coming out in the chilly air, making it look all mysterious, like it was floating in the mist. The little girls tugged at Bryce's arms, their slippered-pajama feet making swishy noises on the concrete steps as they jigged about, buoyant with excitement and shrieking their questions about whether they could play in it or not.

But their aunt only stared at the pirate ship. Mute. Unsmiling.

Ryker's heart plummeted to his knees.

He'd screwed up. What had he been thinking? She was an employee. In retrospect, he shouldn't have put her in this position with his mom. Where the hell was Bryce going to put those boxes when the next delivery came? She'd have to trash them, and then she'd be the bad guy. Or maybe Bryce didn't want the girls playing in the alleyway, because then she'd have to stay out here to watch them, which meant she wouldn't get any work done, and would be more stressed...

Shit. He hadn't thought it through. He'd been hyper-focused on making something awesome for the girls and showing Bryce he was sorry.

Epic. Fail.

While he wanted to slink back to his truck and leave, his Marine training wouldn't allow it. He never shied away from doing hard things. Even if it meant facing a gorgeous woman dressed in a loose-fitting Buffalo Sabres hockey jersey that hung to the middle of her thighs and a blue pair of those fluffy socks that looked like they'd never fit into a pair of shoes. She wore what his mom would call "comfort clothes," and knowing he'd come over and ruined that vibe made his guts churn.

Addison and Cecily abandoned their quest for permission and launched themselves into the pirate ship. He'd made sure to pad the bottom with extra cardboard, ripping out every single box staple and running his big magnetic sweeper from his shop over the whole thing to double check all metal was removed. While he might not have thought out the placement of this ship, he'd made sure it wouldn't give anybody tetanus.

June was the only one still in what appeared to be school clothes—dark jeans, those zombie-stomper boots, and a long-sleeved black T-shirt with a dude in a Jason mask wielding a spoon over a bowl of Cheerios with the words *Cereal Killer* on the front.

"Impressive." June managed to look dazzled and snarky at the same time. "I like the change to the Jolly Roger's skull—giving it pigtails and hairbows was genius. You should start your own YouTube channel: Cardboard My Life, or something. You'd totally win."

Ryker decided to take that as a compliment. He pulled a three-inch-thick rubber-banded pack of paper from atop the file folder on his truck's tailgate and handed it to the twelve-year-old.

"This is for you. It's the proof pages for Drake's next horror book, *March's Madness*. In essence, an early copy." Ryker paused to look at Bryce, who stared stoically ahead. "Full disclosure: I haven't read it. Drake said it's about the wife of a famous basketball player who discovers her husband leads a creepy double life off court. Figured a fan like you would enjoy first dibs."

June took the huge stack of papers, her sarcastic expression fading into one of childlike wonder. She moved the rubber band, reading the hand-scrawled words on the title page.

To June: May you never look at a basketball the same way again. Best—Drake.

The older girl stood there, staring at the printed manuscript in her arms, then clutched it to her chest, finally meeting his eyes. He was startled to see tears pooled there, and her chin wobbled as she spoke three words.

"This. Is. LIFE!"

With that, she bolted inside the restaurant. A moment later, her whoop of joy rang out, rivaling those of her sisters, who were still exploring the cardboard confines of the ship.

"Wow, you're like the Wizard of Oz." Bryce seemed to be looking everywhere but at him as she gave a mirthless laugh. "The bringer of joy. The provider of play. I used to hold those titles. Now I'm a giant fun vacuum, sucking the happiness from my nieces' lives on a regular basis."

He wanted to call bullshit. But he was already mired in mistakes and wasn't about to argue that she was doing an incredible job under some crap-tastic circumstances. Instead, he grabbed the last thing in his truck bed: the file folder.

Breathing through the fear and nausea, he squared his shoulders and thrust the sheaf of papers at her, then adjusted the brim of his ball cap, waiting. In exactly fifteen seconds, he would have completed tonight's mission and could retreat to his garage.

"What's this?" Bryce took the papers, her eyebrows drawing together.

"The rest of my apology. Paperwork is done for me to

transport your nieces to and from school, should you ever need me to. And I did the volunteer stuff, too, in case you needed a tutor or someone to go on a field trip, or whatever."

Bryce flipped through, looking puzzled. "But this says you completed all the volunteer classes and were background checked. How in the world did you do all that since...yesterday? It took me three weeks when I moved here to get that crap situated."

Ryker shrugged. "Small towns. Everyone knows me, my family, my situation. Sometimes it comes in handy to expedite things. Like this."

Bryce dropped her gaze. No smile.

Time to count his losses and vamoose. "I should go. I just wanted to say sorry." He gave a curt nod, slammed the tailgate shut, and climbed into his truck, all the while bitching himself out in his mind. Why had he thought this woman would be different? That he could slide in and do real-boy things? As if.

He'd just backed out of the driveway when he saw Bryce coming after him. He hit the brakes, the rubber squealing a little on the pavement. Ryker rolled down his window.

She leaned through the open window toward him. She wound her fist into the front of his shirt and yanked it until their faces were inches apart. For one wild, glorious second, he thought she was going to kiss him. Instead, she narrowed her eyes.

"I can't stand liars, cheats, and people who don't keep their cooking stations clean. Do we understand each other?" Her face was stern and she looked like some sort of war goddess.

It was hot as hell.

But this was not the time to be aroused. He battled against any facial expression that might give away his feelings, opting for a crisp nod.

"Roger that."

Slowly, she released him from her grip. "Good. Now I want to thank you properly for the epic cardboard ship you created, and for whatever you had to do to get an early copy of your brother's next book. Somehow you managed to single-handedly please everyone in this household." Her mouth curved, finally, *finally* into a smile. The expression brought the sparkle back into her eyes and the teasing lilt to her voice as she added, "Including me."

It was a long beat before he realized the pause meant he should speak.

"Uh, good. I'm glad you—you're all—happy." He glanced toward the pirate ship and he caught sight of the two little girls scampering down the driveway in their pajamas. Try as he might, he couldn't restrain his grin. They were so freaking cute. "Watch out. Two coming up on your six."

"On my what? Oh!" Bryce spun as Addison and Cecily crashed into her simultaneously, all three of them banging into the side of his truck.

"Can we invite Mr. Ryker over for a playdate?" Addison asked, her bent fairy wing quivering as it hung from the rubber-band-like holster over her pajamas. She tossed him an impish grin as she swung herself back and forth with her arms anchored around her aunt's waist. "Puh-lease?"

"Please, please?" Cecily joined in, tugging on the opposite side of Bryce. He noticed that the middle girl's face and arms were clean, and she smelled faintly of Lava soap.

"Oof, quit tugging on me, you two. I was going to ask if he wanted to come over Friday so I can cook him an *adult* dinner when you're at Nana and Pop-Pop's church." She gave him that frank, assessing gaze he found so alluring. "I do my best thank-yous with my pots and pans. You free on Good Friday for dinner?"

Bam.

Just like that, he'd gone from the dog house to a dinner invite. He thanked whatever ancestors were watching over him for Bryce's ability to forgive and move on.

"Totally free." He made a mental note to reschedule his meetup with the Rochester exec to deliver the Mercury Cougar. No way was he missing out on his first date in ages for a car. "What time do you want me?"

One of her expressive eyebrows quirked up, as if she were ready to pounce on his comment and make a lewd joke. Instead, she glanced down at the girls, who were making it clear they were disappointed with the whole "adult dinner" decision, and then she made a wry grimace as she caught his gaze.

"How about you come over when the girls leave at five-thirty and help me cook. Gotta keep my skills sharp." Bryce spoke over her nieces' objections; they wanted to help. "And if two girls I know are *really* good and listen to their aunt until then, they can join us for dessert."

Cecily and Addison whooped in delight, promising every good behavior in a rush of high-pitched words.

"But after dessert, can he play pirate with us on the ship? Please, will you play with us, Mr. Ryker?" Addison's sky-blue gaze pinned him as effectively as a wrestler, the pleading look making him want to say anything so he could tap out.

"Aye. But only if I can borrow yer cutlass, lassie." He did his best Jack Sparrow impression, squinting one eye for effect. "I lost mine during a fight with Davy Jones."

Addison gasped. "I wonder if that's Sammy's dad! I have a Sammy Jones in my class, and he kept liftin' up my dresses so everyone would see my underwear and laugh."

Ryker wasn't sure how to reply. So he leaned in on his pirate role, keeping the accent.

"Sammy sounds like a scallywag. If he did that on my ship, he'd walk the plank."

The little blonde bobbed her head. "Yeah, I punched him in the throat. Only I got put in time-out afterward. Then Aunt Beamer called up my teacher and tol' her boys who lift up girls' dresses without permission deserve a throat-punch all day long."

Ryker wasn't sure whether he wanted to laugh or figure out who the skirt-lifting twerp was and scare the bejesus out of him.

He opted for more pirate. More pirate was always safe.

"Arrgh! Yer aunt be a wise lass."

Cecily's eyes rounded, and she pointed at Ryker. "Ooh! You did a swear. You've gotta do ten push-ups. That's what Aunt Beamer does when she swears."

Bryce laughed. "He said 'lass,' which is some sort of Scottish slang for young lady. It's not a swear, and besides, ten push-ups is hardly a punishment for a guy this strong. C'mon, you two. Let's get out of the road so Ryker can get home. See you Friday at five-thirty."

She reversed in giant, sumo-wrestler-like steps to the sidewalk, lifting the girls who hung, one on each leg, like living ballast. Both girls shrieked with laughter as she shuffled back up the driveway, towing them along with her. She gave one last wave before heading inside.

Ryker glanced in the rearview to make sure they were gone before he pulled away, and he caught sight of his expression.

Smiling. Again.

Shaking his head at himself, he headed back to the garage, whistling. It took a few bars before he realized what song was in his head.

"Yo ho, yo ho, a pirate's life for me."

CHAPTER 9

Thanks again for inviting me," Bryce said the next morning, sighing as her feet soaked in a scented pedicure bath. Imani sat in the chair on one side and Kate Sweet-Matthews sat on the other side. "This is the most relaxed I've been in...honestly, I'm not sure."

Imani squeezed Bryce's hand. "Self-care is not selfish. It wasn't too long ago that I felt like you—overwhelmed and frantic on a daily basis. I promised myself I wouldn't neglect my mental recharge again, and since then I've been careful to carve out pockets of me-time. Whether it's dancing by myself in the studio or getting a pedi with friends, it's important to remind yourself you deserve good things."

Kate nodded. "Mmm. I needed this reminder. It's harder to be a working mom than I expected. I feel so much freaking guilt. All the time."

Bryce's ears perked up. Kate looked like she always had everything under control when she met up with Imani at PattyCakes armed with spreadsheets and planners. "You feel guilty? Why? I mean, you're the picture-perfect working mom. You're all I aspire to be in a mom-like creature."

Kate popped open one green eye and shook her head.

"I don't feel like anyone's aspiration. When I'm with Elise, I worry I'm neglecting my business or putting too much off on Carl or Imani. But then when I'm working at an event, all I can think of is if poor Elise is suffering in some way because she doesn't have her mother there. I feel like I'm never where I'm needed, never doing what I should be doing, and I'm always feeling guilty. Work-life balance is a myth. Both are never equal on the effort scale and they're rarely harmonious—one side or another is always needing more attention. It's toxic to imply an equal balance between work and personal life exists. At least for me."

"Jesus. It's like you're living in my head," Bryce muttered and was surprised when they both laughed. "The difference is, we all know *you're* a great mom-like creature. It's pretty unanimous that I'm failing in that regard."

Kate scowled, her auburn head tilting. "Not true. Imani told me the other day how she loves the way you interact with your nieces."

Imani nodded. "I see the other moms—dads too—watch you chase your girls after dance class, playing like you're a monster. Their kids beg them to do the same, and it's hilarious to watch some of those parents attempt to be lighthearted and silly with their own kids. You're naturally gifted at play—freeing my inner child is something I had to learn from Zander. I never met Bentley, but Heather was one of my volunteers at my first-ever recital, and I think she'd be happy they'd chosen you as the girls' guardian."

Bryce flushed under the compliment. She'd never had many female friends growing up, always playing football with the boys or tinkering on cars with her dad. Working at Chez Pierre, it was all men with her in the kitchen.

Her time around other women was limited, so when Imani invited her for a girls' day out while her nieces were at school, she'd asked Patty, who'd readily agreed, saying it was about time Bryce took a few hours off.

"I appreciate you two saying so, but Heather's parents think otherwise. They've filed papers contesting me as guardian, because they don't think I can provide the stable home environment the girls need." Bryce grimaced, thinking of the upcoming meeting with the judge. "Fun is synonymous with slacking, and they feel that they'd be a better choice to raise the girls. Honestly, some days, I think they're right."

Both Imani and Kate objected, their voices indignant.

"Have either of them had the girls for any significant chunk of time?" Kate asked. "Because parenting is exhausting, and they're retired. They've already raised their child."

"And she died," Bryce reminded herself and her friends. "Heather was their world, and she's gone. The girls are all they have left of their daughter, and they want to raise them."

Imani jutted her chin the way she did when the dancers weren't listening. "It's one thing to think your way of loving them is the best way. But Kate's right. They haven't done daily caregiving for more than a couple days at a time, have they?"

Bryce pondered this. "When Bentley and Heather were in the car accident, it took me four days to give my notice, pack my apartment, and drive up. During that time, the Paynes were in the hospital by Heather's bedside. If I recall, the girls stayed with their friends' parents until I got to town. They kept them for three days while my dad came up and helped me figure out funeral arrangements and settle Bentley's plumbing business."

"It's one thing to be the grandparents who get to whisk in and spoil the kids rotten, but another to care for them full time," Imani insisted as the pedicurist put on her color choice—one called Salsa Red. "Trust me. After my mom died, Gigi became a second mother to me, but she only had me summer vacations and that was enough for her. My dad still did the daily parenting, and during the year after our house burned down and we lost everything, Katie's folks stood in full time. I'll always be thankful for how they took me under their wing, although I was moody and angsty and it was a heavy lift to parent a grieving teen."

"You weren't so moody and angsty as you think." Kate admired her nail polish being applied—a happy pink color called Party Dress. "But your point is valid. I wonder if the Paynes know the saying 'Be careful what you wish for,' because I'm not sure they're ready to parent three young girls."

"Well, it's up to the judge." Bryce kept her tone easy-breezy, but her heart thudded every time she thought about the upcoming trial. "We'll find out soon enough if the Paynes are up to the task of parenting for more than a weekend. When the girls are off school for spring break, I'm taking my paid vacation week from PattyCakes to go to a Niagara Falls restaurant and fill in as sauté chef for some extra cash to pay my legal fees. Harvey and Adele will watch the girls while I'm gone and then the judge will decide on guardianship."

"It'll all work out in the end," Imani said with conviction.

The pedicurist tapped Bryce's leg. "What color do you want?"

Bryce fingered the binder ring fat with multicolored plastic strips of long, fake nails spiraling out like a technicolor medieval weapon. She'd been cycling through color choices as they talked. Salsa Red and Party Dress weren't for her. She was drawn to the purple shades, and she recalled the picture of Ryker in Patty's shop, decked out in his Silver Star and Purple Heart.

"This one." She picked a deep purple that matched the medal in the picture. "Purple is the color for bravery, and I'm going to need all the courage I can muster these next couple of weeks."

The color—called Plum Perfect—went on deep and rich, and Bryce grinned as she looked at her toes. They looked like amethysts and made her feel fancy. And sexy.

Something of this must've shown on her face, because Imani leaned over and gave a hum of approval.

"Nice. Seems a shame to have those toes hidden in your black sneakers all day while you cook. I heard a rumor there might be a special dinner happening this Friday?" Imani raised one dark eyebrow. "A dress-up dinner?"

"Gotta love small towns." Kate laughed as Bryce's cheeks grew hot. "Everybody knows your business. But also, everybody is there for you. It's a double-edged sword, but having the small-town support system beats out the lack of privacy. Most days."

Bryce cleared her throat. They were her friends. Girl-friends told each other things, right?

"I'm cooking for Ryker Friday night when my nieces are with the Paynes. He's been so kind to me and the girls.

After he made them a pirate ship out of cardboard and brought Drake's printed manuscript over, I figured a dinner was the least I could do." Bryce squirmed in her seat, then blurted the rest. "I really like him. Plus, he's hot."

Both Kate and Imani nodded, chuckling.

"Those Matthews boys are like cinnamon rolls—sinfully decadent, but sometimes you've got to unwind them to see what's inside," Kate said. "I'm glad you can see the sweetness underneath Ryker's gruff Marine exterior. I think he cultivates his RBF, just like Drake used to hide behind his Knight of Nightmares title, and how Zander used to play up his carefree philosophy. They use their reps as a shield from the world."

Bryce nodded. "That makes so much sense. I've only begun to peel back the outer layer. I wish I could get him to open up to me."

"Keep at it, and he will. My dear friend gave me a piece of advice last summer that I'm going to pass along to you." Imani winked at Kate, then nodded at Bryce. "Get you a Matthews brother. They're the good ones, and worth the effort it takes to unwind the knotted-up layers."

"Speaking of knots, when are you and Zander tying the knot? You've been engaged for months and haven't set a date." Kate narrowed her eyes. "You'd better not be thinking of using another wedding planner. I will literally kill you."

"What? You once told me, 'If I plan my own wedding, I won't enjoy any of it,' so why would I book you for *my* wedding? Besides," Imani held up a hand to stop her best friend from arguing, "we're saving up for a house. Eventually, we'll set a date and do a casual backyard thing, and I'll invite you both as guests. Not hired help."

Both Kate and Bryce objected, and soon they were chattering away about Imani's future wedding plans. Bryce's chest filled with a sudden feeling of belonging. Of having a place and people to look out for her. It wasn't the same as having Bentley alive. But for the first time in a long time, she felt good.

* * *

Surprisingly, the rest of the week went smoothly. Well, if you didn't count having to pick up Cecily at school for scrapping with one of the boys in her class who'd said there was no such thing as volcano vomit soap. Then there was a major emergency before school Wednesday when the yellow stretchy material covering the left wing of Addison's favorite fairy wings completely separated from the wire frame and she was refusing to leave the house. Not to be forgotten, June declared on Thursday that none of her shoes fit anymore except flip-flops and then got sent home from school for a dress-code violation.

Bryce was proud of how she handled each crisis. She sliced a hunk off the Lava soap for Cecily to take to school and show the boys they were wrong. She found a pair of nude pantyhose to repair Addison's wing, and while one was yellow and one was nude, she set her niece down with glitter glue to decorate the nude wing and pointed out that lots of fairies had different-colored wings. June's shoe-tastrophe was valid—the girl's feet had grown two miles since the start of the school year, so Bryce gave her a budget to buy two new pairs of boots and a pair of Vans online, as long as she crammed her feet into the old shoes until the new ones arrived.

Thankfully, school was closed for Good Friday, minimizing the external chaos. With Patty's permission, the girls spent the day "helping out" at PattyCakes. While Bryce had to wrestle Addison and Cecily apart after a fight over who got to spray the dishes with the wash hose before putting them in the dishwasher, it had been nice to have them with her as customers streamed in, grabbing quarts of soup to have with Easter dinner. Even June was pleasant, working side by side with Willow to learn the register, lending a hand in the busy café, which allowed Bryce to sit with Patty in the tiny cubicle of an office to learn more about the behind-the-scenes work involved in running a shop.

"It's perfect," Patty said, reviewing the online food order Bryce had meticulously put together after creating next week's menu and doing a quick inventory of their current supplies. "You're a natural at this! Even though we're ordering more food since expanding the menu, the expense is more than covered by the increased revenue. Plus, you have an uncanny ability to use up every single leftover. I swear, you were born to run a restaurant, and I am thrilled to have you aboard—so thrilled that I'll actually keep the place open when I go on vacation next month. Something I have never done, but I trust the place in your hands."

Bryce flushed with pleasure at the compliment. "When you first offered to teach me all the sorcery that goes on behind the curtain here, I was intimidated. I thought the skills required to have your own place were way above my head. But you've shown me that it isn't as impossible as I once thought. It's actually . . . kind of awesome."

Patty closed out the computer screen and swiveled her office chair to face Bryce, her blue eyes alight with curiosity.

"Have you thought about your next career move? Because I think in another year or so, I'll have taught you everything and you'd be ready to run this place, if that's what you want."

"I can barely plan ahead to next week, let alone next year," Bryce scoffed.

Patty nodded, then put her hand atop Bryce's. "It's easy to get lost when all you see is your feet on the path in front of you. If all you're doing is avoiding the next obstacle, you'll never find your way out of the forest. At some point you've got to find the time to create a map. Pick your head up, figure out where you are and where you want to go. It's easy as a caregiver for your needs to be subsumed by your children's. Even I still have to remind myself I'm on my own path. I have my own goals. Take it from me—once you orient yourself in the right direction, things tend to fall into place."

Unexpected tears welled up in Bryce's eyes. She blinked, sniffing and nodding. "You're right. It's just been tough..."

"I know. I went through something similar when I lost my husband. I had three boys to care for, and nobody was going to figure it out for me. As awful as Hawthorne's loss was, it taught me that I could do hard things. So can you, Bryce." Patty smiled. "For what it's worth, I think you'd be an excellent restaurant owner."

"I appreciate that," Bryce said, allowing her heart to fill with the possibility of Patty's words. "It's been a fun challenge. I like seeing how things work."

Patty's face crinkled in a smile. "Reminds me of someone else I know. Someone I heard is coming over for an amazing home-cooked meal later?"

More blood rushed to Bryce's cheeks, this time with embarrassment.

"It's a thank-you meal for his help with the girls, but we'll also be cooking vegetables to freeze for soups while I'm in Niagara Falls. It's not...a date, or anything."

"Oh, that's too bad," Patty said, winking. "Because if it was a date, I'd tell you to run upstairs and get ready and I'd watch the girls for you down here as we close up. But since it's just work..."

Bryce shook her head, laughing. "Okay. Maybe it's sort of a date. Your son...he is a pretty special guy. He makes me laugh, and he's like a sorcerer when it comes to figuring out my nieces. But mostly I just enjoy the way I feel when I'm with him. He makes me...value myself as a person again. That sounds stupid, doesn't it?"

"Not at all. I've heard he's just as smitten with you. Now, scoot." Patty shooed her from the office with a grin. "We've got things under control. I'll bet I know three girls who will love to take turns running the floor polisher while you get ready for your 'sort of' date."

* * *

By the time the Paynes arrived to pick up the girls at four o'clock, Bryce was feeling optimistic. She loved her work, and maybe there was some career potential here in Wellsville—opportunities she hadn't dared to think about flitted through her head. She'd handled the girls' chaos this week like a champ and had some excellent moneymaking weeks on the horizon. Maybe she was cut out to be a working mom-like creature after all?

"Well, if you're heading out, you're going to want to put on more sensible shoes" was Adele's greeting as Bryce let them into the empty café, with Patty and Willow having closed the shop and left a few minutes earlier. "It's starting to sleet outside, and the roads are sloppy with slush and salt. Don't you watch the weather forecast?"

Bryce bristled. She'd dug deep into the recesses of her closet for clothing she hadn't worn since Tampa, and after sending a slew of messages to Imani, complete with pictures of each outfit, she'd finally chosen a grayish-blue wraparound dress with an opening in the back that required her to shove her double Ds into a terrifyingly strapless bra. She picked out a pair of dark-gray, teardrop-shaped earrings made of leather, and on her feet were a pair of chunky black sandals. She'd never mastered walking in heels, but she was determined to wear something to showcase her Plum Perfect pedicure, despite the weather. Although it was weird to cook in something with her toes showing— a kitchen no-no, and dangerous to boot—she'd wanted to dress to impress Ryker. Looking down at herself, she hoped she hadn't missed the mark.

"Mr. Ryker's coming over for a dinner daaaaate." Addison sang the last word before flitting over to hug her grandparents, then twirling to Bryce to pluck at the fabric of the gray-blue dress, dancing it back and forth before gesturing up to Bryce's head. "Doesn't her hair look beee-eautiful?"

Self-consciously, Bryce patted at her hair. Thanks to Patty's offer, she'd had time to shower and do something other than throw her hair in a braid. She mustered the patience to blow it out straight and smooth, the way the hairdresser did when she got it trimmed. June had even offered up her hair spray, shellacking the hair until Bryce worried she wasn't going to be able to pull a brush through it later.

"It's not as beautiful as you three girls!" Adele pinched Cecily's cheek.

Cecily swatted her hand away. "Hey! Pinching isn't allowed. I got in trouble when I pinched people for not wearing green on Saint Patrick's Day, and Aunt Beamer said it's rude. Right, Aunt Beamer?"

"Mmm," Bryce hummed in a noncommittal way, then changed subjects. "Okay, girls, we'll see you later for dessert. Have fun at the church dinner with Nana and Pop-Pop, and don't eat too much junk. Behave yourselves."

As Adele ushered them out the door, Harvey cleared his throat. "Do, uh, should we call before bringing the girls home? We don't want to, uh, interrupt anything."

Bryce shook her head. "Not necessary. We're only eating. Pretty G-rated stuff, Harv."

He nodded. "O-okay. Maybe we'll text, though. Just to be safe."

Bryce closed the door behind him, then did a bunch of those box breaths the therapist was always raving about. Four counts in, hold four counts, then release for four, wait for four...

Afterward, Bryce felt calmer. She retreated to the kitchen and flipped on the lights. As they blinked to life, illuminating the stainless-steel stove, the gleaming surfaces of the prep area, the spotlessly clean wash sink, the muscles in her chest relaxed.

It was time to do what she did best. Cook.

She selected a fun '80s playlist on her phone, starting

with "Don't Stop Believin'" by Journey. Listening to it brought back memories of riding with her dad in the long-haul truck and flipping burgers with Mom on the line at the truck stop. She checked the time—only a little after five o'clock. Impulsively, she grabbed her cell, stopping Steve Perry in mid-chorus, and dialed her father's number.

"Hello?" he asked with genuine curiosity in his voice, as he did every time she called, despite the fact her name appeared on his cell phone. "That you, Little Beamer?"

"Hi, Dad." She smiled at the nickname, propping the cell on the plate shelf to talk hands-free. "What are you two doing?"

"Oh, you know us. We got nothin' to do, and all day to do it. Took your mom to her doctor's appointment, and she's lying down now. Doctor visits wipe her out."

In the best of times, Shelby Weatherford had white coat syndrome, her blood pressure spiking merely by entering the doctor's office. Now that each doctor's visit was accompanied by more tests and trial medications for her worsening dementia, trips to their general practitioner would do her mother in for days.

Bryce winced, imagining her father's stress and her mother's anxious confusion. She wished she was there to help. But experience had taught her that the last thing Hudson and Shelby wanted was to feel like a burden to their children, and they were fiercely independent—a trait she admired but that also caused her worry.

Before she could ask any follow-up questions, her father changed the subject. "How are my granddaughters? Still giving you hell on a daily basis?"

"Too many Weatherford genes in them to not give me a

good run for my money," she said. "But this week wasn't a complete disaster. I don't want to jinx myself, but I think I might be getting the hang of this gig."

"That's my girl." Hudson's words lit up the place in her that glowed only under her father's compliments. "Wish we were there to help, but it's probably a good thing I'm not in town. I'm afraid I'd go throttle some sense into Harvey and Adele. But at least they're giving you a little break this weekend."

Bryce snorted. "Yeah. Lucky for the Paynes their church has built-in kids' activities and sitters to play with them all day. They've got the grandparent thing down to a science. But I am thankful for some of the night off."

"Right, tonight's your big date with that Ryker fellow. The mechanic. What are you making him? Your mother won me over with her cooking. Every time I came into the truck stop, she'd say I was skinny as a string of suckers, and then she'd ply me with food. Meatloaf. Chicken Divan. Chili. Scalloped potatoes and ham. All were delicious, but the day I lost my heart to her, she'd made a ribeye steak cooked in butter with—"

"Garlic and rosemary," Bryce finished, her cheeks heating. She'd forgotten it was the dish that had brought her parents together at the diner. Talk about a Freudian moment; her subconscious had taken over at the grocery store as she'd decided on this menu. "It's only a date, Dad. I'm not gunning for a relationship. I just felt like cooking a steak."

"Mm-hmm." His voice was unconvinced. "But remember, you deserve happiness. No time is ever the right time to begin a relationship. Okay, Little Beamer. Be good. And if you can't be good..." Her father paused for their ritual closing.

' "Be good at it," Bryce finished, grinning at her cell phone. "Gotta go, Dad. Love you!"

Suddenly, a knock came at the alley door where Patty got food deliveries. Her heart did a whirling stir as she glanced at the clock.

Five-thirty p.m. On the dot.

Bryce took another box breath, her father's words echoing in her head. She repeated them to herself, like an affirmation.

You deserve happiness. No time is ever the right time to begin a relationship.

She eyed the ribeye resting on her cook station.

She wasn't sure whether tonight she was preparing to be good...

Or just be good at it.

CHAPTER 10

Ryker felt like a kid counting down to Christmas as he crossed each day off his calendar until at last, the week was over and he was driving his truck to Bryce's place. His left leg was still aching, but he'd taken a few ibuprofens, beating the pain down to a negligible level.

What had really changed this week was his internal dialogue. Being with Bryce and her nieces this past month had shown him that he still had it in him to experience happiness. Unexpected moments of joy. That little window was enough to push him to be a bigger advocate of his own mental health journey. He'd admitted the same this week to Dr. Kirkland, his therapist.

"I'm suiting up for the game," he said on their telehealth call, jamming all the doc's favorite football metaphors into the sentences. "I'm blitzing your office in person next week, so have your playbook ready."

Doc's face lit up on the video call.

"Excellent choice. Having you here in person allows us to dig into how your leg pain might be ramping up your PTSD-related night terrors, and come up with some offensive strategies." The man was practically vibrating with enthusiasm, and Ryker felt his mouth twitch in an answering smile. "There are multiple game plans for mitigating PTSD. Which reminds me—any word yet from your Paws of War application, and have you told your family yet that you've applied for a service dog?"

"Negative on both counts," Ryker said. "I don't want them to get their hopes up. I love my brothers, but they tend to...take matters into their own hands. Solve problems that aren't theirs to solve."

"Sounds like someone else I know," Dr. Kirkland said. And Ryker had enough sessions with the man to know that the doc was referencing Ryker's own hero complex. "Consider, though, how good it makes you feel to help someone out—to solve their problem. Your family are no different."

While the therapist's words echoed in his brain, involving his family in his PTSD battle and encroaching HO was the last thing he wanted to think about tonight. Not when he'd finally gotten the opportunity to spend time alone with a woman who'd occupied his every waking thought since meeting her at the grocery store.

"C'mon in! It's unlocked," she called out at his knock, and he entered.

The layered aromas inside made Ryker's mouth water. The smell of butter, braising meat, and herbs was almost as tantalizing as the sight of the chef herself. Almost, because once he'd caught sight of Bryce, her blade flashing as she chopped something on her cutting board and her cheeks flushed from the heat of the stove, his heart gave a mighty squeeze in his chest. Was there ever any woman so stunning and capable in all this world as Bryce?

He closed the door and came to a dead halt as he saw what she was wearing. A storm-cloud-colored dress lay against her curves, making the skin it revealed in the V-neck at the top look like it was glowing. The dress ended a few inches above her knees, hugging her hips and thighs in a way that made him jealous of the fabric, wanting to skim his palms, then his lips, over that same area, kissing all the way to the insides of those sweet thighs. The dress cinched in the middle, and for a long, hot moment, he found himself staring at the knot of fabric tied to the side, willing that sucker to come apart...

"Hey." Her voice thankfully interrupted him before he stared long enough to be a real jackass. Her eyes sparkled and she gave him that frank assessing head-to-toe examination only she made sexy as hell. "I hope you aren't a vampire."

Ryker set the bottle of red wine he'd grabbed at the liquor store on the stainless-steel prep island, well away from the bowls of vegetables and cutting boards arrayed on top. His thoughts, still chugging in L1 gear after being gobsmacked by her appearance, ground out no clever rejoinders. Not for the first time he wished he was one of Drake's main characters in those new romance novels he was writing between his horror books—those guys were never at a loss for words, and they could charm the pants off everyone without breaking a sweat.

But he wasn't the hero of a romance. He was more like the hapless dude in one of Drake's classic horror books— the throwaway secondary character who got killed off to amp up the external conflict.

"Uh," he began, feeling the back of his neck get hot

under the flannel shirt he'd thrown on with a pair of jeans and what sufficed for fancy shoes—his specially modified Chuck Taylors—after his post-work shower. He'd opted not to wear a baseball cap, and hoped he'd chosen attire appropriate for a cooking date. However, at the sight of her outfit, he felt very underdressed and worried this was sending the wrong message. Did women assume if you dressed casually you thought they weren't important? He wished he'd consulted Zander before coming tonight. Kicking himself inwardly, he focused on her vampire comment. "I don't bite, if that's what you mean."

Bryce looked up from the pan where she'd shaken a bunch of mushrooms in that cool chef way where food flies in the air but miraculously lands back in the pan, all flipped to cook evenly, and she grinned. "No? Not ever? Too bad."

The flirty words startled a smile out of him, and he immediately felt more at ease. She must have forgiven him for wearing all the wrong things if she was flirting. Right?

Then he spotted the garlic cloves lined up on the cutting board, and her question made more sense.

"Oh, garlic. I love garlic. And you. I mean, being with you," he began, and then, to his horror, his mouth kept running, spewing out words as if his brain had lurched from L1 to sport-mode without a clutch. "I feel like I owe you a huge apology. I'm not good at talking to women. Or people in general. Unless it's about cars, my conversation skills are rusty. I guess what I'm saying is I'm sorry for my bonehead actions. For leaving you to assume things because that was easier than explaining them. It was a dick move, and that paperwork I got signed wasn't to be creepy or presumptuous, but my way of saying—"

"Shhhh."

Bryce stepped up to him, putting a finger against his lips. It smelled like rosemary—invigorating and delicious. He hadn't been sure where he was going with the rambling explanation-slash-apology-slash-weirdo-come-on, but his whole being went on high alert as her finger trailed down his mouth to his chin. When she traced it down his neck, splaying her palm on his chest, his breath stalled in his throat.

Bryce edged closer, closing the gap between them, her gaze never leaving his as she tilted her head up...

And she kissed him.

It wasn't a sweet, "aww, you're such a nice pal" kind of kiss, either. Her lips were soft, yet, after meeting his briefly, almost questioningly, she came in hot. Her hand gripped the back of his head, and when his tongue traced her lips, she opened her mouth, allowing him to taste her.

God, was she good.

His momentary surprise evaporated, and he wrapped his arms around her, feeling the heat of her through her dress. His palm splayed over her back, moving up to cup her neck, bring her closer, closer.

"I—I'm burning," she gasped against his mouth.

"Mmm," he hummed agreement, kissing down the sweet curve behind her ear. "You are smoking hot."

She gave a breathless laugh, tipping her chin away from him and patting him twice on the arm, like she wanted to tap out of a painful wrestling maneuver. He let her go, and she backed away, grabbing her tongs.

"No, I mean I'm burning, and I can't ruin a nice piece of meat because I'm distracted by a nice piece of meat." She clicked her tongs, her smile morphing to a wince. "Sorry. That was crass. It's my inner trucker coming out. But I can't let this steak get overdone. Here. Come make yourself useful and chop these veggies. While I'm making us dinner, I'm also prepping next week's soups."

As she busied herself flipping the steaks on the stove, Ryker positioned himself behind the middle island she'd gestured at, with its cutting board, knife, and bowls of carrots, celery, and onion. He surreptitiously adjusted himself in his jeans, but it was useless. The kiss was on mental replay and, in the middle of cutting carrots, he sliced his thumb.

"Ow. Shit."

Bryce looked over, her eyes widening. "Oh, no. Are you okay? I should've given you a knife lesson before I set you loose—like you said at your garage, dull instruments are dangerous, and my knives are sharpened weekly. Come over to the sink and let me see."

He gripped his finger to stop it from bleeding on the vegetables and followed her to the sink, where she thrust his hand under the cold tap.

"It's fine." He rinsed it off. The sucker was a bleeder, oozing despite the cold water and pressure he was applying, but he wasn't worried. He was trying not to move. Because if he moved, Bryce might take her hands away, and it felt so fantastic having her hands on him he'd gladly bleed another two pints' worth for the privilege.

Bryce shoved up his sleeve so his shirt didn't get wet, and after dunking his hand under the water, she had kind of paused, her eyes glued to his forearm.

Worried that she might be like Drake—a fainter at the sight of blood—he shifted his weight and stepped away from the sink and behind her. In case she fell, or slumped forward, he could catch her first.

"Hey, I'm okay." The blood finally stopped. "Are you . . . are you feeling dizzy? Do you want to sit down?"

"What?" She blinked, then released her grip on his forearm with something like reluctance. "Oh. Sorry. Your freaking arm . . ."

He looked down at his arm. It wasn't bleeding. There wasn't a thing wrong with it.

" . . . it should come with an R-rating," she finished, ducking around him to the stove. "Band-Aids are in the kit behind the sink. They're probably all girly ones—my nieces go through a mountain of them each month, and nothing eases a boo-boo like a princess Band-Aid."

He twisted the water off and got a paper towel for his finger. He rummaged through the kit, finally selecting a red, white, and blue Wonder Woman one. It wasn't until he'd wound it around his finger that he finally figured out what Bryce was saying about the R-rating.

She liked looking at his arms.

His lips swerved from a frown to a smile.

And before he resumed chopping the carrots, he pushed both sleeves up higher.

* * *

Cooking alongside her in the kitchen was as easy as breathing. After he'd been reprimanded twice not to make a mess on his station, they began to talk. At first it was mindless chitchat about their week, what was going on with the girls and with his Mercury restoration, but soon they were trading stories on everything from rock concerts they'd attended to listing all the cars they'd ever driven. Turned out, her list was longer than his on both counts, and he found that fact delightful. As they chatted, chopped, and sautéed their way toward dinner, he began to realize this woman had begun to carve her way into his heart—a place he'd thought had been destroyed along with his left leg years ago.

Finally, Bryce expertly plated the steaks, nestling them next to the vegetables.

"Okay, the steak is done, the zucchini is perfectly grilled, and the Parker House rolls are warm. Let's go sit down and eat."

He carried the dishes as instructed and followed her out into the dining area. The lights in his mom's restaurant were off and the shades on the front windows were drawn. With only the light from the kitchen, the area was shadowed in a comfortable gray.

"I should've gotten some candles." She frowned as she set down their wineglasses and the bottle he'd brought. "We can barely see our food."

"I don't need to see it." He slid into the booth. "I already know it's a hell of a lot better than my usual protein shakes."

She snorted. "Well, that's a low bar."

Instead of taking the seat opposite him, Bryce slid into the booth with him, and his inner teenaged boy howled with triumph. Her leg was touching his, and she was so close he caught a whiff of her delectable lemony scent.

Bryce fiddled with her phone, then held it up. A single candle's flame flickered on the screen there, and she balanced it on the table's salt and pepper dispensers.

"There. Now, dig in before it gets cold."

Bryce carved into her steak with gusto, eating with un-apologetic hunger and enjoyment. It was so. Damn. Hot.

"Mmm." She sipped the cabernet sauvignon the liquor store guy had recommended. "This is the perfect wine. Nice job. Try a roll. I'm not much of a baker, but my mom taught me how to master Parker House rolls. They're a bitch to make but worth it."

She gestured to the basket of rolls, and he obediently took one, popping half of it into his mouth. It was buttery and yeasty, and he immediately reached for the little container of refrigerated butter pats she'd set on the table.

"These are amazing. You'll have to give my mom the recipe." He spoke between bites, slathering butter on the roll with his knife.

"No way. Patty bakes everything better than I do, and a gal's gotta have some dishes she makes better than anyone else. That's what my mom always told me. She'd say, 'Bryce, honey, fastest way to a man's heart is through his stomach, but don't you be giving anyone a shortcut. Keep your best recipes to yourself.'" Bryce took another bite, then shook her head, her eyes soft with memory. "Do you know my mom still won't give me her recipe for her chili? It's Dad's favorite, and she won an award at the Florida State Fair one year for it. The blue ribbon still hangs in her kitchen, right above her spice rack."

"I'd like to meet her sometime," Ryker ventured, then shoveled another bite of steak into his mouth, playing for time as Bryce's blue-gray gaze speared him. He wasn't sure why she'd paused at his words, so he blundered on. "I love chili. Maybe I can get her to give the recipe to me? My mom gave Kate her recipe for Pumpkin Maniac cupcakes, and she still hasn't given it to my Aunt Cathy, so sometimes it works if someone other than family asks."

Bryce shrugged "She might. I worry if I don't get the chili recipe from her soon, it might be lost forever. Dementia is a cruel, cruel disease."

Ryker kicked himself for bringing up the subject. He'd forgotten her mother was ailing. Tentatively, he put down his utensils and reached for her hand, loving how smooth her skin felt against his.

He dredged up one of his therapist's sayings. "It's okay to be sad."

"Who has the time, though?" She swiped her eye, where he was horrified to see a tear coming down.

No freaking way was he going to be responsible for bringing up shit that triggered this strong woman's tears. He racked his brain for something, anything, to say to make her feel better. But he didn't have Drake's way with words. He didn't have the suave sensitivity of Zander, either.

Ryker was just the middle brother—the jarhead turned gearhead who was more comfortable with action because it was easier than conversation. He'd opened his mouth, hoping something perfect would come tumbling out, but after an awkward beat, he closed it.

He had nothing to say to make it better.

Instead, he opened his arms to her, the tips of his fingers motioning her in. "C'mere. I got you."

Her head and chest hit him so hard he thunked against the back of the booth until he braced himself for her unexpected hug onslaught.

"Sorry." Her voice was muffled by his flannel shirt. "I came in a little hot, didn't I? Do you...do you have any idea how long it's been since I've had a hug? From anyone taller than my hips, anyway? Literally months."

He held her, silent, worried she might cry. But all she did was sigh and burrow her nose into his neck in a way that made him both ticklish and aroused at the same time. He didn't want to embarrass himself with the massive collection of blood vessels who'd chosen that time to gather for a frontal assault in his jockey shorts, so he cleared his throat, digging for words to distract himself from the warm, soft, very female body in his arms.

"It's been longer for me." He searched his memory for the last time he'd hugged or been hugged by anyone. "Not counting when Cecily hugged me at the grocery store a few weeks ago, it's been . . ."

He didn't know. His mom bussed his cheek every time he stopped by, and his brothers knew he was a big advocate for personal space. Bro handshakes or a quick one-armed hug that ended up with a fist smack into the biceps was their love language.

But a full-on hug? By a woman he wasn't related to? His mind finally sifted through and found the memory.

"Approximately three years ago. It was Tammy Rodriguez, Paul's wife. Widow." He corrected himself. "We'd gathered for a dedication in his honor—a plaque at his high school alma mater along with a yearly scholarship for one student to attend art school. That's what he was going to do when he got done with our tour—enroll in art school—and he was talented enough to do it. Tammy hugged me at the event, and that was the last time."

Bryce pulled away but stayed in the circle of his arms, tilting up her face to look at him.

"You haven't hugged another person in three years?"

He shook his head, unsure how to read her voice. Figuring his expression was in its usual resting bastard face, he attempted to rearrange his features into something more suitable. But after trying on a scowl, then a teensy smile, he gave up.

"Well, shit. I had no idea. Why didn't you tell me this was a hug emergency? Come here, you!" She yanked him to her, grasping him tightly.

Something about her earnestness—the fact that she wasn't kidding at all—struck his funny bone. He felt a chuckle bubble up from his diaphragm, held it back as long as possible, not wanting to be perceived as laughing at her, but it was like a tumbling snowball of hilarity, picking up speed until bursting from his mouth in a loud belly laugh.

She pulled away, and would have released her hold around him had he not held her arms, guffawing and shaking his head in apology at the same time.

"A...hug...emergency?" he gasped out between laughs he hadn't known were bottled up. "Is that...a thing?"

Bryce's concern melted away, and her mouth slid into a smile. "It is when you haven't been hugged in three years, jerk-face. I can't believe you're laughing at the hug-aid I'm administering here. Clearly, you need more. Stat!"

She flung her arms around his neck again, thumping him in a rough parody of the back strikes given to a choking victim.

He laughed and coughed at the same time, barely able to get enough breath.

"Uncle, uncle," he said, weak with the goofiness of it.

When was the last time he'd laughed so hard it'd made him weak? It'd been much, much longer than the last hug, he was sure. The thought sobered him, and when he felt her pull away, he let her go.

"Thank you." He breathed deeply to alleviate those residual laugh-spasms from his diaphragm. The lemony scent of her filled his lungs, and he rested his forehead against hers as he took a minute to compose himself. "That was fun. You're fun."

To his surprise, she made a terrible face.

"Ew. I don't want to be 'Fun Bryce' to you. I didn't wear this god-awful strapless bra and get my toes painted Plum Perfect so you'd think I was 'fun.' My high school English teacher said the adjective 'fun' was the lamest one in the book, because it really gives you nothing."

His urge to laugh vanished. "Fun was the . . . safest word I had for what I think of you." The back of his neck prickled with embarrassment.

"Then give me the less-safe words. Tell me the dangerous ones."

"Pretty," he said, then realizing it made him sound like a sixth-grader, he amended himself. "Gorgeous. Talented. Kind. And you make things lighter. Brighter. Maybe 'fun' isn't the right word, but when I'm with you, I feel happy. Whole."

The last word slipped out before he'd realized it was queued up in his mouth, and he regretted it instantly. But, to his surprise, her eyebrows arched in that delighted way he adored.

"Then I'm mistaken. Fun is the best adjective in the book."

With that, her mouth tilted to his, and then he was kissing her.

He felt as though she were tasting him, like a fine wine, savoring each breath, each moment their lips were together. Her hands—those strong, talented hands—gripped the back of his head as if she were ensuring he stayed right where she wanted him. Like that was a problem. There was nowhere else in the world he wanted to be other than in this booth, holding this woman close.

Until she slid her hand down the front of him.

When her palm traced his chest, those dexterous fingers working at the buttons on his flannel shirt, unbuttoning the first two buttons and slipping her hand inside, then he absolutely wanted to be somewhere else.

Like a bed.

He moved his mouth to her neck and was rewarded by a low, sweet groan.

"Mmm, that feels amazing." She tilted her head to give him deeper access as she captured his hand, guiding it to her breast.

Now it was his turn to groan. The rough skin on his hands snagged a little at the fabric on her dress, but by the way she pressed herself into his palms, she didn't seem to mind. His mouth moved down the smooth column of her neck to her chest, and he had just pushed aside the fabric to her shoulder when he heard a muffled noise.

"Aunt Beamer? Are you in there?"

The high-pitched voice was followed by a loud clamor at the front door.

Ryker slid away from Bryce, both of them laughing nervously as they saw that it was Addison and Cecily, their mouths pressed onto the glass door, blowing their cheeks out like puffer fish as they bashed their small fists to be let in.

"Coitus interruptus." Bryce laughed, skootching out of the booth they sat in to go and unlock the front door.

Ryker had no idea what that meant. Maybe it was a cooking term?

Before he drew his next breath, the girls all piled inside, June bringing up the rear with her phone in front of her face, thumbs moving a mile a minute on the keypad.

Their grandparents came inside last, and Mr. Payne said something to Bryce under his breath.

"I told you we should've texted you first" was what he thought the older gentleman said, but Bryce acted like she hadn't heard him.

Ryker followed her lead as the girls crowded around, peppering him with questions about his dinner, telling him about what they ate at the church, then asking if he knew what dessert Bryce had planned for them. He fended off their questions, one by one, as Bryce talked to the grandparents.

Soon the Paynes left. Bryce relocked the front door.

"Only, you promised to play with us. 'Member that?" Addison asked Ryker, her mismatched yellow and tan fairy wings flapping at her back.

"I remember, and I brought something for you." He dug into the front pocket of his jeans. He'd had a minute between customers and had carved out two ovals from an old piece of leather upholstery he had in his shop from an interior restoration he'd done and used an awl to punch holes on either side. He'd had to rummage through his office junk drawer before finally finding an extra pair of shoelace strings, which he'd strung through either side of the leather, creating a crude eye patch. He presented them to Addison and Cecily. "Thought you might want to be pirates with me. We can rule the seas together."

"Can you be one of the Lost Boys, instead?" Addison asked, her face pleading as she yanked his hand to stand up from the restaurant booth.

Then two things happened at once. The girl's tiny leg got wedged in between his feet as he stood, and she did one of her fairy spins. As she twirled, her foot smacked the inside of his prosthetic.

Then he heard the click—the noise that meant the button releasing his prosthesis had been triggered—and suddenly the pin at the end of the socket was freed from its moorings in the prosthetic leg . . .

And he was falling.

Right into Bryce and her nieces.

CHAPTER 11

Look out!" Bryce shouted as Addison tripped Ryker, and he fell out of the booth.

He'd been coming straight at them, but at the last second did some sort of midair Simone Biles maneuver, twisting to land on a nearby table, knocking over the chairs instead of the girls. When his shoulder hit the table, it wobbled like a boat in strong waves but didn't flip. Ryker balanced on the top, lying splayed like a starfish until the motion stopped.

The two little girls gasped, and Bryce was momentarily frozen in shock as the man lay sprawled on a table next to a tumble of upended furniture.

"Is everyone okay?" he asked.

The sound of his voice broke the paralysis. June dashed over at the same time as Bryce, both of them righting chairs and pushing them out of the way.

"Wow, did you see him fly across the restaurant? He was like Superman!" Addison exclaimed, doing a twirl-like movement herself in midair and landing on her butt. She stood up, rubbing her backside, fairy wings bent at a severe angle. "Hey, how'd you do that? Can you teach me?"

Ryker's face went red as he levered himself onto his elbows, surveying the scene.

Bryce eased him down as he sat up, sending the table tilting again.

"Before you stand up, are you okay?" she asked. "I don't think you should move if you hit your head. Lie still for a second. You might have some sort of concussion."

"I'm fine," he growled, but June, Cecily, and Addison rushed over, pestering him to listen to her, and he eventually leaned back, his head barely held up by the corner edge of the table. He rolled his eyes as the girls fussed over him. "The pin got released and I stepped out of . . . my foot."

"His eyeballs look good." Cecily leaned two inches over Ryker to peer into his eyes. "They're real blue, like Wendy's dress in *Peter Pan*. I don't see any blood, 'cept there's a couple skinny squiggly liney-things by the corner. Is that normal?"

"Those are veins." Bryce bit her lip, trying to remember any first aid at all.

Cecily continued her evaluation. "His nose is pretty straight-ish and isn't bleeding. He's not crying, either."

"I got his special foot!" Addison picked up the prosthetic still in its sneaker, waving it in the air.

"Give it to him, Addie," Bryce said, frowning with worry. What if he'd hurt his leg or twisted his knee when he'd come out of his prosthetic?

"Here you go, Mr. Ryker." Addison plopped the leg on Ryker's lap.

"Oof," Ryker grunted, his body curling up on itself into a half crunch, sit-up maneuver.

Addie had thumped him right in the junk.

Addison's little face puckered in a serious expression as she scanned him. "Sorry, Mr. Ryker. Did that hurt?" She reached over and patted his cheek in reassurance. "There's no blood, sweetie-heart. You're okay."

It was completely uncool to laugh right now. So Bryce reined in the giggles by taking in a shaking breath as Ryker removed the sneaker from his groin, holding it as he looked at all of them.

"Did I hurt any of you girls as I stumbled?"

"No, we're all good." Bryce offered her hand and helped him slide off the table onto his solid leg. "Cici, can you get some ice from the ice machine and put it in a towel for Mr. Ryker? Addie, go help her find a clean towel."

The two little girls were up and sprinting before the last word was out of Bryce's mouth.

"I'll grab the first-aid kit." June sprinted toward the kitchen.

Which left her alone with Ryker.

"I don't need any of that stuff." His tone was a little grumpy. But then again, he'd just been knocked in the balls.

She righted a fallen chair for him and pushed him down to sit into it. Then she leaned over, cupping her palms on either side of his face. His slight beard felt gloriously scratchy against her skin, and he smelled like pine and the warm scent that was deliciously Ryker. His eyes were the color of soft, faded denim, and his lashes were thick and almost girlishly long, the tips a little golden in the light. His mouth curved in the tiniest smile, as if he were imagining the naughty things they could be doing, just like she was...

She banished her lustful thoughts and focused. He looked okay. But how could she tell?

"Are you really okay?"

He rolled his eyes but didn't pull away. "I'm embarrassed. Worried I scarred your nieces for life. Other than that, I'm fine."

She released a breath she hadn't realized she'd been holding. Then she leaned in and kissed his forehead, then his lips, in the briefest of kisses. When that wasn't enough—not even close to enough—she groaned and leaned in to slide her tongue into his mouth.

"Got the first-aid kit." June charged into the dining room, skidding to a halt when she'd interrupted them kissing. Bryce had straightened, looking at June guiltily as her niece made a face. "Ew, gawd! I guess he's okay if you two are getting all physical."

"Phys-cle? What's that mean?" Addison came skittering into the dining area, a dirty, wrinkled dish towel in her hands.

Cecily came in behind her, trailing ice cubes as she ran, her palms full of chopped ice.

"Oh, I know. Fizz-kill is when your Sprite loses all its bubbles." Cecily gave Ryker a stern look. She grabbed the food-stained dish towel from her sister, poured the ice into it, wadded it all closed, and plopped the thing on the top of Ryker's head. "You can worry about your Fizz-kill later, Mr. Ryker. Right now, we need to see if you're hurt."

Then the ice poured out of the bottom of the dish towel, cubes raining down on Ryker's shoulders like massive hailstones, piling onto the floor beneath the chair.

Addison shook her head. "Only I think you were 'posed to hold that on your boo-boo."

Ryker threw his head back and laughed.

The deep baritone sound made something within Bryce light up. God, what would it be like to make this man laugh like this every day?

She shook off the impossible thought. "Let me get the broom and sweep this up."

As she went toward the utility closet, she heard Ryker reassure the girls.

"I'm fine. I just stepped out of my foot and tripped."

Bryce swept up the ice into the pan and tossed it into the garbage. As soon as the field was clear of debris, Cecily and Addison crowded around Ryker, their faces curious. They stared at the empty end of his jeans on the left side.

"Can we see you put on your special foot, Mr. Ryker?" Addison asked. "We help Grandpa Weatherford with his stand-up-tall leg all the time."

Ryker gave her a questioning look.

"My dad has a leg-length discrepancy, and he has special orthotics and custom shoes to correct his gait. Girls, this is different from Grandpa Weatherford's shoe. Maybe Mr. Ryker doesn't want—" Bryce began, but Ryker interrupted, his voice soft.

"It won't bother me. As long as it's okay with your aunt." He waited for Bryce's nod before continuing. "See, I think there shouldn't be a stigma about amputees, which is why I don't wear a prosthetic with a fleshy cover. I let the metal show, like I'm a robot, because I sort of am. A bunch of smart men and women designed this thing, and I think it's a shame to hide it."

He pointed to the black plastic-looking cup above the rod that acted like the shinbone, connecting the foot to the apparatus above.

"This is the socket that snaps my new foot onto the rest of my leg below the knee, like a LEGO."

"Hey, that's the same as your tattoo." Cecily pointed to the eagle, globe, and anchor etched on the black plastic cup of the prosthetic. "So your leg goes in there?"

Ryker nodded and slid up the jeans on his left leg, revealing a gray, sock-like sleeve covering his leg from mid-thigh to the four inches remaining beneath the knee. He pointed to the tip of the gray sleeve, where a blunt silver bolt extended about three inches farther from where his limb ended.

"See this pin? It goes into the socket and locks in at the bottom, keeping my foot on."

"Can't you ever change shoes?" Addison asked. "Or do you keep a bunch of different legs in your closet?"

Ryker chuckled. "Nope. I can change shoes whenever I want, just like you, as long as the heel is three-eighths of an inch—Chuck Taylors aren't normally suited for amputees, but I have a lift inside to level them out."

He slipped the sneaker and sock off the prosthetic, revealing a peachy, flesh-toned foot. Then, to Bryce's surprise, he peeled back some of the foot to reveal a glint of black and metal beneath.

"This is a Kevlar sock, which covers my metal foot to make sure the sharp edges don't poke through and ruin my cosmesis—that's this part here." Ryker tapped on the realistic flesh-like prosthetic foot.

"Isn't Kevlar what they make bulletproof vests out of?" June asked. Although her arms were crossed over her chest in that eternally defensive posture she seemed to have these days, she peered over her sisters' heads with interest.

"Correct," he said.

"Wait. Under that pretend foot, you've got another foot that's...bulletproof?" Cecily asked, her eyes wide. At Ryker's shrug and nod, she raised an arm in triumph. "See? I told you he's like Superman!"

"What's under this sock up there?" Addison poked at the gray, almost foamlike cover on Ryker's left leg.

Bryce opened her mouth to intervene, but Ryker was already rolling down the tight-fitting sleeve from his thigh.

"My leg. I was hurt in Afghanistan by a bomb, and they had to operate." Using his palms, he slid the gel-like inside sleeve over his knee, then down the three inches that remained of his shin below the knee. "This is the scar where the doctor took the hurt part of my leg."

Bryce saw silvery-white scars decorating the flesh on the outside of his leg down to a few inches below the knee, where the limb ended just below a neat, smile-like scar that extended from one side of his calf to the other. The only other evidence of injury was a red, angry-looking spot on the front of his shin, a little below his knee, and indentations in his flesh where the prosthetic hugged his limb at the sides of his calf.

"Does it hurt?" June's question echoed the one in Bryce's head.

Ryker shrugged. "It hurt when it happened. Sometimes I can feel my old foot down there and it'll itch, burn, or tickle, even though it's gone. Like right now I feel like I'm wiggling my big toe—except it's invisible. My phantom leg thinks it's all still down there."

"Like my wings." Addison nodded. "When I take these off at night, I can still feel them fluttering on my back.

I think I'm growing invisible wings, and maybe soon I can fly!"

"Don't be a dope," June scoffed, leaning against the nearby booth, her phone in her hand. "You can't fly."

"Once you put that on, can you come play with us?" Cecily asked, bored. "This is our last night with the ship, 'cause deliveries are coming tomorrow. Aunt Beamer says it's gotta go in your truck to be recycled."

Ryker nodded. "Give me two seconds, and we can play whatever you want."

With fast, efficient movements, he'd slid the squishy, gel-like sleeve over his residual limb and knee, all the way to mid-thigh. Then, lining up the socket like you would to put on a pair of stiff pants, he slid the limb into the black, decorated shell. Bryce envisioned the metal pin on the end slipping into the socket, then the hole in the bottom.

Ryker pushed his leg down until it clicked a few times. Then he stood and gave one more, mighty shove with his left leg until the thing clicked twice more.

"Okay, all set. So, am I the mean pirate, then?" he asked, pushing down his jeans. The leg clicked one more time as he took a step, holding out his hand to Bryce. "How about if I'm the bad guy who took this lovely lass hostage, and you two pirates have to come in and save her?"

Cecily snorted. "No way. You aren't the bad guy. You're the good guy. Everyone knows that."

Bryce felt Ryker's hand tighten, and his expression morphed into one that could be best described as touched. Maybe verging on...overwhelmed?

"He *is* the good guy," she said, leaning in to plant a loud, obnoxious kiss on his cheek. "Okay, who's going to toss us into the ship's brig?"

As the two little girls shepherded them to the cardboard contraption on the back loading dock, Bryce watched Ryker's carefully guarded expression evaporate as he laughed along with the girls' antics. The man *was* the good guy.

Yet as their eyes met, and his sultry wink made her stomach go all fluttery, Bryce realized this man was also a pirate. A tall, blond Viking-looking pirate who'd literally swept her off her feet in the baby aisle of the grocery store, and now—not a month later, and despite the wretched timing—was beginning to carve a way into her heart. The thought was simultaneously thrilling and terrifying.

Bryce was starting to realize that while she was a whiz in the kitchen . . .

She might have gotten the recipe for love all wrong.

CHAPTER 12

Hey, I know this is last minute," Ryker said later that evening, loading the remains of the cardboard boat into the bed of his truck. As soon as he began speaking, he wanted to smack himself in the forehead for starting so lamely, but now he had to finish his sentence. "I was wondering if you're busy tomorrow? I thought I might take you with me to Rochester, since the girls are at their grandparents'."

"Are you asking me on a date?" She gave that saucy grin, one eyebrow raised.

"Yes. I mean, no. It's also work. I have to deliver the Cougar to my client, and I thought you might want to ride up with me." He rushed to continue, realizing this sounded like he was taking her on a lame date in his truck with a trailer hitched to it. "After we drop off the car, I thought we'd go to dinner. A buddy of mine got me reservations on a dinner cruise, and the chef on the boat is some hotshot—"

"Wait. You're taking me with you to drop off the Eliminator? Absolutely I want to go, but can I drive it off the trailer? Please?"

He barked a laugh. She'd done it again—surprised him.

He'd hoped she'd be lured by the thought of a meal by a hotshot chef, but she'd been sucked in for the chance to drive a muscle car.

God, if she wasn't perfect in every way...

"You can drive whatever you want. Do we have a date?"

"Hell, yes." Then she tilted her head, the streetlamps highlighting her pained expression. "But do we *have* to eat at the fancy boat dinner cruise? I've got a better idea. There's this place I've been craving—my dad took me once when we were in Rochester on a delivery."

"Sure." He pushed away the feeling he'd somehow missed the mark on the grand gesture his brothers insisted was necessary. "We can go wherever you want. Where would you like to go?"

"I want to get a Garbage Plate at Nick Tahou's." She speared him with a look when he laughed. "What? It's the best greasy spoon in the area, and they're known for their Garbage Plate special."

"I plan a romantic dinner cruise with a big-deal chef and you're just as happy to get a Garbo at Tahou's." He was trying to play it off as if he were disappointed, but the huge grin on his face was probably a dead giveaway of his true feelings. He felt vindicated; he'd been right after all when he'd told his brothers Bryce wasn't going to be into a showy display of intentions. "You're on. Meet me at my garage after you drop off the girls, and we'll head out."

He'd pulled her into his arms for a kiss when the door slammed open and Cecily stuck her head out.

"Aunt Beamer? Addison was jumping on her bed tryin' to fly, and she barfed all over."

"Ugh. This happens every time I send them with their

grandparents. They eat junk like starving wolverines, then puke all night long." Bryce groaned, giving him the briefest peck on the lips. "Coitus interruptus strikes again. But tomorrow...the girls are gone all day long. Just saying. Gotta bolt."

And then she was gone.

Ryker flipped up his truck's tailgate to secure the pirate ship and slid into the driver's seat. His leg had begun to throb about an hour ago, and he was overdue on taking the ibuprofen, but all that could wait.

Snagging his phone, he Googled "coitus interruptus" and read the definition.

And then he grinned the whole way home.

* * *

Saturday morning, Bryce met him at the garage after dropping the girls off at the Paynes'. She wore a pair of black jeans and a watermelon-red shirt that hugged her chest and scooped tantalizingly low in the front.

After climbing up into the cab of his truck, she leaned over to give him a kiss on the lips so full of promise he had to resist the urge to drag her onto his lap right there in the parking lot.

"For the first time in forever, I am a free woman for an entire twenty-four hours. I'm giddy with the possibilities." She buckled herself into the passenger seat. "I had a light breakfast to save room for Tahou's after we deliver the Cougar. Did you eat yet?"

Ryker held up his Tervis. "Protein shake. Breakfast of champions."

Bryce made a face as she blipped the key fob to lock her BMW, where it sat outside of his garage. She arched her neck to sniff at his Tervis. "You're always drinking one of those. They must be good, huh?"

He shrugged, starting the truck, his eyes automatically going to the rearview to gaze at the trailer behind him. The Cougar was already loaded up, but he intended to make good on his promise to have her drive the baby off when they got to the man's house.

"I don't mind them."

He backed out of the driveway as she snagged the drink from his hands.

"Let me taste."

She took a big gulp, then her eyes bulged. She pivoted in the seat, threw her shoulder against the door and leaned out of his truck, only the seat belt holding her inside as she spewed the mouthful of greenish liquid onto the pavement of State Street.

"Are you trying to poison me? Or yourself? What in the hell is in there?"

"Kale, protein powder, egg whites, and blueberries for sweetness." He laughed, taking a big swig as she gagged, rifling through her purse until finding a stick of gum.

Popping it into her mouth, she shook her head. "Uh-uh. No way. That's swill. Throw it out, and swing by Modern Diner before we hit the highway. Don't you know how to eat healthy and have it not taste like dirty sink water?"

He did as told, and as soon as they pulled up to the tiny diner, Bryce swung out of the truck and told him to wait as she went in to order. She came back with one small Styrofoam container.

"Here. Egg whites, Canadian bacon, and a slice of lightly grilled tomato on an English muffin. Comes in around three hundred calories and is healthy and will keep you full without chemicals and whatever other crap is in your shake." She popped open the container for him, and the scent of the breakfast made his stomach rumble in anticipation. "You don't have to drink your meal to be healthy."

This morphed into a conversation where he lamely put up an argument of the benefits of blending your foods as a meal replacement, while she hotly argued if God had intended you to drink every meal, He'd never have given you teeth.

The mention of teeth had triggered a whole talk about her fear of dentists and the bad experience she'd had as a teen getting her wisdom teeth pulled—and how she hadn't been able to blink for two hours and had to use her hand to force her eyelids together so her eyes didn't dry out. This talk of medical procedures had prompted her to ask about his surgeries, and while it had been like starting an old, wheezy engine, once he got going on the topic, he found it amazingly easy to talk about the first trauma surgery in nearby Kabul, where they'd attempted to re-rig his foot back onto his leg but it had ultimately failed. The second surgery in the States was at Walter Reed when they'd originally amputated, and the third surgery was about eight months later to remove a bone spur forming on his femur. That was when he'd discovered he was one of those few people prone to HO.

At the mention of HO, and after his explanation of what heterotopic ossification was, Bryce sobered.

"So is surgery the only option when you get these cells growing bone into your soft tissue?" she asked. "It must be nerve-racking to wonder when the next time you'll be under the knife. Isn't there something else they can do?"

"There's radiation treatment." His palms grew clammy. This was the time to tell her he might be due for another surgery in the not-too-distant future, as well as the sterility likelihood from the radiation at his hip, thigh, and lower leg. "But having prophylactic radiation treatment comes with its own risks, like—"

"Take the next right and you will arrive at your destination on the left-hand side," came the voice from his phone's GPS, interrupting Ryker's train of thought.

"Yay, we're here." Bryce practically bounced in her seat. "You sure you're still okay if I drive it off the trailer?"

"Absolutely." Ryker swerved from his planned confession, relieved that the GPS had interrupted him. He'd find a way to drop that bomb another time. Who was he to bring up having kids when they were only on their second true date? He was thankful he'd avoided the conversational tripwire.

Unloading the Cougar went without a hitch, and Ryker wasn't sure if he was more impressed with Bryce's careful handling of the muscle car as she reversed it off the trailer, or the fact that she knew exactly how to unhook the Mercury from its canvas tire tethers. She'd had her side's tires free before he was done with his.

"It's been at least ten years since I've done that, and look—my skills are as good as a pro like you," she crowed in the car after they'd given the Kodak exec his new ride.

"I wasn't aware it was a competition, or else I'd have moved a little faster," he countered, then laughed as she squawked with indignation. "How about a rematch?"

"You're on. I want in on the next delivery." She crossed her arms over her chest, narrowing her eyes in what he assumed was a playful challenge. "And I will hand your ass to you again."

They bantered through the drive into the city, and Ryker's heart felt as full as a newly inflated tire.

This is what Drake had meant when he'd said his relationship with Kate had been effortless. This was the full-bellied, joyously floating feeling Zander had described that came over him whenever he spent time with Imani. He got it now.

And damn if he wasn't going to do his level best not to blow it.

By the time they made it from the parking lot to Nick Tahou's for lunch, there was a line stretching around the building. It moved faster than he'd expected, and it wasn't long before they were out of the brisk spring air and inside the restaurant.

"My God. It's just like I remembered," Bryce said. The atmosphere of the place had distinct "dive diner" vibes and was packed to the gills. "Mmm, smell that grill. Do you have any idea how well seasoned that grill top must be? I'm salivating so hard for a cheeseburger Garbage Plate with the works. What are you getting?"

"Same but without onions."

"No onions? Okay, then I'll do the same. Can't have a root vegetable taking me out of whatever little game I might have," she said cryptically.

They ordered as the line snaked around and finally made it to the register.

"We need more bread up here!" called the guy at the

register. Then he gave Ryker his change as a skinny kid brought up a black garbage bag.

"Wait," Bryce whispered to him, her eyes popping in disbelief. "I think that garbage bag is filled with the bread."

Sure enough, the register man reached in, pulled out two hunks of Italian bread.

"Oh my god. Never have I ever eaten bread stored in a Hefty bag," she breathed, and then she squealed. "This is so exciting!"

"Want to eat in the truck?" he asked, noticing when she gave the diner's tables a once-over. The customer turnover was so rapid, patrons didn't wait for someone to clean off a table. They merely brushed away the last person's crumbs with a napkin and sat down to dig in.

"Yep."

Ten minutes later, they were in his truck balancing to-go containers on their laps as they ate. The Garbage Plate was layered like a trippy lasagna, with baked beans, home fries, and a generous scoop of mayonnaise-heavy macaroni salad that was the base of the dish. Flopped atop that goodness was the cheeseburger patty with hot sauce, mustard, ketchup, and mayo drizzled over everything. He'd had his first taste of the dish after a long, hard night of partying with some Marine buddies on leave, and it was true what they said: grease helped cure the hangover.

But this was the first Garbage Plate he'd eaten stone sober, and it was as good as he remembered.

"So?" he asked, when she was silent. "What do you think?"

"It's unbelievable it all tastes good together, but it does.

It's like a rave in my mouth. The chill cool of the mac salad balances the burger, beans, and home fries." She swallowed, then grinned at him. "This is the best lunch date. Ever!"

After they polished off as much of the Garbage Plates as possible, tossing the rest into a bin in the parking lot, he reluctantly started the truck. He was sad the day was over and they were returning to Wellsville. He knew how busy she was with her nieces—how rare it was for her to have time to herself—and with working at PattyCakes, plus her catering side business, she likely had mounds of things clamoring for her attention.

Damn, though, he didn't want this date to end. As if reading his mind, Bryce tapped his arm, her fingers lingering on his forearm.

"Do you have to get right back? There's a car expo over at the convention center. Want to go?" Bryce asked, and the way her eyebrows arched in that delighted expression, she could've asked to attend a detailed lecture on cooking in the Middle Ages and he would've said yes.

As it was, she was speaking his love language.

"Spend the day looking at cars with a beautiful woman at my side? Sign me up." He leaned in for another kiss. It was as if he couldn't get enough of tasting her; sampling her kisses was like being given only one taste of some amazing culinary delight—it was incredible, but not enough at the same time.

The auto show was busy and well attended. Vendors lined the edges of the floor, and Bryce delighted in tugging him into each booth. She made him pose with her next to all her favorite cars. By the time the show ended at eight, her phone was full of pictures of the two of them, and as she scrolled through, showing the best ones to him on the drive home from the expo, he was struck by how different he looked. It took a while to realize that the difference was due to one simple fact: in every picture, he'd been smiling.

The trip back to Wellsville flew by, and as they passed the sign welcoming them to the village, he hated that the night was ending. It had been the best date he'd ever had—no contest.

"Thanks for coming with me."

"This day has been so..." She paused, as if searching for the right word. Then she grinned at him, reaching over to place her hand on his forearm, the fingers cool against his skin. "...so absolutely perfect."

It was as if he'd been given the gold medal in dating. Ryker's chest puffed out like a balloon filled with happiness and pride. "For me, too."

"That's how I know you're trouble for me," she said.

And just like that, the balloon of happiness popped.

But she hadn't removed her hand from his arm. In fact, her fingers had gone from resting there to softly tracing the veins in his forearm, her eyes glued to the work, as if she were memorizing a topographical map, following the blue line of his vein from the hand on the steering wheel all the way to the crease at his elbow.

He cleared his throat. "In what way?"

She didn't answer for a minute. Her face was thoughtful, focused, as she traced his veins with one cool finger up and down his arm. Her touch was maddening, but any desire he might have felt was tamped down by her words and the cautious expression on her face.

He'd seen that look before in women. It was the look they gave right before they uttered the words he dreaded.

She looked like she was going to break up with him.

Then she spoke. "I really like you."

The words were the opposite of what he was expecting and exactly what he wanted to hear...yet her face wasn't wearing the delighted expression. It was frowny and pensive. He searched his mind for what Drake's romance hero might say in this situation but had nothing other than the obvious.

"Good. Because I really like you, too."

"No. I mean, I really, *really* like you. A lot. But more than that, being with you makes me feel sexy, and strong, and more like...myself. Like the me I was before Bentley died. Before I came up here to try and fill two massively big pairs of shoes. I look forward to every second with you. Like every single second." Bryce's face was mostly in shadow in the dark cabin of his truck, and he couldn't read her expression as she looked at him.

"I feel like there is a 'but' coming in this conversation," Ryker finally muttered in the silence of the truck. "Why is looking forward to spending time with me—a problem?"

"Because my life is currently a dumpster fire, and I don't know who I am anymore, let alone what I'm doing. Your mom is very wise, and she told me to pick my head up and make a map for myself, but I'm scared that if I stop looking where my feet are in the forest, I'm going to face-plant into a tree." Her words spilled out, tripping over themselves in a rush. "That's why liking you as much as I do spells only trouble. Being with me right now is a heavy lift."

Ryker felt his brain struggling, like an engine running on gloppy expired oil. There was so much to unpack in that sentence. He ignored the part about his mom and her career advice—he'd heard the same lecture once or twice. However, the rest of Bryce's words sounded like the preface to a breakup...yet her fingers tracing up and down his arm generated the best sort of sexual tension and gave the opposite impression.

He waited until he pulled next to her BMW in the small parking lot outside of his garage before he broke the silence between them, wanting to look into her eyes when he spoke. He unhooked his seat belt and took her hands, holding them within his own until he found the right words.

"I've only known you about a month, but I've seen enough to say *you* are not a dumpster fire. Is your life complicated? Affirmative. Whose isn't?" He squeezed her palms, her skin smooth against his callused hands. Her face looked skeptical and he grimaced, knowing he had to dig deeper, unearth things he tried hardest to bury: his feelings. "Look, I don't casually date. I suck at the whole...courtship dance. But this, whatever we're doing, is not a heavy lift. It's pretty amazing, and I'd be lying if I said I didn't want to take the next step with you."

"The inside of my head is a mess, like a clean room after unleashing my nieces for an hour. Parts are strewn everywhere," she said.

He reached out, carefully tracing his thumb along her jawline. "I happen to be excellent in a room filled with spare parts, and as for the mess...well, I have plenty of Lava soap."

Her lips quirked, like she wanted to smile. Wanted to believe.

He was quiet, waiting for her to speak, but she stayed silent, her fingers pressing his vein as if testing a piece of meat on her grill top for doneness. Or maybe she was testing to see if he was a puppet or a real boy?

Suddenly, she unhooked her seat belt and scooted to him. She wrapped her arms around his neck and kissed him with feral intensity. The impact of her enjoyment, her desire, took his breath away. Her mouth tasted sweet, like the chocolate bar they'd split before leaving the car show, and as he stroked her face and neck, deepening the kiss, the scent of her lemony shampoo tickled his nose.

Next, she was crawling onto his lap, her mouth never leaving his, and then she was straddling him, her palms skating down his chest, and then over to his hands, dragging them to her chest. When he cupped her breasts, her groan was so raw, so unfiltered, so *Bryce*, it lit him up inside. He pushed up her shirt, replacing his hands with his lips, leaning her back against his steering wheel as he kissed his way around the lace of her bra, finally pulling the fabric down to take first one nipple into his mouth, then the other, repeating the same flick of his tongue, the same scrape of his whiskers against her flesh that elicited gasps and those sexy moans.

She was like a feast in his arms, and he was a starving man sitting down to dine. He wanted to tell her this, but when he finally, finally, finally managed to drag his mouth from her chest, all he managed was a single sentence.

"I could do this all night long with you."

She gave a shaky laugh. "Not me. I am not cut out for this prolonged Tantric-like foreplay. Does that apartment of yours have a bed? Because this is more serious than a hug emergency."

He took in her flushed face and the way her pupils in

her gray-blue eyes dilated when she caught his gaze and gave him a smile so smolderingly sexy the breath caught in his lungs.

"H-how serious?" he managed, his hands unable to stop caressing her breasts.

"Super serious. This is a full-on 'better get me naked and in your bed' type of crisis. The critical sort of emergency that involves you between my legs. For like a half hour. Maybe more."

"Roger that."

He'd leaned into her for another kiss when, suddenly, his truck horn sounded one long, angry blast.

She laughed in her full-throated, hot-as-hell way, her hands fixing her clothes as she collapsed off him onto the passenger seat. "Get me inside before we're caught out here by the cops for indecent exposure."

Kissing, they fell inside his garage, hands everywhere on each other. Clothes came off as they headed to his apartment, his shirt being the first to go, followed by hers as they stepped into his private quarters in the back. His mouth explored the curves of her neck and shoulders as he slammed the door behind them, hitting the light switch with his elbow as he dropped his keys onto the counter by the door.

"I cannot wait to get you into bed." He used his hand to work on the clasp of her bra. It was black and lacy and he wished he had a moment to appreciate the sight of her in it, but then it was off, and he was glad it was gone. Her breasts filled his hands, the skin there exquisitely soft. She lay back on his bed and he followed, raining kisses across the silky expanse of her chest.

"Yes," she hissed in his ear, her hands gripping his arms. He took her nipple in his mouth, teasing the flesh there with his teeth and tongue until he heard her groan. "Pants. Off. Now."

He chuckled, switching his attention to her other breast, but at the same time unbuckling his own pants and hers. Thankfully, she helped, and soon her jeans were tossed to the side, revealing the most delectable pair of plum-colored lacy underwear he'd ever seen.

He groaned, levering himself up on his hand, pulling away from her kiss.

"Let me look at you. Jesus. Those panties are enough to kill a man."

She gave a gasping laugh. "Want to see something better?" She lifted the leg opposite him, bending her knee until it was practically at her ear, and his hand skimmed down her smooth skin from her beautiful breasts to the sweet indent of her belly button to the lacy creation half revealing and half hiding the wonders beneath. "My toenail polish matches my underwear. Isn't that fun?"

"Fun? Your English teacher was right. That word doesn't even come close to describing it," he growled, feeling like he might burst out of his jeans if he didn't get them off, pronto. "Do not move. Not one inch."

He twisted away from her to sit on the bed. Yanking up the cuff of his jeans on his left leg, he smacked the button to release the pin from the socket on his prosthetic. He slid it off, along with his right sneaker, followed by his jeans in two breaths. He'd begun to unroll the sleeve on his left thigh when he felt her hand.

Ryker froze. He'd hoped to get everything off and get

back to business before she noticed. But as she sat up, he realized his expectation that she'd wait there, all docile-like, wasn't realistic. Bryce, thank God, was anything but docile—she was the kind of woman who went after what she wanted, who was as fearless as any Marine in the field. It's what he adored about her. But damn. Being vulnerable—revealing everything to her like this—was hard.

"You moved." It came out sounding a little more defensive than he'd intended. He scrounged for more words. "I...have to take this off. So I can do the things I want to your beautiful body."

Her cool fingers traced maddening patterns on his arms and then up his shoulders. Soon her lips joined in, and she was kneeling behind him, kissing his neck, her arms coming around his front, pressing her naked breasts into his back.

"By all means. You do whatever you want—limber up, do some stretching, whatever prep you need, I am here for it." Her mouth found his ear, the one left ragged and uneven from the shrapnel from the IED—and she traced the notch there with her lips, trailing the tiniest kisses down to his earlobe, where she nibbled softly. He groaned as her breath fanned his neck, tickling there, as she whispered in his ear. "Because I have been waiting to get you all to myself in a bed for weeks, and I mean to make you put in some work. Maybe even some overtime tonight."

He closed his eyes briefly in an attempt to slow the cranking gears of his lust at her words. Then, battling his self-consciousness, he eased the sleeve off.

Bryce stopped her attention to his ear and neck briefly to gaze down the front of him. She sighed, then twisted herself around him to sit on his lap. Her palm grazed the whiskers on his cheek as she cupped the side of his face to look into his eyes. He moved to kiss her, anything to distract from his awkwardness in this moment, but she held his face still.

"Your body is beautiful," she said. "Every last inch of it."

He exhaled in a whoosh, unaware until then that he'd been holding his breath, waiting for her reaction. Her word—the fact she'd called him "beautiful"—expanded and filled the lonely warehouse of his heart, bolstering and fixing all the tiny bits he hadn't realized were lingering, broken and hurting, in there.

"I—uh, thank you," he finally managed.

She placed a feather-light kiss on his lips, then his forehead, cheeks, and finally his chin, like some sort of benediction, before pulling away. Then she gripped his forearms.

"Now. Ryker Matthews, can we have sex? Or are you going to keep me waiting on your lap forever?"

In answer, he lifted her, spinning to bounce her back against his mattress. She laughed, shrieking in delight as he growled playfully, burying his face into her neck, moving his whiskered face across her skin there, kissing her until her laughs morphed into a long, low moan.

That. That was the sound he'd been imagining, wishing for, all these weeks.

Laughter, and the sounds of desire.

They were the best gifts he'd been given in a very long time. As his lips followed his hands down her body and he parted her legs, positioning his head between thighs as smooth as silk, he vowed to do everything possible to keep this woman in his life.

"Don't stop." She gazed at him, catching her bottom lip between her teeth.

He gave a low chuckle, his lips grazing her flesh. "Roger that."

This woman, and her talent for life and laughter, was everything. Until he could work up the courage to tell her...

He'd show her.

He slid her panties off and began.

CHAPTER 13

Bryce was pretty sure the air inside Ryker's apartment, specifically in the proximity of his king-sized bed, was a nanosecond away from combusting. It had to be. There was no way the vibes between them could be any more sexually charged than right at this moment.

Damn, but this guy was *good*.

She enjoyed sex. Very much. But something about Ryker put this experience at next-level hot. She wasn't sure if it was because he made her feel good about herself as a person, or if it was simply because he had skills. Physical skills. His fingers and hands were callused and rough in all the right ways, and then he'd done this thing with his tongue...she was seconds away from bursting.

"Hey," she panted, tugging on his hands, his arms, finally his head until he reluctantly dragged his mouth from between her thighs. "I'm going to explode if you don't stop."

He gave an evil chuckle, making her insides spasm in longing. "That's sort of the point."

"But I really, really want you in me when I do." She sent a look toward the spartan side tables. "Tell me you have condoms hidden in some secret drawer somewhere?"

He nodded, pointing his chin to the bathroom. "In my medicine cabinet. Hold on, be right back."

He got off the bed and grabbed a pair of crutches leaning against the wall by the headboard. A couple seconds later, she heard the creaky, metallic sound of a door being opened, then closed.

Then she heard a curse, followed by a loud bang on the bathroom wall.

"You okay?" she called.

Then another curse, and finally Ryker returned. Instead of answering her, he began to methodically ransack the room, rifling through drawers in a dresser against the far wall, grumbling under his breath as he yanked each one open, then closed it with more force than necessary.

"What's wrong?" Bryce brushed the hair from her face, the glow of foreplay evaporating from her in a slow-rising mist. "Don't you, erm, have anything?"

Only after he'd gone through all four drawers in his dresser did he turn to her. He tossed a box to the bed, and she made a fumbling catch.

"Oh, you found some."

"They're expired. By two years, so they aren't safe to use. If this isn't evidence of the fact that I don't date casually, I don't know what is." His face was a portrait of misery as he thunked his fist into the wall, making dishes rattle in a nearby cupboard. His glance went to the clock on the wall. He gave her a pained smile, returning to the bed in only his navy-blue jockey shorts, erection jutting prominently inside the tight material. He set his crutches against the wall and sat down next to her with a sigh. "It's past ten o'clock. Unfortunately, everything's closed in town, or I'd run and grab more. Can I...can I ask for a rain check?"

"Hardly," Bryce snorted, shaking her head. She rolled her eyes, desire battling with embarrassment, until finally lust won out. "I'm not a rain check kind of girl. I'm a 'finish what you started' kind of girl."

Ryker frowned as Bryce got up. "I don't want you to leave, Bryce."

"I'm not going anywhere."

She retrieved her purse where she'd dumped it next to the apartment door and unzipped it, going for the inside pocket. She fished out a strip of three condoms, tossing them to Ryker, who caught them one-handed.

A big grin spread across his face as she lay back down on his bed.

Bryce shook her finger at him. "You are damn lucky. I bought these this morning, just in case. And inquiring minds want to know—are you coming off a three-year dry spell?"

Ryker whooshed out a breath and nodded. "Couple of near misses, but that's about the extent of it."

She brought him down to her, helping him ease off his jockey shorts until there wasn't a stitch of clothing between them. Kissing his mouth, she moved under the delicious hard length of him, reveling in the weight of his body against her own. "Let's end this dry spell of yours, shall we?"

He returned the kiss, his blue eyes soft. "Whatever good thing I did in the world to deserve a woman like you, I'm damn grateful."

Then his mouth was on hers, gently at first, his kisses

light as rain, then with more urgency. His hands—those strong, callused hands—skated over her skin, cupping her breasts, squeezing, kneading her until she ground up against him. Then his hand was between her legs. She was beyond ready. But he continued to stoke the flames higher, until she finally gripped his shoulders.

"More," she said, breathing hard. "I need you in me. Ryker—"

His breathing was ragged as he kissed her nose.

Then he rolled half off her, snagging the condoms. Faster than she thought possible, he had one ripped off, slid it on, and was back between her thighs.

"Time to finish what I started," he said, that crooked half smile on his lips.

"Yesss." She sighed as he entered her slowly at first, as if he were afraid of hurting her. But when she began to move her hips under him, her knees coming back, opening herself wider, and wider still, she thrilled to hear him groan.

"Jesus. You are so wet."

He began a rhythm then, and when his hand crept around to cup her ass, gripping there to thrust harder, deeper, the motion catapulted her to the edge.

A climax broke over her in a tide of sensation, the pulsing inside surprising her with the fierce intensity.

She cried out, arching into him, riding him as the spasms racked her body. He stilled above her, and after she'd wrung every last pulse from her orgasm and collapsed back on the sheets, he kissed her on the lips. A mischievous grin crept onto his face as he gazed down at her.

"I'm about to clock some overtime. You ready?"

His mouth and his hands began their rough, but oh so

gentle exploration of her body, and he kept a slow, steady rhythm in and out of her, as if he had all the time in the world. By the time he rolled her nipple in his mouth, she felt that familiar aching hunger, and as her hips began to writhe under him, she felt herself growing more and more taut, until she was like a rope stretched to its limit, pulsing with need.

A second orgasm tore through her, and she arched up, holding her breath as the pulses of pleasure rippled through her, and she was still grinding against him when suddenly he gripped her hip and drove in one last time, shuddering. They were so close, so joined into one being, she felt every spasm as he emptied himself inside her with one low, long groan.

They lay entwined until their breathing returned to normal. Finally, he levered himself onto both elbows, and she grinned at him, kissing those luscious lips.

"You get the prize," she said. "I feel like you got robbed—I got the better end of your two-for-one special."

"I was going for three. Next time." Although his lopsided smile reappeared, she knew from his tone he was dead serious.

"I love y—I mean, I love that you're an overachiever." She quickly pivoted, aghast she'd almost said the l-word. You did *not* tell a guy you loved him after he'd banged two orgasms from you. Besides, it was too soon for that anyway. Yet, as she searched her heart, she wondered how far off that mark it was. Not much. It might not be "love," but the way she felt when she spent time with him was far north of mere "like." But now was not the time to be that heavy lift that he'd just insisted she wasn't—she needed to keep it light. Fun. "Three next time. You're on."

His face had grown still when she'd almost uttered the l-word, but when she lamely amended her statement, he cautiously nodded.

"And there will be a box of *non*-expired condoms next time," he added. "Glad you had my six."

She fixed her face, smiling cheerfully as if she hadn't almost accidentally told him she loved him. Then a yawn overtook her, exhaustion from the week finally catching up.

"You rest." He kissed her forehead, carefully rolling off her. "I'll go take care of this. Can I get you anything? A drink?"

She smiled, rolling to the side to scoot under the covers on his bed, suddenly chilled without his warmth. She yawned again.

"Sure—a cold beer would be amazing. But only if you're drinking with me."

"You got it."

He sat on the side of the bed, snagging his boxers and his crutches, but before he stood, he looked back at her.

"Will you spend the night with me, Bryce?"

Something about the simple, boyish sincerity in his tone made her heart melt into an ooey-gooey mass in her chest.

"Try and kick me out," she said, forcing herself to ignore the rising panic in her chest that things were moving too fast. Way too fast for the dumpster-fire mess that was her life.

She heard the water running in the bathroom and closed her eyes, vowing to worry about that later. Right now, she was tucked into the bed of a man who had lit up her body like a Christmas tree—twice—and his pillowcase smelled like spicy pine laced with his unique scent. All she wanted to do was enjoy tonight. She'd think about the rest tomorrow.

A few minutes later, she felt the bed dip, and soon his arm was around her waist. She mumbled something, but it was too much work to open her eyes. Instead, she snuggled closer, holding his arm hostage with her own until at last sinking down into sweet oblivion.

* * *

Bryce was startled awake by the sound of someone yelling. A man.

Ryker.

The words were garbled and sounded like he was in the garage. She levered herself up on an elbow, the faint light from the windows in his tiny place confirming that she was alone in his bed.

"What time is it?" Grabbing her cell phone from the wooden crate that stood in for his nightstand, she checked the time. Two-fifteen a.m. Why was Ryker out of bed and in the garage in the middle of the night?

Fearing some type of family or car emergency, she fumbled on her shirt and underwear. Then she toggled on her cell's flashlight, casting its illumination across the spartan apartment. She saw his dresser, the television on top, and the kitchen, which consisted of a teensy countertop, microwave, sink, and one lonely cupboard. No Ryker.

The door leading into the garage stood ajar. She padded barefoot to the threshold, pushing it open.

The garage lights were off, but it was partially

illuminated thanks to the bright security halogens outside shining through the windows. Nothing moved, and she heard no sound. A quick check into Ryker's tiny office showed it was empty.

"Ryker?" she whispered, shivering in the brisk temperature of the uninsulated garage space. She figured he might be on a phone call and didn't want to be too loud and interrupt. There was no response, but she heard someone moving.

A clunking noise came from behind the VW front end. It sounded like someone had bumped an elbow or leg into the metal. She was starting to get freaked out. If Ryker wasn't here, where was he, and who was in the garage?

"Hello? Who's there?"

"Stop! Look to your left, your left! Get down!" Ryker's shout filled the garage, his tone urgent, commanding. Scared.

Bryce jumped, then ducked, crouching instinctively at his warning. She hunkered by the entrance to the tiny office, half in and half out of the doorway. Her heart boomed as she looked to her left, adrenaline making her breath fast and her senses hyperalert. Shaking, she directed her cell's flashlight in that direction.

Nothing.

Slowly, she traced the phone's light in an arc to include the rest of the garage. Shadows fled under the bright glare, but she saw nothing menacing lurking under a vintage Mustang Ryker had on the lift, nor anything in the periphery.

Seeing no threat, she released her death grip on the doorjamb. Before she called out again, a sound came to her. It started out low, like a moan, then grew into a cry of pain and anger.

"Noooo. Tarun, stay with me, man. Where's Paul? Shit! My leg..."

It was definitely Ryker. His anguished tone brought Bryce to her feet, and she was running toward his voice, behind the VW's front end, before she registered the intent to do so. She dove around the edge, the cell phone's light bringing the tiny area in full view, and what she saw stopped her cold.

Ryker lay huddled in the corner made by the front end being fastened to the garage wall. His big body was crammed into an impossibly tight package of limbs, as if he were a child hiding from the boogeyman. He wore no prosthetic, and both his hands were gripped around the scarred skin above his amputation, like he was trying to stop a bleed.

"Ryker, are you hurt?" She cast her light onto his leg, dreading what she'd see... but there was nothing. The flesh on his residual limb was intact. No blood. No sign of recent trauma or injury.

Ryker didn't answer. His eyes stared straight ahead, as if he were watching a movie projected on the metal of the VW's front end. His breath came in harsh gasps, and his hand shot from his knee to shake the bundle of blankets on the floor.

"Tarun? Paul's not... he's not moving. Tarun, damn it, open your eyes! You've got to stay with me, man!" He shouted the last two sentences, his voice straining until it gave out at the end.

He was dreaming, but it wasn't like any dream she'd ever had, nor any nightmare, either. This felt like a horrible reenactment from his time as a Marine.

"PTSD," she breathed. What should she do?

"Ryker?" she whispered, not wanting to startle him but hoping to wake him out of this state. "It's me. Bryce. Are you okay?"

He looked at her then. His blue eyes were blank. Staring. While his expression never altered, the raw pain in his expression triggered tears of her own.

"Shh," he said, staring at her but not seeing her at all, "as soon as they clear the area, they'll be back for us. You need to stay awake, Tarun. Ah, God! My fucking leg..."

His gaze left her and he groaned, both hands around his left knee, squeezing the skin red there.

Slowly, Bryce backed out of the fort-like area behind the VW. She retreated to the stool on the other side, sitting shakily as she flipped the flashlight app off to see the cell phone's screen.

Her fingers flew as she brought up the Google search bar, typing in *What do you do if someone is having a PTSD flashback?*

Google immediately returned several websites with information, and a quick glance confirmed that her instinct not to wake him was right. She scrolled through the .org sites Google had listed, her eyes scanning fast as Ryker continued to give a pep talk to a guy named Tarun and ask about someone named Paul.

She clicked on a bunch of links until she could summarize their advice:

- Put your safety first. Be cautious and keep your distance to avoid getting hurt.
- Stay calm. Avoid sudden movements.
- Tell them they're having a flashback, that it's not real.

- Gently instruct them to breathe deeply and slowly.
- Wait for them to become aware of their surroundings. Ask them to describe what they see to ensure they are awake.
- Support them afterward without judgment; invite them to talk about their experience, yet don't press them if they don't.

Bryce shivered. Was she equipped to deal with this? Hell, no. Would it be better to call Imani and have Zander come over? Maybe. She thought she recalled Ryker telling her Zander had been his recovery coach at Walter Reed.

Then she put herself in Ryker's shoes. He wasn't in any immediate danger. Besides blankets, there was nothing in the space behind the VW he might use as a weapon. He wasn't posing a threat to her or himself. Ryker hated pity and any attention surrounding his war injury. If she called his relatives, there would be hubbub, embarrassment, and negative attention he definitely wouldn't want. If he wasn't in any danger or posing a threat...why should she make this situation worse for him?

Quietly, she walked to the garage's tiny office and flipped on the desk lamp. The puddle of light barely illuminated the space, but she could see enough to notice the office had a door that locked from the inside.

Good. If things went south and she needed the extra security of a door barrier, she'd have it, but she'd still be close enough to keep an eye on him.

Her eyes lit on the coffee maker in the corner, and she got up to start a pot. She would watch out for him tonight, wait for him to awaken fully, then be there for him when...if...he wanted to talk.

CHAPTER 14

Ryker woke to the smell of coffee, toast and...*mmm*. Bacon. Inhaling the scents of breakfast deep into his lungs, he yawned, smiling. Bryce. She was cooking for him—her self-proclaimed love language—and that thought made him happier than her spending the night. He yawned, raising his arms to stretch.

Clunk.

His hand connected with metal, and he opened his eyes, blinking twice as he realized he wasn't in his bed. He was curled up on a pile of blankets, wearing only his jockey shorts, behind the VW's front end in the garage. His leg socket, sleeves, and his everyday prosthetic—the boring one with the faux Pinocchio-like foot at the end—lay in a neat stack where the VW's fort-like entrance led to the garage.

Shit. What had he done last night?

He remembered Bryce. Remembered the fantastic sex. Remembered drinking his beer, then the one he'd opened for her, reluctant to wake her up after he'd returned to bed and found her asleep. He recalled eventually crawling under the covers next to her, feeling blessed as she rolled over, throwing an arm across his chest, her breath warm and sweet against his skin as he held her in his arms...

And then he remembered nothing.

He'd gone to sleep, relaxed by the beer and the wonderful lethargy from making love to Bryce. Yet, sometime during the night, he'd wandered out here.

The metal man and his metal security blanket...

He grabbed his head with both hands, then dragged them down his face, fingers pressing into his eyes, his cheeks, and all the way down his chin as he prayed, prayed, prayed for God or whatever cosmic force that ran this PTSD shit show to please pick this moment to take him.

But his heart continued to beat.

After a moment, he let out his breath in a defeated, curse-filled whoosh.

"Ryker?" Bryce's voice came from the apartment, and he wanted to die all over again as he heard her approach the entrance to his weird safe space. Before his hand did anything but twitch toward his prosthetic, she'd popped her head in and around the VW's front end.

She was dressed only in her watermelon-colored shirt from yesterday. A tiny bit of those incredible purple, lacy panties peeked out from beneath the hem, and the thought of being between those thighs again was almost enough to overcome his embarrassment.

Almost.

Her mouth was smiling, but there was a wariness in her stormy blue eyes that said he'd done more than sleep behind the VW last night. The thought twisted like a serpent in his guts. What had he done? What had she seen? Or, please, no... had he scared her?

His mouth worked up and down without making much noise until he finally ground out a word. "Hi."

Because, really, what else was there to say? How did you start a conversation about why you left a beautiful, naked woman sleeping in your bed to go curl up behind a car part in your garage? How could he know if he'd done anything to make her feel afraid last night? He closed his eyes, summoning the courage to finally ask—

"Hi to you, sleepyhead," she interrupted his thoughts.

His eyes flew open, and, as if she'd read his mind and understood his dilemma, she gave him a huge wink. Then, to his delight and confusion, she whipped her shirt up in one move, flashing her naked breasts to him and then quickly covered herself.

Her saucy grin appeared as she next spoke. "Quick quiz: what did you see? The PTSD website said to make sure you could accurately describe your surroundings to make sure you're really awake."

The words battered at him. PTSD website. She'd had to look up what to do—get some cautionary advice. He must've had a doozy last night. Yet...she was smiling. And she'd flashed him? Jesus. What did it all mean?

"Listen, Bryce, about last night—"

"Nope. We're gonna listen to the experts and follow the rules. What did you see?"

Her expression told him that while she was being playful, she was serious as hell. Okay. Now which word to choose? Did he say boobs? Or was that too middle school? Maybe tits? Too crass? How about breasts...but that felt like Drake writing a love scene in a romance novel where the writer is tippy-toeing around anatomical names to avoid pissing off a reader.

"Your chest," he finally blurted, heaving himself up to stand, one-legged. He felt naked without his prosthetic on, but this barely registered over the shame of being found hiding behind a metal shield all night long. "I saw your fucking gorgeous chest. And the front of those amazing lace panties that I'd like to see up close and damn personal again. But I also see your pretty blue eyes. The worry there. Please, tell me if you're okay. Did I . . . did I hurt you?"

"No. As if. Now, come closer and tell me more about my fucking gorgeous chest. I need those big arms wrapped around me for a sec."

Grabbing on to the top of the VW front end, he used it as leverage to move himself to stand in front of her.

"Don't you want to talk about what happened?" he asked.

"It's a hug emergency, damn it!" Her cheeks were flushed under a mop of unruly brown hair. "Hug me!"

He did as he was told. Wrapping his arms around her, he held her carefully, then more forcefully as she clutched at him, her hands a little cold on his bare skin. Bryce's ribs expanded under his hands, and she burrowed her nose into his neck, breathing deeply and sighing. Her body was soft, molded to him. Her silky hair tickled the underside of his chin but he didn't move a muscle, not wanting to break the spell.

Because once she started to talk, he knew things were going to go sideways.

Suddenly, the sound of beeping came from his tiny apartment. It wasn't the high-pitched noise of his fire alarm, but more subdued, like a . . .

"That's the microwave timer. Breakfast, such as it is, is ready." She pulled away with what seemed like regret. Was this where she gave him the speech of why it was better if they were still friends?

He did the most chivalric thing he could think to do— say the hard part for her.

"You've probably got to go, huh? Don't worry about breakfast—"

She pulled his head down to hers, planting a long, fierce kiss on his lips.

"There are three facts you should know. Fact one: I'm free until the girls are dropped off after church and their Easter brunch with their grandparents. Fact two: I'm hungry. I worked my ass off putting together a meal in that sad, sad area you call a kitchen, and I want to eat the fruits of my labors. Fact three: We need to talk about last night, and then I need a shower. So hustle up—you've got two minutes while I plate everything and bring it out here to eat since you have no table in your whole freaking apartment."

She gave him one more kiss on his lips, which he returned with something between confusion and wonder, then disappeared into his apartment.

His arms and legs moved automatically. He grabbed his prosthetic, socket, and sleeve and, using the VW for stability, hopped to the nearby bistro table and chair. Sliding on the sleeve, he wondered what explanation he'd give Bryce...and what would be her reaction? Sure, she'd been cool. Remarkably so. But there was only so much crazy one person could take, and he'd been shoveling about ten pounds of it into a nine-pound bag if he was right about last night.

When was she going to tell him he wasn't worth all this?

The prosthetic clicked home, and then it clicked once

more as he put his weight on it. He gritted his teeth at the stab of pain. This morning it seemed more localized to the front of his residual limb, below the kneecap, but he didn't have time to deal with this HO flare-up. He had to solve this PTSD thing first. Only one war-related crisis at a time.

Sooner begun, sooner done. But damn, he didn't want to go there. He didn't want to see her kind face fold in on itself when she determined that the math of him plus her didn't add up. Yet he'd done hard things before, he reminded himself. He would do this, then lick his wounds later.

Bryce approached with two plates balanced on one hand and holding two mugs of coffee by the handles with the other. He reached out to help her unload it all onto the table.

"Dig in." She sat next to him, gesturing at his plate with her fork. "This isn't my best work, but I should get hella extra credit for using mostly packaged military rations as ingredients and cooking with one pot, a hot plate, and a freaking microwave."

He cleared his throat, feeling like he had to apologize for the accommodations. "My apartment used to be the former owner's staff break room."

"Ah. That explains why there's a full-sized refrigerator but no stove or range." She took a bite, gesturing he do the same.

Ryker shoveled the egg stuff into his mouth. Flavors exploded on his tongue and, like it always was with Bryce's cooking, eating erased everything else. There weren't enough cylinders in his brain to handle anything other than this culinary enjoyment.

"Wow. You used my MREs for this?" he asked, mentally attempting to catalog what had been in his cupboards, fridge, and freezer besides frozen berries, kale, egg whites, and milk for his protein drinks. The MREs were there as a last resort if he had no leftovers from dinner at his mom's or takeout. "This is incredible."

"Thanks. You finally fell asleep about four-thirty this morning and really started snoring around five." Her abrupt shift in topics made him swallow hard as she continued. "So I thought it was safe to leave you. I went through your food and pretended I was in a Zombie apocalypse–style cooking competition. I'm naming this dish either MRE breakfast medley or stressed-the-fuck-out soufflé. I haven't decided which."

Ryker carefully set down his fork. It was time. No more pussyfooting around. He owed her an explanation.

"I don't usually drink. Especially at night. Because sometimes when I do, I have vivid dreams. PTSD episodes, where my mind relives memories." He reached for her hand, not daring to breathe until she took it, squeezing lightly. Her direct, "don't bullshit me" gaze held his and he continued. "Those episodes usually center on that night in Afghanistan. April nineteenth."

"When you lost part of your leg?"

"When we lost Paul. Almost lost Tarun, too, and my leg was the least of our worries."

Her gaze never faltered. "Would you tell me the story?"

So he did.

He told her of their training to scan the area for IEDs, and the fact that they were the second team through this blown-out section of Sangin, Afghanistan. How they'd been up playing cards the night before.

"We weren't at our best. I'd goaded them into a poker competition, and we pulled an all-nighter. I figured we deserved the mental health break. Cards all night is frowned upon, but it's not forbidden, either. I was razzing Paul about being the night's biggest loser, and he turned to flip me off when I saw it."

"A bomb?" Her gray-blue eyes were wide, the rest of her breakfast forgotten.

"A wire. Sticking out of the ground as we rounded a blind corner. Perfect place for an IED, and we were all trained to spot the signs. To be wary. But our guys had already cleared this the day before. And we'd been up all night messing around, and I spotted it a half second too late." He paused in his story, the picture of that moment frozen in his mind, how Paul's expression had gone from hilarity to a blankness full of horror. Ryker shook his head, willing the image away like erasing a giant Etch A Sketch in his mind. "My buddies say I grabbed Tarun and tossed him behind a burned-out hulk of a 1970s VW bus in some feat of jacked-up strength, and I'd begun to leap behind the VW myself when the device exploded, a half second too late for my left leg. And way too late to save Paul."

Bryce swallowed. She took another bite of her egg, motioning for him to do the same, but in a distracted way, like she was playing for time. Her eyes slid to the VW next to them.

"Is this the same VW bus? From Afghanistan?"

Ryker shook his head, his finger reaching out to trace the emblem, the pocked area where a bullet or a bit of shrapnel from the IED had put a hole close to the center.

"No. After... Tarun and I had been medevaced out, the

guys in our battalion had to clean up and sweep the area for any other devices. Our buddies pried this and the mirrors from the VW that saved our lives and sent them over to Tarun and me at Walter Reed. Tarun got the driver's-side mirror and I got the emblem and the rearview mirror. I was at the scrapyard one day looking for car parts for a 'sixty-eight Camaro, and I saw this VW front end. Same model as the one in Afghanistan. I figured it was a sign. I brought it home and drilled it into the brackets on my wall, welding the emblem on and installing the rearview mirror as a daily reminder of why I'm alive. Or at least *how* I'm alive."

He wanted to tell her more. Tell her how the VW was his reminder not to let his guard down again, because when he did, bad shit happened like it did with Paul. Like it could have last night when he was in his night terror. What if he had hurt her?

Bryce reached over and squeezed his hand, the gesture centering and calming him.

"Thanks for sharing that with me. It's awful, what you went through, and I'm thankful for your service. But Paul's death was no more your fault than it was mine when Bentley died." She grimaced, her eyes swimming with sudden tears she sniffed away, almost angrily. "But I get the allure of an easy target. Self-blame seems to be our specialty, huh?"

Ryker put another bite in his mouth, but it tasted like dust because he still had to ask the hard question. Putting on his mental Kevlar, he finally blurted it out. "My extra-curricular activities last night ... they didn't scare you?"

Bryce cocked her head. "Did June's first period scare you? Or Cici's lack of bathing? Addie's plastic sword to the nuts?"

"Those aren't in the same category," he hedged, feeling his mouth twitch a little at the memory of the littlest Weatherford girl's cutlass attack.

"Says who? A lot of guys would've been running for the hills in any of those situations, but you stuck around. I think I can handle an all-nighter as your sentry. We're a team. Right?"

"Are we?" He immediately wanted to take the question back, especially when her eyes grew wary. "I mean, is that...*all* we are to each other?"

Some of the frost thawed from her expression. "If this is your way of passing me a note saying, 'Do you like me? Check YES or NO,' then I'd be checking, circling, and highlighting the hell out of 'YES.' But I get the sense you're not...at the same place I'm at, relationship-wise, which totally makes sense. My current situation with my nieces and my job makes the thought of committing to one more thing tough. Honestly, I didn't intend to start anything with you, but you sort of snuck up behind my defenses. My time with you has been amazing." She paused for a long moment, her cheeks going pink. "Now would be a good time for you to say something. Anything."

Ryker took another bite, stalling for time as he got his words to line up. Hell, yes, he liked her. But he wasn't sure she was as chill about his baggage as she pretended to be. Hell, *he* wasn't as chill about his baggage as he pretended to be. He decided to give as much of an answer as he could. "Relationships haven't been my strong suit for...a long time. I'm rusty. And I'm pretty sure I'm going to screw this up."

"Well, that's not defeatist thinking at all—"

Bryce stopped talking, and he heard a phone vibrate. She pulled up her watermelon-red shirt, revealing that she'd stashed her cell phone like a gunslinger into the waistband of those sexy purple panties at the hip, as if the device were a weapon holstered by the elastic there. Her brows drew together as she read a text. Then she groaned, slapping her forehead with her palm in a gesture so cliché it would be funny if not for the stark horror on her face.

"What's wrong?" he asked, immediately alert.

"We're going to have to table this talk. I've—damn it, I've got to go." Bryce pivoted, heading toward the apartment.

"Did something happen to the girls?" He leaped up, following as she picked up her clothes and began to dress.

"I forgot today was Easter," she said, yanking on yesterday's pants. "I mean, I remembered Adele and Harvey wanted the girls overnight so they could take them to church service and the big luncheon afterward, but I forgot it was a holiday. Adele says she took the girls to the apartment to change into fancier dresses suitable for Easter Sunday, and they're wondering where I am, and what time they should have the girls back to celebrate Easter with me. I've got to get over there... but I don't have anything planned!"

Ryker pulled out a clean pair of jeans for himself, a plan of attack coming together neatly in his mind. "If you can whip up breakfast using military rations, you can make something from your own kitchen. I can help chop things—I'll even keep my station spotless."

Her grin was quickly erased as the phone buzzed again. Bryce's eyes widened as she read the next text, then gazed at him in something like panic.

"June is asking if she should allow the little girls inside the apartment because she doesn't want them to hunt for their Easter baskets until I'm ready. I don't have any frigging baskets, or candy, or those plastic eggs—I assumed if they were at their grandparents', they'd do that. When Bentley and I were kids, all my parents did for Easter was make a really nice ham dinner. We sometimes went to church, but we never did baskets or egg hunts. Bentley and Heather must've had different traditions, and now I'm letting my nieces down. Again."

At the first mention of the problem, the gears of Ryker's mind whirred to life. Talking about PTSD and his feelings—he sucked at that. But fixing shit? That was right in his wheelhouse.

"Tell them you're out getting a surprise ready for when they get home."

Her face was a portrait of misery. "But it's Easter Sunday, and all the stores will be closed."

He strode over to snag his phone from the charger. "Text her and trust me. Between my brothers, my sister-in-law, and my mother, we'll give them an Easter to remember. Let's hustle. We've got to get to PattyCakes and boil some eggs."

CHAPTER 15

Adele texted. They're heading to brunch, and should be here in about forty minutes," Bryce called out over the hubbub in the café, her heart soaring. She felt—for the first time in ages—excited about the day. The future. The... everything.

And it was all thanks to Ryker. Well, Ryker and his entire family.

As the man promised, his brothers came out to help, if in the most unexpected ways. Drake and Kate raided their attic, bringing over old Easter baskets and miscellaneous spring decorations. They drove them to PattyCakes, where they proceeded to decorate every spare inch of the café dining room in flower garlands, bunnies, and all things happy.

"Patty gave me permission to deck this place out for spring," Kate said as a greeting when she walked into PattyCakes. She looked like she'd walked off the cover of *Working Mom* magazine, wearing a mint-green dress and juggling bags of pastel-colored decorations. Kate's ready smile and can-do attitude made Bryce weak with relief. "I brought along a crap-ton of bubble wand favors left over from the last wedding I planned. Bubbles make everything better. So does glitter, but that's hell to clean up."

Bryce gave the petite woman a one-armed hug. "You are a rock star. Go nuts, and I'll make sure Patty's place is spotless afterward."

"Uh-oh," said Drake, looking exactly like his pictures on the café's walls in a black shirt, khakis, and dark, chunky glasses. "You may regret those words. I should know."

Kate's green eyes crinkled in a grin as she shoved her husband with a hip. "Patty is baking cupcakes, and Zander is stuffing himself into the Easter Bunny costume he begged from Ray at the dry cleaner's. This is so much fun. I haven't planned something for kids in forever."

Ryker, who'd lugged the rest of the bags from Kate's car, gave Bryce a chin nod as he set everything down.

"See? Told you Kate would be game to throw together a last-minute party."

"Event!" both Kate and Drake said in unison, then laughed in a way that told Bryce it was an inside joke.

"Okay, let's get moving." Kate leveled Drake a playful look. "Carrying Elise doesn't exempt you from helping. Come hold my tape dispenser."

Drake gave an up-down waggle of his eyebrows. "I'll hold your tape dispenser. Best offer I've had all day."

Kate rolled her eyes. "Ignore him. He's just spunky because he finished the final edits for *March's Madness*, and he's in his one-day honeymoon between one book and the next."

"Can I hold Elise?" Bryce asked, reaching for the chubby redheaded baby.

Drake handed her over, and Elise chortled as Bryce snuggled her. She smelled like baby powder and Cheerios, and she was so squishy and yummy that Bryce couldn't resist giving her a raspberry on her cheek, making Elise shriek with joy.

"You're a natural." Kate beamed, adjusting Elise's frilly white Easter dress. "And you say you're a hopeless mom-like creature. I disagree. See how she's holding her, Ry? Elise likes to face outward and see the world."

Ryker made a noise that could be a grunt of agreement or a scornful scoff. His face was in its usual rigid lines, but this time Bryce didn't sense a smile lurking under the surface. Maybe he felt Kate was calling him out? Remembering his earlier admission that he was rusty at relationships, she rushed to rescue him.

"It's not natural. I had a year of practice. Before culinary school, I was a nanny for this executive in Tampa. The boy's name was Quinn, and he had two dimples you only saw when he belly laughed. So I spent my days seeing how many times I could make him giggle." Bryce shifted Elise from one arm to the other, catching Ryker's gaze and smiling. "Don't you love babies? I used to say I wanted ten, but now I realize four is more realistic."

Ryker's face went funny, like he suddenly had indigestion. "I'd better go check on the cupcakes. Mom should be here already." He pivoted, then vanished out the front door.

Bryce tried not to be hurt by how abruptly he'd turned away. After all, he clearly cared, since he'd called in the Matthews cavalry for this impromptu Easter bash. Why was she always so sensitive? But she felt validated when Kate whispered under her breath.

"Ryker gets a little stressed out in crowds, or hectic situations. Don't let it bother you."

There wasn't any time to be bothered, because between hanging bunches of flower garlands and taping up Easter Bunny and egg pictures to the front store windows until it looked like something out of a Martha Stewart Easter catalog, thirty minutes flew by. Bryce's heart did a nervous flop as her phone binged with a text notification.

"It's Imani. She says, 'Hey, sorry but we're not going to be able to make it to the party. Zander jabbed himself in the eye applying the Easter Bunny's eyelashes and whiskers, and we've spent the better part of an hour at the ER.'" Bryce scanned the rest of the long text from her friend and the girls' dance teacher. "Oh no! Zander has a lacerated cornea. But they're picking up eyedrops from the pharmacy and the doc say he'll be fine in a couple of days."

"That means we won't have an Easter Bunny," Kate said, disappointed. "He got the only costume Ray had."

Bryce's spirits fell. She'd wanted to give the girls an epic holiday, but fate was conspiring against her. She shrugged, trying to look on the bright side. "It'll be fine. The girls will have eggs to hunt and—oh, crappers—the eggs!"

She raced to the kitchen. The eggs sat in the pot of water, but both were stone cold. She'd never turned the burner on.

"Nooo!" Bryce grabbed the sides of her head.

"What can I do?" came Ryker's voice from behind.

She spun, throwing her hands up. "Sprinkle magic dust and make these eggs cook in the next thirty seconds, and heal your brother's cornea so we can have a bunny here today." She hated how high her voice sounded. "Honestly, if there's a way to screw up a perfectly good plan, I'll find it. Kate and Imani had everything under control—all

I had to do was cook some freaking eggs. You think I'd get that right. And now the Easter Bunny isn't coming because Zander poked himself in the eye. At least there's decorations. Thank goodness for that."

Ryker said nothing, just opened his arms to her.

She threw herself into them, her nose buried into his neck, inhaling his soothing scent—he smelled like cars and tools and strong soap. She grew calm, breathing him in, and, after a moment, she pulled away.

"Hug emergency?" he asked as his hand cupped her cheek.

She nodded. Tears threatened, and she blinked rapidly, refusing to cry. "Thank God you were here, saving the day. My hero."

His shoulders dropped. He chuckled wryly, kissed her forehead, then released her.

"Start the water. Blow bubbles to occupy the girls. I'll be back in thirty minutes."

"Where are you going?"

"Doing hero shit," he muttered. "Time to nut up or shut up."

With that odd non sequitur, he left.

"Bryce?" Kate stuck her head around the wall into the kitchen. "They pulled up out front. The girls are here."

Flipping the burner to high under the eggs, Bryce grabbed a handful of the tiny bubble wands Kate had brought and went out into the dining area.

Ryker was right—she hadn't ruined the day. She'd cook the eggs, hide them hot, then by the time the girls found them, they'd be cool enough to decorate. There was no reason to freak out. She'd blow bubbles, as instructed. Whatever Ryker was up to, well, Bryce's spirits were buoyed by the fact he'd come through for her. Because that's who he was.

The Paynes entered first, followed by her nieces, and Bryce grinned as Addie shrieked at a goblet-shattering decibel. "Aaah! It looks like a fairy garden in here!"

Her new white fairy wings were perky and looked like they were made for the frilly, pink-and-white Easter dress. She was like a pixie come to life, and someone had done her hair in a braid that went around her head, like a crown, the end hidden by a white spray of flowers.

"You look beautiful, Addie-bell." Bryce gathered her up in a quick hug and kiss, the stress melting off at the transported look in Addison's eyes.

"Nana braided my hair like Mommy used to," Addison said, and Bryce hid the pang she felt at not measuring up. Aware of Kate and Drake standing in the nook by the front windows, she called her niece's attention to the decorations.

"Doesn't it look wonderful in here? Ms. Kate and Mr. Drake did all of this as an Easter surprise. They brought bubbles for you, and when the eggs are done cooking, we're going to hunt for them, and then decorate—"

"Aunt Beamer, I don't feel good," Cecily said, and it was only then Bryce noticed that her eight-year-old niece was practically green—a shade that matched her camouflage-patterned dress.

Bryce put a hand to Cecily's forehead. No fever. That likely meant the stomach upset was due to bad food choices—a common theme when the girls were allowed to graze freely in their grandparents' care.

"Oh, Cici. What did you eat? I told you not to eat junk."

Bryce sat Cecily in a chair and headed to her purse, but the tube of Tums wasn't in there.

Cecily lay her head on the table. "It wasn't junk. I had two peanut-butter-and-jelly doughnuts, an' I had fruit to be healthy."

June snorted. "You had an apple fritter. That doesn't count as fruit, wise lass."

"June Shelby Weatherford." Adele's voice was shocked. "Language!"

"It's not a swear. It's pirate," June shot back, looking at Bryce for backup.

But it took all Bryce's effort to keep her mouth shut and not jump down the Paynes' throats. It was like her nieces' grandparents refused to set any boundaries on purpose—so the girls would choose them as guardians when the time came.

She looked at her oldest niece, who stood in her chunky black boots, black socks slouched down over her skinny bare legs under a black T-shirt dress that was two sizes bigger than she was, and gave her an apologetic look. "June, can you run upstairs and get the Tums? They're in the medicine cabinet on the top shelf."

June rolled her eyes. "Fine. Can I get my phone, Pop-Pop?"

"We had to take her phone because she was using it. At church." Harvey's tone was scandalized as he handed over the device, implying June's phone obsession was somehow Bryce's fault.

Bryce bit back a defensive reply.

It was Easter. She wouldn't let Adele and Harvey goad her. Besides, they looked frazzled. Adele's butter-yellow sheath dress had a gray smudge smack-dab in the middle of her right breast in a shape that looked suspiciously like a shoe print, and Harvey's matching shirt had a smear of chocolate—at least she hoped it was chocolate—on the collar.

Catching her stare, Adele swiped at her chest. "Addison decided to twirl. While sitting in my lap."

"Only, I got stuck halfway and had to push off," Addison explained, flitting over to grab Adele's hands. "Don't be mad anymore, Nana. Aunt Beamer has a magic pen that makes everything come off."

"Tide stick," Bryce explained at Adele's confused expression. "Addie, come blow bubbles with me."

Addison sprinted over, clapping. Even Cecily dragged her head off the table to take a bubble wand, blowing through it listlessly as her sister rushed to pop the bubbles before they hit the floor.

"Ooh, look at the pretty bubbles, Elise." Kate brought her daughter over to try to grab one out of the air. Drake picked up a bubble container, nudging his black-framed glasses up his nose to help blow bubbles for the girls.

Bryce was thankful for her new friends and their subtle efforts to defuse tension. The knot in her stomach eased as the girls giggled. Cecily perked up as Drake managed to create giant bubbles, and both girls dashed over to help blow air under one to keep it aloft until Elise's chubby hands smashed through it. The day was starting to turn around, and Bryce was thinking about checking on the eggs when Adele spoke.

"Bryce, we need to talk about your behavior management techniques, because I cannot believe how badly these girls acted. I had to remind Cecily four times to stop running, Addison twirls everywhere she goes, and only June uses an indoor voice." Adele looked at her husband. "The only time they sat was when they ate. Harvey and I know how restrictive your diet is for the girls, so we let them choose their brunch and they enjoyed having baked goods as a treat. Cecily probably just has a bug."

Anger bubbled inside of Bryce until her face felt scalded. Seeing Kate shift nervously, Bryce forced herself to take a box breath before answering—four counts in, hold for four, then four counts out.

"I am not restrictive." Bryce chose her words carefully. "I simply don't offer junk food and processed garbage as the first option at every freaking meal."

Her tone rose at the end and she struggled to ratchet down her anger, but it was like a kitchen fire, hot and blazing from the pan, igniting the spilled grease of her words.

"Now listen, Bryce," Harvey said, but she was over listening. Both girls stopped chasing bubbles as their aunt's voice rang out loud and full in the restaurant's dining room.

"Cecily does *not* have a bug, and neither did Addison when she threw up after she ate too much chocolate pudding for dessert under *your* watch."

Adele's cheeks bloomed with circular rose-colored spots.

"Don't tell us how to parent these children. You can't even keep them in shoes and clothing that fits, and almost nothing in their closets is appropriate for church—"

"Let's talk about church—the only place you take your grandkids, because they have built-in babysitters," Bryce spat, and a small part of her brain told her to stop now, stop before she went too far, stop at least until it could be a more private conversation. But her frustration and anger boiled over and no lid in the world was strong enough to contain it. "How will you manage while I'm in Niagara Falls working all week, with no school, church, or childcare to do the work while you sit on your—"

The front door flew open, and a woman holding a massive stack of pink boxes entered.

"Sorry I'm late, but I've got goodies," Patty said.

Then two things happened at once.

First, Cecily opened her mouth. And spewed. The pinkish goop arced in a trajectory that included the shoes, pants, and legs of Adele, Harvey, and Patty.

Unaware of the dramatic reversal of Cecily's jelly doughnuts, Patty kept moving forward, boxes blocking her view. She stepped in the stinky pile and slipped. Yelping, Patty tossed the pastry containers, arms pinwheeling for balance. She flailed into Adele and Harvey, and all three senior citizens shuffled together, sliding and hanging on to each other.

They managed not to fall, but the cupcakes weren't so lucky. All four boxes flew with enough oomph to launch the lids off. Bunny cupcakes were ejected into the air...

Until splatting like wet, poofy grenades on the puke-covered floor.

One box of cupcakes managed to stay shut, and landed unscathed by the door.

"Oh, Cici." Bryce breathed through her mouth to avoid inhaling the bilious stench. She reached for her niece, who was miraculously clean, putting an arm around her frail shoulders.

Addison tiptoed, her fairy wings trembling as she leaned over the river of vomit.

"Only, guess what? This box didn't land in the puke. An' I can see the cupcakes! They are the cutiest little bunnies. Can we have one?"

Bryce guided Cici to the nearest chair, biting the inside of her cheeks as she gazed over at Adele and Harvey.

They stood there, the wide-eyed victims of instant karma. Their shoes and legs were splattered with pinkish-red, chunky bits.

"H-hold on, I'll get you all a towel." Bryce bit back the inappropriate giggles welling up inside. But a few bubbled out.

"Is she *laughing* at this?" Adele hissed in what had to be the world's loudest stage whisper.

Choking off more giggles, Bryce grabbed clean towels from the kitchen. Wiping at her leaking eyes—she wasn't sure if they were tears of slapstick mirth or the impending guilt storm she sensed coming her way—she snagged the mop bucket, sticking it under the industrial sink faucet to fill. By the time she returned with the bucket and cleaning rags, she'd regained control over her emotions.

Kate had handed out napkins and produced an empty, sparkling gift bag. Patty, Adele, and Harvey were busy mopping themselves up, tossing the dirty paper napkins in the party bag.

"Here." She handed Patty a towel, wincing at the barf on the poor woman's pretty beige dress shoes. "If it doesn't come out, I'll pay for them. Thanks for making those, and I—I'm so sorry, Patty. I'll get it all cleaned up in here."

"No harm, no foul." Patty's amiable smile was in place as she wiped off her shoes. "Addison is right—one box survived unscathed. It's our own Easter miracle!"

Bryce smiled her thanks at the older woman who'd been such a help to her since arriving in Wellsville. She handed a towel to Adele and Harvey, who were both looking way less forgiving and genial. Aware that she should apologize to them for her rant—if not for the words themselves, then at least for her tone and the fact that she'd blasted it all in front of everyone—she opened her mouth to try, but Harvey spoke.

"We've had enough. We're going to go."

That settled that. The apology evaporated from Bryce's lips. She'd spun and gone to retrieve the mop bucket when she passed Cecily.

Her middle niece was using her arm, combined with the sleeve of her camouflage dress, to wipe her mouth before declaring to everyone, "I feel much better now. Can I have one of those bunny cupcakes, Aunt Beamer?"

"Let me mop this up, and then—"

Bryce caught a glimpse of black blurred movement from the corner of her eye before her oldest niece came charging into the café. June's attention was locked in awed fascination on Drake Matthews, not registering any of the mess on the floor before her.

Smash!

The only remaining box of bunny cupcakes fell victim to the bottom of June's zombie-stomping boots. It crumpled into a wad of pink packaging and white frosting, a few sugar eyes staring out of the mess.

Cecily shrieked as if June had crushed a nest of real baby bunnies, and Addison raced over to tug on her oldest sister's leg.

"Get off, you're smashing the cupcakes, Junie!"

June looked down, and her eyes bulged. "Who put those there?" She raised her boot. The cupcake box had formed around it, so the entire thing lifted as a unit until Addison pulled it off June's leg with a wail.

Tracking through the puddle of vomit, she set the cupcake box on a nearby table, and yanked off the lid.

Not a single bunny cupcake had survived.

Addison began to wail, her face pointed to the ceiling, tears streaming down her cheeks. Soon Cecily joined in, her cries listless and heartbroken.

June looked at her sisters and huffed. "Happy Freaking Easter. Great job, Aunt Bryce."

Bryce felt her face go scalding hot. Her lips trembled, and she stood there in yesterday's black jeans and wrinkled watermelon-red top, unsure whether to cry, laugh, rail at the gods, or just get the damn mop. She might have stayed there forever, frozen in indecision, if it weren't for the sound of the alley door opening and closing, followed by a loud male call.

"Weatherford girls!" a man said, his voice as commanding and brusque as a drill sergeant's. "Front and center. The Easter Bunny is here, and we have eggs to find."

Then, lumbering into the dining area, came the tallest, pinkest, loudest Easter Bunny Bryce had ever seen.

It was Ryker.

Although, if it weren't for the oval cutout for the face, allowing her to see his brilliant blue eyes, she might've wondered. Because the face in the oval was decorated as if he'd prepped for a day terrorizing people at a horror house versus cheering up some girls.

Ryker had drawn black circles around his eyes, probably in

an attempt to make them look cartoonishly big and fun. But without a white ring around them, the dark circles made his eyes into two eerie holes of nothing, and when he blinked, showing off the fact that his lids were painted matte black, too, the effect of him being eyeless intensified. What made it worse was his attempt at whiskers. Instead of using black, he'd chosen to use a bloodred paint, and the whiskers were drawn on in thick lines, uneven and jagged across his whiskered cheeks. They read more like wounds than fine hairs.

It looked like the Easter Bunny had come across a pack of feral cats and barely made it out alive.

"Oh my god. Who booked Goth Bunny?" June shot a picture with her cell phone. Her mouth twisted into a smirk. "Never mind. My socials are going to blow up."

Addison's sobs took on a more desperate note as her youngest niece flung herself at Bryce, clutching her legs.

"There's a s-scary bunny, Aunt Beamer!"

"Ry? That you?" Drake squinted at the bunny in face paint.

Ryker, in his big bunny costume, put his pink furred paw out in an "it's okay" gesture to Addison. "It's me. Ryker."

"Make the scary bunny go away, Aunt Beamer!" Addison's white wings crumpled as she squished herself into Bryce's crotch area. "Make it stop!"

"Addie," she said, trying to extricate the child from between her legs and balance the wet mop before she tripped. "It's Mr. Ryker. It's okay."

Cecily picked her head up off the table. She took one look at the bunny, waved, then leaned over the other side of the chair.

And barfed again.

Bryce and Addison were in the splash zone. Splatters of gunk flecked both of them, including the perfect white fairy wings, which made Addison's shriek louder than an air-raid siren. Over the din she saw more than heard Harvey and Adele step over the stinky puddles of gross to leave, but Bryce didn't have the time—or the desire—to say goodbye. She was doing her best to shove Kate's sparkly gift bag in front of Cecily in time to catch the contents as her niece threw up again.

After that, Bryce was so overwhelmed, so embarrassed, and so angry at the world that she decided the safest course was not to talk to anyone or do anything other than clean up. Busy always filled the void, and every time she was tempted to look at her nieces, or the abject pity on her friends' faces, she forced herself to look at the next dribble of vomit to be mopped up. She might be the world's worst guardian-in-training, but she could clean like nobody's business.

As she dragged her mop over the dirty floors, wringing it out after every terrible swipe into the goop, she saw Drake having a quick side conversation with Ryker, whose eyes were as round as saucers in his scary-bunny makeup. She'd finished the floors, deposited Addison and Cecily at the least-contaminated table in the café, and begun to lug the bucket of disgusting water toward the back alley door when Kate caught her sleeve.

"We bleach-wiped the tables and got most of it out of Addison's wings for you. Patty left, but she, Adele, and Harvey are all fine. They'll send their clothes to Ray. He's amazing with stains." Kate's face was composed and serene, as if there hadn't been a disaster of epic proportions only five minutes earlier.

"Thank you," Bryce mumbled. "I-I can't tell you how much I appreciate all of your hard work. I'm sorry. For everything."

"It's not anyone's fault. Things happen. But you've got to promise me a do-over." Kate bundled up a crying Elise as a white-faced Drake took the bags of unused Easter décor out of PattyCakes. "If I had enough time to prepare—put together a spreadsheet, at least—I could've created such an epic event. I need to make it up to you and the girls. Promise I get to do the next event for you all, okay?"

"Sure." Bryce nodded, but in her head she was pretty sure there would never be a do-over.

Kate waved as she left. "Next time, the event will be perfect. I promise!"

Bryce shut the door and faced her nieces. Addison was trying to straighten her stained fairy wings. She'd stripped off her puke-and-frosting-covered dress and wore only her white undershirt with a picture of Tinker Bell on the front, along with a pair of matching Tinker Bell underwear. Cecily's head hung over the garbage can, and she was moaning about how she would never eat peanut-butter-and-jelly doughnuts again, while June was swiping dejectedly at her only boots—the black soles and sides of which were smeared with white frosting.

Bryce's chin wobbled. Then she caught sight of Ryker. He was standing there, in his scary-as-hell bunny outfit, his arms outstretched.

"Hug emergency?" he asked, and before Bryce could move, Addison flew over, pausing only briefly at his pink fluffy bunny feet.

"Only, I don't like that bunny head. Can you take it off?"

Nodding, he lifted it over his head with some effort. The result smeared the eye-black up his forehead, and made the red whiskers on his cheek look more like really heavily applied cherry-red blush.

"Better?" he asked.

She nodded, wrapping her thin arms around his right leg, her voice muffled. "This is the biggest hug emergency ever."

Then Cecily staggered over, saying nothing but hugging Ryker around his pink bunny waist.

Finally, although she was snickering the whole time, when Ryker motioned to her, June shuffled over in frosting-covered boots, accepting a one-arm hug around her shoulders.

The three kids most important in her life were in the arms of the demented Easter Bunny. Bryce had wanted to cry. But the longer she stared, the more the tears receded, and in their place was...laughter? A giggle bubbled inside of her at the sight of Ryker and her nieces looking like they'd win the prize for worst Easter picture ever. It was too freaking funny.

She snorted a watery laugh. "This moment should be captioned, 'People who are having a worse Easter than you.'"

Ryker extended his left arm to her, hand beckoning her in.

"C'mon, Aunt Beamer," June said. "I know you need a hug from the Easter Bunny, too."

Surprised that it was June—not the little girls—speaking and smiling kindly at her, Bryce moved to them. Her eyes locked with Ryker's as she joined her nieces for a hug from Goth Bunny. She pulled her cell from her pocket.

"C'mon. Everyone lean in. There's no way in hell we'll ever beat this new low, and I feel we need to record it."

June barked a laugh, but she reached out to squeeze her aunt's arm in a gesture that was almost a hug, showing she meant her words to be funny and not snarky as she spoke. "Yeah. It'll be one of those memes. We might go viral. It's too bad Drake Matthews left already, or it definitely would. Let's all look extra miserable, and you can take one picture, and then I'll do one with my phone, Aunt Beamer. It'll be awesome."

It wasn't some overt "it's okay you failed" acknowledgment from June, but it wasn't hostility. Bryce's heart soared. Progress.

They took the pictures, working hard to look miserable. Something about the situation—despite how awful this last hour had been—struck them all as funny. Or maybe it was Ryker, who was doing his level best to look menacing as the Goth Bunny, even putting on his head for a couple pictures. Afterward, Addison screamed in delight when he pulled a white floppy-eared stuffed bunny from a hidden pocket and presented it to her, and before Cecily could squawk, he magically produced another one, in a grassy-green color. Bryce felt like her face was a giant heart-eyed emoji as she watched both girls hoot with happiness at the unexpected gift. Then he pulled a third gray one from his pocket, tossing it to June.

"Tried to find a black rabbit, but this was the darkest stuffed animal the gas station had this morning," Ryker explained.

Bryce inwardly braced for the tween's derision. To her surprise, instead of a sarcasm-grenade, June's face softened.

"It's cool. Thanks for... thinking of me."

Bryce's insides went as gooey as warm caramel. The guy said he was rusty at relationships—had made it seem like his PTSD made him emotionally unavailable—yet here he was, doing the most to bring them smiles.

They were posing for their last shot with their new stuffed animals when Cecily said, "Is it me, or does it smell like stinky broccoli?"

Bryce, who'd been leaning against Ryker, his woodsy cologne and spicy yumminess filling her nose, picked her head up from his pink bunny shoulder and sniffed.

"Oh, no! The eggs." Bryce sprinted to the kitchen.

Most of the water had boiled off, and they sat in a half inch of foaming liquid. Their shells had burst, and they were nothing but white blobs of sulfurous mess.

She flicked off the burner, shaking her head. Thanks to the gesture from June, and the giggles from Cecily and Addison—not to mention the amazing gift of bunny awesomeness from Ryker—her urge to cry was gone. As the large pink bunny made his way into the kitchen, she tipped the pot to show him the contents before dumping it into the trash.

"No eggs to decorate or hunt. No chocolate bunnies or cupcakes for the girls' baskets." She set the pot down and came over to touch him on his red-stained cheeks. "But we have a bunny whose kindness saved the day, and your family who decorated this place to look like a spring garden. Thank you, Ryker. For everything."

His mouth twisted into a wince as he made a circle motion around his face. "Sorry about this. Zan gave me the face makeup and told me how to apply it. But art is not my thing. Or makeup. I didn't mean to make Addison cry."

Either because she'd heard her name, or by coincidence, Addison appeared in the kitchen in her Tink underclothes, her white bunny tucked under an arm as she held out her ruined dress.

"Aunt Beamer, can I take a tub? I've got yuck-o on my legs, an' can you fix my dress?"

Bryce nodded. It was time to be the mom-like creature again.

"Yep. You and Cici both are hopping in the tub. Help your sister up the stairs, and tell June I'm closing down the kitchen." She thought quickly about the supplies she had upstairs. "Tell you what: you two get in the tub and don't make an unholy mess of the bathroom, and when you're all squeaky clean, I'll have a surprise snack waiting for you, okay?"

Addison's face lit up. "Only I like to know what the surprise is. So I can get excited."

Bryce held Ryker's hand as she ushered Addison from the kitchen to tell the other two the same bribe—clean up, get on jammies, and when you're done, treats will abound.

All three perked up at this, and even Cecily, carrying a small empty garbage can with her, trooped up the steps to the apartment as Bryce turned off the lights and locked up the restaurant. Standing on the sidewalk in the mild, spring sunshine with Ryker, who was still carrying his bunny head, she gave him an apologetic smile.

"I'd invite you upstairs, but it's going to be mayhem, and I'm pretty sure Cecily isn't done vomiting—she usually pukes in multiples of four. Plus, I was in the last splash zone, so I've got to wash up once the girls are done. But I don't want you to think that I don't want to spend time with you, or—"

"Shhh," he said, and kissed her. His lips were soft, and he tasted like peppermint. She was suddenly conscious of how wrinkled and terrible she looked and probably smelled and tasted at this point. But he didn't seem to mind, kissing her so deeply a passing car beeped before they ended it with a laugh. "I had a great weekend with you, puking kids and all. Every day with you is a good one in my book, Bryce."

The words hit her directly in the feels, and she threw her arms around his broad and furry pink shoulders. "How do you always know what to say to make me feel better? It's one of the things I love about you."

He froze, and Bryce quickly realized what had plopped out of her mouth. Had she really said the l-word to Ryker...when he was dressed in a freaking bunny suit?

He pulled away, his face in that Marine-serious expression, his voice devoid of emotion. "Bryce, we need to talk. About us. Our relationship. I've been avoiding this conversation, but I have to tell you I'm not—"

Cutting him off, she quickly backpedaled. She absolutely could *not* hear him say he wasn't feeling the same way she was. Not here. Not now. There was only so much she could take in one day, and hearing those words might break her. "I meant to say it's one of the things I *like* about you. How you make things better. How you're so freaking solid, and present, and how you..." Bryce paused, editing her words mid-sentence. She'd been about to say "you complete me," but realized that was a rom-com movie line, and, even though it was true, it was too much to say on a sidewalk. To a man in a bunny outfit who was clearly trying to tell her he wasn't at the same emotional place she was. She chose another phrase. "...you make me feel like I'm not a total loser in life."

His face—the one he'd coined his RBF for good reason—lost some of its rigidity. "You're not a loser. You are amazing, and I enjoy spending time with you. And your nieces. You all have been the highlight of these past few weeks."

Bryce sensed a "but" in his tone. Of course there was a "but"—they'd only known each other for what? A month? Nobody fell in love that quickly.

She braced herself for his words, but just then June came thudding down the apartment stairs to the sidewalk.

"Cecily puked in my room!" she screeched. "It's smooshed into my carpet, and I am *not* cleaning it up."

Bryce had never been so thankful for vomit in her whole life. Stepping away from Ryker, she squeezed his hand.

"Gotta go. Text me. I'll see you for lunch this week? And...are we're still on to run during the girls' dance class Thursday?"

He nodded and waved.

Bryce fled upstairs before he could reveal the "but" in their conversation, before he could say that he wasn't ready, or that they were better off as friends. She didn't want their bubble of happiness to pop, but how long could it last?

Bryce shook her head. She'd had enough of feelings for the day. Grabbing the scrub brush, carpet cleaner, and some rubber gloves, she got to work.

Busy was the antidote to feeling, and if there was one thing her life was full of, it was being busy.

She'd deal with his potential breakup talk.

Later.

CHAPTER 16

For Bryce, it was as if Easter Sunday kicked off a week of awful for the Weatherford females. It began on Monday, when her nieces were home for the last day of Easter break. Unlike having them in the restaurant Friday, the girls were no longer excited to work at PattyCakes and squabbled the entire time. Even Willow, who wasn't easily rattled, finally took Bryce aside.

"I know we're shorthanded, with Patty being off," she said, "but maybe you can start a movie in the back office for the girls? It might be...easier if it's just you and me today."

Willow was tactful but accurate. Addison and Cecily had come to blows twice in the last half hour, arguing first over who got to use the broom to sweep the dining area, then about who got to hold the dustpan and brush. June, no longer enthralled with working the register, had short-changed one customer and mistakenly forgotten to ring up two drinks for another. Operating a restaurant— even a small one like PattyCakes—was tough with only two people, but Willow was right. It was less chaotic to have them out of the customer area. Besides, June wanted only to curl up in a corner and finish reading the Drake Matthews manuscript Ryker had gotten for her.

Ryker. He was another reason things were off lately—she kept reliving that moment when she'd accidentally blurted the l-word on Easter and then had to retract it. His expression—and his unspoken "but"—was on repeat in her mind. She didn't know which was worse: his face when she'd basically said she loved him, or his face when she took it back.

She'd been so distraught she'd called Imani. After asking if Zander's eye was okay, Bryce spilled everything about Sunday's events.

"Well, have you seen or talked to him since then?" Imani had asked after listening to Bryce's story.

"Sort of. He stopped in for lunch. But I had six deep in line, and another five customers waiting for me to assemble their orders, while I was busy pulling Addison and Cecily apart from a spat over who got to use the spray bottle on the table." Bryce huffed out a breath, remembering how hectic it was.

"Well, did you talk to him? What did he say?"

"There wasn't time for talking. I gave him a quick kiss, but it was really awkward. I don't know if that's because I was using my leg to separate the girls who were pulling each other's hair, or if it was a vibe I was getting from him."

Imani gave a musical laugh. "Ryker's not a fan of crowds. Even if it's his family, he sometimes gets anxious. I think it has to do with his PTSD."

"What if I spooked him with that slip of my tongue?" Bryce asked, while in her head she wondered if it was a slip at all. Were those her true feelings coming out when her filters were set to "off" position after the day's chaos?

"I wouldn't overthink it. Just text him and schedule your next get-together without the girls. I've got an idea. He'll be operating the sound and lights for this year's dance recital, and since your girls will be backstage, you can spend time with him then. But don't distract him too much—we've got a rehearsal and recital to get through!"

After Bryce hung up with Imani, she'd texted Ryker with the idea, and he'd replied with a thumbs-up, saying he'd see her Thursday for what had become their weekly run. He wasn't able to come to PattyCakes for lunch because he'd had to work on a car towed to his shop. While he'd sent her a couple of mechanic jokes and she'd sent him some of the best pictures of the two of them together at the car show this past weekend, she couldn't shake the feeling that something was off. He seemed...distant. Like he was looking to put some space between them— cool it off.

By the time Wednesday arrived, life with the girls became a shit show of epic proportions, eclipsing any relationship thoughts altogether. It was parent-teacher conference night. After booking Shama Patel to watch the girls, Bryce had headed to Wellsville Elementary School for conferences. First, she had Addison's pre-K teacher, Mrs. Stackowitz, followed by Mrs. Dawson, Cecily's second-grade teacher, then she had to scoot over to the middle school across town to meet with June's four teachers.

The Paynes had insisted on attending each conference.

"We need to know how our only granddaughters are

doing," Harvey said. "Academics were very important to our Heather—"

"And to Bentley," Bryce had interrupted hotly. "Just because he came from a blue-collar family doesn't mean he didn't want the best education for his girls."

"Which is why it's important for us all to be there," Harvey had continued, as if he hadn't delivered a put-down of omission toward his former son-in-law. "We won't make a peep the whole time. We'll let you do all the talking."

For the most part, they had done just that. Which was worse than having their two cents, as with every constructive or negative piece of news from the teachers, their body language was all crossed arms and disappointed indignation.

Bryce felt like she was just barely hanging on for Thursday's dance class, when she finally got to see Ryker. As soon as she'd deposited the girls with Imani and ensured her cell phone was in the pocket of her yoga pants, she met Ryker in the parking lot. She threw her arms around him, breathing in the scent of motor oil, Lava soap, and his warm goodness underneath. He returned her embrace, kissing her deeply until one of the dance moms beeped at them, the sound as judgy as the stare she gave their public display of affection.

They both laughed, and as Bryce launched into a retelling of the past few days, it seemed as though the weirdness from her Sunday evening outburst was behind them.

"I couldn't even look at them when June's teachers—every one of them except the language arts teacher—said she was close to failing," she told Ryker as they jogged over the bridge and onto Maple Avenue.

"Failing?" Ryker asked, scowling.

Bryce elaborated. "I've been doing my best to help her, but I wasn't a star student myself. It's been years since I've done algebra, and how am I supposed to help when I can't look at a book—it's all on her iPad. I've been watching freaking YouTube videos on the quadratic equation in my spare time, which only happens to be when I'm sitting on the toilet at this point!"

It was probably TMI, but she didn't care. She'd waited all week to see Ryker, knowing she could off-load all of this to him and he wouldn't judge. The wind gusted chilly from the overcast day as they jogged through the back streets of Wellsville. Most of the houses had spring gardens, with green shoots of irises and tulips peeping out from clumps of snow next to daffodils whose yellow petals drooped with the day's earlier sleet and wind. The flowers were much like her life—she wanted to be hopeful, but fate's hailstorms kept wreaking havoc.

"I can help tutor. I'm volunteer checked with the school, so I'm legit," Ryker offered, but he seemed distracted as they ran, constantly looking down at the sidewalk pavement, lending a feeling of obligation to his words.

She was quick to decline. "That's sweet, but I'm not even sure when we'd fit it in. I can barely get June up for school, and afternoons are hectic between waiting for the little girls' buses to arrive, finishing my shift at PattyCakes, then fixing dinner. What I need is a freaking life partner. If you know of anyone who can fit the bill, I'm accepting applications."

As soon as those words left her mouth, she regretted them. When she looked at Ryker, his concerned expression morphed into a blank, ready-to-receive-orders Marine RBF. She'd meant to highlight how hard it was parenting alone, not to push him to declare himself to her in any way.

"I've been meaning to talk to you before tonight, but this week has been nuts," Ryker began. "It's about us. Well, really it's about me. Shit. I'm not doing this very well. Let me start over."

But before he could, a vehicle slowed, beeping at them. It was Drake's vintage black truck, and the Knight of Nightmares himself was behind the wheel.

"Sorry to interrupt." Drake leaned toward his open passenger window to talk, pushing his dark-framed glasses up the bridge of his nose. "I've been looking all over town for this guy. Ry—Mom's at the house and wants to speak with all three of us. She's acting...strange. Zander's with her, and she sent me to find you when you didn't answer your cell."

Ryker pulled out his phone, grimacing. "My bad. I must've had it on silent. I'll jog back to the studio with Bryce, then I'll be right there."

"No, you go ahead." Bryce read the worry etched on Drake's face. "I'm literally a block away from the studio. I'll be fine."

Instead of hopping into Drake's truck, Ryker took her by the shoulders, capturing her gaze. His work-callused palm cupped her cheek, the caress sending delicious shivers like electric shocks through her skin. From the intensity of his expression, Bryce expected something big when Ryker spoke.

But all he said was "We need to finish this conversation. I'll call you later."

The words hit like a punch.

"O-okay," Bryce said, her chest tight. She returned an all-too-brief goodbye kiss from Ryker, their lips barely touching before his scowl was back in place.

He hopped into the passenger seat of Drake's truck, giving one last wave before they drove away. She headed back to the dance studio, wondering at the exchange. Was Ryker just worried about his mom? Or had he hinted at something else that was bothering him with his "We need to finish this conversation" comment? Although they'd spent quite a bit of time together learning the most impactful, devastating details of each other's lives, she wasn't sure where he stood in the relationship. There were times, like at the restaurant in the Easter Bunny costume, when she was certain they had something permanent and amazing. But then there were times, like now, when she felt like a tiny gear in the complex mechanics of his life. Before he'd been interrupted, it sounded very much like he was queueing up an "it's not you, it's me" breakup speech...yet he'd kissed her in a way that seemed to imply something else.

She mulled this over as she picked up the girls. She fixed them dinner, supervised their squabbles, and insisted on dental health while standing at the bathroom vanity to time how long the toothbrushes were in Cici's and Addie's mouths. She put the little ones in front of *Tinker Bell and the Pirate Fairy* on the portable DVD player, then sat with June, frantically Googling how to determine the radius of a circle with only knowing the degree of the circle's arc. Finally, after these tasks, she checked her phone.

No texts. No calls. Nothing from Ryker but radio silence.

Crappers.

She wondered what Patty had wanted to speak to them about. Was she sick? Was that why the sweet woman had been urging Bryce to take on more responsibility at the café? Although her boss hadn't seemed ill, Patty had been taking more time off lately, and there'd been those mysterious dates she hadn't wanted to tell her sons about.

Then Bryce wondered if Ryker's silence was more than whatever family situation he'd been called to tonight. Maybe she'd scared him off with her stress off-loading? Damn. She had to be better about not word-vomiting all over the guy every time they were together. Although she was always asking about his day at the garage, he never had much to say. Doubts crept in on silent feet until her head was overrun with worries and she was replaying his last words to her with all sorts of inflections.

Did his words "We need to finish this conversation" mean he had something important to say? Something unsavory? Something that would require him to cup her cheek, as if he were prepared to give her a breakup speech?

Eager to banish those thought demons, she threw herself into tonight's reading of *Peter Pan*, putting what little acting skills she had into every role, from Wendy's delight at flying to Captain Hook's commands to his crew to attack Peter. Afterward, the little girls clapped and cheered, and Bryce's heart was full as she kissed Addison and Cecily good night and knocked on June's door to wish her the same. Then she brushed her own teeth, washed up, and shut herself in her bedroom.

Pulling out her phone, she bit her lip, wondering what to text. Finally, she decided on just checking in—he had, after all, been picked up by Drake for some emergency family meeting. It was totally normal to check in—it wasn't stalkerish at all.

Convinced she was doing the right thing, she decided on an opening.

> Bryce: Hey there. Checking in to see if every-thing's okay?

The dots on her phone danced immediately, and her heart lifted.

> Ryker: Just a family thing. I've got to head out of town for a few days. Marine business. I want to talk with you when I get back.

Bryce frowned at her phone. What the hell did that mean? And what happened to wanting to finish their conversation tonight? She'd been so open—probably oversharing—with the chaotic details of her life. Why didn't he trust her enough to do the same? She wanted to reply she hated sudoku and any other cryptic puzzle, including this freaking text exchange. She wanted to demand he tell her what was happening.

But maybe that was overstepping? They'd dated a few times. They'd slept together once. She'd spilled the beans that she'd kind of fallen for him—was this his way of cooling things down? Telling her she was feeling too much too fast?

> Bryce: Um, ok. Is it a hug emergency?

She finally tossed out this half joke, half plea, hoping he'd read her insecurities in the message—hoping he'd reassure her. When his reply arrived, his words hit her square in the chest.

Ryker: Call you soon.

Her mouth dropped open. He'd call her soon?
She texted him back, fingers flying over the keyboard.

Bryce: Is there anything I can do to help?

Ryker: Negative.

Biting her lip, Bryce debated what to write next and if she should use emojis, or if sending a heart, or a heart-eyed face, was too much. Finally, she opted for just words, matching his energy.

Bryce: Travel safe.

Her guts churned like a stand mixer on high as she waited for those dots to appear, showing he was replying.

But they never did. After thirty minutes of checking, she finally flipped her phone over. She was done worrying about the weight of her feelings for him and how much they probably outweighed his for her. And she was going to do her best to put out of her mind his request to talk when he returned. It sounded ominous—worse, it seemed to point emphatically to her fears being valid. The guy was going to break up with her.

Flipping off her bedroom light, she huddled inside her bed, listening to the angry splatter of the sleet against her window. She'd been convinced that Ryker was different. He was the guy who returned her smart remarks. The one who kept pace with her on a run, who never blinked in the face of her nieces' emergencies, who was the steadying force she thought she'd finally, *finally* found.

But she had gotten it all wrong.

CHAPTER 17

Boys, I have something to tell you," Patty said after Ryker followed Drake into the house. She wore a black blouse with sparkly bits sewn all over the front paired with dark blue jeans that appeared to have a crease down the front, as if she'd ironed them that way on purpose. Her hair was curled, she had on makeup, and she looked way fancier than she normally did for work. "Two things, actually."

Two things.

Ryker forced his face to remain neutral as his anxiety ratcheted up twenty notches. When Mom counted, that was bad news in the Matthews household.

"Where's Zan?" Drake asked, following their mom through the kitchen and into the yellow room Kate called the Reading Parlor, looking around and stifling a yawn, apparently oblivious to any stress vibes. "I thought you wanted to tell us all something?"

"He's out walking Sasha. Honestly, getting the three of you in a room to talk is like stacking marbles." Patty and Drake headed toward the Victorian's front door, both disappearing onto the porch to call for Zander in the growing dark.

Stress curled around Ryker like a poisonous fog. He wasn't sure if it was from his mother's tense body language or just his own internal distress. Ever since he'd read the email this afternoon from Paws of War notifying him that he was eligible for an immediate service dog training spot, he'd vacillated from a state of excitement to one of down-right dread. What if he went up there, spent all that time with a dog, and they didn't match? The worry was enough to make him queasy, but worse was the second alternative: what if they did match? The thought of the change in his daily life involved with having a dog—a creature who'd rely upon him for every meal, every walk, every...everything— was that an emotional investment he could handle? His leg was killing him, and between the pain there and the turmoil from the email notification, Ryker felt like his heart was pounding out of his chest.

His phone buzzed in his pocket and he pulled it out. It was a text from Tarun.

Tarun: How's the leg, man? Any better?

The guy was some sort of freaking psychic—it was as if their experience in Afghanistan had bonded them in some weird wizard-y way. Somehow he always seemed to know— as if he felt Ryker's pain during tonight's run with Bryce in some phantom form.

Bryce. She was the one bright spot in these past few weeks. Who was he kidding? Being with her made him feel lighter than he had in years. He knew she'd sensed that he'd been off tonight. Between the HO pain and the indecision surrounding the email, he'd barely been able to focus on what she was saying. He'd had a hard time holding up his end of the conversation as he concentrated on picking the best footing on the uneven pavement, every misstep blasting white-hot fire down his leg, as though his prosthetic was filled with broken glass. Considering what the bone scans showed, that wasn't surprising. While he'd have to wait to see what his surgeon said, the fact that the growths were larger had been weighing on him, just like the talk about his potential sterility. He'd meant to tell Bryce everything, but she'd had so many other things going on, it didn't feel fair to burden her.

His mom, followed by his brothers, tromped up the steps and into the house. Before they came into the room, Ryker typed out a response to his friend.

Ryker: Same old story there. Got other news, tho. Someone dropped out last minute, and I got offered a service dog training slot. Gotta go to Long Island tomorrow for a 5 day training.

Ryker finished the text and saw the message indicator go from Sent to Read in the moment before Zander came up, delivering a healthy jab to his arm.

"Dude," Zander said, his right eye totally bloodshot. "I saw a picture of you subbing in for me as the Easter Bunny for the Weatherford girls. Scared the shit out of me."

Ryker rolled his eyes, giving his younger brother a good thwack in the stomach. "We all know your eye injury was from trying to force the costume over that big melon of yours."

"Boys, take a seat," his mother said, gesturing to the

leather sofa, her lips pursing as she gazed at them both. "Why is it every time you two are together, a wrestling match breaks out? Can't you just sit down next to Drake so we can talk?"

"Why do I feel like we're going to need some alcohol with this news?" Zander asked, and as his brother reached for the whiskey glasses on Nana's old teacart, Ryker took the opportunity to sit, exhaling with relief as he propped his left leg on the coffee table.

Sasha, Drake's tiny shih tzu, immediately jumped up onto his lap, her tail wagging for pets. Ryker focused on her sweet, caramel-and-white furry face and the thudding of his heart became more modulated.

"Here, dude." Zander handed Ryker a tumbler with two fingers' worth of alcohol, then one to Drake. Zander offered the third glass to Mom, but she only raised an eyebrow at him. "Okay, fine. I'll keep this one."

Ryker held the drink but had no intention of imbibing. Alcohol this time of night, triggering another PTSD episode, was the last thing he needed. His phone buzzed in his lap, and he juggled Sasha around to peek at it.

Tarun: Ok. I've got the weekend off. I'll be at your house at 06:00, sharp. Then, we ride!

Ryker snorted, recalling his friend's obsession with old western movies. He was about to reply, telling him he didn't need Tarun to drop everything and hold his hand on this road trip, which might amount to a big nothing-burger, when Mom's voice snapped his attention up like it had when he'd been a boy.

"Think you can tear yourself away from that phone, Ryker? I have something important to discuss with all of you." Mom's face was flushed—a look she got only if she was nervous or ticked off.

Neither one boded well for the message to come.

"Sorry, Mom." He stuffed the cell into his pocket. Then he shoved his worries to the side, making an effort to replace his usual RBF with something...more open to accepting whatever bombshell his mother was about to drop. She never called them together unless it was an emergency.

His mind immediately went to Nana Grace—his grand-mother was in assisted living and had celebrated her one-hundredth birthday a few months ago. Was that it? Was Nana dead? Dying? Or was it Mom? Was she sick?

He stroked Sasha, who immediately rolled over, her eyes closed in blissful appreciation as he rubbed her pink belly. Ryker smoothed the fur on her chest, forcing his mind to focus on the task, blocking out the Paws of War opportunity, the aching area below his left knee, and his worries about his relationship with Bryce.

"I've made some life decisions recently. Been making a new map of my goals." Mom's blue eyes snapped with determination. "I have two things I want to say that I've been keeping a secret until I was sure. And now I am. So I need you to be the good boys I raised and keep an open mind."

In normal circumstances, this would've been the ideal opportunity for Zander to make some dumb-ass joke about how Ryker's mind was so empty it was better than open for all that went on between his ears.

But his kid brother was uncharacteristically silent. Zan's

blue eyes widened, and he ran a hand through his shaggy hair in the nervous gesture he'd had since childhood.

"Of course." Drake cleared his throat, doing his big-bro thing and attempting to shoulder all responsibility. "What is going on, Mom?"

"First, I'm cutting back my hours at PattyCakes. I'm working like I'm still in my twenties when I should be thinking about retirement. It's my hope that Bryce might take it over completely in a few years. But if she isn't interested, or able to do that, I'll cast my net out for someone else."

Ryker blinked. Bryce had mentioned that his mom was teaching her things about the business side of the café, but she'd never said she was taking over PattyCakes. He hadn't even known his mom was getting tired of being a small-business owner, as she seemed as gung-ho about PattyCakes as when she'd started the business soon after his dad's death. What else had he missed, being mired in his own feels?

The cell phone in his pocket buzzed again, but he ignored it.

Figuring it was his turn to be a real boy in the conversation, he ventured the only question circulating through his brain. "What will you do instead?"

"I'm starting a new chapter in my life." But her stiff demeanor said that wasn't the whole story.

"That's great news, Mom." Drake's voice was relieved, and Ryker wondered how his brother's writerly mind couldn't sense there was more to the tale. "I mean, we'll miss PattyCakes, but if you're not working there, you'll have much more time to..."

Drake paused, as if stumped by what activities Mom

might want to do, but Zander picked up the thread, not missing a beat.

"Do whatever you want." His baby brother nodded with approval. "Find your Zen. Chase your dream. I dig it, Mom, and I support you on this journey."

Mom's face got that pursed-lip expression she used when fed up and annoyed but trying not to show it.

"I'm not going on any journeys, Zander. I know who I am, and, more importantly, I know what I want. I'm going to sell my house, buy a condo in Florida, and be a snowbird, with—with..." Mom trailed off, her face going brick red.

"With our blessing!" Zander's grin gleamed as flashy as the front grille of a Cadillac. He stood, his arms open to give Mom a hug. "Aw, congrats, Mom! I'm putting in my vote for a beach condo, preferably on the Atlantic, so when we visit, there'll be some surf lessons—"

"Sit down." She batted away the hug. "I'm not finished. What I'm saying is—"

Suddenly, Drake's doorbell rang, and Sasha—who'd just fallen asleep on Ryker's lap—went berserk. The dog rolled off and was on her feet, galloping to the door in mere nanoseconds after the noise. Her tiny nails pawed at the front door as she barked in her most strident shih tzu voice.

"Hold on." Drake took his whiskey with him as he strode to the door, scooping up the frantic dog. "I thought the front gate was locked. I don't know who that is. C'mere, Sasha."

"Wait, Drake, don't!" His mom's voice strained to carry over the dog's barking. "I'm trying to tell you...I'm getting married!"

It was as if the air had been sucked out of the room and they'd been thrust into the noiseless vacuum of space.

Even Sasha, tucked in Drake's arms, stopped barking and wriggled silently as she stared toward the frosted window of the front door. The motion-sensor porch light flickered to life, illuminating the shadow of a figure in a fedora-style hat.

"You're getting married?" Zander asked, still standing there, holding his whiskey after his rebuffed hug attempt. "To who?"

"Whom," Drake automatically corrected, juggling his whiskey to unlock the door, but it was clear he didn't know the answer, either.

Then the front door swung open and the answer was there, standing inside Drake's doorway.

"Mr. Penny?" Drake asked in greeting, at the same time his mother blurted, "To Frank Penny."

"Good evening," said Mr. Penny—whose first name was apparently Frank, a fact Ryker had never known of the curmudgeonly neighbor. The older man beamed, his eyes taking in the tumblers of alcohol in everyone's hand. "Are we having a toast, then? To Patty! The woman of my dreams who said yes, making me the luckiest man alive. Cheers!"

With that, Frank Penny snatched the tumbler of whiskey from Drake's hand and downed it in one gulp.

* * *

The next hour and a half went by in a blur of loud talking, food, and, thankfully, very little standing. The muscles around Ryker's shinbone ached. His flesh was as swollen and fluid filled as if he'd eaten the sodium equivalent of ten double cheeseburgers and fries. Ryker yearned to remove the prosthesis, slide down the liner, and put his leg up to relieve the constant pain, but there was a virtual stranger in the room. Frank Penny kept giving him the side-eye as it was—definitely not a time to get comfortable.

"I had no idea you were seeing...my neighbor," Drake said, offering the man his seat on the couch before leaning against the fireplace. "As a writer, I need the backstory around how you two...got together."

His mom plopped down next to Frank on the sofa, which left only Ryker sitting next to the new couple. He scooted down to the farthest end of the leather couch, the black carbon blade on the end of his left leg still propped in what he hoped was a nonchalant way on the coffee table as his mom began to explain.

"We first started talking after that whole debacle with the town council, when they turned down Kate's permit request to allow the haunted maze and the mechanical spider for Drake's book launch for *Halloween Hacker*," his mom said. "Frank came into the café and I confronted him, mad as a hatter because it was his vote that influenced the other members to decline the permit. I felt he was responsible for ruining Kate's plans for Drake's big day, and—"

"And I explained I'd done it to protect your mother from embarrassment." Frank took over the story in the way couples did when they'd spent years finishing each other's sentences. Ryker resisted the urge to narrow his eyes at the man and saw that his brothers were doing the same. "After I spotted Drake and his party planner cavorting on his lawn, I was worried the whole book launch would be a debacle. I didn't want some redheaded harlot coming in and coordinating a ridiculous fiasco that would end up besmirching Patty's good name in town."

At the words "cavorting" and "redheaded harlot," Drake fixed Frank Penny with his fiercest scowl.

"That redhead you're maligning happens to be my wife. And the mother of my child. Call her a name again and I'll escort you out by the short and curly hairs of your—"

"Turns out, I was wrong about your party planner, and I'm not too proud to say it," Mr. Penny interrupted, with a nod of apology at Drake. "Your Kate is a lovely woman, and not a harlot at all."

Drake made a move toward the couch, and Zander smoothly inserted himself between his brother and the old man. He put a hand on Drake's shoulder, the gesture casual, but Ryker saw by the white tips of Zander's fingers that he was actually having to restrain his oldest brother.

"Well, I'm sure Kate will be thrilled she's off the harlot list." Zander gave his trademark easy laugh. "But let's talk more about you two. What, exactly, are your plans?"

As Ryker listened to his mom chatter about how they intended to spend winters in an as-yet-unpurchased property in Florida and summers in "Frankie's" house, he decided he wouldn't tell his family about his trip to Long Island. He knew damn well they'd all lurch into crisis mode when he said the words "PTSD" or "therapy dog." They always were in crisis mode for him, it seemed—Zander had lost almost an entire working year of his life being Ryker's coach at Walter Reed, and Drake had stood tall for him as creditor when he'd returned to civilian life. He didn't want to get their hopes up and have them dashed. It would be hard enough for him if he and the dog didn't bond—he was counting on this being the bridge he needed to fully engage in civilian life and be the man Bryce deserved. No. He wasn't going to tell his family. No need to let his stupid PTSD ruin his mom's celebration.

He'd just have to figure out how to leave town for a week without freaking them out.

That's where Tarun came in. His best friend could take him to Walter Reed and get him home without arousing too much suspicion. Tarun was always coming to town, whisking up Ryker and insisting they attend some Marine event or another. He'd pretend this was another one of those innocuous visits.

Soon the conversation about Mom and her new fiancé's relationship wound down. He caught Zander's eye and gave him a chin nod to show he was ready to make an exit.

"Well, congrats, Mom." Zander embraced their mother, then shook Mr. Penny's—Frank's—hand. "We gotta roll. Ryker's hit his level of social interaction tonight, and any more might send him into some sort of RBF attack."

For once, Ryker was thankful for Zander's goofiness. He pretended the wince he gave when he stood was due to his younger brother's smart mouth.

"Shut up, bro," he growled, because it was expected of him. He gave a nod to Mr. Penny and kissed his mom's cheek. "I'm heading out with Tarun tomorrow. Road trip for a few days. Marine stuff."

He walked toward the kitchen, his left leg feeling as though someone had taken a blowtorch to the end of his residual limb. His missing left ankle throbbed in time to his heartbeat.

"You sure you're okay, sweetheart?" His mom had crept up behind him as he'd followed Zander toward Drake's back door, where the Prius was parked by the carriage house garage. "You look like something's bothering you."

He kept his face forward. No way could he pull off this lie if he were meeting his mother's blue-eyed gaze. She had a built-in bullshit meter, and it would start to ping if she saw his face when he spoke.

"I'm just sore from jogging tonight. I'll be fine. Love you, Mom."

A text blipped on his phone as he made his way out of his grandparents' old house—the place Drake and Kate had made their own, filling it with so much love it seemed to glow from within—and as he climbed into Zander's Prius, he pulled it out.

It was Bryce.

Bryce: Hey there. Checking in to see if everything's okay?

Ryker looked at the text. How could he respond in a way that wouldn't worry her but wasn't a bald-faced lie? He wished for the millionth time he'd finished what he'd wanted to say when he was dressed in that god-awful Easter Bunny costume. Because then he'd have told her he felt the same about her. He grinned every time he thought about her, counted down the hours until he could see her at the café or on their run. Yanked his phone out of his coveralls with the expectation of every one of her texts. No doubt this woman was carving her way into his heart. But she had to know what she was signing up for. She'd said she wanted kids at Easter, and before they went further, deeper in this relationship, she deserved the truth about his probable sterility and about the realities of his life with PTSD. But there hadn't been a good opportunity to say what needed to be said. PattyCakes was always busy with customers, and telling her in between making sandwiches or ladling out soup orders wasn't cool. He'd consoled himself with the knowledge that they'd be alone when they jogged, and he'd planned to bring it up then.

But when he'd finally met up with her outside Imani's dance studio, Bryce was clearly so upset about the girls' parent-teacher conferences he'd let her talk first. Then he'd gotten caught up in figuring out how to help June— Zander was ridiculously good at science and history, and Ryker had been good at math—and in his head he was thinking of a possible tutoring arrangement. Thoughts of telling her about his years of radiation treatment and how they'd likely negatively impact his ability to ever father children had fled his mind, as had thoughts of telling her about his potential service dog for his PTSD.

He looked at her question. Telling her all of this via text didn't seem right, neither did telling her on the phone. They'd talk when he got back from Long Island, whether he got matched with a dog or not.

So thinking, he tapped out a neutral response with his thumbs, screwing up the spelling twice until he hit all the right keys.

Ryker: Just a family thing. I've got to head out of town for a few days. Marine business. I want to talk with you when I get back.

Bryce: Um, ok. Is it a hug emergency?

His heart chugged in his chest—she knew him. She sensed there were things he wanted to say.

He wanted, more than anything, to be with this woman. Maybe forever. But if they were going to be a real couple, she deserved to know what she was signing up for first. PTSD, therapy dog, potential sterility, and further surgery for his leg—that was all a conversation best left for when they were together.

Until then, he would do what Marines did best—endure. He would do the right thing by Bryce. He replied.

Ryker: Call you soon.

Then he pocketed his phone as Zander started the Prius. "Everything okay, dude?"

Ryker fixed his face. Forced his lips to curve on the ends, his best real-boy smile.

"Yep. Everything's great."

Zander snorted. "I'm not an idiot. Neither is Mom or Drake. We know something's up, and for your information, you'd make a crap spy. I saw your text to Tarun over your shoulder when I handed you the drink—the one you didn't touch tonight. A fact I also noticed."

"Do you notice what I'm doing now?" Ryker gave his brother the bird, dodging when Zander shot a playful punch in his direction. "What I do isn't any of your—"

"Business? Is that what you're going to say? Because I beg to differ. What you do is my business." Zander shook his head, his tone lowering. "I was with you all those weeks after your surgery, was the one helping put your ass on the throne every day as you recovered, and I know more than anyone how tough you are. And how that toughness makes you stupid."

Ryker snorted. "Stupid?"

"You let that hero cape flapping at your shoulders blind you to the fact that you aren't a superhero, and you aren't alone. Me, Drake, Mom—we're all your support network, just like you are part of ours. And it pisses me off when you shut us out of your life in some misguided attempt at, what? Saving us from worry?"

Was he that transparent? Probably. Ryker felt heat prickle the back of his neck and ears and was thankful his brother's gaze was on the dark streets.

"Why is that so bad?" Ryker finally asked, his tone sounding peevish even to his own ears.

"Because, you lunkhead, we love you." Zander pulled to a stop outside State Street Garage, his hand shooting out to grip Ryker's shoulder. "Tell me what's going on."

Ryker looked at Zander. The light hit his brother's face, highlighting the laugh lines as well as the worry grooves in his forehead. Although he could still see the little brother—the one who was gullible and goofy as a kid—lurking under the surface, what he saw now was the capable, caring man he'd become.

Suddenly, Ryker felt the heaviness of all that he'd been bottling up. It was like getting stuck under the bar with twenty more pounds than he could handle. He wouldn't hesitate to ask Zander for a spot, a hand in lifting that work-out weight off his chest. How was this any different?

So he began to talk, rewinding time to five months ago

when his leg had started to hurt and the increasing night terrors related to his PTSD. He told him about Tarun convincing him to finally apply for the Paws of War program, and about this week's unexpected opening in their training program.

"That's excellent news, bro." Zander clapped a hand on his shoulder. "Why are you stressing out, then?"

Ryker shook his head, gazing out the windshield of Zander's Prius at the moths frantically flapping around the streetlight. His chest felt tight, like the emotions inside him were as confused and aimless as the moths.

"It feels so high stakes. I...I want Bryce. I want how I feel when I'm with her and her nieces. I want to be someone's everything without the constant fear. I want to function in a grocery store, in a busy café, without my hands sweating, and my mouth tasting like sand and regret." Ryker met Zander's gaze, surprising himself with how good it felt to empty his bucket of worries. "Matching with this dog might be the miracle I need to function again as a civilian."

Zander's mouth lifted in a smile. "And even if it isn't, spending this week in therapy with a dog is a massive step for you, man. You're taking time away to focus on you. Finally, you've discovered what we've known all along."

"What?" Ryker asked, half expecting a joke.

"That you're worth it."

Ryker swallowed the sudden lump in his throat. After a moment, he forced himself to tell Zander the rest.

"I've been struggling to find the right words to tell Bryce about everything all night—no, since we slept together this past weekend," he said, putting up a hand to forestall

Zander's surprised exclamation, "a relationship fact which you will not be repeating. To anyone."

"It's not my news to share," Zander said. "But for the record, I think you should call Bryce. Tell her what's rattling around in that jarhead of yours. Explain why you're motivated to work on your PTSD and the side effects of your HO prevention. Tell her how you feel. All of it."

The thought of calling her—saying all of that again—made his palms sweat. Suddenly, his cell phone buzzed. Pulling it out of his pocket, he read Bryce's last message, then showed Zander the string of recent texts.

Bryce: Is there anything I can do to help?

Ryker: Negative.

Bryce: Travel safe.

Ryker grimaced, taking in the time on his cell phone. The girls would be in bed, and knowing how early Bryce had to get up, she'd likely be asleep.

"She seems okay with everything. Besides, it's too late to get into the rest of it tonight. I'll call tomorrow after I get to the training center," Ryker said, but the thought made his chest constrict. "Or maybe I'll wait until I get back home. Just tell her it's Marine stuff and leave the rest for later."

Zander shook his head. "Whatever you think, dude, but in my experience, bad things happen when you don't communicate. Speaking of which, what are you telling Mom and Drake?"

"Nothing. Seriously, man," Ryker pleaded. "The story is: I'm with Tarun on Marine business. It's not entirely a lie, and it's all the truth they currently need. No reason to tie everyone in knots, especially if I don't match with a service dog. The disappointment will be easier if nobody knows. Okay?"

Zander's expression conveyed his disappointment. "Let the record state I'm against this, but okay. Your news, your rules."

"It'll be fine," Ryker said, and hoped the confidence in his tone made it a reality.

CHAPTER 18

But why can't I wear *my* wings onstage?" Addison whined as they headed to the Nancy Howe Auditorium for Saturday's dance recital rehearsal. While this rehearsal was for the younger dance groups, June was riding along, because where else was the older girl going? The Paynes had a golf tournament, and Bryce couldn't leave June at the apartment alone. Who knew how many ways that could be twisted against her in court? It seemed cruel to hire a babysitter for a twelve-year-old, so June sat slouched in the passenger seat glaring alternately at her aunt, then down at her phone.

"You can't wear fairy wings because you're a butterfly in the dance," Bryce explained for the millionth time. "Your costume has special wings, Addie. You're going to be beautiful."

Bryce turned onto Main Street. These past days had been a test of her as a person, as a caregiver, and as a chef. She was exhausted. Her body was in a dead sprint from the moment Addison crawled into bed with her at five a.m., until she finished helping June with homework and figured out next week's buying and menus for PattyCakes, around midnight. As a result, she was spacey, forgetting yesterday to add seasoning to her soups, and she struggled to keep the girls' schedules straight. As a result, neither Addison nor Cecily was wearing the right color tights for rehearsal, and Bryce dreaded the judgy-mom looks she knew were coming her way.

Guilt and a sense of failure seemed to be Bryce's constant companions, and she felt as though a horrible storm system had settled over her. She wished for something to blow it all away, letting the sun shine on her again.

To top it off, she hadn't heard from Ryker since his mysterious texts Thursday night about having to go out of town. Granted, it had only been two days, and it wasn't like they'd officially defined their relationship. He was under no obligation to explain himself.

She'd asked Patty about it this morning at work.

"Where's Ryker?" Bryce ignored the way her face flamed in a blush. "He hasn't texted or called since Thursday, and I was hoping everything was okay."

Patty told her about the surprise engagement announcement as they finished piping the frosting on her Butterscotch Bliss cupcakes. After accepting Bryce's congratulations, the older woman patted her on the arm. "I think my engagement to Frank was a shock to all my boys. In retrospect, maybe I should've told them we were dating, but I wasn't sure how they'd react. It could be that he left town to come to grips with this. But more likely, Ryker had this trip with Tarun planned in advance—they're always taking off to meet up with Marine buddies. You should call him. He's very taken with you, and I'm thrilled. He deserves happiness with someone as wonderful as you."

While part of her was cheering that Patty approved

of their relationship, Bryce's mind went to Ryker's PTSD moment in the garage.

"Is he . . . is he okay?"

Patty paused before answering. "He says he's fine."

Then the café had gotten busy and she hadn't had the chance to ask her boss further questions. But Bryce got the distinct impression that Patty was withholding information. As she escorted the girls into the auditorium, Bryce brightened. Maybe Imani had the scoop from Zander? The two brothers were very close.

"Hey, do you know where Ryker is?" Bryce asked as her friend—dressed in a floaty dancer's skirt over a black leotard—came gliding over to hug her in greeting.

"Your guess is as good as mine." Imani grinned at the girls, reassuring Addison her wings were backstage and ready to be perched on her cute shoulders soon. Then she gave Bryce a side look. Her chocolate-colored eyes were a little wider than normal—the only sign the dance teacher was stressed. "Zander's being all cryptic. When I asked if Ryker would be here to run lights, all he'd say was I'd need to get someone else because Ryker was doing something therapy-related out of town. But I heard through the grapevine that he's canceled his garage appointments next week. I thought you might know why he disappeared?"

Bryce swallowed at the words.

Did his disappearance have anything to do with her? Or what she'd said? Also, what therapy required a whole week?

Realizing Imani had stresses of her own, Bryce changed the subject.

"If you still need someone to run lights, June is amazing

with technology, and she's a quick learner. She mastered the
cash register in five minutes when Willow taught her at
the café. June would rock the sound and light job. I mean,
if she wants to?"

She winced, realizing belatedly she'd put June on the
spot. But June's eyes lit up, and she beamed first at Bryce,
then at Imani.

"Um, sure. I'll try."

Imani's relief was palpable. "Oh, June, thank you. I'll
pay you—same as I would have paid Ryker. I'll take you up
and show you how everything works. Just let me tell the
dance moms where I'm going."

Imani hustled off, and June gave Bryce a shy glance.

"Did you really mean that, Aunt Beamer?"

"What? That you're a quick learner and good at tech?
Yeah. You remind me of...of your dad. You're so freaking
smart and pick things up quickly, like he did." Bryce
hugged her niece around the shoulders, elated when she
didn't pull away. "You're an incredible kid."

June's happy expression vanished. "I'm not a kid."

Before Bryce could apologize, Imani raced back to them,
her gauzy black dancer's skirt streaming like a banner
behind her.

"Okay, let's go. You can practice using the spotlight as
we position the classes..."

As they left, Bryce kicked herself, vowing to do better in
showering June more with her heartfelt compliments.

But at the moment she had two little girls who were
racing around the auditorium, playing a game of tag that
involved scaling the theater-style seats and riding them
down as they went from closed to open.

"Weatherford girls, follow me." She snapped her fingers but finally had to grab them both to get them to stop surfing the seats.

Bryce guided her nieces to the prep area, where a team of moms were set up, assembly-line fashion, to put up the girls' hair in identical buns and makeup. She sat Addison down with a mom doing hair, and then had to practically drag Cecily to the makeup station.

"I don't like makeup," Cecily grouched. "It's too girly."

"It's so they can see your face under the bright stage lights." Bryce grunted as she wrestled with her niece. "Have a seat."

Reluctantly, Cecily sat down in front of Mrs. Foltz, Imani's grandmother, who all the dancers called Ms. Gigi. The older woman was dressed in a zebra-print shirt, her hair done in orderly gray-blond curls over her head.

"That you, Cecily? Don't think I've ever seen you clean. I like it. Now, let's put some greasepaint on you, shall we?"

"Greasepaint?" At the phrase, Cecily's resistance melted away. "I thought it was makeup?"

Gigi snorted. "I call it what it is. This stuff's the same consistency my late husband used when he'd camouflage his face to hunt turkey. You'll have a devil of a time getting it off. Tomorrow morning when you get up, it'll look like you got into a brawl with a pack of wolves."

Cecily brightened. "Can you put it on extra heavy, Ms. Gigi? I want to be the greasiest, paint-iest one onstage."

"You got it." Mrs. Foltz winked, and Bryce escaped before her niece changed her mind.

Since Imani had a bazillion adult helpers, Bryce wasn't needed until pickup, so she headed back to her apartment.

It was the first free two-hour stretch of time she'd had since the Paynes had taken the girls before Easter, and she found herself wishing Ryker was around. She missed being with him, watching him work on his latest car renovation, or having him help chop veggies in his slow, methodical way. A good hour in bed with him would've been amazing as well.

But he'd disappeared, apparently for something therapy related. Did his therapy crisis have something to do with her? What else could it be? Maybe he was getting fitted for a new prosthetic? But why would that be all secret and covert?

Bryce knew she could obsess about it for hours, but luckily she had mountains of distractions. First up was a call with her lawyer in preparation for the guardianship trial soon after she returned from working at Niagara Falls as a guest chef for Cascade.

"Are you sure you're ready to do this in two weeks?" asked Lillian Goodwin in her no-nonsense court voice. "Because things are bound to get messy with the Paynes. They will come with their guns blazing. I expect they'll use the babysitter snafu and the girls' bad grades against you. Also, the Attorney for the Children is getting mixed messages from June as to where she wants to go—with you, or with their grandparents."

Steeling herself against the sting of betrayal, Bryce spoke with grim determination.

"I don't doubt it. This transition, coupled with her roller-coaster teen angst, has been hard on June. The girls are still reeling from losing their parents. The counselor says it's normal for them to lash out and resent me." Bryce fought against the knot in her throat. "I've had a steep learning curve, going from a single woman to a caregiver for three, and I know I've made mistakes. But nobody—not even the Paynes—can deny I've worked my ass off and tried my best. I love my nieces. And both Bentley and Heather named me as guardian in their will, not the Paynes. That should count for something."

"Of course," Lillian replied in her crisp, calm voice. "The burden is on the Paynes to show extraordinary circumstances on why they have a superior right to guardianship, or prove you're deficient enough to disregard the wishes of the deceased. The goal of the trial is to determine what is in the best interest for the children."

Bryce winced at the word "deficient" but made sure her voice was calm when she replied. "I know they have a longer history with the girls, as they lived here while I was in Florida, and they'll use the fact they're more financially stable against me. But after the funeral, Adele and Harvey have only had the girls a total of . . . what? Seventeen days, and only two overnights? I've been the one shouldering the daily tasks. By myself. We're going to point that out to the judge, right?"

"By the time of the trial, they'll have had them while you're at the Niagara Falls job, so we'll increase that number of days to twenty-four, but, yes," her lawyer said, "we will use math to our advantage. However, a good counterargument is that they didn't feel they could ask for more time with the girls, or that you displayed hostility toward them having their grandchildren."

Her breath whooshed out as she realized Lillian was right. They *would* use that argument. Worse, it was true.

Images of arguing with the Paynes at Easter came to mind, and Bryce grimaced at what they could use against her in the trial. She laughed half-heartedly.

"You don't suppose it would help if I treat the whole Surrogate's Court to an amazing lunch of homemade soup and sandwiches, do you?"

True to form, Lillian Goodwin, Esquire, never broke character. "No. That won't help. You'll catch a charge if you try to bribe the judge."

Emotions boiled in her chest, and Bryce held it together until she'd finished the call with her lawyer and pulled into the back of PattyCakes.

Then Bryce let out a howl that echoed inside the BMW. "Whyyyy? Why is everything so hard?"

Her phone pinged with a new voicemail message.

Ryker.

"Hey, uh..." He paused, as if wrestling with what to say. "I just wanted to call. If I don't talk to you before you leave, drive safe. Good luck in Niagara Falls. Knock 'em dead."

That was it.

Growling in frustration, she tried to call back, but she was sent to voicemail.

She texted, instead.

Bryce: Sorry I missed your call. Was on with my lawyer about the trial. Is everything okay?

She really wanted to type *Are we okay?* but her insecurity prevented her from asking.

An hour later, Ryker finally replied with a yellow thumbs-up emoji. Nothing else.

Fortunately, she was so busy with prepping for Patty-Cakes, packing the girls' suitcase for their time with the Paynes, washing up her white chef's coats for her time at Cascade, that she didn't have time to obsess over his terse reply. The hours flew by, and suddenly it was nine o'clock and she was rushing the girls into pajamas and bed. Giving them strict instructions to stay put, she ran downstairs to ladle the extra soups she'd made into freezer-safe containers, all neatly labeled for Patty to use while she was gone. She hurried, knowing she'd left her suitcase for Niagara Falls half packed and she still had emails to write to her catering clients. She was loading the freezer when she heard running footsteps and shrieking giggles from upstairs.

"Addie and Cici, I hear you. Get to bed!" she hollered to the ceiling, listening as the giggling grew hushed. "I mean it!"

Scampering footsteps headed in the direction of the girls' bedroom, and she heard the sound of their door slamming. The laughter and giggles continued, but she figured if they were in their bedroom, they were fine.

Shutting the freezer, Bryce headed to the café's makeshift office for the list she'd scribbled on a piece of notebook paper. Harvey and Adele had asked her to write down the girls' schedules outside of school, and Bryce was doing her best to give the grandparents every tip she'd learned. Much as she might hope the week was tough for the Paynes, in her heart she wanted her nieces to enjoy their spring break. They deserved this good time. Bryce nibbled on the pen, considering her scrawled list she'd written like a recipe.

INGREDIENTS FOR THE BEST POSSIBLE WEEK:

- 1 set of fairy wings on Addison at all times. Tell her they need to rest at night, and put them to bed next to her.
- Cici's Lava soap is in her bag. Nobody else is allowed to use it but her. Say this often for the best results.
- Read the little girls *Peter Pan* before bed, using different voices for Peter, Wendy, Hook, etc. The more dramatic you make it, the better they sleep.
- 1 pull-up on Addison before bed.
- Make June put her phone on the charger in the kitchen, or she'll doom scroll all night.
- Be sure June brings her small backpack with her at all times.

She'd debated being a little clearer with the last point—if her calculations were right, June should be getting her second-ever period while Bryce was away. She'd already reminded her oldest niece about the timing, telling her to bring her small backpack with her period supplies everywhere, just in case. But she decided not to be explicit in the last bullet, to avoid angering or embarrassing June if she saw the note.

She tapped the pen against the paper, trying to think of any other tips. She'd packed the girls' school workbooks and homework assignments due at the end of break, including June's three-page paper for language arts. She debated on detailing exactly what needed to be done, by girl, but then figured it was overkill. The Paynes had raised a child—they'd see the schoolbooks and ask the obvious questions.

She added one last point:

- Be sure to run them around during the day for at least an hour, or they get squirrelly. Call me whenever you need me, and tell the girls I'll check in with them every day.

Bryce folded the paper and stuffed it into her pocket to add it to the girls' bag later. Then she tackled the rest of the pile on the desk. As part of teaching her how to run the café, Patty had delegated paying the invoices to Bryce, and she also had to order food for the following week. She wondered for the millionth time if working in Niagara Falls during her paid vacation from PattyCakes was worth the extra money, a worry she'd voiced to Imani when she'd picked up the girls after recital practice.

"Maybe I should give up the Cascade gig and stay in town while the Paynes watch the girls so I can get caught up?" Bryce had said as she crammed her nieces and their dance gear into her BMW. Her small car was jam-packed with Addie's booster seat and the girls, but a larger vehicle was definitely not in the budget. "I mean, it's almost a vanity thing to go and be their saucier. It's not like I'm résumé building at this point."

"No, you need this time for you." Imani's tone had rung with certainty. "I used to go hard at life, or, as Gigi says, 'Full-Tilt-Boogie,' so often it became a health hazard. I suffered from panic attacks, and my anxiety was through the roof. I'm thankful I took that time away from my job to help Gigi recover from knee surgery, because it forced me to take some time for myself. You loved being a saucier, so this is like self-care for you."

Now, as Bryce paid the bills, she told herself Imani was right. She began to look forward to the time alone. It would be amazing to just cook all day. She could even use the time as a detox from her feelings toward Ryker—she'd obviously been the one who'd fallen first, but maybe after she returned she could put some context to that. Maybe she'd fallen for him because he was the ideal problem solver. The ultimate fixer. The man who excelled at doing that superhero thing, flying in to solve a crisis and whisk her and the girls out of danger.

She definitely needed a reset, because Ryker hadn't reached out again. She recognized that dating a girl in the midst of a dumpster fire was one thing, loving one was quite another. He just wasn't there yet. Although that thought gutted her, maybe what she needed was time to process this? Surely if her feelings were real, she'd be willing to wait until—

Suddenly, there was a massive thump overhead.

Then Addison gave an unearthly shriek.

She'd heard the girls scream enough times to discern the difference between when it was in play or for real.

This yell was real—Addison was hurt.

Bryce was already sprinting to the stairs as a twin shriek split the air. Cecily. She sounded scared. But it was June's wail that injected the final burst of adrenaline into Bryce's steps.

Heart pounding, Bryce threw open the door and flew down the hall to the little girls' room. She halted.

Lying in the middle of the floor was Addison.

She was dressed in her yellow Tinker Bell nightgown, her eyes wide as she clutched her leg.

"Oh my god, what happened?" Bryce's knees bashed

into the hardwood floors as she dove to gather Addison in her arms.

As she held her, Bryce noticed two things at once: Addison's leg was buckled oddly below the knee. It was puffy and bulged in a way that meant more than a bruise.

Addison had broken her leg.

Bile filled Bryce's mouth, and she wanted to scream. Instead, she pushed Addison's hair from her eyes. "Looks like a pretty good boo-boo on your leg. Did you fall?"

"She thought she could fly and she jumped from the top of the bunk bed." Cecily's face was the color of skim milk as she wrung her hands. "I told her not to."

Cecily burst into loud, braying tears.

Bryce fumbled in her pocket for her cell, but she'd left it downstairs.

Bryce looked at her oldest niece. "June, it's first-aid time. Find two strong, straight things—long wooden spoons, rulers, whatever—and grab the girls' tights so we can make a quick splint."

June nodded and vanished.

Bryce turned to Cecily, who was wailing louder than Addison.

"Cici, stop crying. I need you to be brave and help your sister." Bryce waited until Cecily had calmed enough to listen. "Go grab my phone from Patty's desk in the café. We need to call Nana and Pop-Pop to ask them to watch you while I take Addie to the hospital."

Cecily dashed away, her sobs jittery as she took the stairs down to the restaurant level.

"Hospital? I don't wanna go to the hospital," Addison cried.

"Shh, it's okay Addie-bell. We're going to visit the doctor, who will make it all better." She held the tiny girl close, feeling her small body shake in her arms. Bryce snagged the blanket from the bottom bunk to wrap around her thin shoulders.

"Aunt Beamer," Addie sobbed against her chest, her fists bunched in the fabric of her T-shirt. "I thought my invisible wings were ready to fly, but they didn't work, and now it hurrrrrrts! Can I have a princess Band-Aid?"

"I'll bet the doc has really neat Band-Aids. Does anything else hurt except your leg? Did you hit your head?"

Addison shook her head. "No. I flew for only a minute, then I crashed on my leg."

Bryce held her, making soothing noises until June raced in, eyes wild as she held a wooden spoon and a metal ladle. "Will these work?"

"Perfect." With remarkably steady hands, Bryce wound the girls' dance tights around Addison's leg, bolstered by the ladle on one side, the girls' hardcover copy of *Peter Pan* underneath, and the wooden spoon stabilizing the other side. It had been decades since she'd been a Girl Scout, but she recalled the makeshift splints they'd made out of sticks and bandanas at camp. She went as gently as possible, yet Addison sobbed.

Cecily came in with Bryce's cell, holding it out. "I called Nana and Pop-Pop, and they want to talk to you."

"What happened?" Adele's greeting was frantic as Bryce motioned for Cecily to hold the phone while she slipped a sweater over Addison's pajamas.

Cecily spoke first. "Addie jumped from the top of the bunk bed 'cause she thought she could fly. Now her leg has a bad bump, but Aunt Beamer put a spoon and dance tights on it, so it'll be okay."

"What? A spoon? What is going on?" Harvey yelled, as if he thought they were having trouble hearing them. "Someone get your Aunt Bryce on the phone."

"I'm here, Harvey." Bryce grunted, picking up Addison. "Addie jumped off the bunk bed, and she may have...broken her leg. Can you watch Cecily and June while I take Addison to the hospital?"

Addison screamed again, and June stroked her sister's hair, fat tears rolling down her cheeks. Her oldest niece said nothing, but the look she gave her aunt—part horror, part accusation—spoke volumes.

"What?" Adele's voice. "Where were you? How did it happen?"

Bryce carried Addison carefully down the hallway, waves of guilt crashing around her. "I was in the restaurant finishing up the bills. I was gone for ten minutes. They were in bed—I put them to bed first."

The excuses sounded lame, even to her own ears. There was a shuffling noise, then Harvey spoke.

"I'll call Pastor Stan and his wife to see if they'll watch the girls. We'll meet you at the hospital." He disconnected.

"I don't want to go with Pastor Stan," June said, immediately. "I want to stay with Addie. I took first aid. I can help."

"I want to help, too," Cecily said.

"The way you can help is to find my purse and car keys. They should be on my dresser."

"I want my wings," Addison managed between sobs.

By the time she made it downstairs with Addison, June

and Cecily were racing behind with her purse, keys, and Addison's fairy wings. They helped load their sister into the BMW for the ride to the hospital.

Pastor Stan and his wife met them in the parking lot, with Harvey and Adele, the latter of whom immediately took charge, ushering an angry June and weeping Cecily into the back of the pastor's car.

"I bet you're gonna get a really cool cast," Cecily said, hanging out of the car window.

"I want to be the first one to sign it, okay?" June said, glowering once more at her grandparents and Bryce before being driven away.

"Only..." Addison's voice was quavery as the ER attendants loaded her into a wheelchair. "I don't want to get a cast all alone. You'll come with me, right, Aunt Beamer?"

"Let them try and stop me." Bryce fervently hoped they'd let her be with her niece the whole time. "We'll make sure they patch you up good as new."

Addison gave a mewling cry. "It hurts. I want Mommy and Daddy. Why won't they fly down from heaven and help me, Aunt Beamer? Why?"

How was she supposed to answer that question? She glanced over at Harvey and Adele, but their faces were just as pained.

Bryce finally opted for words she hoped a five-year-old might understand.

"I know they're watching over you, and that they love you very, very much. Just like I do." Gripping her niece's hand, she rushed into the ER. "It's all going to be okay."

And she prayed she was right.

* * *

Sitting in the wretched peach-tinted waiting room at Jones Memorial Hospital waiting for Addison to get out of X-ray was the longest half hour of Bryce's life. The intake process, with the online forms to complete, the insurance cards to drag out, and the initial examination from an ER doc, had taken over an hour, then they were told they had to wait for an orthopedic consult and the X-ray. Thankfully, Bryce and the Paynes had been able to be with Addison the whole time, holding her hand and comforting her, until the X-ray, when they'd all been shuttled to a waiting room.

If her own guilt weren't a heavy enough burden, the accusatory looks Harvey and Adele threw her way practically buried her under the weight of their judgment and scorn.

"For heaven's sake, I wonder how much longer they're going to be with her. She's only a baby," Adele wailed to the waiting room, which was empty except for the three of them.

"She's five. And she's tough," Bryce said, more to reassure herself than to contradict Adele. "The orthopedic doctor needs to see if the fracture was displaced enough to require surgery, or if they have to reduce the fracture under anesthesia."

Both of those options sounded scary, and while Bryce didn't understand medical lingo, she was pretty sure the phrase "reduce the fracture" meant they'd push the hell out of the bone to get it to line up before casting it into place. Yet as rough as that sounded, it had to be better than cutting her niece open. Didn't it?

Worries swirled through her, and it seemed as though

they'd been in this hospital purgatory for endless days, but the clock on the wall ticked only a smidge more than two hours after a sobbing Addison had been wheeled inside the ER. Even though she said her left leg felt like she'd been stung by a bazillion bees, her tears had finally dried up, although she'd been mad the tech wouldn't let her wear her fairy wings in the X-ray.

The wings now lay across Bryce's lap. The yellow left wing was still holding strong, albeit a bit grimy around the edges, but the right wing—where it had broken and Bryce had slid on a pair of nude pantyhose, using some electrical tape to secure it all together—looked like a frightful, Frankenstein'd piece of trash.

Tears pooled in Bryce's eyes, a few escaping to drip down her cheeks.

Why, oh why hadn't she bought her new fairy wings? The poor girl had been running around with nude panty-hose stretched on a frame, affixed by black electrical tape— and Bryce couldn't find five minutes to order the kid another set?

As if reading her mind, Adele spoke.

"We bought Addison a new pair of wings at our house. We thought she'd be happy to have pretty new ones, considering those have gone around the bend a few times." Adele's words jabbed Bryce.

"The white ones she wore at Easter were new, but they got splattered with yuck," Bryce retorted, then because she was feeling guilty, she threw them a conversational bone. "I haven't bought others because I've been hoping to wean her off them. She jumped tonight because she insists she's growing invisible wings...ones that'll let her fly to heaven to visit Heather and Bentley. I'd...I'd love your help talking to her about angels, and how we won't see any."

"But I believe we will," Adele said. "We will see them both in heaven."

Bryce fought the urge to roll her eyes.

"That's not what I meant. I thought you could explain we can't fly like angels, no matter how long you wear wings." Bryce worked at her voice being level. "They might understand your explanation better than mine."

They sat in silence, taking turns staring at the door or at the room's clock. Then Harvey spoke, his voice gentle.

"We'd like you to reconsider us having the girls full time. As their guardian. Perhaps this accident with Addison is a sign that guardianship is too much right now. You're a young single woman." Harvey's face wasn't accusatory but earnest. "You've done your best, but maybe with this job in Niagara Falls, you'll have another door opening for you. Adele and I are ready to be the girls' full-time guardians, which would allow you to live your life."

Bryce wanted to shoot back *I am living my life. And this is what Bentley and your daughter wanted—me as their guardian, not you two.* But she refrained. Much as she didn't want to admit it, a part of her missed her old life. This internal conflict must have shown on her face, because Adele spoke up, her face growing soft with kindness.

"Please, just think about it. We don't meet with the judge until after you return from Niagara Falls. Wouldn't it be nice—more peaceful for everyone—if we came to the trial wanting the same thing?"

Left unspoken was that the judge would hear about this broken leg and the fact that Bryce was in another part of the building when it had happened. While no parent was realistically with their wards every minute of every day, this accident had happened on her watch. Nothing she said would change those basic facts.

Then the door opened and a petite woman in a white coat entered, heading to Harvey and Adele.

"I'm Kiersten Sweet, the medical student on rotation with Dr. Morelli. Are you Addison Weatherford's guardians?"

"Yes," Adele and Harvey said, and Bryce's face went hot as she cleared her throat.

"Technically, I'm her legal guardian at the moment. They are her grandparents." Bryce stepped over and shook Kiersten Sweet's hand. The med student had a strong grip and wore her dark brown hair cut in a shoulder-brushing bob. Yet something about her face looked familiar. Maybe she'd come into the restaurant? "I'm Bryce Weatherford, and Addison is my niece and ward. How's she doing?"

"Oh, Bryce." The woman's face brightened. "You're the woman my sister, Kate—Kate Sweet-Matthews—told me makes the best soups in town. Your niece is fine, and I have good news. Dr. Morelli was able to get her fractured tibia aligned without having to take her to the operating room. You're welcome to come be with her as they cast her leg."

As they followed Kiersten out of the waiting room and down the hall, Bryce ventured a question. "How long will she be in a cast? Does she—can she walk on it?"

"She's non-weight-bearing right now. Dr. Morelli will give you more details, but the break was clean and, given time, will heal with no issues." Kiersten chuckled. "Also, your niece has charmed the socks off everyone.

She's wheedled her way into a rainbow-colored cast, which requires five different boxes of colored fiberglass material to be opened and is *never* done. But your niece has a way about her. She's delightful, and you should be so proud."

"When can we take her home?" Harvey asked. "I'm guessing she'll need to be in a place without stairs, correct?"

The woman shrugged. "Stairs are a definite no for a few days until she learns how to get around on her crutches."

"Then she'll recuperate at our place." Harvey sounded smug, and Bryce resisted the urge to glare at him. "We have a ranch-style house with no stairs. That would be best, wouldn't it?"

"For now," Kiersten agreed, and Bryce felt as though the universe was conspiring against her. But when the door to the casting room opened, Bryce pushed aside her mounting despair. She visualized the Bentley wings tattooed on her lower back and reminded herself of her brother's belief in her.

And she tried to ignore the mounting evidence showing he might have been wrong.

CHAPTER 19

Although Ryker had meant to call Bryce on Friday as soon as he'd checked in to the hotel, the drive from Wellsville to Smithtown had taken hours longer than expected with the heavy Long Island weekend traffic. As soon as he and Tarun had downed a couple of burgers for dinner and gotten into their respective rooms, Ryker had flipped on ESPN, dropped into bed, and immediately fallen asleep. Saturday proved even harder for him to carve out time for a call to Bryce. The morning flew in a whirlwind of paperwork and orientation classes at the Paws of War training center with other vets and first responders who, like him, were getting a service dog. They spent all day learning what to expect from their dog, dos and don'ts, and got to meet and chat with several area vets who'd already been matched with dogs and heard their experiences and words of wisdom.

"I'd plateaued in my recovery with my psychiatrist, and I battled PTSD, as well as my TBI," one young Army vet said, referring to his traumatic brain injury received in combat. "The statistics are that almost twenty veterans take their lives every single day—double the rate of civilians— and while they tell you here that the dog isn't a cure-all for everything, it's been nine months since I matched with Liberty. And I credit this dog for me being here today. I can go out in crowds without the anxiety, my night terrors have lessened—this guy wakes me up before they escalate—and I'm off all medication except for aspirin."

Ryker watched the veteran, a stocky, tough-looking man in an Army sweatshirt who stood in the center of the gymnasium-like space as Liberty nudged at his hand. The guy's stoic expression softened as he reached down to stroke the flanks of his brindle Rottweiler–Jack Russell mix. The dog had a scar crisscrossing his face from above his eye to the side of his snout.

"Liberty was taken from a group that operated a dog-fighting ring. This dog was used as bait to train bigger, fiercer dogs. It makes me sick to think what he went through," the man said, and the dog head-butted his thigh until the Army vet reached down to pet him again, his hands caressing the dog's ears as the Rotty mix panted and turned his grinning face back to the crowd. "Just there, Liberty sensed my anxiety, and he's trained to head-butt me, or lick my hands, even jump up on my chest, until I pet him, which in turn eases my stress. It's true what they say here—their work helps on both ends of the leash."

Ryker's heart squeezed at their obvious bond. Sunday—tomorrow—he and the other vets in his orientation class would meet their dogs, and see if they matched. He'd never wanted anything so badly in his life.

After Saturday's session, he and Tarun had stuck around, chatting with the vets who'd come that day to pay it forward to the organization. He'd forgotten all about his phone, having put it on silent for the day of training, and it wasn't until he was in his room after showering that night that he pulled it out. In addition to texts from Zander, Drake, and his mom, all variations of "Hope everything is okay," he saw that he had a missed call and a text from Bryce.

Bryce's text said she'd been on the phone with her lawyer discussing the upcoming guardianship trial and hadn't been able to answer his earlier call. She finished by asking if everything was okay and, knowing her plate was full, he'd sent her a thumbs-up—the same response he'd sent to the rest of his family. He wanted to call Bryce back, but a glance at the clock showed it was past midnight. He knew she was driving to Niagara Falls in the morning and he didn't want to chance waking her—she had a busy day with dropping the girls at their grandparents', then hitting the road for the almost-three-hour drive.

Instead, hoping to be that bright spot in her Sunday morning before she left for Niagara Falls, he sent her a mechanic joke before bed.

What's the name of every mechanic's favorite movie?...Lord of the Springs. Drive safe.

He'd woken once, jerking with a start at the sound of a car alarm in the parking lot, panic gripping his lungs until he finally recalled where he was, and he drifted in and out of sleep until his phone alarm went off. He'd barely gotten dressed when Tarun was at his door.

"Wakey-wakey," his buddy said, giving his outfit of jeans, a T-shirt, and Bills ball cap a once-over as he walked in. "You ready to roll? I picked us up some bagels. Because no way in hell am I drinking some protein drink of yours this morning."

"Ready." Ryker followed him out to the truck, a smile turning the corners of his mouth as he thought that Bryce would absolutely agree with his Marine buddy. He flipped his phone over to confirm—no further texts from Bryce. No news meant good news, right?

"Your mom called me this morning demanding to know where we were," Tarun said as Ryker started the car and plugged in the directions for the Paws of War training center, and he was so surprised he choked on his bite of bagel. Tarun laughed, clapping him on the back. "You didn't warn me that this mission was covert, but I covered for your ass, anyway. I told her we were in Long Island."

Ryker waited until he'd pulled out and was on his way to the training center before asking, "Did you tell her why?"

Tarun shrugged. "I always stay as close to the truth as possible. I said we were checking out some therapy options. Today is the big day. When are you going to tell your family? And Bryce? Trust me, man. Texting and voicemails are relationship napalm. If this woman means something to you—and by the way you were talking about her on the way up here, she clearly does—you need to call her. Tell her what's going on. That way, nothing is lost in translation."

Ryker nodded. "You're right. I'll try her at lunch—she should be in Niagara Falls by that time and maybe I can catch her before she goes in to work. At that point, maybe I'll know if the dog . . . likes me, or whatever."

Tarun rolled his eyes. "When did you get so dramatic? It's going to be fine. I'll stick around to see your new mate, then I have a car coming to take me to the airport and back to work."

Ryker put his truck in park, noting that the place was jammed with cars, vets, men and women in civilian clothes, and people holding leashes with dogs everywhere. "Thanks for coming with me. Putting up with my bullshit."

"I'm honored to be here for this, man." Tarun grabbed his duffel and opened the door. "Let's go meet your match."

Ryker squared his shoulders and entered the facility behind the main offices. Tarun gave him a salute as he went to sit on the metal bleachers they had set up for family and friends to watch the ownership ceremony, while Ryker joined the other vets who'd been asked to sit in a line of chairs in the middle of the vast space. He sat, gazing at the opposite wall, where a bunch of men and women stood with dogs on leashes whose harnesses were exactly alike: blue with white stars and red piping along the sides, with the words "Service Dog—Do Not Pet" emblazoned on the harness as well as on the leashes themselves.

There were seven dogs, some breeds recognizable and some not so much. He saw a muscular German shepherd, two dogs that had the same blocky, massive head as a Rottweiler, a furry golden retriever, two others that appeared to be some combination of Labrador, and one squatty little fellow who looked like he had corgi blood.

Ryker watched as the dogs sniffed either each other or the floor, or nosed up against their handler. All except one. The golden retriever. She sat still as a statue at the feet of a thin, middle-aged man, completely calm but alert. Unlike the other dogs, whose trainers had their leashes in hand, the golden held the end of the leash in her own mouth, as if preparing to walk herself to the next destination.

Ryker grinned. He did love an independent woman who

knew her own mind. He gazed at the dog, and he swore she met his eyes. Her golden coloring was lighter in a triangular shape around her dark eyes, like blond eyebrows, and when combined with her mouth open in that retriever smile, it created the impression that she was gazing at him with delight.

"What a sweetheart you are," he said under his breath.

Although it was impossible the golden heard him from this distance, her tail wagged, thwapping against the feet of her handler.

Breaking eye contact, Ryker made himself study the other dogs. It wouldn't do to fall in love with some dog that wasn't meant to be his. The shepherd looked like a tough dog who'd be thrilled to join him on any run, and he could see any of the Labs or Rotty mixes fitting right in with the dirty hands, grease, and grime of his garage. Even the corgi guy, with his squatty little legs, would be easy to love, although he'd likely have to lift him in and out of his truck.

He half listened as the owner of Paws of War, a tall woman with her hair in a clip, spoke about the organization, touting all the facts he'd read about before applying, and were reiterated in yesterday's orientation.

"About one million shelter animals are put down every year, and it's estimated that almost three hundred thousand vets suffer from PTSD. While the math is in our favor, the funds and outreach are not," she said, ending her fundraising appeal with a gesture to the dogs at the side of the gymnasium-like space and the vets sitting in a line in the middle. "While service dogs are a holistic approach and not a cure-all, we know from experience that these honorable

men and women will benefit from this relationship immediately, as will these dogs. Without further ado, let's meet
the pairs who will be getting a new leash on life."

The woman handed the microphone over to the head
trainer, a man named Robert, who read from a series of
white index cards.

"First up, we have Rory Kline, a ten-year Navy vet who
has been matched with Javelin, a German shepherd rescued
from a kill shelter in North Carolina."

The crowd cheered as the man next to Ryker leaped up,
meeting Javelin halfway across the floor, catching the dog
as he jumped up into his arms, a kissing, wriggling mass
of fur. Ryker's hands tightened at his knees as the next
name was called, and the next, with both Rottweiler mixes
going to soldiers Ryker had met yesterday in training. The
medically retired Navy woman got one of the Lab mixes—a
bounding ball of energy named Hero—and the wheelchair-
bound firefighter got the other Lab, named Lana.

It was down to the corgi and the golden. Besides Ryker,
there was only one human left unmatched—a smiling
Marine named Amal, whom he and Tarun had grabbed
dinner with last night. Amal was already down on one
knee, ready to receive whichever dog came his way.

Ryker felt like he'd been turned to stone as he heard
Robert say his name on the microphone.

"Next up, we have Ryker Matthews, a highly decorated
Marine veteran, who will be going home with Six, a golden
retriever—one of six in her litter—rescued from a storm
drain after a tornado in Alabama."

The golden. Six. He had matched with the one he'd
accidentally fallen in love with already.

Ryker knew he should stand. Or kneel. Or run over to meet the dog, like all the others were doing. But he felt glued to his chair, frozen with a deadly combination of joy and fear as the trainer behind Six said something and the golden stood. She stepped over the concrete floor, the rubberized handle of her leash firmly in her jaws, her dark-brown eyes locked on his as she approached. She never even glanced at Amal as she stepped around him to Ryker.

Dropping her leash at his feet, the dog put her paw on Ryker's right knee, as if sensing that his left knee was sore above his prosthetic.

"This is Six," her trainer said. "The shelter named her that because she was the sixth one pulled out of the drain. You can change it if you want."

"Negative. The name is perfect," Ryker breathed. The dog immediately licked his hand, tail wagging fiercely, and it was as if her motion set his gears back into alignment. Ryker lifted his hands off his knees, burying them in her soft, golden fur. He lowered his head to hers, scratching and petting behind her ears. "In the Marines, if someone has your six, that means they're watching out for you. Watching your back. She is...my Six."

The dog barked once, then leaped into his lap. Although she was much too large to be a lapdog, especially in this office chair that had arms penning her in on both sides, she somehow managed to smoosh her body into Ryker, bending like an elbow macaroni.

"That's how she gives hugs," the trainer said. "She is clearly in love with you already."

Ryker's throat was tight. He buried his face in Six's fur,

breathing in her warm, doggy scent until he finally found his voice.

"Ditto."

* * *

After Amal was matched to the corgi, whose name was Biscuit and whose superpower seemed to be rolling over to show his belly, tongue lolling out of his mouth at every opportunity, the crowd of well-wishers for the ceremony were asked to leave so the veterans could have their first handling lesson.

"You got the prettiest bitch out there," Tarun joked, meeting Six and giving Ryker a hard, back-thumping hug of congratulations. "Gonna give Bryce a run for her money."

"Hey, not cool."

"Kidding. But seriously, you'd better call her. Your family, too. They deserve to know and they'll be thrilled for you."

Ryker agreed, and after they'd had their first lesson on walking with their dogs and the best ways to fend off well-meaning people who wanted to pet them while they were on duty, the group broke for lunch. Ryker and Six's trainer—a retired air-traffic controller named Gary—grabbed a sandwich together while he told Ryker everything he knew about the dog.

"She was originally trained for another Marine combat vet with PTSD and some mobility issues," Gary explained. "So she's trained to stand still with the command 'Hold' if you need help getting up, or finding your balance. Soon she'll learn your scent, your heartbeat, your anxiety triggers. She's first trained to bump you with her nose, then if she doesn't sense your anxiety lessening, she'll escalate to jumping on you and licking your face. She's relentless. Until she senses you're calm, she's going to apply the doggy-therapy as thick as peanut butter."

Ryker ruffled Six's ears. "I like peanut butter."

When they finished eating, Gary suggested Ryker walk Six alone in the fenced area outside, to start getting acquainted. He took her outside, walking along the back of the yard, allowing Six to sniff and squat in various places. She looked back at him with that doggo grin as if to make sure he was still with her, and he felt like he had as a kid at Christmas that one year when he'd been given a motorbike—like he was on top of the world. Recalling his promise to Tarun, he pulled out his phone, ready and wanting to share his news with Bryce.

She didn't answer.

He tried not to get anxious about it, but knew he was failing because just as he was about to leave a message, Six stopped her joyous exploration of every sniffable surface in the yard and pivoted, her snout bashing him in the balls.

"Um, hi, Bryce," he began the voicemail, pivoting Six's head out of his crotch, "I know you're working today, but I'd like to talk to you. If you get the chance, can you call me later?"

Six jumped up, licking at his hands as he tried to end the call, and Ryker chuckled.

"Hey, Six-y. Go easy on me, sweetheart," he said, wrestling with his cell phone to hang up. "Bryce means a lot to me, and I'm not great at talking to women. We'll try her again later, huh?"

Ryker shook his head at himself. He'd never thought he'd be the guy who talked to his dog. Yet here he was.

Worries began to swirl in his head once more. When he told Bryce he was sterile, would that be a relationship deal-breaker? If she was cool with that, what if he brought home Six and it turned out Bryce hated dogs? He actually had no idea—they'd never talked about it, and he'd never seen her interact with Sasha at Drake's house. Worse, what if she or one of her nieces was allergic?

Suddenly, Six jumped on his chest. Her furry, blond face with those all-knowing chocolate-brown eyes stared into his, as if saying, *Chill. I've got your six.*

Ryker felt his eyebrows relax from their bunched position, and he shook his head, ruffling her fur. Inspiration struck, and he knelt down next to Six. Accepting her kisses on the side of his jaw, he worked to get his phone into camera mode.

"Tell you what: let's send Bryce and my family a picture of you and me. Nobody can stay mad when they see your beautiful face."

He took three pictures until finally getting a good one where Six was staring at the camera, but before he could send it, they called everyone to return from lunch. Ryker put his cell back in his pocket. He'd send it later.

"Hold," he said, giving the command Gary had taught him to use the dog's back as a bit of leverage and balance when standing. Six stood stock-still until Ryker was upright.

"We need to get you some dog treats," he said, walking back inside.

CHAPTER 20

It was two in the morning before Bryce got Addison and her rainbow cast to the twin bed at her grandparents' house and the Paynes had retrieved Cecily and June from Pastor Stan. Once the girls heard they would be staying with their grandparents, they cheered, sending a spasm of hurt through Bryce.

"I can't wait to eat doughnuts for breakfast in the morning." Cecily grinned. "Can you get me Boston Creams this time, Pop-Pop? I'm a little grossed out by jelly ones, after Easter."

"You can have whatever you want," Adele cooed, kissing her on the head, and Bryce felt her jaws clench. "We're going to have a great week together and then... well, we'll see."

She gave Bryce a pointed look, which Bryce chose to ignore, focusing on her nieces instead. "I'll... bring over your bags tomorrow before I head to Niagara Falls."

"Oh, don't worry about those. We have a key if we need anything. Besides, we're going to take the girls shopping. They all need new clothes, and we'd love to treat them to a day at the mall." Harvey smiled as June squealed with delight. "Won't that be fun?"

Feeling exhausted and useless in the face of all this extravagance, Bryce forced a smile, giving each girl a hug and a kiss.

"Have fun as guest chef, Aunt Beamer." Cecily yawned. "I know you're gonna do great because you make the best things."

June's send-off was much chillier. She gave her aunt the driest of kisses on her cheek. "Bye. See you...whenever."

Only Addison clung to her neck as she bent to kiss her goodbye.

"I don't want you to go," she whispered, her lower lip buckling as she tried hard not to cry. "I need you, Aunt Beamer. I need you to be my mommy."

Bryce knew it was likely the pain medication making her say that, but the words pierced her chest. Before she responded, June snarled.

"She's *not* our mom. She's our aunt, and she has to leave."

The room went silent. Bryce gave Addison one last kiss on her forehead. She avoided June's glare, instead looking at Adele and Harvey as she pulled the folded paper from her pocket.

"I wrote up some tips about the girls' schedules to make the week easier for you."

"Thank you." Harvey took the paper. Without reading it, he stuffed it into his pants pocket. "But it's not the first time we've had our granddaughters. I'm sure we'll manage. Now, who wants hot chocolate with marshmallows?"

Bryce let herself out the front door, feeling like the world's worst caregiver.

* * *

Five restless hours of sleep later, she was on her way to Niagara Falls, the feelings of inadequacy having quadrupled. Bryce's guilt over Addison's injury made her question her choices. Who was she to parent three kids? These past months, she'd barely stayed afloat. It was probably only sheer luck that her incompetence hadn't resulted in an injury to her nieces before. Maybe the Paynes were right—maybe the girls would benefit by living with someone with time and experience as a parent? Not to mention that there were two of them, so they had her beat in sheer number of bodies working to care for the girls.

She'd tried to call Ryker after leaving the girls at their grandparents' last night—she'd been desperate to have someone she trusted to talk to. Yet his phone went directly to voicemail, and she hung up without leaving a message, figuring that was for the best. He was an excellent problem solver and a generous man—but he didn't love her. Although he'd sent a mechanic joke late last night, his lack of a return call felt deliberate. He obviously didn't want to talk.

Thoughts and doubts swirled in her head as she checked in to her hotel, changed into her chef's coat, then drove to Cascade, the farm-to-table high-end restaurant she'd be working at this week. Her phone buzzed once on the way.

Ryker.

Unfortunately, she was using her phone for GPS and couldn't take the call without losing the display in downtown Niagara Falls, and just as she pulled into the restaurant's employee parking lot, the call went to voicemail. Ten seconds later, her phone buzzed with a message. Exiting her car, she breathed in the crisp air, the roar of

Niagara Falls in her ears, although it was blocked from view by the restaurant. As she walked toward the swanky eatery, Bryce played Ryker's brief voicemail, her eyes going up to watch the gulls diving in the sky overhead.

"Bryce, if you get the chance, can you call me later?" Ryker's voice sounded jubilant. Almost buoyant. It confused her. Her chest ached with missing him, but from the sounds of it, he was having the time of his life. "I know you're working, but um...we need to...I'd like to talk to you. Okay, bye."

Then, instead of the voicemail ending, there was a smooshing, wet noise, followed by the deep rumble of Ryker's voice, like he was talking low and personal to someone standing close to him. The phone sounded far from his mouth, but she could clearly make out his voice right before the call disconnected.

"Heyyyy, sexy," he said. And then, he gave a deep, throaty laugh—the hot one that always made her breath catch. "Go easy on me, sweethea—"

What. The. Hell?

She played the message three times, but she couldn't figure out who he was talking to, except another woman. He wouldn't use that tone with a Marine buddy—or if he did, he had more going on with Tarun than just friendship. And he was using "sweetheart"—a word she'd never heard him use. Not to his goddaughter, Elise, not to her nieces. Not to her.

Even if the "sweetheart" comment was innocent, which was a debatable point, nobody left a voicemail like that, saying they needed to talk, when they had anything good to say.

She pressed Delete. Closing her eyes, she battled the widening hole in her chest—the place where Ryker lived, the place where her nieces had taken up residence. She took a box breath, breathing in four counts, holding four, releasing in four counts, then nothing for four. Patty had been right. She needed to make a map. Get above the trees and figure out her life. Her priorities. Her next steps. No matter what change of plans next week might bring with her nieces, or with Ryker, she needed to take this time and discover what she wanted.

Imani said to use this time as a gift. Gazing down at the phone in her hand, at Ryker's number, Bryce decided to give herself another gift. The gift of a week without worrying that she'd have to hear a breakup speech. A gift of time to figure her own shit out before returning to Wellsville.

Before she could talk herself out of it, she blocked Ryker's number, then, with a swipe of her thumb, deleted his contact from her phone entirely. Although she knew it wasn't permanent—hell, she could call either Imani or Patty and have his number again in a heartbeat—it felt momentous. Now she couldn't drunk-text him, or—in the more likely case—lonely-stressed-out-text him.

For the next five days, she would think. Make a map. Discover herself. Just. Be.

Opening her eyes, she took the steps to Cascade two at a time.

As soon as she walked into the place, the proprietor, a tall woman named Collette Elias, came out to greet her, a huge smile on her face.

"We are overjoyed to have you at Cascade as guest saucier this week," she said in a French accent. "Pierre recommends you highly, and I cannot wait to taste what you present to us. Come. I will show you the kitchen."

Bryce followed the woman clad in her elegant red sheath dress through the dining area. The woman's heels made a subdued click on the gleaming hardwood floors as they passed white, linen-covered tables with banquette seating done in sumptuous turquoise velvet and set with snowy white china and real silver that sparkled like candlelight. The tables all faced the vista—the tumbling waters of the American Falls with the Horseshoe Falls on the distant Canadian shore.

But it wasn't until they passed through the swinging doors into the kitchen that Bryce's heart thumped at the view. Rows of gleaming stainless-steel workstations, cutting boards stacked clean and ready for use next to silver bowls arranged by size. Ringing the perimeter were Vulcan stoves, most off but some in use, their yellow-orange flames burning merrily under copper-bottomed pans. Chefs and cooks, clad in spotless white coats, worked chopping, cooking, or prepping in readiness for tonight's dinner. As they entered, Collette clapped her hands.

"One of our most esteemed colleagues is here, Chef Bryce Weatherford."

As if they'd rehearsed it, every person in the kitchen called out at once. "Hello, Chef."

Bryce bobbed her head in greeting.

Then Collette threw out her hand, as if offering the kitchen to her. "Please. Feel free to walk around and explore. The storeroom is in the back, the wine cellar is through that door." She pointed to an old wooden door at the far end of the kitchen. "You may help Chef Nassur tonight, or you may merely observe as a way of orientation."

Bryce lit up. "Are you kidding? Who would waste an opportunity to work with Chef Nassur?"

A throaty voice behind her spoke.

"Ah, it's the saucier from Tampa." At the sound of the male voice, she turned to see the robust form of Chef Nassur—the man who'd brought two different restaurants their first Michelin Star, and the retiring head chef for Cascade—standing behind her. His ruddy cheeks and white eyebrows buckled in disapproval. "The same one whose toasted orzo soup was hailed the best in the East."

"Don't believe everything you hear." Bryce grinned at the older man. "It's the best in the entire United States."

Chef Nassur's lips twitched, almost toward a smile. The man, all scowls and serious, reminded her of a much older, grizzled version of Ryker, and, as she'd done in Wellsville, she searched for a way to crack that hard, prickly exterior.

"Chef, do you know, my parents once took me to Lacy Elaine's for my sweet sixteenth? I ordered your eggs Benedict." Bentley had been there, and she remembered feeling so special, all dressed up at a fancy restaurant, able to order whatever she wanted. Her voice softened in memory as she continued. "Your hollandaise sauce was like tasting happiness. I've never been able to duplicate it. Would you believe me if I told you I took the offer to work at Cascade this week in hopes of watching you make an eggs Benedict?"

Chef Nassur waved his hand in dismissal, yet his eyes sparkled. "Nonsense. Now, will you cook tonight, or will you...spectate?" The last word was spat out as if it were a curse.

"I'd be delighted to cook, Chef."

She was shown to a workstation and given the menu.

Bryce breathed in the smell of fresh herbs and produce—the sweet scent of thyme, the solid punch of garlic, the unmistakable tang of chopped onions—all of it danced along her nose and in her mouth, and she exhaled.

Finally. A place she understood.

A place where she belonged.

She put worries about her nieces, finances, and about her relationship with Ryker out of her mind. Instead, she picked a bowl of potatoes and selected a knife.

Busy is the enemy of sadness.

So thinking, she got to work.

CHAPTER 21

We need more diced shallots," Bryce called out to the cooks around her in the small lull between breakfast rush and lunch crunch on Thursday.

"Yes, Chef!" The resounding answer echoed off the tile walls, swirled in the metal prep bowls, and rose like the scent of something decadent and caramelized above the kitchen's din.

"Very few chefs match your work ethic and talent," Chef Nassur had told her this morning when she'd asked to come in early to watch him prepare the day's hollandaise sauce. "You have a job here, should you want it."

Bryce had spent the past four days cooking for crowds of food lovers. That was four days of waking to her alarm, versus Addie leaping into bed, rousing her with a recounting of last night's dream of Neverland. She'd had four mornings when she had to bathe only herself, no wrestling matches with Cecily, and she could eat a bowl of granola for breakfast instead of crafting the ultimate French toast to entice June to eat. Her white chef's coats remained immaculate, no spatters, dirty hand smudges, or accidental glitter smears from Addie's wings.

In fact, she'd rocked this gig. On her debut night at Cascade, she'd wowed a Toronto food critic, who'd called her toasted orzo chicken soup "enough to make you weep over the years you wasted eating subpar creations."

Today, she stood before the Vulcan range in her spotless attire, supervising three soups she'd started for dinner, two that were ready for the lunch crowd, and one front burner with hollandaise sauce—the creation of which she'd done with the express supervision of Chef Nassur himself.

She'd charmed the prickly chef into allowing her to watch him create his signature eggs Benedict; he had shown her exactly how he'd made the velvety hollandaise, the taste of which brought back that same contented feeling of happiness she'd had at her sweet sixteen brunch years ago.

"The week working as guest chef was just a ruse to learn this sauce recipe," she'd said, only half joking. "Thank you for this gift, Chef."

He'd grumbled about having to mollycoddle young chefs, but Bryce could tell he'd been pleased.

Now here she was, basically told she'd be given the position as sauté chef of Cascade—one of the most prestigious restaurants in Western New York. She'd been a hit with her colleagues here, and in control of all she surveyed. This would have been the pinnacle of her career.

If she weren't so miserable.

It was more than the blow from hearing Ryker's last voicemail—his calling another woman "sexy" and "sweetheart" hit hard. Worse than that was her ache for Addison, Cecily, and June. Missing the girls felt like an open wound in her chest. She'd called them every morning and every night, but for the past two days her calls to June had gone to voicemail, and this morning June's message indicated that her voicemail was full. She'd tried both Harvey and Adele, but they'd hurried off the phone with her, and she hadn't gotten to talk with any of her nieces. It was as if they'd all forgotten her.

Bryce dipped a tasting spoon into the hollandaise sauce. She added another smidge of white pepper before ladling some over four orders of eggs Benedict, garnishing them with a sprinkle of sliced chives.

"Go." As she waved the server off, Bryce dropped her tasting spoon. She'd picked it up and was heading to toss it in the dirty dish bin when her gaze caught on something glimmering in the nearby garbage. It was a metal saltshaker, the top dented as if it had been accidentally mangled by the dishwasher or hit by the wheels of a serving cart. It was silver—not real silver, but restaurant-grade sterling, like the utensils—and it looked abandoned, sitting there atop potato peels and kitchen waste.

Bryce plucked the shaker from the trash, using a nearby towel to wipe it down. It was roughed up, but it still worked. Crystals of salt glimmered against her palm as she flipped it upside down. She frowned. Cecily would've rescued it. With a little work, the dent could be hammered out. It might not be good as new, but it was still beautiful, despite its imperfections.

Maybe because of them?

Tears pricked her eyes as she thought about her nieces and the girls' grandparents. That situation was dented. Some might say it wasn't salvageable.

Yet, all she'd been thinking about this week was missing the girls, and she was downright miserable. What was she doing here?

No doubt, cooking brought her joy. It was something she was effortlessly good at, unlike being a daily kid-wrangler. But as she stood there looking out over the massive kitchen, the rows of Vulcan ranges, the cooks and servers and chefs, she missed the tiny, cramped area behind the swinging doors of PattyCakes café. She missed the challenge of coming up with new menu ideas with limited budgets, of ways to use leftover ingredients to make something spectacular. She missed watching the kitchen clock, counting down until her nieces were done with school, whipping up a snack for them, figuring out ways to prepare their favorites and introduce new delights, expanding their limited palates.

Gazing down at the dented saltshaker, she realized that after Bentley's death, after her world had been forever changed, what brought her the most joy and healing hadn't been cooking. It had been her time with her nieces. Being silly, playing sumo wrestler as they grabbed her legs, or being the hapless victim in the endless game of Tinker Bell and pirate. It was the times she'd cajoled a smile from June, successfully gotten Cecily bathed, or heard Addison's sweet voice saying, "I love you." Her nieces melted her heart.

She may be a disaster as a mom-like creature.

But that title was the best prize.

It's what made her happy.

Carefully, she slid the saltshaker into her pants pocket. With shaking hands, she untied the apron around her waist.

"I've got to go," she said to Chef Nassur, whose white eyebrows bunched together in confusion. "I'm sorry. I've got to get back to my ... my kids."

* * *

Two hours later, and after a pep talk from her father, she'd pulled beside the Paynes' big SUV in their driveway, the large vehicle practically hiding her BMW from view as she walked to the front door.

Her father's words from earlier echoed in her mind.

"Little Beamer, nobody's born knowing how to parent. And no parent, or parent-like creature, is perfect. Your mother used to say there wasn't a recipe for success as a mom. Like cooking, you've got to stand at the stove every day and do your best." Her dad's words, and the memory of her mom comparing everything to cooking, brought a smile to her face.

But more importantly, it brought the steel back in her spine.

She might not be a perfect mom-like creature, but she adored her nieces. Her kids. Bentley and Heather had chosen Bryce to raise their children, and Bryce was going to do everything within her power to prove to Adele, Harvey, and the judge that her late brother and sister-in-law had chosen correctly...but that she'd rather do this as a team. Together, they could figure out a way to make their dented relationship not only work, but show that its beauty was because it wasn't perfect. It was unique. Strong. And worth saving.

Gathering her courage, she rang the Paynes' doorbell.

Shouts and cries sounded from within—some of them from her nieces. Some could be from...the Paynes?

Adrenaline spiked, and without thinking of the consequences, she twisted the knob and burst inside the white ranch-style house. The foyer and living room looked like a pack of rabid raccoons had rampaged through, and her eyes darted everywhere.

Crayons, scissors, and construction paper lay on every available surface. One of Cecily's black sneakers lay by the door, the other a footstep away, as if she'd literally walked right out of them upon entering the house. Coats, sweaters, and socks littered the chairs and floor, and two plates of half-eaten sandwiches and potato chips sat forgotten on what had previously been an immaculately kept coffee table but now held a riot of LEGOs, Barbie dolls, and a motley assortment of rocks and leaves.

"Hello? Harvey? Adele?" Bryce called out and was rewarded by the sound of the Paynes coming down the hallway.

"Bryce, thank God!" Harvey and Adele rushed to her. Both wore wrinkled clothing, and Adele's face was devoid of makeup. They had bluish bags under their eyes, as if they hadn't slept.

"What's wrong? Where are the girls?" Bryce peered around but saw no kids.

Adele threw herself against Bryce, who staggered back, stunned, as the older woman began to cry.

"The girls have b-barricaded themselves in the guest suite and haven't been out to eat since Wednesday morning." Adele sobbed against Bryce's chest. "They won't talk to us. W-we don't even know if they're alive or dead in there!"

"Adele, let's not get dramatic," Harvey said. "We hear all three voices when they fight."

"They've... locked themselves in a room since Wednesday morning?" Bryce asked as Adele pulled away, taking the handkerchief Harvey handed to her. "Why didn't you tell me? I've talked to you twice a day and you didn't say anything was wrong. I'd have come home last night if I'd have known."

"We were going to call you if they didn't come out by dinner. This week...this week has been more challenging than we could have ever imagined." Harvey's normally clean-shaven face was heavy with fatigue and silvered with whiskers.

Unsure what to say, Bryce ventured a question. "Why did the girls lock themselves in the guest suite?"

"It's all a jumble, but we think it was Cecily's doing, at first," Harvey explained, following Bryce as she walked toward the guest room. "She spilled chocolate pudding on her camo pants, and when we said we'd go over to the apartment and get her another pair, she...she melted down. They took all our cardboard boxes—the ones we used for storage in the basement—and they dumped everything out. Then Addison came out, crying that her leg itched and she needed us to fashion a coat hanger to scratch inside the cast—"

Adele took over the story. "But that was just a ruse. While we were in the bathroom, June raided our cupboards and refrigerator. They've been holed up in there—the only room with an attached bathroom—ever since."

"Mmm." Bryce nodded to show she was listening, but really she was wondering whether to panic or to laugh. Her nieces had basically commandeered the Payne household, waging some sort of mutiny. If it wasn't so concerning and terrifying, it might be funny.

"And I...I don't want to scare you," Adele began, "but

one of the girls raided Harvey's toolbox, and he's missing his duct tape, plus his—"

"Box cutter," Bryce said at the same time as Adele, then smiled in reassurance. "Don't worry. June knows how to use it. I think...they might be making a pirate ship."

Bryce knocked on the guest room's door.

"It's Aunt Beamer. Can I come in and talk to you for a second?"

Addison was the first to answer. "Nope. We gotta talk to you through the door. June says if we open it, the gig is up. An' we want to keep gigging until Cici feels better. Also, did you know Nana and Pop-Pop won't let us watch anything but news and the Weather Channel?"

Harvey made as if to retort, but Bryce gave an "it's okay" gesture to forestall him.

"Sounds like you got really bored. What's going on with Cecily? Is it her tummy?"

This time June answered, her voice ripe with sarcasm, but holding a note of...was it sadness? Worry? Whatever it was, Bryce strained to hear what was between the teen's words as she replied. "There's been *a lot* going on with Cecily. I thought building her a pirate ship might fix it—like when she played with Ryker's. She's eating just fine, but she keeps looking at Mom and Dad's photo albums and crying..."

"Yeah," Addison piped up, filling the silence. Bryce heard a *thump-thump* sound that must've been her crutches moving closer to the door. "Only I think she might be getting curvy because we haven't had any fruit since you left."

"Scurvy," June corrected. "Not curvy. And that's not what's wrong with Cici. She...she keeps saying it's her fault that Mom and Dad are...are gone."

Adele, listening behind Bryce, clucked her tongue, her voice kind as she called out. "Honey, a stranger ran a stop sign and caused the accident. It's not your fault—"

"It is my fault!" Cecily's shout, all broken and jagged, sliced through the air. "I spilled yogurt all over my shirt when I was eating the rest of my breakfast in the car. I was crying because I wanted a clean shirt and when Mom and Dad dropped me off at school they promised to go right home and get me a clean one. That's why they were in the accident—because I wanted a clean shirt."

Everything clicked into place in Bryce's head: Cecily's refusal to bathe, to have her clothes washed, her panic whenever she'd forgotten something at home. This poor child had been living with such crushing guilt—it broke Bryce's heart.

"Aw, Cici." Bryce shook her head. "You can't blame yourself, because it's simply not true. You weren't there. You weren't driving the other car. Nothing you did caused the crash."

"They wouldn't have been at that road when the man hit them with the car if it weren't for me."

The three adults looked at each other, helpless. Bryce thought about trying to call the girls' therapist, but it was almost seven o'clock and the office was closed. To her surprise, it was June who spoke up.

"Was it Aunt Beamer's fault you got stuck under the shelves at the grocery store that time?"

"No," Cecily said with a huff. "I was getting my lucky rock that rolled under."

"But what if the shelf had fallen and you'd gotten really hurt? Would it have been her fault then?" June persisted.

"No. But it didn't fall. It's not the same."

Catching on to June's logic, Bryce spoke. "Was it my fault Addison broke her leg? If I'd have been upstairs, maybe she wouldn't have jumped off the bunk beds."

"It wasn't your fault," Cecily mumbled. "I told her not to, but she didn't have her listening ears on."

Even through the door she heard Addison click her tongue. "Only, I was testing my invisible wings that day, and my ears weren't really part of that."

"Don't you see? Accidents just...happen. Nothing was your fault, Cici." Bryce waited, but all was silent on the other side of the door. After a moment, she dug into her pocket and pulled out the item she'd grabbed from the trash. She knocked the silver saltshaker against the door, making a tinny metallic clink. "Hey, I found something at the fancy restaurant. It reminded me of you, Cecily. All of us, really. Can I come in and show it to you?"

Several gasps and a whispering flurry of conversation came from behind the door. Bryce was pretty sure she'd heard June argue to open the door, and was just as certain it was Addison arguing that opening the door for trash wasn't as good as waiting until there was chocolate. Yet it was clear after a few minutes that the impasse was continuing.

"Give it to us through the door," Addison said in her best Captain Hook voice, and the door opened a crack. Bryce slid the saltshaker through the narrow space, barely getting her fingers out of the way before the door slammed shut, locking again.

Slumping to the floor, Bryce gave the Paynes a wan smile as she directed her voice to the girls beyond the door.

"I left my station at work in Niagara Falls, and do you know why?"

"Because Nana and Pop-Pop called and tattled on us!" Cecily said, her voice hoarse. "We told them not to."

"No, they didn't tattle on you. I'm here because I saw that saltshaker in the garbage and figured something out." Bryce leaned her head against the door, closing her eyes to best listen to her heart. "Your dad, Bentley...he used to collect things, too. As a plumber, it was useful—he'd keep spare parts from one job, like bits of pipe and washers and things—because he said you never knew what would come in handy and the next customer might need that exact piece to fix their sink, and it would save someone some money. When I saw the saltshaker in the garbage, I knew you'd want me to rescue it."

There was the sound of snuffling from the other side of the door.

"Yeah," came Cecily's watery voice.

"You and your dad are alike in that way. Bentley was the best brother anyone ever had, and he was an amazing father. Heather was incredible, and I'll never be the mom she was. I'll never replace your parents. But my love for you three is as vast as the moon and stars. I came home because I'd rather be here, cooking for you three Weatherfords, than cooking for anyone else in the entire world." Bryce blinked away tears. "While it isn't fair that the accident happened and I'm here and they aren't, you girls are the best gift I ever had. I'll always miss my brother, but I feel blessed for this time with you. For making this new family together. We're like this dented saltshaker—a little banged up, but still good. Me, your Nana and Pop-Pop—we love you all so much—"

Bryce's voice caught, and she gulped back a sob, trying to work words around the lump in her throat.

Suddenly, the door fell open, pitching her off-balance. She fell into the room, into the arms of the three girls she couldn't imagine life without, and then they were all hugging, all crying, all speaking at once.

"I missed you, Aunt Beamer." Cecily squeezed her around the neck.

"Only," Addison said, falling against her, "you can't believe how good I can walk in these things. I've been practicing, so I'll be able to use the steps at home. I miss my wings. And I missed you."

June let her sisters crowd in first, but then came over when Bryce opened her arms wider. The tween hugged her, whispering in her ear. "I got my period again. It was awful without you, and I would've texted but my phone charger cord broke. We've...we've missed you so much. Can we go home?"

Home.

She'd said home. Not the apartment.

It wasn't everything, but it was a start.

Bryce nodded her head, not bothering to hide the tears. "I've missed you all, too, and we can go home—but," she amended her statement as her eyes cleared and she got the full picture of what the girls had done with the guest suite. A massive, ship-like structure dominated the room, balanced on the edge of the two twin beds, which showcased the number of empty containers and discarded clothes, toys, and wrappers underneath. "...but we need to pitch in and clean up first. And I think you need to give Nana and Pop-Pop a big hug and an apology. You gave them quite a scare. Nobody likes a mutiny in their house."

The girls, surprisingly, did exactly as told, hugging their

grandparents. Soon they all had garbage bags and suitcases and began to pile items in each to clear out the room.

Harvey pulled Bryce aside, his gray-whiskered face earnest as he spoke in a low voice.

"Adele and I...we thought we were up to the task of parenting our grandchildren, but these past few days have reminded us that two seniors in their sixties are no match for three Weatherford girls under the age of thirteen. At least, not full time."

Adele chimed in, reaching for Bryce's hand. "All this bickering between us...that's not what Heather or Bentley would have wanted. We got caught up more in what we thought family should look like instead of what our granddaughters needed. We won't...we won't contest the guardianship."

Bryce squeezed the older woman's hand. "You weren't the only one getting caught up in things. It's pretty clear raising my nieces isn't a one-person show, and someone very important to me said I need to learn to ask and accept help. I think, together, we can figure out a great arrangement for you, Harvey, and me—but especially for the girls. They need all of us in their lives, and I want to be sure the guardianship paperwork has written stipulations for your time with them. They are lucky to have you as involved grandparents."

Adele's eyes misted over. "Thank you, Bryce. We can say the same for you as their guardian."

Just then the doorbell rang, and, noticing the mess of luggage in the hallway, Bryce held up a hand to the older couple.

"No need to scramble over this stuff. I'll get that for you."

She wasn't sure what she expected when she opened the door—maybe the UPS guy or a neighbor who'd heard all the caterwauling? But when she threw it open, she was struck dumb.

Standing on the front porch was Ryker Matthews.

And he wasn't alone.

CHAPTER 22

When Ryker returned to town Thursday, his elation over going home with Six tanked as he drove down Main Street. Although he knew Bryce was working in Niagara Falls until the end of the week, he couldn't help but feel his heart slide in his chest when her BMW wasn't outside PattyCakes. It would've been nice to see her and introduce her and his mom to Six at the same time—two women, one apology, and potentially zero casualties because they were in a public place with witnesses.

He'd been trying to call and text Bryce all week, but first the picture of him and Six bounced, and he figured it was something to do with his data plan, or the size of the photo. But when his family got the picture, and the onslaught of questions and congratulations came pouring in, he tried to send it to Bryce's phone again.

No dice. And all his texts came back Undeliverable.

At first, he wondered if her phone might be out of range, being close to the Canadian border, or maybe she'd forgotten to pack her phone charger or something. But when he mentioned his guesses on the phone to Zander, his brother disagreed.

"Shit, man. She must've blocked you."

Ryker's eyes bulged. That scenario hadn't even entered his head. "No. Something—something must be wrong."

"Well, I mean, Addison did break her leg, and from what Mom said, she's worried Bryce may not come back to PattyCakes at all," Zander said nonchalantly. "Apparently, they fell in love with her at Cascade."

Ryker's voice shook as he finally got his thoughts aligned. "W-what? Is Addison okay? When did this happen? Why didn't anyone call me?"

"I figured she called you, same as she called Mom. If I were you, I'd get over to PattyCakes. Not only can Mom fill you in, you owe her an in-person apology. She is royally pissed you didn't tell her the real reason you were leaving, and so is Drake. You put me in a hell of an awkward position, dude. Even Imani's mad at me."

"Sorry, Zan. I..." Ryker paused, glanced at his dog, who'd just woken up from an hour-long nap in his front seat, blinking first at the view outside the window, then at Ryker. Just having Six in the car comforted him enough to share it all. "I'm sorry. Making you promise to stay silent was a dick move, but this week gave me clarity and I feel like I will be a better version of me, with Six by my side."

Zander gave a low whistle. "Whoa. Who are you? And what have you done with my emotionally unavailable brother?"

Ryker rolled his eyes. "You're a douche. I've got to go, but swing by later and meet Six."

"Sweet. Can't wait. Good luck with Mom, and ... I hope you and Bryce get things worked out. I like that one. She's spicy and doesn't put up with your bullshit."

They hung up, and Ryker pulled into the alley next to PattyCakes to park. Originally, he'd wanted to go home, take Six out, and get something to eat. Plus, he needed to get out of these jeans and the long-sleeved black T-shirt he'd thrown on this morning—it was one Zander had gifted him one Christmas that said *I'm a ~~makanick. Mecchanik. Mekanic~~. I fix cars*—and change into something cooler for the warm spring day.

But after he heard the news from Zander, nothing was more important than answers. Ryker slammed his palm against the steering wheel. He thought he'd been doing the right thing by handling this by himself.

Six whined, putting her paw across the truck's seat to land on his thigh.

"I know, girl. I'm okay," he said, making himself breathe. He turned off the truck and stroked the dog's head, running her soft ears through his fingers. "Our first mission: meet Mom. Do your best to look adorable as I apologize. Then we'll strategize about Bryce. Got it?"

He was holding out hope that it was all a giant misunderstanding...but his gut told him otherwise. As he walked Six through the door of PattyCakes, he recalled the last voicemail he'd sent to Bryce:

We need to talk.

In retrospect, he should've been more forthcoming— he'd probably sounded ominous, but what should he have sent? *Gotta bolt. Might be matching with a dog, but maybe not. Oh, btw, I probably can never give you kids. Talk soon?*

First, he'd never strung together a text that long in his life. Plus, it was a topic he thought better discussed as a face-to-face deal, not in a text where things could be mis-construed. But he couldn't shake the feeling he'd screwed up, and when the comforting smell of baked goods hit his face when he and his dog entered PattyCakes, he felt his throat closing up.

Freaking feelings, again. Damn it!

Six bumped her nose into his thigh, and he automatically reached down to pet her just as his mom spotted him, rushing out from behind the counter.

Her eyes immediately landed on the golden retriever at his side.

"Sorry, Mom." He opted for a fast, surprise offense. "I screwed up. I should've told you I applied for a service dog. I was on a two-year waiting list, so I figured I'd have lots of time, but another vet opted out at the last minute for training, and I got his spot this week. I wasn't sure we'd match, and I didn't want to get your hopes up or worry you—"

To his horror, his throat closed off, as if a lump of sand had congealed behind his Adam's apple. Tears clouded his vision, and he blinked rapidly.

Six whined, licking his fist until his hands uncurled at his side.

"Ryker, honey, I'm glad you're okay." Mom kissed his cheek, then led them both to a table in the corner, away from the other patrons. "I've been worried sick."

"Mom, I'd like you to meet Six. She's a rescue from Alabama..." Ryker sat, telling his mom all about the golden retriever's origin, her skills, their match and training together. All the while his mom knelt next to the golden retriever, cooing over the dog until Six rolled over, presenting her belly in ecstasy at all the attention.

When he ran out of words and his mom sat at the table again, he asked the question he'd dreaded most.

"What's going on with Bryce? Are the girls okay?"

His mom gave him a pitying smile, and he wanted to die. Pity. The worst emotion ever.

"It's been...quite a week." She stood, patting his hand. "Sit tight. I'm going to get us both some food before I tell you everything I know. I even saved a chicken breast from last night's dinner, just for my newest grand-dog."

She left him at the table to stare alternately at the boomerang pattern on the top and at his phone, which was eerily silent. He pulled up the last string of text messages from Bryce, cringing at his terse replies, the way his protection instinct had backfired.

His mom returned carrying two plates. One with a massive slice of carrot cake, the cream cheese frosting an inch high, and the other with two golden-brown rolls in the center.

She slid both plates toward him, giving him a fork for the carrot cake—his favorite. Then she sat opposite, as Willow poured them two cups of coffee.

"Ryker, I love you more than anything, but your actions—or your inactions—have consequences." His mom sipped her coffee, waiting for Willow to leave before continuing. "While you were gone, Addison jumped off her bunk bed and broke her leg. She's fine, and while Bryce didn't tell me the whole story, I got the impression she's worried the girl's injury will somehow be used against her in court."

Ryker groaned, grinding the palms of his hand into his eyes. "She...she tried to call me, and I've tried to get in touch with her, but we kept missing each other. I wish I'd been here for her."

"There's more." His mom lay an index-sized card on the

table, covered in a sheath of plastic. "She stopped by before she went to Niagara Falls to work at Cascade during her vacation week, and she gave me this—her recipe for Parker House rolls—the same delicious rolls on the plate in front of you. She said you'd know what it meant."

Ryker felt the back of his neck grow scalding hot, as if he'd been standing at attention for hours in the blazing sun. He knew what this card meant. Bryce's mother had told her never to share a signature recipe that got you a man unless you were prepared to give up that man.

He swallowed, taking the card. "Yeah. I do. It's not good."

"Tell me what happened." His mom patted his hand. "You may be full grown, but you're still my boy. Let's see if I can help."

Ryker's words came haltingly at first, like an old lawn mower starting, but then, as he relived these past weeks, they came faster. He talked about meeting Bryce in the grocery store. Getting to know her and her girls at the garage, at her house, and the ways in which he'd made himself vulnerable, coming out of his shell because of Bryce and her nieces. Whether it was that day he'd allowed them to put him in full Barbie makeup, or when he'd stepped out of his leg, or dressed as a pink bunny, time with them had left an indelible impression on his heart. He explained to his mom how he'd tried to tell Bryce about his PTSD, his radiation treatments and what that meant for a future family, as well as the fact that his HO kept returning, which might mean further amputations.

"I wanted to tell her everything," he said, anguished. "Now I'm worried it's too late."

"When you left town without explanation, I imagine

that might have something to do with the fact she's not taking your calls. Women aren't like engines, to turn on and off at will."

"I—I thought I was protecting all of you. I wanted to handle it myself, because your lives are busy, and you don't need any added worries—"

"Any added worries? Is that what you think this is about?" The disappointment in his mother's eyes made him want to curl up inside and die. "Ever since you returned from Afghanistan, you've built up this wall around yourself. It's as if after your injury, you did your best to make sure you'd never get hurt again. You distanced yourself from your family, kept friends at arm's length, and you barely interact with the community, all because you were scared to expose your heart to hurt. We worry because we love you, and when you shut us out like you did this week, you're not protecting us—you're protecting yourself."

Six sat up, putting her paw on his lap, and Ryker stroked her head, processing his mom's words.

He recalled Zander's texts, Drake's words at the garage a few weeks ago, when he reminded Ryker he had a support system. He remembered both Tarun and his family practically having to drag him out of his garage and be social. He'd thought it was just his family being busybodies. Now he could see how destructive his PTSD had been. And poor Bryce...

"I've been such a selfish prick." He hunched over his coffee. The weight of this admission was almost too much to bear.

"No." His mother took his hand. "It's like when they tell you on the airplane to put on your own oxygen mask before securing others'. You just took a long time to do this for yourself. To take this step and put on your own oxygen mask. And I can't tell you how proud I am of you, son."

"But I never told Bryce...I love her." Ryker shook his head. "I didn't tell her, even after she basically told me."

Patty squeezed his hand. "You aren't perfect. But here's something else: you're not dead. And unless you want to die alone, you'd best figure it out."

Mom was right. It was time to nut up or shut up.

"Is she still in Niagara Falls?" He sighed in relief when his mom nodded. "What hotel is she at?"

"I'm not sure. But her nieces' grandparents know, and you can ask them." Patty stood, brushing off her pink apron. "I suggest you get a move on."

He stood and held out his arms to his mother. She hugged him fiercely, and he breathed in the scent of cookies and vanilla—the aromas of his childhood.

"Thanks, Mom. I love you."

He loaded up Six and they drove to the Paynes' house.

"New mission," he said to Six as the golden gazed out the window, panting happily. "Convince Adele or Harvey to tell us which hotel Bryce is at, then it's road trip time again."

He hauled himself out of the truck and gathered up Six's leash, making his way to the Paynes' front door. He heard the girls inside, squealing and laughing, and the sound—that sound of joy—was like a candle flame to the darkness inside. He drew nearer and, screwing up his courage, rang the doorbell.

He had words all queued up in his mind—he'd say, "Hi, can you give me the name of the hotel Bryce is staying at in Niagara Falls?" and then if they balked, he'd tell them he wanted to introduce her to his service dog. Whatever it took, he was going to get the name of the hotel.

But when the door opened, it was neither Harvey nor Adele standing in front of him, nor was it one of the little Weatherford children.

It was Bryce.

His planned speech halted as he stared at her. She wore her white chef's coat, but her face had tear tracks and her eyes were bloodshot. She'd been crying. His mouth dropped open, and he wanted to reach for her, take her in his arms, hold her, tell her he'd fix everything.

But she speared him with that direct blue-gray gaze, scanning him head to toe.

"Well, well, well. If it isn't Ryker Matthews. The jerk-face who couldn't be bothered to return my calls or texts, then has some sexy sidepiece he calls 'sweetheart.'" Bryce's eyes narrowed. "Give me three reasons I shouldn't punch you in the throat right now."

His mouth opened and closed, confusion barricading his voice. He wasn't sure what the hell she meant by the sexy sidepiece, but the rest of her accusation was valid. So he squared his shoulders, bracing for the onslaught.

"I got nothing. Swing away."

CHAPTER 23

Fine," Bryce said to Ryker. "Why did you go MIA? And I want the truth."

Even as hurt and angry as she was, the sight of this man still made her insides cartwheel with delight. She also noticed that his face was scruffy and looked like he hadn't slept well in days.

Sensing that she had an audience—the Paynes had come into the living room, followed by her nieces—Bryce stepped out onto the front porch, crowding close as they shared space on the step. She tried to keep her scowl on her face, but it was tough with that sweet golden retriever wagging her tail so hard it banged against the Paynes' screen door. "Also, why do you have a dog?"

Instead of the one-word answer she expected, he launched into a detailed, almost blow-by-blow account of his week. Her anger quickly morphed into concern, then to incredulity when she heard about how his trauma-induced HO had resulted in radiation treatments whose side effect might be sterility. But even with treatment, he worried more of his leg might be amputated, and on top of all that, he was concerned about his escalating PTSD episodes and how all this, combined, might be a relationship deal-breaker for her.

She opened her mouth to tell him how ludicrous that was, but he held up a hand.

"I know. I'm an ass. I've already been briefed by Drake, Zander, and my mother about that fact." His face held remorse and also... was it fear? "I'm sorry I didn't figure out a way to tell you, and I'm even sorrier that I went off for this service dog opportunity without explaining what was going on in my head. I didn't tell you how I was doing this for me, but also for us—to give me the confidence that I can be there, be wholly there, for you. I guess a part of me was worried that my sterility, my HO, my having a service dog to help my PTSD—all that might... freak you out. Make you think..."

Bryce wanted to reach out to him, put her arms around him, or maybe shake him in frustration. Instead, she used her words. "That I had too much on my plate, and that you might be a heavy lift for me right now?"

He nodded. "Exactly."

"Like hell you are," she said. "What's the rest? I hate people who lie, cheat, and don't keep their stations clean, so tell me the truth and quit protecting me. Do I look like the kind of woman who needs protecting?"

This elicited a small smile. His rigid, stand-at-attention posture loosened, and he fiddled with the dog's leash before gazing directly at her to answer. "No, you're tough as hell. It's one of the reasons I love you."

Her eyes bulged. "What did you say? How can you say that when in your last message to me you were romancing some other woman?"

Ryker's eyebrows drew together. "What are you talking about?"

"After your cryptic-as-hell voicemail, you thought you'd hung up the phone." Her chin trembled as the memory brought back the hurt and anger. "But before it disconnected, I heard you call someone else 'sexy' and 'sweetheart.' Why don't you admit you're seeing another woman?"

His face went from confused to understanding, and then morphed into amusement. When his face broke out in that "sun from behind the clouds" smile, she almost flung herself at him, fists flying. But then he spoke.

"Because I wanted to introduce you to her in person. Bryce, meet the newest lady in my life. This little sweetheart is Six," he said, taking a step away from the golden to allow the dog to approach Bryce, sniffing and panting as her tail wagged frantically. "I've already become that guy who talks to his dog, and although I think her name is perfect, I sort of nicknamed her 'Six-y' because...well, the same reason I like to call my goddaughter Lisi versus Elise. I think it fits."

As his explanation sank in, Bryce's hurt evaporated—he hadn't been seeing someone else, and the dog was absolutely a sweetheart. She knelt down to pet the golden retriever, who licked her face as thoughts swirled in Bryce's mind. He'd been gone this week to make himself more whole for him, but also for her? All this time she'd thought his emotional distance meant he didn't have feelings, but all along he'd been worried she'd toss him aside if she knew his whole story. And he loved her. He had said that, hadn't he?

As if he heard the thoughts tumbling through her head,

he cupped her face in his hands, guiding her to stand until he could gaze directly at her.

"I love you, Bryce. I think I've loved you from the moment you and your nieces came to my garage. You make me feel connected. Real. Whole."

Bryce leaned against him, bracing herself on his strong forearms, bringing them close enough so she saw every fleck of navy in his soft blue eyes. "I've been waiting a long time to hear those words. I told you a week ago that your kindness was one of the things I loved about you, but I should've said what I meant: I love you. I don't care if you can't have kids. I'm blessed to hopefully soon have three of my own, and besides when I say I love you, that means *all* of you. The parts that are here, and the parts that aren't."

Ryker swallowed, his Adam's apple bobbing. "So . . . you don't still want to throat-punch me?"

She grinned, tossing her arms around his neck. He was solid and beautiful, and perfect.

"I do love you, Ryker Matthews. But I reserve the right to throat-punch you if you ever leave me a vague-as-hell text and voicemail string ever again. Got it?"

"Roger that."

He kissed her, gently at first, then groaned as she melted against him. His arms wrapped around her, holding her close as his kiss deepened, his tongue finding hers . . .

The door flew open. Standing on the threshold were all three of her nieces, who gasped as they spotted Ryker and Six at the same time.

The golden retriever took it in stride as the girls screeched in delight. As soon as the door opened, the dog looked back at Ryker once, then took up the handle to her leash and let herself in to be swallowed up by a trio of fawning girls.

"Sorry," Ryker said to the Paynes, who waved as they followed the dog into the house, but the grin on his face belied his words. "I . . . I hope nobody's allergic. This is Six, and she's my service dog."

It was like watching a tornado of fur as Six eagerly licked the girls' hands, faces, and even Cecily's bare feet as they petted her, until the golden finally rolled over on her back, letting them scratch her belly. Finally, her nieces calmed enough for words.

"Hi, Mr. Ryker," Cecily said. "We've missed you this week, too. And that volcano vomit soap makes my skin itch. You happen to have anything better?"

"Look at my leg." Addison thrust out her cast with its rainbow striping of fiberglass. "We're twinsies! I tried to fly with my invisible wings and it didn't work out. Hey, can we have your dog be Nana next time we play pirates?"

Adele's face reddened, and Bryce rushed to explain. "She doesn't mean you. Nana is the name of the dog in *Peter Pan*."

June cleared her throat. "Uh, Mr. Ryker? Do you have your tool kit in your truck? Because . . . we may or may not have accidentally broken one of the beds in the guest room."

Ryker's smile grew with each girl's question, and when they were all done, he hugged Bryce's shoulder as he patiently answered.

"Yes, I have more soap. Yes, Six will be with me all the time, and I'm sure she'll love to join our next pirate adventure. And yes. I always have my tools. They're in my truck, I can get them—"

"That won't be necessary," Harvey said, shaking his head. The older man was smiling at them all, his eyes misty. "Adele and I can handle the rest of the cleanup. You two— no, all of you—have some catching up to do. Bryce, we'll call you later and set up some time to meet with all the lawyers. The judge is going to love that we got this whole thing buttoned up by ourselves."

The girls hugged their grandparents goodbye, and Bryce stepped up to hug them, too.

"Thank you. I'll make us all an epic lunch when we get together."

Soon they'd gathered up all the backpacks and found everyone's shoes and headed to the BMW. Ryker helped her strategically pack the girls' things in the trunk, and Bryce just managed to wedge Addie's crutches in there before getting it closed.

"Ugh. I love my Beamer, but I think it's time to get a bigger vehicle. One we can fit in. Maybe even take a road trip with—I love road trips. Are you and Six game to come along someday?"

Ryker reached down to pat the dog's head as she took her leash in her mouth, sitting patiently by his side, her gaze flicking alternately at the girls still waving at her through the BMW's windows and at Ryker and Bryce. "This sweetheart just rode with me the entire eight-hour drive from Smith-town to Wellsville like a boss. She's up for anything."

"How about you?" she asked, winking at him as she tilted her face up to his. "After I get life sorted out this week-end and get the kids back into school on Monday, I think it's going to be a hug emergency, a kiss emergency...and maybe another emergency. If you're up for it?"

He took Bryce a few steps away from the BMW, then he brought her to him for another sizzling kiss. Bryce felt herself melt into him—this man who had figured out the way to her heart, despite the chaos. This wonderful guy loved the dented areas of her life, of her, and found her worth the effort. She deepened the kiss, her tongue finding his...

Addison and Cecily immediately broke out into a singsong voice.

"Aunt Beamer and Ryker sitting in a tree...K-I-S-S-I-N-G."

"Coitus interruptus." She laughed, pulling away from him. "By the way, you didn't answer my question."

He grinned, then whispered in her ear. "Oh, I'm up for it. Leave your calendar open Monday morning. After the girls are in school, I plan on addressing every single one of the emergencies you mentioned. Many, many times."

EPILOGUE

C'mon girls." Bryce ushered Addison, Cecily, and June down the courthouse steps and into her BMW, cranking the air-conditioning in the vehicle to offset the stifling July heat. "Patty called, and before we can go out and get ice cream to celebrate, we've got to swing into PattyCakes. There's something wrong with the Wi-Fi, and the new QR menu code doesn't seem to be working, so, June, I'm going to need your tech expertise."

The girls all groaned.

"But today was 'posed to be a vacation day," Addison said, folding her arms across her chest.

"The joys of restaurant ownership," Bryce said. While she'd been thrilled when Patty had presented her with an ownership agreement that allowed her to transition out of the business with enough time to teach Bryce everything she knew in two years' time, all this meant she hadn't had time off in a while. She'd wanted this one day to celebrate officially becoming her nieces' permanent guardian. She and the girls had plans to enjoy a massive hot fudge sundae, and then browse Wellsville's Main Street, which was filled with vendors gearing up for the upcoming balloon rally this weekend. But even Willow had sounded frantic in the background, and that woman never got flustered. It must be pretty bad.

She pulled into the alley, using her keys to open the service door. The kitchen lights were off.

"Whoa. They must've had a power failure. Patty? Willow?" Bryce called, blinking for her eyes to adjust to the dark. Addison grabbed on to her skirt on one side, Cecily the other, and June crowded behind her as the metal door clanged shut.

She used her cell phone's flashlight to find the light switch and tried it, not expecting anything.

But the kitchen lit up.

Suddenly, the dining area lights flashed on, and there were hordes of people standing there.

"Surprise!" everyone shouted at once, and Bryce dropped her keys in shock.

"Happy Forever Family Day!" Patty, dressed in a snappy pantsuit and without her normal frilly apron, bustled up to hug her and the girls. "Sorry about the drama, but Kate insisted we keep it all hush-hush, and Imani swore you wouldn't be mad at me."

Bryce hugged her, then Imani, who glided up next.

"She's not mad—she knows it's important to celebrate and enjoy the moment." Imani's lips were done in a festive shade of pink-red that perfectly matched her sundress. Zander—the tallest, sturdiest of the Matthews men—came up and took his turn hugging Bryce.

"My fiancée is right. Soak this in—this party is for you."

"It's not a party, it's an *event*," Kate said, waiting her turn to give Bryce and the girls a squeeze. She wore a kelly-green dress, her auburn hair in an immaculate chignon. "And there will be no lacerated corneas, no thrown pastries, and there are enough healthy food options to ensure no vomit, either. Told you I'd give you an epic redo! Girls, come and see everything!"

Kate took Addison and Cecily by the hands, with June and Bryce following her out into the café's dining room, where everyone waited. Bryce spotted Harvey and Adele, who immediately swooped in to hug their granddaughters, and then she saw Patty's new guy, Frank Penny, as well as some of the girls' friends from dance class and school. Bryce's attorney, Lillian Goodwin, gave a cheerful wave as she stood next to the Paynes' lawyer. Drake gave her a chin nod from the corner, where he was holding little Elise, and next to him, her tiny frame hunched into a chair, was Nana Grace, the Matthewses' one-hundred-year-old matriarch.

Finally, she spotted Ryker, standing off to the side with Six until everyone had their turn hugging and congratulating her. Dressed in a pair of faded jeans and a black T-shirt that clung to his chest and shoulders, Ryker leaned against the wall, arms crossed. But instead of his RBF— a look she rarely saw anymore—his mouth was stretched in a smile that melted her insides. Bryce flew to him, her heart skipping in her chest like it did every time she saw the man.

"Hey." He wrapped her in his arms, kissing her, his blue eyes sparkling.

"Keeping secrets from me again?" she accused as she kissed him back, then burrowed her nose into his neck.

"Surprises are supposed to be secret," he said. "Besides, I should get extra credit for this mission. You four Weatherford females are hard to ambush."

She inhaled the scent of his skin, smelling his clean warmth along with those delicious notes of car and garage underneath. She could stay there, arms wrapped around him, all day, but she pulled away as Six nudged her knee.

"Hey, Six-y," she cooed to the dog, dropping to one knee to accept her kisses as she nuzzled her back, stroking her soft fur. "I've got some diced chicken I set aside just for you, my VIP."

"Speaking of VIPs, there are two more here to greet you."

Bryce looked up from loving on Six, scanning the dining room in curiosity. Then she saw the couple sitting in the booth. The woman had salt-and-pepper bobbed hair, and she sat looking around at the hubbub with a confused smile on her thin face. Next to her sat a stockier man with thinning hair and a port-wine stain on his left cheek and chin.

Bryce shrieked, Six barked, and the restaurant went momentarily silent.

"Dad! Mom!" she yelled, springing up to throw herself at them. Tears sprang from her eyes as she hugged her father first, then her mother, who patted and kissed her cheek. Bryce gasped out the words, "When did you...how did you...I didn't think you could travel?"

Her dad wiped her tears with his thumb before nodding his head in Ryker's direction. "It was all his doing. He and that wonderful dog of his flew down, then drove us up, all in one day to make it easier on your mother. She and Six rode in the back seat and slept almost the whole way. That dog is a miracle worker. Shelby is having a good day today."

"Why wouldn't I be having a good day?" her mother asked, giving him a grumpy look. Then she put her hand out to touch Bryce's cheek. "Oh, my sweet girl! I am so happy to see you. Which reminds me, I have something for you."

Bryce wiped the tears from her face, leaning in to hug Ryker as he and Six approached. "You didn't have to bring me anything, Mom. Just having you here is gift enough."

Undeterred, her mother pressed something into Bryce's hands.

"This is for you."

Puzzled, Bryce examined the piece of paper furled along the edges, as if it had been folded and unfolded numerous times over the years. The white paper was covered in handwriting, the top written in organized columns, with writing underneath, almost like a . . .

Recipe.

"It's . . . it's your chili recipe." Bryce's breath caught in her throat as she read the ingredients. "Mom, thank you."

"Took me a while to recall where I put it. But this young man of yours asked me about it, and then I remembered. It was at the bottom of my jewelry box with some things I'd meant to give you. But it's yours now." Her mother nodded happily as Bryce bent to kiss her again.

"Thanks, Mom." Bryce brushed back tears, catching Ryker's eye to smile when he shrugged, as if to say *Told you I could make her give it up to me.*

Mom followed her gaze to Ryker. "But I see you won't be needing it to catch a man—is that an engagement ring on your finger?"

Ryker kissed Bryce on the forehead, urging her to sit with her parents. "I'll let you catch up. I'm double-parked, so Six-y and I are going to go take care of that. Be right back."

Bryce did as told, telling her mother—again—the story of how Ryker had proposed to her. But this time she enjoyed repeating old news, because she got to see the thrilled expression on her mother's face as she listened to how Ryker had slid the ring on a raw carrot, which he'd hidden in a fresh bunch Bryce was using for the next day's soup.

"But it was almost an epic fail, because it slipped off and down the drain as I washed the carrots." Bryce soaked in her mother's bright peal of laughter at the mishap. "He had to tear apart the plumbing and fish it out of the U-bend, and when he presented it to me, it was covered in gunk. But I slid that sucker on my finger anyway. He said it was an RSVP for my hand in marriage when the guardianship was finalized, because the girls came first. After his proposal, I'd have slid a twist tie on my finger and been just as happy."

Between drinking in the sights and sounds of her parents—whom she hadn't seen since Bentley's funeral—Bryce accepted congratulations, hugs, food, and a piece of the cake she and the girls had cut together. It was a massive one Patty had made with the words *To the Weatherford Family: We Love You* written in beautiful icing calligraphy surrounded by piped-on hearts and bows.

Before she knew it, an hour had passed, and guests were saying their final congratulations before leaving. Soon, the only ones left were Bryce and her family—Mom, Dad, and her three sweet girls, plus the entire Matthews clan…all but Ryker.

"Hey, where'd Ryker go?" Bryce asked Imani as she helped clean up some of the guests' leftover plates and cups. "He was here, then he disappeared with Six. Is everything okay?"

"He's...coming right back." Her friend flushed, then grinned, clearly up to something. "Just stay right here in the kitchen for a few minutes more, okay?"

She gave her friend a "what are you up to" look, but she nodded. A minute later, Imani returned with the girls. Her forever family. Bryce's heart gave a lurch every time those words went through her head—she hadn't thought a piece of paper could make a difference. But it had. Bentley and Heather would always be listed on the girls' birth certificates as their mom and dad—Bryce would never want their names erased from any document or from their memories—but now she and her nieces could officially start this new chapter of their lives.

Harvey and Adele waited out in the dining area, and Adele threw her a wink. She was obviously in on the surprise. Bryce grinned at the couple, who'd become the best allies she could have ever hoped for these past couple of months. After that fateful spring break week, it was like the dam of communication had finally been thrown open. They'd postponed their trial date to allow time to have discussions about their hopes for the girls and their wants, finally hammering out an agreement for guardianship that included language for time with the Paynes every week, as well as taking the girls for a vacation every summer. Bryce took Ryker's advice to ask for what she needed, and the Paynes had really stepped up. They took the girls to school every day, giving Bryce time to prepare food and soup for the expanding PattyCakes menu, and were always happy to help FaceTime with June when Bryce was flummoxed by an assignment. They took the girls any weekend in which Bryce had catering events, as well as every Thursday for beef on wecks after dance class—

a fact Ryker took advantage of by staking his claim for Thursday date nights with her.

Bryce gazed over at her nieces, reflecting on the amazing changes these past months. Addison still wore her fairy wings, but only on weekends when she played Tinker Bell Defeats the Pirate with Ryker. The Lava soap had given Cecily terribly dry skin, and had to be replaced by a black foaming bar that smelled like an old man. But she was clean after her many misadventures, which included helping Ryker with routine oil changes in the garage. June, while still prickly and objecting when her sisters called Bryce Mom instead of Aunt Beamer, had all A's and B's in school—thanks to tutoring from Ryker in math, and Drake in English. She'd also taken on the responsibility of being the restaurant's tech guru. She'd built a web page for PattyCakes, which included a link to a site for Bryce's catering business, and took pride in updating the café's social media pages.

Bryce knew she had changed most of all. While she often got overwhelmed with juggling her catering business with parenting, she reminded herself that the girls were happy and had many people who loved them, including their New York and Florida grandparents—all of whom spoiled them rotten, which was as it should be. While the thought of taking over PattyCakes in another eighteen months was scary as hell, there was nowhere else in the world she'd rather be...and nobody she'd rather be with than the man who loved the chaos of her life as much as he loved her.

Just then, a horn sounded outside.

"Sounds like your surprise is here," Imani said in her singsong voice.

Curious, Bryce opened the metal door, her girls peering around her.

Idling in the alley was a pretty, yellow-and-white vintage VW bus. As soon as they came out to the landing dock, she saw Ryker in the front seat, Six riding shotgun. He beeped the shave-and-a-haircut staccato on the horn.

"Hey, is that from Ryker's garage?" Cecily asked, squinting.

Bryce gasped. It was!

She recognized the gleaming VW emblem—with its little nick in the side of the V—as the same front end bolted inside Ryker's garage. The very one Ryker called his "metal security blanket."

Ryker's eyes met hers over the girls' heads. Then he opened the driver's-side door, stepping out.

"Thought you ladies deserved something a little bigger than the Beamer. It's big enough for road trips, too. Happy Forever Family Day."

Bryce gasped, blinking back tears. "Are you kidding? That's for . . . that's for us?"

"Dude," came Zander's voice from behind them. Bryce turned to see that the entire party—both of their families—had filed outside. Zander gave a low whistle, and Drake did a slow clap as he spoke.

"Now that's a grand gesture. Well done, bro."

The girls screamed and piled onto the VW bus. In two seconds, they'd already figured out how to pop the metal latches on the tiny side windows and were climbing on and over the seats, hooting with delight.

"Are you serious?" Bryce whispered to him, and as he nodded, she flung her arms around him. He kissed her lips, his light blue eyes dancing as he spun her around.

"Go check it out."

As she climbed into the driver's seat, she spotted the same rearview mirror—with its little haze around the edges—that his platoon had brought back from Afghanistan.

Ryker climbed in to sit on the passenger side, moving Six to sit on the floor between them. The dog's head whipped back and forth as she looked at one, then the other; her tail wagged so hard it banged the leather seats like bass drums.

"I don't need it anymore." He smiled, nodded to the front end and mirror. "Those mirrors are for looking behind, and all I want is to look ahead at the future. With you."

"I have half a mind to drive back down to the courthouse and marry you right here and now," she said, her voice low, meaning every word.

"Let's do it." He grinned. "You're in the driver's seat. I'm just waiting for you."

She smiled. He'd told her the same when he'd proposed with the gunk-covered diamond.

"Not today. Today's about them." She gazed in the rear-view mirror at her sweet girls laughing and battling over seats, begging to have Six come back and sit with them. "But soon."

"Hey, is there room for all of us grandparents in there for the maiden voyage of the Weatherford bus?" her father, his arm around Mom's shoulders, called out.

Cecily threw open the bus's back door. "C'mon in, Grandpa and Grandma! You, too, Nana and Pop-Pop. We can all fit, because this bus is huge."

All the girls' grandparents were loaded up, with Addison changing seats three times until declaring she'd gotten the one she wanted.

"Okay, everyone's buckled in?" Bryce asked. Her heart was full as she started the VW, the vintage engine turning over and catching easily, wafting through the open windows the intoxicating smells of gas, grease, and possibilities. The sight of her nieces—her children—happy and chattering with their grandparents in the back seats of the vintage bus caught at her heart. She blinked furiously.

"You good?" Ryker's finger caught and brushed away her stray tear.

She shook her head. "It's...a hug emergency."

He chuckled, drawing her to him. "Love you," he said, kissing her lips.

Her lips smiled against his mouth as she answered. "You'd better. Because I love you more."

Six leaped between them, all grinning golden smiles and doggo breath as she inserted herself in the moment.

Bryce laughed, petting her sweet head. "Aww, Six-y. Don't worry." She kept her hand on the dog as she met Ryker's gaze. "There's no reason we can't both have this guy forever."

As she leaned over, stealing one last lingering kiss from Ryker, she heard her girls whispering to each other, coming to some sort of agreement.

Then they started singing.

"Ryker and Aunt-Mommy sitting in a tree, K-I-S-S-I-N-G..."

SHELBY'S BLUE-RIBBON SWEET CHILI

Once thought lost forever, here is Bryce's mother's blue-ribbon chili recipe. Shelby Weatherford only knows how to make chili to feed a crowd, so this one will satisfy even your heartiest eaters. Done in thirty minutes, this chili is chock-full of vegetables, making it an easy one-pot meal. If I had to describe Shelby's chili, it is much like this book: Satisfying and sweet with just the right amount of heat! Enjoy! —Dylan

Serves 6–8

Ingredients

- 2 tablespoons olive oil
- 1 large green bell pepper, cut into ½" chunks
- 1 medium yellow onion, diced
- 3 medium cloves garlic, minced
- 2 lbs. lean ground beef
- 1 8.75 oz. can whole kernel corn, drained
- 1 14.5/15 oz. can peeled tomatoes, undrained, rough cut
- 1 15 oz. can tomato sauce
- 1 16 oz. can your favorite baked beans (we use Bush's Original Baked Beans)

- 1 15 oz. can black beans, drained and rinsed
- 3 tablespoons brown sugar
- 2 tablespoons chili powder
- 1 teaspoon sweet paprika
- 1 teaspoon fine sea salt
- ½ teaspoon ground black pepper
- ½ teaspoon onion powder
- ½ teaspoon ground cumin
- sour cream (optional)
- 1 pkg. shredded cheddar cheese (optional)
- 1 green onion, sliced for garnish (optional)
- 1 bag of corn chips, like Fritos (optional)

Directions

In a large pot add the olive oil over medium high heat. Add the green pepper, onion, and garlic and sauté until almost tender. Add the ground beef and cook until it's browned. Then, stir in corn, tomatoes, tomato sauce, baked beans, black beans, brown sugar, chili powder, sweet paprika, sea salt, black pepper, onion powder, and cumin.

Bring to a boil, then reduce to a simmer. Let it thicken and the flavors combine for at least 30 minutes, then ladle into bowls. Top chili with optional garnishes of sour cream, cheddar cheese, sliced green onions, and corn chips. Dig in!

ACKNOWLEDGMENTS

If I had to name two women who influenced this book the most, it would easily be my fabulous agent, Cori Deyoe, and my talented editor, Leah Hultenschmidt. Cori, thanks for having my Six (this time, literally), and Leah, your editing notes are superb at teasing out a story's layers. I owe you both a drink. Cheers to the end of the Matthews brothers series!

One of the best things about being a writer is also the most frightening: writing about things you have not personally lived. For me, that means the guardianship process, the life of a veteran and amputee, serving in the military and living with PTSD. I am very thankful to those who paused to answer my questions, hear the book's abbreviated plot, and offer their expertise. First, thank you to Jessica Hamm, who vetted the earliest synopsis of Bryce's story—I hope you know how much I admire your grace and selflessness. The adoption/guardianship process is terrifyingly complex, and this book's factual accuracy and background owes so much to Eftihia Bourtis for her legal expertise, and to Margaret Burt for her years as a foster care/ adoption advocate. In addition, I want to thank prosthetist

Jeff Hammen, CP, LPO for allowing me to shadow him, and for sharing his knowledge of prosthetics and experience as an amputee—I appreciated your patience with my many questions. Thank you to Kirsten Barrington-Hughes and Nancy Weaver for their candor and willingness to offer some behind-the-scenes truths, much of which shaped and enriched this story. I'd like to shine a big spotlight on the folks at Paws of War, a real-life group of heroes, for all that they do to serve both ends of the leash. Thank you for talking to me, and for the inspiring work that you do! Lastly, my heartfelt gratitude to the following Marines for their service and for sharing their Corps knowledge, experience, and grit for this story and the series: Sergeant Jonathan da Cruz, Sergeant Michael MacHose, Corporal Jamey Clovis, and Infantryman Josh Langston White. The above experts were an invaluable resource in writing this novel, and any mistakes are entirely mine.

Without my beta readers, I'd be lost. Molly Call, I am so thankful for your plotting help and endless encouragement. Casey Reed, thanks for keeping me grounded and for the "mom-like creature" idea, and a huge kudos to Annette Miller for her eagle eye, and those sanity-saving lunch/scrapbook dates. I have also been blessed with some incredible friends in the community at large—huge thanks to Taylor Keeran, Eric Head, Sherri Feltz, Nic Gunning, Niki Gordon, Erin Bronscom, Lorelei's Lit Lair, and others who helped influence this series. A special, puffy-hearted shout-out to my ARC Leaders/Readers, to the Newton Book Neighborhood, to my newsletter VIPs, and to everyone who has read my books and supported me in this journey—you all are amazing! Congrats, also, to Tina

Goodwin, who won the chance to name one of my favorite secondary characters in the novel.

My family deserves so much gratitude—not only for dealing with me during deadline, but for their help during the writing process. A big thanks to Mark Newton for being the best middle brother-in-law, and sharing all the middle child feels. Praise also belongs to Leslie Ball, who serves as an example of opening one's heart and home, and to my sister, Marly Bouchard, who led me to experts who shaped the story's background. My acknowledgment would not be complete without a heart-eyed emoji for my incredible daughters, whose support and love buoy me through writing and through life. I am so proud of you two, and honored to be your mom-like creature.

Finally, always, this is for Mike—you are my real-life hero and the very best man I know. I am so fortunate to have you by my side.

ABOUT THE AUTHOR

Dylan Newton was born and raised in a small town where the library was her favorite hangout. After over a decade working in corporate America, Dylan quit to pursue her passion: writing books. When she isn't writing, Dylan is pursuing her own happily ever after with her high school sweetheart as they split time between Florida and Upstate New York with their two much-cooler daughters.

Check her out at:
DylanNewton.com
Facebook.com/DylanNewtonAuthor
Instagram @AuthorDylanNewton